Illuminate

THE LIGHT KEY TRILOGY

Praise for *Scintillate* by Tracy Clark

"Clark's novel is a powerful, heart-wrenching adventure."
— *Kirkus Reviews*

"Beautifully written. Keep your eye on author Tracy Clark. She's going places!" —Ellen Hopkins, *New York Times* Bestselling Author of the Crank trilogy

"A lush and atmospheric debut with a scorching romance and a metaphysical mystery. It had me hooked from the start."
—Suzanne Young, author of *The Program*

"*Scintillate* is full of unexpected plot twists and turns. A refreshing, magnificent read." —Beth from Tome Tender Book Blog

"If the publishing world is still looking for The Next Big Thing in YA novels, *Scintillate*: The Light Key Trilogy by Tracy Clark hits all the right notes." —The Bookend Family

Illuminate

THE LIGHT KEY TRILOGY

TRACY CLARK

Entangled Publishing, LLC
2614 South Timberline Road
Suite 109
Fort Collins, CO 80525
Visit our website at www.entangledpublishing.com.

Ember is an imprint of Entangled Publishing, LLC.

Edited by Karen Grove
Cover design by Kelley York

Manufactured in the United States of America

First Edition September 2015

For Mom—I'm always yours. You're always mine.

"But already my desire and my will
were being turned like a wheel, all at one speed,
by the Love which moves the sun and the other stars."

—Dante/Paradiso/canto XXXIII

Chapter One

Cora

The keys to heaven.

That phrase scratched a deep groove in my brain. I fingered the silver key pressing against my chest as Finn drove Giovanni and me to *Brú na Bóinne*—Newgrange, in Yankee speak. The key was much weightier since I found out it had been stolen by my grandmother from a statue of St. Peter at the Vatican. What was the connection between the key in my hand and the fact that it came from the hand of a saint at one of the most hallowed religious sites in the world? My key couldn't be a *literal* key to heaven, could it? At this point, heaven could open through a magical portal in Costco and it wouldn't surprise me. Mom's journal said that the *Scintilla* were *the keys to heaven*. How could either of those things be true?

Death was the only door to that domain.

My parents had both walked through it. Mari, too.

Because my aura had been attacked numerous times by the Arrazi, I knew how they felt when they died. I learned that souls don't bleed warm and sticky. The bleed of a soul is stinging ice.

I bet it doesn't feel that way when you die naturally. I imagine a natural death is like warm steam rising from a bath, languid and ambitious as it stretches its wings and sails upward. Peaceful.

Both my father and my mother died the cold way. Surely I'd be killed likewise. I intimately knew the icy bleed, and every time it felt like the frozen blade of an ice axe stabbing into my chest and splitting me open for my silver aura to spill out.

Pain battered my temples and tension gripped my muscles until they felt bloodless and limp. Soul so angry. Body so damned tired. I'd have to climb the steep stairs out of my weariness to find the truth and use it to stop the slaughter of Scintilla and of innocent humans as well. My circle was shrinking. I had so few people left.

The two boys in the car with me had my love, but my love for them was a receding wave that had swept my heart out to sea.

One was a liar. One was a killer.

The car rolled to a stop in front of the Visitor's Center and Finn jumped out and ran in for admission tickets. We were uncomfortably close to the tomb where, just hours ago, we'd left Clancy Mulcarr unconscious on the floor next to Ultana Lennon's dead body. His grand plan to sacrifice the "maiden, mother, and crone" in the ancient tomb had failed.

After he kidnapped my mother and I as we escaped from Dr. M's facility, he'd tried to kill us—and my grandmother, to boot—but Ultana Lennon, the head of Xepa, showed up to claim Clancy's prize. Ultana's death by her own hands was both shocking and a relief. One major ass-pain of an enemy, down. But I hadn't killed Clancy when I'd had the chance. A mistake that already haunted me. Some part of me felt that Clancy carried my father's soul within him. I couldn't snuff it out. And I just wanted this all to end. No more volleys of death back and forth. My lack of bloodlust meant Clancy was alive and way too close to where we were now. I had to shove that fact into a corner of my mind in order to complete what I had come to do.

Tickets in hand, we entered the ancient ruins and ran up the path that led to the megalithic tomb. Each of us climbed the ladder leading over the large curbstone in front of the tomb's entrance. Finn and Giovanni stayed close to me. Together, we stepped inside the dark, cool monument and stared at the giant stone bearing the marking that seemed to connect the Arrazi and the Scintilla through history.

I reached out with shaking fingers to touch the triple spiral. Would the stone itself tell me the truth?

The energy that swirled from the triple spiral was palpable and robust, tingling my fingertips before I even made contact with the stone. I placed my palm flat on the engraving and closed my eyes, waiting to feel my mind spin into a vortex of memory. But I didn't spin. Visions didn't form a tempest in my mind. I remained stubbornly rooted in the present, where all my questions stacked like bricks on top of me. There was energy in the rock, yes, but it was a scratched record. Like reaching my arm into a swirling hum of white noise. Indistinct residue. So many hands had touched this stone over the years that I could pull nothing clear from the static but a faint image of breathtaking spirals of light.

The grooves of cold stone pressed against my head as I leaned forward in frustration. This damn monument had lured me since I was a child, and now it taunted me by holding tight to its secrets.

Ultana Lennon had convinced Clancy that the spirals represented the *maiden, mother, and crone,* and that if he killed my mother, my grandmother, and me he'd become immortal. She'd tricked him. It was a false trinity used by Ultana's twisted mind to ensnare and kill the remaining few Scintilla. She used Clancy to find us, and in the end, she murdered a most precious Scintilla—my mother.

I stared hard at the trinity of interlaced spirals. My mind stretched for connections, fought to understand a mystery that had been around since before the time of Christ. Thousands of years before. After a few moments of staring and thinking, an astonished breath puffed out. "A false trinity…"

"What?" Finn asked.

A glimpse of his triple spiral tattoo could be seen just at his neck where his pulse fired rapid and steady. When I first saw Finn's tattoo in the hospital in Santa Cruz, I'd recalled that the true meaning of the triple spiral was unknown and that people of various beliefs had hijacked the symbol to suit their own philosophies.

"No one knows what this design really means," I ventured. "But some mistakenly think it symbolizes the holy trinity. The trinity isn't an original idea, though. It's an evolution of ideas from many belief systems, some older than Christianity," I whispered, recalling my mother's writings in her journal and the research we'd done. "If Ultana had been telling the truth that someone won't stop hunting us as long as there's a God on their altar, then all the memories I pulled from the key make more sense. Why would the spiral be in those religious images from the key if it weren't connected? Why would my grandmother steal the key from the Vatican in the first place?"

I grew more excited as I slowly pieced things together. "The religious symbols, the persecution and death of those who dared to believe differently... Those were deeds of the most dominant religion in the world over many centuries."

"Not just one religion," Giovanni said. "Many have killed and still kill for their own special brand of God. I can't see that God would want a thug kingdom populated by murderers, but then, I'm just being logical," he added with a cynical tone.

Finn wiped his forearm across his lip, still bloody from when Dun beat him after he confessed to killing Mari, though he described it as a mercy killing. I swallowed hard. That reality was a coarse lump of salt in my throat, in my heart. It was bad enough my first love was an Arrazi, but that he had a hand in my cousin's death was unbearable.

"According to Ultana," Finn said, "a religious organization—possibly at the Vatican, I'd wager, as that's where your key is from—has targeted the Scintilla and hired the Arrazi to eradicate them. Why?"

"That's the question," I said. "What truth can be so scary to them that they'll break their own commandments to conceal it?"

Giovanni leaned against the stone with his arms crossed. "I still don't understand how the spirals play into this..."

"It's a trinity. Threes… The church has taken many pre-existing ancient symbols and made them their own."

Finn's hand rested over the spirals on his chest. "I'm Catholic," Finn said. "Born and raised. But I know from history that many of the church's symbols were adapted from earlier pagan symbols. It's a brilliant conversion tactic, really. Take something people already believe in and alter it just enough to make it their own. It's how beliefs are stolen." His brown eyes pierced mine. "It's how followers are created."

"Okay," I said. "Confirmation that I'm headed to the right place."

"*If* Ultana was telling the truth," Finn said, eyebrows arched skeptically. "It might have been a deviation from the truth. You could be going to Italy for nothing."

I ignored his comment. They'd already tried to convince me I shouldn't go. I'd lost my father, my mother, and my best friend. I no longer cared about "shoulds."

"Finn, keep tabs on the Arrazi here so we know what they're up to. Giovanni, you have to go with my grandmother to Chile. Keep her and Claire safe. See that Dun makes it home to California. As for me…I'll find out if we're finally on the right trail and, if so, why they want to bury the *keys to heaven*."

We emerged from the chill of the tomb into the morning sunlight, blinking to adjust our eyes. I squinted at the dark outline of a group of people standing directly in front of us, blocking our path out of the ruins. A familiar energy sent a blast of terror through my body, and I clasped both Finn and Giovanni's arms.

As my eyes found focus, the Arrazi came into view.

Before I could utter a word or move, their knifelike energy reached out and plunged icy hands into me and just as quickly pulled back. A chilling greeting.

The gravel crunched under my feet as I skidded to a stop and stared in shock at the Arrazi who blocked our escape from Newgrange. I cringed, bracing myself for the strike of the axe.

Giovanni and Finn both thrust a protective arm in front of me. Pure fear swelled through my palms as I clasped each boy's arm. Dread rippled off them and buffeted my sides. I forced myself to breathe. Beneath a thick layer of fear bubbled molten hate. I stepped forward, shaking with a curious blend of rage and exhaustion that made me feel almost invincible, like I'd lost concern over my own death. I was sick of running, sick of living in fear, sick of losing the people I loved.

"The last I saw of you, you were drooling on yourself in a tomb," I said to Clancy. "Not killing you is officially my biggest regret."

"I told you this was a bad risk," Finn grumbled next to me.

"I'm at risk just waking up every day."

"I won't have that regret, lass. Did you really think I'd not know where you went?" Clancy asked, stepping toward me with a smile, as if we were old friends. "Haven't we been down this road before, pet?"

"Pet?" Giovanni yanked his arm from my grasp and shoved his way in front of me. "Cora will never be something you stake claim to, ever again."

"Stop," I whispered to Giovanni, reaching up to clasp his shoulder. "The *geis* Lorcan put on you. You save my life, you die. Is that such a hard rule to remember?"

His head turned enough that I could trace the noble slope of his nose and see the determined attitude of one blue eye as he snarled, "Yes."

His Scintilla energy sizzled under my palm so ferociously that I fought the temptation to pull away. Instead, I tried to calm him the way he'd done for me so many times, but I was too dark, too angry to produce any positive feelings.

I had nothing to give.

Giovanni's shoulder tensed as I squeezed harder and whispered, "You can't afford to think like that. There's someone else depending on you now." Giovanni had to worry more about taking care of his newfound daughter, Claire, than protecting me. I couldn't blame his lapse. Finding out at eighteen that Dr. M's genetic tampering had produced a child, and that Giovanni was the father, must have been a speed bump to his brain. Insta-father was insta-mind-blowing. There was a slow blink and an almost imperceptible nod from him. He understood.

A series of crunching thuds resounded around us, like sledgehammers hitting gravel. A chorus of shrieks filled the air as bystanders pointed at a group of tourists who lay in a heap, their limbs piled chaotically over the top of one another.

"Stop!" I screamed at Clancy. They were innocents who had nothing to do with our drama and wouldn't believe it even if they were told. But Clancy's bushy white brows were bent in consternation at the pile of dead bodies, and I realized I hadn't seen the Arrazi hook their auras into the bodies to take and kill. Yet, there they lay—dead. *What…?*

I'd thought the Arrazi were responsible for the drop-dead people. Could my father have been right? Was there a phenomenon randomly striking down clusters of people? And was I the antidote, as he'd suggested? My gut still said no. But it seemed like it could have something to do with us, with this ugliness of a war between two unique types of human. I just didn't know how.

The park wasn't crowded. It had just opened, but all the tourists were now packed around the dead bodies, some snapping pictures and video with their phones. I couldn't be caught on film again at the site of another incident. I wanted to turn my head away, shield myself, but I didn't dare take my eyes off the Arrazi.

Their eyes hadn't left us for one second.

Clancy smiled widely. Before I could even guess what he found so amusing, he lifted a finger and, all at once, the Arrazi lashed their ensnaring auras at the living, pulsing crowd and siphoned their colors from their bodies. Giant tubes of color flowed from the tourists into the bodies of each Arrazi.

People died as they ran for their lives, their life force sucked from them, even as they hugged one another for comfort. Bodies fell like crushed flowers. And we could do nothing to prevent it.

Thunder cracked as the Arrazi's auras exploded in white as blinding as the lightning that shot overhead. The cloud of pure white energy surrounded them and reached for us like a misty, noxious vapor.

Chapter Two

Finn

"Enough!" I yelled into the rain that seemed to start from nowhere and soak us in seconds. I positioned myself in front of Giovanni and Cora. Even as I stood to defend the Scintilla, I wondered; could I save them from these others who were deadlier than I knew we Arrazi could be? They'd just attacked and murdered numerous people at once, with ease.

My own hungry Arrazi need shook me as I looked at the bodies around us. Shame raked its dirty nails down my back.

I reached behind me and clasped the hilt of Ultana's dagger, which was stashed under my sodden T-shirt. I thrust the blade toward my uncle Clancy, as well as two other Arrazi I didn't recognize, a woman and a man. They also had two common men with them—non-Arrazi. Amazing how the sight of new, unfamiliar faces heightened my fear. At least with my uncle, I knew what to expect—pure sadistic treachery.

"What'll you do with that toy, lad?" Clancy taunted.

Surely he knew that he couldn't attack my energy without being blown back by it. An Arrazi could never attack another Arrazi. But a knife…a knife didn't play by our rules. I wished Cora had one. From the looks of her and the acrid feel of her aura hitting me like a draft, she'd gut Clancy like a slimy fish.

"What'll you do, uncle? Fight me? Try to kill me? No doubt you would. Nothing means more to you than the power of possessing these Scintilla, right? Even at the risk of your own family." I pointed the dagger at each Arrazi, one by one. "I swear on my life, I will kill you if you so much as breathe unnaturally in their direction. I have no devotion now but to morality and the truth. What the Arrazi are doing is wrong."

Clancy stepped forward and pointed a fat finger at me. "Ignorant, disloyal *muzzie*! Your devotion to save the Scintilla from the natural course of things is as resolute as my devotion to seeing them dead. Your family is the Arrazi."

"I think I liked him better when he was only trying to hold us prisoner," Cora said from behind me.

"Give it up and let's be done with this," Clancy said. "What you see here"—he gestured to the other Arrazi who looked like tigers about to pounce—"are but a fraction of an army bent on destroying the Scintilla for good."

"Whose good, you gluttonous lump of a man?" Giovanni shouted.

I couldn't see the attack, but I could feel the cold wind

of my uncle's energy *whoosh* past me. Giovanni made a grunting sound and lurched into my back. Cora screamed.

Her scared cry was the starting gun I needed, and I leaped forward toward Clancy, whose eyes widened at me and the oncoming blade. I couldn't take them all at once, and they could kill Cora and Giovanni both before the dagger struck. But I had an idea...

I darted past my uncle, who spun to track me, momentarily interrupting his attack. I looked back at Cora trying to help Giovanni up from one bent knee. His hand covered his chest. I threw my energy out toward my uncle. When it collided with his body I was instantly thrown backward into the Arrazi woman and one of my uncle's human thugs—the non-Arrazi with the harelip, Ultana's driver and my uncle's lackey, whom we'd drugged and left in the tomb as well. The force knocked all three of us to the ground.

I bashed the hilt of the dagger into the woman's temple, knocking her unconscious, then pulled the aura from the man until he passed out. The other common man we'd left at the tomb earlier ran to me and reached for the dagger. I yanked at his soul until I was dizzy with the cementing of his foul spirit into mine. My energy surged with the kill. Clancy took but a moment to narrow his eyes at me before he turned around and committed himself to killing Cora and Giovanni. Her black curls flew forward as she stooped, crossing her arms over her chest. Her mouth was frozen in a delicate *O* as not only her breath rushed out of her but her life.

I had no choice.

I leaped up and ran. There was only a moment before the knife drove into my uncle's back, severing the pull of Cora's aura. She gasped and looked up, eyes widening in shock when she saw my uncle fall forward with the hilt sticking from his back.

The world must have momentarily stopped spinning. Everything slowed, and I could only hear my own heartbeat and register the grateful yet condemning look in Cora's green eyes that seemed to say, "Thank you, but this doesn't make up for Mari."

She pulled a weakened Giovanni to his feet, and they began to stumble away around the dome of the tomb. The last Arrazi ran after them. I pulled the bloody dagger from Clancy's back and pitched it at the man. It struck, but not deeply and not in the right place. It bounced grossly in his hamstring as he twisted to grab it.

In one sickening instant, he ignored the knife and pulled at Cora's aura so hard it flung her off of her feet. She landed in the dirt with a thud, writhing in pain. I ran and threw myself onto his wide back. He swung a meaty arm at me, grazing my cheek. I clamped my arms around his neck, but he was much stronger than me. He reached his arm over his head and pulled me forward over his shoulder. The impact rattled the breath from me even as he squeezed my neck to pinch it closed.

He gave a high-pitched yelp and released my neck, twisting to look behind him. Cora's bottom lip was sucked into a grim line. She had apparently swiped the blade from his leg. With two hands clasping the hilt, she skipped forward like a fencer and plunged the knife deep into his side. The bloke immediately fell next to me, sending comets of gravel flying around him when he hit. I jumped to stand in front of Cora.

She shuddered. It wasn't the cool rain coating her skin;

it was pure shock and adrenaline. She'd just killed a man to save my life. Her hands flew up to her mouth. She couldn't speak, just shook her head over and over, tears mixing with the rain coating her face. I'd never seen someone so tortured.

My hands instinctively reached to draw her in. I pulled her against my chest. Images of holding her in California bombarded me: carrying her after she fainted in the coffeehouse. Embracing her as she cried against the rec center wall when she'd found out her mother hadn't abandoned her but had been missing for over a decade. Every memory of holding her against me as we kissed...

Crunches of steps approached, startling us from our embrace. Over her shoulder, I saw Lorcan Lennon—Ultana's *gobshite* son—walking toward us, staring with eyes slashed to thin, speculative slits. What was he doing here? Had Clancy told him of his mother's death?

I gave her a push away from me. "Run! Take my car to the house. My mother and father will keep you safe until I arrive."

"Finn," she said, tugging at the back of my shirt. "Come on!"

As Lorcan drew closer, I heard but mostly *felt* her retreat. He could have attacked her from where he stood but strangely, he didn't. Why? I bent for the blade. "Don't even think about it," I warned him.

He held his hands up in a gesture of surrender as his chest heaved with fast breaths, but he didn't move forward or even look in Cora's direction.

"Why are you here? You don't want any part of this," I said.

"Saoirse caught wind of something about to happen

here…" His voice trailed off as he looked around at the heaps of fallen bodies.

Aye, a desperate *shite* thing had definitely happened here.

Lorcan looked down at the fallen man and his brow bent with a question. "That's my mother's dagger. How the hell did *you* get it?"

Chapter Three

Giovanni

Rain dripped from the black coils of Cora's hair, her feet assumed a fighting stance, and for one moment she looked like an otherworldly warrior, shimmering and fierce. The Arrazi was deservedly, blessedly dead. His aura blinked out like a broken bulb.

I could breathe again.

"To Finn's," she gasped, grabbing my hand. We dodged and swerved around the saturated minefield of dead bodies, still and dark as the stones they came to see.

Cora's silver aura drew in tightly and pointed out in sharp-tipped spikes. Defenses up. Guarded. She dripped adrenaline. She'd been in battle. Seemed an inevitable progression. After she'd left Clancy drugged but alive in that tomb, I figured she'd never kill. But she'd driven the blade so hard into the Arrazi man's side it looked like she'd reached inside him to snap a rib bone as a trophy.

I gripped her hand tighter as we made our escape. "We must leave all these Arrazi *stronzi* behind. It's out of the question for you to go to Italy alone. Doesn't this attack prove it? We will find our way to safety. Together."

It was difficult for us to run, our legs dragging as though we ran through sludge. I tried to infuse her with strength, but after being attacked my energy was as depleted as hers. She pierced me with a cautionary look when she felt my efforts. Her green eyes were wide with fear and something else I'd never seen in them—something reckless and deadly. It made my gut drop uneasily.

"Don't do that. Save your energy," she gasped. "We're both weakened."

"I can help you. I'm not damned helpless." I broke the lie off like a twig tossed at her feet.

Helpless was not something I'd felt in many, many years, but that's *exactly* what I felt.

I'd been helpless as I watched Cora get brutally attacked and could do nothing to help because I had a *geis* put on me by Lorcan to prevent me from saving her life; the cruelest curse to inflict when every instinct in my body was to defend the girl who was singularly one of my own. She was more than that. She had become a part of me.

With every step closer to the car, my hope grew that we'd live another day. Fight another day. Love…someday.

We dove into Finn's car, and I started it up. "Are we to wait for *him*?" I asked, already putting the car in gear, my foot lifting from the brake.

Cora looked through the fencing at Finn and Lorcan

talking. "I don't know," she said, her voice as faded as distant wind. "I don't know..." Then her eyes drifted upward, and she pointed to a security camera on the fence's perimeter. "We'd better get away from here, go to his house. This is his territory. He'll find his way back to us, I hope."

I bit the inside of my cheek. None of my hopes included the Arrazi, Finn Doyle.

Dun paced on the front steps of Finn's manor like a wild horse with his long black mane stuck to his body. He was as soaked as we were and as indifferent to it. He pulled Cora into a tight hug. My gut squeezed. I'd never had friendship like that.

"Mami Tulke already has plane tickets booked," Dun said. "My Spanish is no *bueno*, but she's mumbling about keys and treasures, and I think she's been out-of-her-mind worried about you. Are you okay? Where's Finn?"

"He'll be coming," Cora said, worrying her bottom lip.

"Where's Claire?" I asked him. Claire's little face—a rounder less-edged version of my mother's—flashed in my mind. Claire was the only thing that stopped me from chasing after Cora when she ran into battle against that man. It was no contest to be willing to die in Cora's place. None. But to choose death and leave a little girl, *my* little girl alone, was something I couldn't do. It was characteristically selfless of Cora to remind me of that fact. How was I possibly going to be a good father when I'd been orphaned and didn't really know what a father should do?

"Claire's hanging out in the Doyles' library, reading

books I can't even wrap my brain around," Dun answered. "Smart kid, man."

Even if it had only been some of my DNA that contributed to her intelligence, I felt a burst of pride. I wondered who Claire's biological mother was. *What* the mother was... Claire was Dr. M's experiment and obviously not full-blooded Scintilla. Though I noticed something different about her aura right away; it was broad, expansive, like an explosion in slow motion. People were wary of her, could sense the bomb in her energy.

Though I knew from experience that her mind alone could intimidate. People feared those who roam many rooms of the mind when most are wedged into just one. Cora thought I survived by manipulating with my Scintilla energy and that had been partly true in my life, but most of the time I manipulated with intellect. People are easy to manage.

A spotlight of guilt flashed on my handling of Dr. M. I hadn't been up front with Cora that I was paid by him to find and bring in other Scintilla. But it wasn't a damn bounty. It wasn't price-per-head as she'd accused. Dr. M's company funded my life under the auspices that I was out looking for others like me. He didn't need to know I was already doing it for free as best I could with limited cash.

I'd spent my whole life searching for a blaze of silver.

I accepted his offer because I desperately wanted to find others like me, and I needed the money. I thought he was going to help my kind. That was his promise to me. But I put Cora and everyone else at great risk. There was never any indication that Dr. M was a lunatic when I made my deal with him years ago. How was I to know the Arrazi, by way of Xepa, were involved with his facility and his research? Dr.

M didn't even seem to know. Now I knew how wrong I was, and the price for my mistake was too high—Cora's trust, and maybe her hard-won love.

As I stared at Cora, this new warrior—wet from rain and weary from battle—I wondered if she would ever forgive me. If she didn't, I wondered if I could ever forgive myself.

Chapter Four

Cora

"What have you been doing?" I asked Dun, suddenly noticing the mud that caked the bottom of his jeans and covered his shoes. The mud and the look in his eyes was all it took for me to understand. "But you didn't *finish*…" I couldn't make myself say it. They wouldn't have buried my mother without me?

"No, girl. No. And it was raining so hard, the hole was filling in faster than I could dig it. Freaky weather."

The three of us looked to the sky. The sudden downpour that had started while we fought the Arrazi *had* been weird. The sky was now the slate of so many Irish days, but no rain.

"It was almost as though it had something to do with us," Giovanni said.

"Mmmm…" I mumbled, thinking again of my father's

theory that natural disasters were increasing because of an energy imbalance in the world. I yawned. Exhaustion weighed me down, but the need to lay my mom to rest next to my dad was too strong. I couldn't be *at rest* until it was done. The sooner I finished it, the sooner I could leave Ireland for Italy.

Not caring whether anyone followed, I walked across the drive to the spot where my mother's body lay on the damp ground. Someone had placed a red and green plaid cloth with thin stripes of gold over her, but the rain had soaked it so that her gentle profile showed clearly under the fabric. I sunk to my knees next to her and pulled the cloth from her face. I traced my finger lightly over her nose, coming to rest on her mouth. Pulsing with grief, I kissed my fingers and placed them back on her slightly parted lips.

Of all moments when I most wanted to cry, *needed* to cry, I couldn't. Resentment dripped steadily into my bloodstream as I looked from her still body to the half-dug hole. The Arrazi had made me an orphan. Xepa conspired to exterminate my race. If Ultana's words meant anything, there was a conspiracy somewhere within the most powerful church in the world to sweep us into a hole and bury the truth.

Bury... I'd always thought it was strange to put bodies in the ground. I pictured the round earth with one entire layer of its crust populated with skeletons. A landfill of the dead. I never understood it. But in the short time I'd known her, Mom was happiest with her hands in the dirt. It made sense to bury her—to *ground* her. She and my father would bloom in some new way, together forever.

If I stared long enough at the watery layer at the base

of the hole, I could imagine it was bottomless and she'd sink to the center of the earth and float away on a red river of lava. Was it any better to be cremated and scattered with the winds? Either way, form becomes formless and transmutes into something new.

Nothing ever felt so wrong than to see a Scintilla's spark stolen and her body ground into the earth like ash under the Arrazi's boot. We were givers of light. There *had* to be a purpose for us. Fresh rage heated my blood. This was so wrong. Not just that my mother was murdered but that her purpose was unknown yet so feared. Those more powerful had killed her.

I clenched my fists into the mud at my sides. They would know fear. Their actions inspired a dark drive within me. I wanted to know my purpose and make the fearful quake by bringing the truth to the world.

Hell-bent, I hoisted myself up and jumped with the shovel into the hole that was only as deep as my knees and began digging. I dug until my shoulders ached and my hands were scraped pink.

I dug until I could finally cry.

"There now, luv." Finn's Irish brogue lilted down to me. "Let me," he said, gently pulling the shovel from my hands. I tried to keep him from taking it but barely had the strength to stand, let alone shovel another mound-full. Finn clucked his tongue and fixed sad eyes on me. "I tried doing what you're doing. Turned out I couldn't bury my sadness and anger. I could only find a use for it. I suspect that's what you're after with Italy?"

I nodded. He always seemed to instinctively know what was going on inside me. I once loved that. Now, its futility aggravated me. I brushed my forearm across my tears. "You said you have something you found at Ultana's that might interest me? I'd like to see it before I leave for good."

"Of course." His jaw muscles clenched. "I'll help you... finish..." he said, looking briefly at my mother then back down to the spade. His legs and arms moved in fluid unison to dig, and I thought, of course, he's done this before, for my father.

"Shall I get the others?" he asked after the grave had been dug.

It was ready.

"Just my grandmother." Finn gave me a questioning look. "The Maiden and the Crone will bury the Mother," I said. I couldn't explain it. It just seemed right. We were a broken circle now, but burying her together might forge a stronger connection between my grandmother and I. Clancy's crazy notions about sacrificing us aside, I did feel there was something sacred about the feminine triple we had comprised. "We were her family," I added, as if that fully explained the deeply personal and inexplicable reasons I wanted to do it my way.

I climbed down into the grave, and Finn nodded. With our arms laced together underneath her, we lowered my mother into the too-willing ground. The mud displaced around her, taking her in. She belonged to the earth now.

Finn bent over my mom. *"Ta sé in ait na fhirinne anois."* He had said those words before, after he realized my father had died. His gold-flecked sorrowful eyes met mine. "She is in a place of truth now." Something fluttered in his hand when he stood. He passed me a small scrap of the fabric covering my mother's body. "It's the Doyle family tartan," he explained. I held out my hand, and Finn tied the scrap around my wrist, the one with the marking of my mother's moon.

Handfasting. That was all I could see when he tied the tartan. Handfasting between my parents. Handfasting with Finn in an alternate reality. One where we'd have had the chance to grow in love and connection instead of live as natural enemies. One where he hadn't killed my cousin. I yanked my hand away and climbed from the hole. "Mami Tulke," I said, gulping hard to hold myself in check. Wordlessly, Finn left to fetch my grandmother.

Drifting through me like a daydream was the urge to lie down next to my mother and pull clods of dirt over me. I wanted rest, though not eternal rest, I supposed. I wanted my life to be different. I wanted peace, which was as futile a wish as wanting wings.

Moments later, Mami Tulke ambled across the grass, her folksy skirt floating around her legs. She eyed me with sharp, black eyes peering from wrinkled lids and hopped down into the hole with me. Her agility surprised a smile from me. Unafraid of the face of death, she squatted and peeled the cloth from my mother's head. Mom's black hair floated in the shallow water like reeds in a marsh. She looked like she bloomed from the earth rather than being newly planted in it.

Mami Tulke grabbed my hand and pulled me splashing to my knees across from her with my mother between us. I bent and pressed my forehead to Mom's as she'd done in the tomb when she'd gifted me with her memories of our early life together. I sat upright, startled, touching my forehead, suddenly remembering I'd been marked by her memories but didn't yet know how. "What's there? How did she mark me?"

My grandmother smoothed one finger over the skin above my nose. "It looks Celtic. I don't know what it means, but it's lovely, *mija*. Ask the boy. Perhaps he'll know."

She held her papery hand over the center of my mother's chest and moved it in three circles, small at first but growing wider. A silver spiral of energy hovered over my mother's heart.

"What are you doing?" I asked, genuinely curious about the ritual she was performing.

"I'm connecting with any remaining energy in her heart chakra and releasing it," Mami Tulke said, suddenly flinging the spiral of sparkling energy up to the sky, where it fell over our heads like silver rain. My mother's heart energy shrouded me in sweet, penetrating love that seeped into my skin and into my own heart. Kissing my fingers and touching it to her mark on my forehead was the only ritual I could think to perform before I climbed from her grave.

I couldn't face anyone or anything else.

I stumbled away from my mother's grave in a daze. I didn't care if they could wave a wand and make me suddenly appear in Italy, or Chile, or with Toto back in Kansas… If I didn't sleep, I'd never make it through another minute. My body was giving out. My eyelids twitched uncontrollably. Everything from my neck down was numb and tingling from digging. Every inhale was a yawn. Every exhale was heartache.

I went to the tower where I'd stayed once when I was a guest in the Doyle's home. It was familiarity in the midst of overwhelming uncertainty. Sweet associations: learning how Finn used to sneak up there and teach himself the guitar, it was the place where Finn first called me *críona* — his heart — and one unsettling memory, of Finn's mother the night she took from my aura in my sleep and gained her sortilege to see people's deepest secrets.

I shook off the memories. The tower was isolated and empty, and so I claimed it.

Sleep claimed me.

Waves and seagulls were the soft music that woke me. I turned and lifted onto my knees to peer out my window, suddenly wishing I hadn't. My mother's new grave looked like a scab in the green grass. The gnawing hurt in my chest had become so familiar that I wondered if I'd ever have a day when pain was so absent it would be like the wind blowing through me.

I showered, dressed, and descended the spiral stairs to find the others.

If one didn't know what we'd all just been through, the sounds of the house would have lifted the spirit. The chatter of little Claire in the kitchen as she asked question after question of Finn's mother. Dun and Giovanni talking about tribes, specifically Dun's Apache heritage. Giovanni mused that the American Indians had endured a similar genocide to the Scintilla's. He was right, of course, one warrior to another.

"Sleep well?"

Finn startled me. I spun around, my hand automatically reaching to ward him off and my mind admonishing me for not feeling him approach. Any other Arrazi I'd have felt a mile away. Finn, well, he somehow penetrated that defense. He never felt like an enemy and even then, after what he'd done, I didn't understand why not. I should hate him.

"I slept like a boss," I answered honestly. "It feels wrong to admit that, but my eyes closed at sunset and opened at sunrise, and it had only been, like, five minutes."

"I've had sleep like that, where you wake and it feels like a trick of time."

We stood a couple of awkwardly silent seconds before I noticed what was right behind him. "The *Scintillating Host of Heaven*," I said, pointing. It still amazed me that was the title of Gustav Dore's depiction of one of the scenes from Dante's *Paradiso*. "That's the name of this painting. After being threatened with Dante's words by Griffin when I was in the hospital, then reading *Paradiso* myself, and especially after Ultana said he was killed because he was trying to spread the truth, I know it's not a coincidence. Tell me why it's in your house."

"It's not a coincidence," Finn said. "My mother told me that it was believed that Dante knew the truth about the Arrazi and Scintilla and was trying to spread it to all of humanity. I don't think most people read between his lines."

"If you didn't already know the truth, it'd be easy to see how most would assume it was just an allegory about heaven and hell," I said, looking up at the artwork. It was eerie to stand next to Finn, the way that Dante and Beatrice stood together looking up at the spiraling mass of angels in the sky.

"So, maybe it was a message not to humanity, but to *us*," I said, quickening at the new idea. What message could Dante have been trying to give specifically to *both* supernatural breeds of human?

Though I didn't look away from the painting, I could feel Finn's eyes on me. "Brilliant," he whispered. "I think you'll be very happy with what I have to show you."

"I also believe there's a connection between Dante and Michelangelo," I added, causing Finn's brows to arch in surprise and something more, like a realization. "It's part of why I'm going to Italy."

With an eager and expectant expression, Finn pulled out his phone and showed me a picture of a yellowed drawing—a side portrait of a woman.

"Is that Ultana?" I asked, unsure why the odd depiction of her was important.

He nodded like I'd gotten the right answer. "I believe it is, especially in light of her unnatural lifespan." Swiping to another picture, I saw it was a photo of a triangular scrap of paper in his hand. "I found this in a copy of *The Divine Comedy* in her office. See how it fits the missing corner of the drawing?"

"Michelangelo's emblem," I whispered, staring at the three circles. He was known to use those circles as a signature. "The line of Italian scrawled next to it, what does it say?"

"It translates as, 'We all have our illusions and our mysteries.'"

"Ain't that the truth?" I said, wishing for more to go on, but the fact that it was a note from Michelangelo in Dante's book in Ultana's office was significant. Proof of the connection I suspected.

Uncomfortable with how amiable we were being, not because it felt fake but because it felt…disloyal…to Mari, I hit him with anger. "If you kill me," I said, ignoring the wary look in his coppery eyes, "you take my power and never have to kill again." I motioned to Giovanni and Mami Tulke, whose voices drifted from the kitchen. "If you or your parents kill the three of us at once, you take our powers and possibly live forever."

Finn raked his fingers, still stained from wielding the shovel that had buried my mother in a damp grave next to my father's, through his black hair. I suddenly wondered if he had slept at all, and cursed myself for my concern. My heart constricted. "Why haven't you done it, Finn? Why don't you do it now?" My words blew from me, a fresh, hot wind of anger that I couldn't control.

Finn's murky aura caved like I'd hit him. His gaze and his pause were longer and deeper than normal. He swallowed hard. "Because I don't want that kind of forever."

"But still… Mari…" My dam threatened to crack. "How could you?" I choked out, unable to believe he'd been the one to steal her spirit, unable to believe he had no other choice.

"Hate me, Cora. Do that. I can feel your angry aura. Hate me, if that's what it will take to keep you safe. I deserve every ounce of your contempt. If you insist on going to slay your dragons alone, I'll be here, fighting to unearth Ultana's secrets, Xepa's secrets. People will soon know that she's dead, I'm sure. But we should assume that there are Arrazi out there still set on the tasks she put to them. I'll do everything I can to stop them. Until then, this isn't over."

Spent, I crumbled in on myself. "Will it ever be?"

Finn didn't answer. We both knew the likely ending for

the few remaining Scintilla.

"After what's happened, you think any Arrazi are going to trust you? How can you possibly find out secrets when you're on the outside?" I asked.

"The witnesses are dead."

"Lorcan—"

"He arrived too late to know exactly what happened, but I've got to watch out for him, I know."

"What did you two talk about as we ran?"

"He wanted to know where I got his mother's dagger. I told him she'd given it to me as a gift when—when I killed Mari. She didn't," Finn rushed to say. Whips of darkness flashed in his eyes, and I lashed myself for the war inside me between pity and disgust.

"But I didn't know what else to tell him except that I am in love with a Scintilla and was defending you. He didn't seem to know anything about his mother. In fact, he said he wasn't sure how he'd explain to her what he saw there. I don't think he knew what he was walking into, but someone must have tried to contact Ultana because Saoirse was the one who told Lorcan about it. I don't think Lorcan fully understood what was happening. I don't think Lorcan fully understands a whole helluva lot.

"Perhaps there will be time to find out more about his mother and her connections," Finn continued, reaching into his pocket and pulling out a small satchel and an envelope. "This is what I wanted to show you. I took this from an old wooden heart in Ultana's office."

"Wait," I interrupted. "A *wooden* heart? The one that was stolen from Christ Church?" I'd seen it in the memory of my parent's wedding.

Finn looked surprised when I said this, but he nodded. "Of course… I knew I'd seen it before, on the news three or four years back, I just couldn't place it until you said that."

"She was a thief, you know. That's what the marking was on her face—the brand of a thief. So she stole the heart from Christ Church and these were hidden inside?" I took the objects from him.

"Aye. Fascinating. You'll see."

The delicate and worn paper in the envelope certified that the pouch contained the ashes of Dante Alighieri.

My gaze snapped up to meet Finn's, and he gave an encouraging nod, whispering, "This isn't the only one. I researched it online. There were originally six sacks. Four vanished. Eventually one turned up in the Italian senate in 1987 and another in the central library of Florence, tucked away into the rare manuscripts collection. The rest are still missing."

"Dante was Scintilla. Obviously someone knew that," I said, feeling a connective thread to a man hundreds of years before my time. I slipped my finger into the top of the pouch and coaxed it open to reveal a small pile of gray dust at the bottom. Palpable energy rose up from the powder. My hand shook as I pondered whether to reach inside. My body had become a profane wall of graffiti from the echoes of energy in some memories. I'd never look the same. I'd never *be* the same.

I took a bolstering, determined breath, tapped my finger on top of the miniature dune, and was thrown from the present moment into the past.

A dark room illuminated by candles. A dark time for the feeble man in the bed, whose eyes I saw through as he watched someone approach from the shadows in the corner. At first, he was not scared, but intrigued by her. The woman bent over him, smiling. He'd been ill. He thought she was sent to comfort him, especially after the first words she spoke.

"I've been sent," she said. "To—"

"To steal," he muttered, because he could now see, by the light of the candle, the thief's mark branded on her face. "Could you not wait until I die," he spat. "I will soon enough."

Ultana, a much younger Ultana, smiled amiably but with a tripwire in her eyes. "Yes, dear, you will die. But I need you quite alive now, for the only thing I was sent to steal…is your soul."

Ultana Lennon hooked her Arrazi energy into the great poet's and ripped his aura from his body until the last pearl of his soul floated into her own.

Chapter Five

Finn

I'd never watched Cora use her sortilege before.

Once her fingers reached into the purple sack, her long lashes fluttered delicately, then closed. Her head tilted back somewhat, causing a spiral of black hair to sweep off the ledge of her shoulder. She inhaled sharply with slightly parted lips, and I couldn't help but think that she looked like she did when she was about to be kissed. I clenched my hands, longing to cup her face.

I wished I could see through her eyes, not only for the magic of pulling the past from objects but for the beauty of seeing the light around people. That room at Dr. M's had been extraordinary—a glimpse of the world as Cora saw it, and a glimpse of the silver-tipped soul of a Scintilla. It moved me. Hell, I think it even moved Lorcan, who was with me when we saw it.

Her eyes opened, and she gasped. "Ultana wasn't lying about killing Dante. She assassinated him. She said she was sent to steal his soul."

"Sent by who?"

"Exactly." As the words left her mouth, the inky black impression of three interconnected circles appeared on Cora's skin, as if the symbol had lain dormant under the creamy layers, waiting to rise up. Cora's brows pinched together, and her hand flew to the spot below her jaw like she'd been stung.

"No," she said, covering the new marking that bloomed right before my eyes. "Again with the face? God, this sucks." I gently pulled her hand away so I could see the design that dipped and curved on her neck where the tiny dot of her pulse fired.

Cora pulled her hand from mine. "Can you tell me the meaning of the symbol on my forehead?" she asked, touching it lightly.

"It can be interpreted two ways," I said, examining the small Celtic symbol in the middle of her forehead. "It can be a symbol for mother and daughter," I said. "But it's also said to symbolize new beginnings."

"I wish."

"It doesn't change you," I said, tracing my finger over the circles. "You're beautiful. Always." She pushed my hand away and scowled. I murmured an apology. "You didn't ask about the new marking," I said. "The mark on your neck is the same as Michelangelo's symbol on the scrap of paper in the picture."

"The *giri tondi*?" she said, clearly astonished. "I touch Dante's ashes and Michelangelo's emblem marks me? Wild.

Both he and Dante believed the circles were a metaphor for God. Even across hundreds of years, Dante and Michelangelo were connected and" —her eyes took on a mystified squint— "they had a *thing* for threes."

"They were buried at the same place, you know," I told her, reminded by the way she said "threes". "At the Basilica de Santa Croce, in Florence." I had learned that after my mother and I spoke of Dante. Cora's eyes widened, and I sighed. That information surely wouldn't help my case to stop her from going alone to Italy. "Galileo is buried there, too. Three fingers had been cut off his corpse."

Cora's head tilted in an adorable way, like her innate curiosity weighed down just the right side of her head. "You're kidding."

"I don't kid about severed digits."

The faintest hint of a smile appeared, then faded too quickly before she said, "You know I'm right about going to Italy."

I hadn't had time to respond, nor would it have mattered from the look in Cora's eyes, before my mother burst through the kitchen door and found us in the hall. "There you are!" she said to me. "Why have you been avoiding—"

Unguarded as I shifted my gaze from Cora, my mother caught a deep look into my eyes and grasped the wall next to her for stability. Her narrow face was a blend of stricken grief and disgust at seeing my deepest secret. Her sortilege was bloody scary. "Oh. Jesus, Mary, and Joseph—my—my brother is dead."

"Now you know," I said, shame coating me like sticky film. I'd been avoiding my mother since we returned from Newgrange the previous day. I couldn't discuss the gale of feelings inside me. I had meant to sit her down and tell her about Clancy when we were alone. "Seems I excel at killing people's loved ones."

Cora cleared her throat. "I have to find a way out of Ireland," she said, changing the subject. "I need a passport." Cora's voice faltered, and it was then I noticed a tear running down her cheek. She swiped it away angrily, it seemed. But that one tear of Cora's cut me in half with guilt.

"I'll go to Clancy's," Mum said, her voice shaking on the last word. But I knew her well enough to see she had shifted to Emergency Room mode. She'd roll up her sleeves and do what had to be done. "Perhaps Cora's belongings are there somewhere from when he kidnapped her." Her gaze flitted to the new marking on Cora's neck, but she didn't inquire.

"Thank you, Ina. Look for my grandmother's belongings, too, since he kidnapped her as well. God, I hope our passports are there."

"I have mine and Claire's," Giovanni said, emerging from the kitchen with the little girl, who peered up at us with her abnormal eyes. It was hard not to be unsettled by anyone with three irises. "We've got Dun's passport, too. We took them from Dr. M's vans when we escaped." He took notice of her new marking and skimmed his fingers under her jaw. My own clenched. "Michelangelo's seal? How? Why?" he asked her.

"Finn found pouches with remnants from Dante's grave," Cora explained. "They were hidden at Ultana's. She killed Dante. I saw it."

My mother scoffed. "Impossible."

Hot anger flashed in Cora's eyes. "I know what I saw," she said, sounding more sure of herself than I'd ever heard her. "An Arrazi killed a Scintilla, that's not news." Her tone was acidic, meant to burn. "But that she was sent by someone to do it because he was trying to tell the world the truth. That *is* news."

"Could Ultana herself have known what that truth was?" I wondered aloud.

"If she did," Cora said, "then do her children know as well?" Her expression pressed me to be the one to find out.

Giovanni slapped my shoulder. "Looks like Finn has his marching orders."

My jaw clenched. "I know my business, mate."

Mother crossed her arms, taking in the group of fugitives we harbored. "Right now, I'm afraid you're all in the business of escape."

Chapter Six

Giovanni

I'd been a homeless orphan roaming Europe for most of my life and that difficulty paled compared to getting a child to fall asleep when she didn't want to.

Claire missed Dr. M and his research facility—the only family she'd ever known. She was too smart and too old to sugarcoat the circumstances of our escape. She'd seen the bodies and the blood as I carried her from the place. I did my best to explain our situation with such frankness that she'd understand that running away was our only option. I also told her I was her biological father. That's when I realized that there's a vast difference between mere intelligence and emotional intelligence. She cried like the little girl that she was.

I understood her longing for her "family" better than

she knew, having lost my own just a few years older than her five. But my familiarity with loss couldn't ease her pain. It was my first lesson in the very new practice of parenting; my daughter was going to have her experiences and her own losses. I couldn't save her from that.

None of us get out unscathed.

Her mass of blond curls spilled over the pillow, and her fist curled in her sleep in a way that reminded me of Cora. I sat on the edge of the bed, watching Claire's peculiar light. It was the most volatile aura I'd ever seen, constantly changing color, shifting shape and texture. It seemed to push at the air around her, competing for space in the room. Very infrequently, I thought I detected a flash of Scintilla silver, but that might have been my wishful thinking. Or not. Would I really wish her this life of being hunted?

Claire's aura curled in like a multicolored flower petal as she drifted deeper into sleep, and I vowed I'd do everything I could to create for her a world in which she never had to run, hide, or be afraid of the murderous Arrazi. I wanted the same for Cora. For a brief, ridiculous moment, I let myself wonder if we three might someday live together as a family.

Once I was sure Claire was out for good, I tiptoed from the room and went to find Cora. Ina had retrieved Cora's and Mami Tulke's passports, and all travel arrangements had been hurriedly made. Cora would see us off in the morning before we left for the airport, but I needed to see her now. I needed to say good-bye privately.

Every step up the spiraled stairs made my legs and my heart heavier. I was torn between protecting my little girl and protecting the woman I loved, and I wondered, would Claire and everyone else be better served if I went to Italy with Cora?

Our lives might depend upon what we found in my home country, and Cora's life might depend on not being alone.

I squared my shoulders and knocked on the whitewashed wood of the old door.

Cora answered immediately. I couldn't decipher the drop of her eyes when she saw me, but hoped it wasn't disappointment. "Hey," she said, her arm crooked to lean on the edge of the door. "What do you need?"

"Such a big question."

"There's always a big question, isn't there?" We smiled at her use of my phrase, but we both knew it was a diversion.

I stepped past her into the room. A packed backpack sat on her bed like a deflated balloon. She had so few possessions. For the first time, I considered what we'd both lost from our previous lives. "*There is no home for the hunted*," was something she'd said to her mother once as we were escaping the shack on Finn's property where her father was killed by his uncle, and I believed that was when I felt our bond cement.

In that instant, Cora became my home.

Behind me, I felt her stillness, felt the guardedness in her aura and that she was so very tired. It radiated off of her like fumes. "No one but you can *see* what I need," I said, still facing away from her. I knew that if I faced her, I'd blow everything by sweeping her into my arms and burying my face in her deep brown curls.

"I can't give you what you need," she said, and didn't sound sorry.

Only then, when I knew the firing squad I was facing, could I turn. "Forgiveness? Trust? Love?" Every word I threw bounced off her. She was so defended; her aura was an impenetrable shield. "I need to go with you to Italy," I said, more sure than ever of what I had to do. "I need to be with you, *need* you to be safe."

Cora Sandoval had enfolded me back into humanity. I wondered if she knew that. An incredible feat after all my years surviving alone, trusting no one, and admittedly looking out for only myself. Now, I wanted nothing more than to look out for her.

"We both know you can't keep me safe." She stepped forward, tilting her heart-shaped face up to me. "I want to forgive you…trust you…"

My insides squeezed. She didn't say love.

"I'm going to try to do both, and I'm asking you to do something for me." Cora took my hand and squeezed my fingers, sending tides of electricity up my arm, through my body, into my heart. "Please go to Chile with Mami Tulke. She's the only family I have left. The thought of her there alone, defenseless… We might be the only Scintilla remaining in the world, and I'm afraid they'll come for her. I need you to look out for her, keep her safe. Please do that for me?"

"But you—"

Cora's finger lifted to my mouth, and I remembered the first time we met, how I'd done the very same to quiet her, sending her aura into spasms of nervous excitement. I'd loved seeing her reaction to me then and was sure she observed my intense reaction to her now. Her pupils dilated a bit as I reached to skim my fingers over the pulse firing under the *tiri gondi* on her neck. She was crazy if she thought our responses to each other were simply our Scintilla blood.

"Please," she said, and I answered with a kiss, wanting utterly to believe that was her request.

Chapter Seven

Cora

Why is it that the fire of anger and the fire of passion burn alike?

Both consumed me when Giovanni kissed me. I was angry at myself for not pushing him away sooner. "None of this matters anymore," I managed to say through uneven breaths and a thrust to his chest, as if those words would cool the hurt in his blue eyes. He only looked more wounded.

I wanted it to matter. If it did, it would mean my life was mine, and I'd be normal, worrying about what book to read next and staring at my fully realized butt in the mirror to see how my new jeans fit. I'd be pondering which college I'd attend in a year. I'd be bouncing to have romance in my life and the "problem" of choosing which boy to love.

I shook my head. "It doesn't matter, G. Not my confused

feelings. Not my bruised love for both of you." I noticed the hurt in his eyes when I said "both." "None of it matters. The only thing that matters to me is uncovering the truth that will set us all free."

"Maybe then, you'll be free to love me," he said with so much hope in his voice.

"Maybe I'll never be."

A dark look passed over Giovanni's face, which I thought would precede some type of battle, but he just cast his eyes to the door and announced, "Finn is coming." Seconds later, there was a soft knock.

Finn and Giovanni regarded each other in the doorway, and Giovanni leaned to say something to Finn. I turned, pretended I was still packing. Their Love Olympiads were beyond me now. None of it mattered, I told myself again. Not the burn of my still tingling lips from Giovanni's kiss, or the fact that Finn's sudden presence unhinged me.

"Why are you here?" I asked when I heard the door close. When no one answered, I looked over my shoulder and saw I was alone. Even that didn't matter.

"You're not coming."

The hinges of Dun's jaw clenched, and his nose flared bullishly.

"Does it really have to be said?" I began, knowing what I was about to say would kill my best friend and also knowing I had to say it to protect him. "If you and Mari hadn't come to Ireland, she'd still be alive. Do you think I can handle something happening to you, too?"

A tear that could drown the world slid down his brown cheek. "If I'd been with Mari and Teruko that day, she might still be alive." I admired his swagger in the face of an Arrazi foe. "If something happens to you in Italy, do you think *I* can handle knowing I might have prevented your death, too? You're being a selfish brat. This isn't a party I'm asking to crash with you. This is a war. You think I'm just going to cruise on back to Santa Cruz and surf and eat corn dogs on the boardwalk and hit on girls and ignore that my best friend's in a battle on the other side of the world? I'm a part of this now."

"You shouldn't be a part of—"

Dun punched the wall, tilting a framed print of a pear and leaving an imprint of his fist in the drywall. "I'm a fucking part of it!"

The tremors of his outburst shook us, then quieted us. Dun had never yelled at me before. "I know you want to keep me safe." I slipped inside his muddy-red aura and wrapped my arms around his waist. "But I don't think there's a person on this planet who can help me now."

Mami Tulke buzzed into the room, her silver aura flashing with impatience. "I must talk to you before I go, Cora," she said.

My room was a rotating door of good-byes.

Dun left us with a silent, defiant look, which I'd seen before, usually when Mari bossed him around and he wasn't having it. He was going to have to deal with my decision. Thankfully, time for arguing about it was running out. My flight to Florence was leaving two hours after my grandmother, Giovanni, and Claire would depart for South America. There'd also been a lengthy debate between Finn and his father about whether I'd make it through airport security and the option of sailing from Dublin to France and trekking to Italy from there. They sounded like smugglers with me as the cargo.

My grandmother took my hand and pulled me to sit next to her on my bed. "I understand why you are doing what you're doing, and I know you have enough of your mother in you that I can't stop you." She patted my hand consolingly, peering at me with dark eyes the exact shade of my father's. "Your childhood is over."

Hearing it stated so firmly, blatantly, was like a guillotine blade slamming down on my youth.

"I will pray to God every day that you return safely to me, *mija*."

"Do you believe in God?" I asked, suddenly curious. "I mean, after everything that's happened…"

Mami Tulke's eyes turned soft and sad. "I don't know why the Scintilla were created any more than I understand the purpose of a fly. Maybe there's no purpose but to be pesky." Her old-apple face lifted into a smile. "Maybe a fly is just another expression of life and I'm not meant to know. But I believe the Scintilla are divine creations and that we have a divine purpose. I believe our enemies know what it is and are trying to stop us from fulfilling it."

"Maybe we're just pesky flies to them."

"People don't pay gold for flies."

We scanned each other's faces. Memorized every line and freckle, every fleck and pocket of color in the eyes. Took in the face of family, one that might not be seen again.

There were questions I'd wanted to ask her, and this might be my only time. "Dad said you were able to use your sortilege to shield me most of my life. How did it work?"

"It's like a force field," she said, and for the umpteenth

time, I marveled at how supernatural terms were becoming commonplace in my world. "I can wrap a shield around one person so that supernatural abilities can't penetrate."

"Why did it suddenly stop working on me?"

Mami Tulke sighed. "I wish I knew. Your father wondered if it was the sickness that was causing people to die because your blood showed the same cellular abnormality."

Except I didn't drop dead. I still had no explanation for that.

"We also thought it could have been the high fever that put you in the hospital." She surprised me by pulling out a hand-rolled cigarette and pursing it between her craggy lips.

"What, like burning the connection?"

She shrugged and blew out a puff of earthy smoke. "I can't protect you any longer. You're on your own."

Suddenly, I could see where Mari inherited her outspokenness, and it made me miss her so much that I felt my insides hollow out. At the same time, a roaring affection bubbled up in me for Mami Tulke. I wish she knew how much of me just wanted to run away to Chile and hide with her there forever.

She blew another puff of thick smoke toward the window. "Listen, I followed clues and my instincts and it led me to seek the highest seat of the keys to heaven that I know of—to St. Peter, to that key you wear now around your neck. I don't know what it opens. I don't know if you'll live to find out." Her chin trembled as she gazed into my eyes. "But follow your instincts. Use your gifts. You," she said, lifting my chin, "might hold the key to our salvation, the *world's* salvation."

"No pressure or anything..."

"Eh. You can handle it. I have a feeling about you, grandchild."

Chapter Eight

Finn

Cora steeled herself as she said good-bye to her grand-mother, Claire, and Giovanni at the edge of the airport security line. I could tell by the set of her shoulders, the abnormally high lift of her chin. She was trying to convince them she was capable enough, strong enough, and right to go it alone.

Or trying to convince herself.

Giovanni looked back at us once as he and Claire entered security. I felt myself breathe deeper with his absence, and it made me wish I had days alone with Cora—hell, a lifetime—instead of less than an hour.

Every few minutes, Cora would cast a paranoid glance at security guards who were out in abnormally high numbers. The "tragedy" at Newgrange was all over the telly, but this worked in her favor. They were allowing non-citizens a three-day window to leave Ireland. Unfortunately, it also meant that the airport video was once again circulating, making all of us edgy and afraid she'd be recognized and seized.

"You don't have to stay with me," she said, meeting my eyes for a split second before looking away with her brows puckered.

"You know why I do," I answered. "We both know I can help you if trouble comes. I can protect you." We sat together in the quietest corner we could find. Our backs were blocked by windows, and we could see anyone approach from the front. I glanced at my mother, who sat a few feet away, pretending to read a magazine. We were on alert. Ready.

"Helping me might mean killing." Cora's chin dipped and she spoke toward her feet. "Watching you kill once was enough," she said. Every time she recalled it, she probably thought that's how it happened with her cousin. But it wasn't like that. It was…sacred. With Ultana it would have been brutal. Though telling myself that didn't dislodge the guilt from my chest. Killing Mari was the most terrible thing I'd ever done, and the most merciful. "And who will protect me from you?" she said, stabbing me with her words.

"You didn't ask why I came to see you last night," I said, changing the subject. She leaned forward on her knees, and I snuck a look at her. From the side, her lips looked full, pouty, but the way she bit them told me she was thinking something she didn't want to say, likely that she didn't care why I'd gone to see her the night before, nor why I left so abruptly.

I'd not taken one step into her room when Giovanni leaned in and whispered, "You saw us together. She should be with someone like her—her own kind. Stop tearing her heart in half."

I hated the git.

Beneath the intercom calls for flights and the bustle of people panicked to leave Ireland, I extended my cupped palm to her. In it was my favorite ring. It was a replica of one found on a Roman soldier buried in Denmark. My father had brought it back for me after visiting the Viking museum there. Damn Vikings, so sure that what was ours was theirs for the taking. The ring was silver, with a two-headed snake winding three circles around the finger, wide enough to cover her ivy marking—the one the authorities were on the watch for.

Cora's face looked like I'd just asked her to marry me, and not in a good way. "To cover your finger," I quickly said, degraded to my bones. "I know our days of promise rings are over."

Sorrow coated her face like rain on a window as she took the ring from me and rolled it around in her fingers. "Thank you," she said, slipping it over the black ivy marking. When she did, I noticed the underside of what I'd thought was a simple gold band on her other hand.

"What is that ring?" I asked, wondering if Giovanni had given her one as well.

"It was Ultana's. My mother had buried it in her garden at the cottage after she cut off Ultana's hand in a fight."

"Japers! That's how Ultana lost her hand? Why do you wear it?"

"It's Xepa's symbol," she said, holding up her palm, allowing me to see the engraving in the gold: two triangles joined at their tips. I'd be looking into that symbol right quick. Saoirse might be able to shed light on it for me.

Cora glanced at the clock on the wall, and I felt the gravitational tug of time ready to pull her from me. "I want to say something before you go," I said, drinking in her face, her skin, the markings that she wore with dignity and that somehow made her more beautiful to my eyes. "Remember when I said I could *feel* you in the forest in California? I could. I just didn't know what I was feeling. I didn't know it was your aura. I thought that's what falling in love was supposed to feel like. I felt my heart swell, my mind, too, to accommodate the constant thoughts of you. Your shy but strong spirit, your beauty…"

My mouth went dry, but I pressed on. If this was my last chance to tell her how I felt, maybe she'd believe in some part of her charred heart that it was real for me. "I felt light, like a balloon barely tethered. I felt like the string was in your hands."

She said nothing in response, but her chin quivered slightly and her green eyes snapped up to mine, but she too quickly looked away.

"Cora, don't you ever wonder *why*?" I felt like a whimpering mutt, but I couldn't help asking. "*Why* two people who are supposed to be mortal enemies felt so instantly and deeply connected?"

She opened her mouth to speak what I was sure would be the same awful words she'd thrown at me before: that I was only attracted to her Scintilla aura, that what I felt wasn't love.

May God strike me dead on the spot if it wasn't.

"I'm going to tell you what I told Giovanni last night," she said in a measured tone. "It doesn't matter anymore. If we're lucky, we'll all have our whole lives to ponder the whys of love, but right now I have bigger questions to answer."

She looked at her watch before her eyes held mine. There was so much in that look. Naked vulnerability, anger, regret…and under the coals of that messy fire, love. I saw it like a flag hoisted over her heart.

"But yeah," she finally said, "I've wondered the same thing."

She stood to go, and my cell vibrated. "Shite," I murmured, pulling it from my pocket. It was a text from Saoirse.

Where are you?

I neglected it to focus on my good-bye with Cora. She'd once clung to me, wrapped her sneakers around my waist, held me tightly to her, all while whispering pained good-byes between kisses. That good-bye was so beautiful and full of truth, a bud compared to the shriveled pale petals of this one with my cautious kiss to her wet cheek. Still, like then, as I watched her walk away—maybe for the last time—it never truly felt like good-bye.

Chapter Nine

Giovanni

Claire tugged at my hand, pulling me through the Jetway from the airplane. The impression was that of a tiger who'd never been allowed to roam free. The flight had been long and confining. She was ready for action and expected us to be as well. Mami Tulke shuffled behind. I yawned. Children required stamina.

She looked like a wild thing, too, with her flyaway waves twisting together like weeds. What did I know of doing a girl's hair? What did I know about taking care of her at all? A memory came to me of my father brushing my mother's hair as she sat on the floor in front of his chair—to warm his feet, she would say teasingly, but I knew it was because of the way her lids drooped as he ran the brush down her blond waves. A sudden ache of missing my parents hit me. It was as unfamiliar as it was unwelcome, because I normally never allowed it. I looked down at Claire through blurry eyes.

I had no idea what to expect once we landed in the coastal city of La Serena, Chile, after the ninety-minute flight from Santiago, but I wasn't quite prepared for the luxury car that awaited us outside the airport. "I made arrangements with someone I trust," Mami Tulke said. "I was taken at the airport in Dublin when I went to collect Cora. That's how the *cabrón* caught me."

"How did Clancy know you were going to be in Dublin?"

"I now know that he was the one who called me and told me my son was dead. He said that Cora had asked him to contact me. He arranged for the car to pick me up and, of course, it took me straight to him. He later taunted me that he'd found out about me from Gráinne's journal." A string of Spanish cursing followed, mostly at herself for being *estúpida*.

A young man in linen pants and a fedora greeted Mami Tulke and took her bag while a weathered older man, who looked like he'd rather be on horseback than driving the black sedan, sucked on a toothpick and eyed Claire and me with unabashed curiosity, especially Claire. I was used to being the stranger and didn't mind his stares, but my stomach clenched with protective flares that spit like a volcano when he saw her eyes and tried not to look stunned.

Rather than her aura pulling in shyly as most children's do when met with people they don't know, Claire's reached out like another appendage, stroking the energies of those around her. They felt it, and in some cases their aura shrunk back in response. It was an energetic social breach to blend so blatantly with the auras of others, and I chalked it up to her very sheltered existence within the confines of Dr. M's facility.

About a hundred kilometers east from La Serena we entered the Elqui Valley, a narrow belt across Chile through which the Rio Elqui flowed from the Andes to the Pacific Ocean. *Pisco* and wine vineyards hemmed the bottom of the arid mountains like a ruffled green skirt.

"I like the way this place feels," Claire announced.

"It's said to be the earth's magnetic center." Mami Tulke explained the wash of energy I felt all around me. The very air was saturated and charged with it. "This valley is known for its energy. Absorb it, Giovanni. You will feel very at home, I promise," she added with a hint of mischief, making me wonder what she *wasn't* saying.

I imagined there were worse places to hide in obscurity and raise a daughter than this sunny stretch of valley, but I thrummed with a restless desire to be out in the world fighting. Cora was out there, fighting in her own stubborn way, and I felt like a coward, hiding in a South American village as far away from the world of Arrazi and Scintilla as could be.

"Cora said her parents met here," I said, recalling Cora's account of her mother's journal entries. "Why did Gráinne come to this place?"

Mami Tulke stared off for enough strung-together moments of memory that I felt bad for asking about them. "The triple spiral led her to research ancient pre-Columbian spirals. As is the nature of spirals, her search fanned out to key places all over the world. The body of earth is scarred with evidence." Mami Tulke halted for a moment, and I wondered if we were both thinking of Cora and the evidence marked on her body.

I tenderly kissed those markings once…

"Grace…Gráinne showed up at my door, looking for a place to sit out a storm." Mami Tulke smiled sorrowfully. "The moment she saw me, she cried. She had never seen another silver one in her life."

"Weren't you just as shocked?"

Her old face lit into a secret smile. "No."

The car stopped at a clay-colored adobe ranch house with a covered portico supported by wooden beams painted the orange-red of an unripe pomegranate. The curved roof tiles looked like stacked turtle shells. It was a modest home but well lived-in, with vibrant colors like the skirts and scarves Mami Tulke wore. Her house was stacked with personal mementos. We were shown to two simple rooms across the hall from each other. Mami Tulke plopped into a worn leather armchair and exhaled loudly. "*Mis montañas.*" She sighed. Her mountains. Her home. What it must feel like to have a place so deeply impressed on you that you could use the sacred word *home*.

As energetic as Claire had seemed when we got off the plane, she suddenly drooped like an unwatered flower. I put her to bed and went out to talk to Mami Tulke, but she snored softly in her chair with her hands folded over her round belly. I covered her with a blanket and went to bed listening to the crickets and marveling at the impossibly bright moon that turned my room blue-white, and wondered if Cora was gazing at the same light.

"I should be doing something," I told Mami Tulke. "There are Arrazi enemies out there, and I want to find them before they find us. I don't want to be on the run. I want to fight." I'd woken from my fitful sleep, plagued by dreams of Cora, sure that she needed me. Regret was a sour ball in my stomach.

"You feel like a babysitter to an old woman and a child," Mami Tulke said, sprinkling tobacco in a thin line in the rolling paper perched in her fingers.

"I feel like I should be with Cora."

"Love is just one of the wars you're waging," she said, licking the paper and twisting the ends into puckered points. "I'm not sure you'll win either if you're too intent on fighting."

"You're not suggesting we sit here in these craggy mountains and do nothing? They killed your son, your daughter-in-law. They'll kill your granddaughter next." The sour ball grew and rolled as I said those words. My outburst earned me a ferocious look, and for the briefest flash I saw an older version of Cora.

"You assume I'm doing nothing," Mami Tulke said but didn't seem to think she needed to explain what exactly it was that she thought she was doing. She struck a match on the table next to her and lit her homemade cigarette. "Come with me," she said with a puff of smoke and an abrupt scoot of her chair.

We left Claire with the housekeeper, Yolanda, and rode a rickety golf cart farther down into the green basin of the valley. Houses dotted the valley at sparse intervals between *pisco* vineyards and farms. Soon, a cluster of tiny geodesic domes and small modernistic angular buildings came into view. They looked like individual houses for an alien race. "Where are we going?" I asked.

"To exercise."

"To *what*?" Exasperation rose up in me. I wasn't visiting a country club. I'd agreed to look after Cora's grandmother, and I knew I had an obligation to Claire, but every second away from Cora, away from doing something important, was wearing me down to a useless nub. "What kind of exercise?" I finally asked, surrendering only because if I ever was going to go after the Arrazi, I might as well stay as fit as I could.

"Qigong."

I stifled a groan and rode in silence until she skidded to a stop at the top of an incline in the road. I offered my hand to help her down, which she took without comment, just pointing with a finger that we were to walk through a break in the vineyard along the side of the road.

Inexplicably, my heart sped up as we descended along the narrow dirt path. The place truly was an energetic enigma. As we stepped through the trees, I saw one reason why. Approximately sixty people stood, evenly spaced, in a lush meadow. Simultaneously, their arms swooped and dipped in elegant Qigong moves. I stood frozen, openmouthed, and stared.

Above and around the dozens of people were clouds of pulsing, sparkling platinum.

Mami Tulke motioned toward them. Her voice was soft. "This is how *I* fight. I keep them hidden. I keep them alive."

Her face beamed as she looked upon the Scintilla below us. A lineage, a continuation of our kind. She saw herself as a savior of our race, and she was. I had to admit, she was. "I believe the energy of this place masks the Scintilla's energy like auric camouflage."

I blinked and tried to breathe normally. Her words shoved me back into my worst childhood memory. Mami Tulke was hiding the Scintilla in the same way—albeit naturally and on a much larger scale—that my parents had hidden me in the electronics cabinet when the Arrazi came for them. They'd hoped to conceal not only my body but the pull of my aura as well.

Mami Tulke surveyed her kingdom of Scintilla with pride evident in her face. She should be proud. It was a miracle to see so many Scintilla alive in one place, but when I looked out among them I saw something else...power in numbers, the makings of a Scintilla army.

Chapter Ten

Cora

"My name's Joe, I work for the dough. If I don't have money, can't keep my honey. No honey, not funny. You say my cab go so fast, that's 'cause I press the gas, slow taxi man can't last."

Of all the taxi drivers in Italy, I got the one from India who thought he could rap. The drive through Rome was enough to convert me to lifelong pedestrianism. Mopeds jockeyed for position at the front of every light, and when the light changed, everyone blasted off like they heard the shot of a starting gun. Preservation of life and limb was apparently not on the Italian menu.

Funny, that was *all* that was on mine.

My two days at the *Basilica di Santa Croce* in Florence to see the tombs of Dante, Michelangelo, and Galileo had been interesting, though I'd left Florence with a numbing sense that I might never find the answers I sought, like the answers were written on the bottom of a teacup that could never be drained, but I could get flashing, teasing glimpses beneath the murky liquid.

It was no coincidence that Dante and Michelangelo were buried together. Nor did I believe it was a coincidence that Galileo had three fingers cut from his corpse. No freaking way was it chance that carved reliefs of three interlocked rings—Michelangelo's monogram I now wore on my skin— were prominent all over his tomb.

The facade of the Catholic Church had surprised me because the Star of David adorned the pinnacle. I'd always associated the symbol with Judaism. When I stared at the triangles, visions of Clancy and Ultana would return with emotions so violent, I'd felt nauseated. Actually, I felt that way most of the time. Fear had worn my insides so I felt my gut had been scraped out and carved like a pumpkin.

I'd run my hands all over that church, feeling for memory like a nearly blind person gropes for their glasses. There was much memory in the building and in the monuments but none that illuminated the truth, and none had marked me. A small blessing as people had begun to blatantly stare at my forehead, neck, and hands. It made me want to rip off my shirt and give them some knife.

For the first time in my life, I pondered wearing makeup. "Concealer" sounded exactly like a product I should become acquainted with. Case in point, an older woman in the *piazza* had asked me if my "tattoo" was of the Borromean rings. She was kind about it, said it symbolized "strength in unity." The stripped, exposed feeling I had, lifted slightly as I thought about what she'd said. *Strength in Unity?*

Dante, Michelangelo, and threes... My inability to comprehend the meaning of these repeating coincidences frustrated me.

Also frustrating was my inability to speak Italian. More than once, I'd wished Giovanni were with me to translate and help me get around. In my more still and honest moments, I wished simply for his presence. I missed him: his confidence, his intensity, his...touch. God, his touch. I fought an internal battle over my feelings for Giovanni *and* for Finn and had to repeatedly tell myself what I told them: it doesn't matter.

My heart called bullshit and squeezed like a punishment at the thought of never seeing either of them again. "Never" was a hatchet cutting choice to the bone. The only choice I had left was to move forward.

In general, I played the part of the post high-school backpacker on a European jaunt before starting college. I found that talking to other tourists—well, talking *and* utilizing the play of energy I learned from Giovanni—yielded results: directions, assistance, and information.

I'd been judgmental and skeptical when Giovanni first showed me what he could do with his Scintilla energy, explaining that people would do almost anything for a hit of what they wanted most: happiness. It wasn't my nature to manipulate that way, but I shocked myself with how easily it came to me.

Because of this newfound ability, I'd had a very fortunate exchange with an art historian who'd also noticed the marking on my neck as we stood staring up at the circles on the tomb and asked if it was the *giri tondi*, which I'm sure made him think I was some kind of fanatical Michelangelo groupie. He arranged for me to tour the Vatican with his friend, Professor Piero Salamone, one of the foremost experts on Vatican art, particularly Michelangelo's. It would be better than roaming the Pope's pad on my own, hoping to blindly stumble upon clues or a big door that just happened to have a lock fitting the key around my neck. Arrangements were made to meet Piero Salamone on my second day in Rome.

Ina and Fergus had graciously given me money—quite a lot of it—and a new cell phone, and they arranged for a hotel room for me in Rome. My palms sweated every time I put the key in my hotel door, afraid the Arrazi had Finn's family under surveillance and had a way to trace their credit cards. I knew my thoughts were dramatic and paranoid, but more than once in Italy, I'd had the slithering feeling that someone was following me. I saw no flashes of a telltale white aura, but I couldn't be alerted to an Arrazi who hadn't recently killed unless they were close enough to feel—close enough to kill.

Joe, the cab driver, was now beatboxing, either that or he had a nasty cough. I asked him to drop me at Vatican City, where I made my way through the throng of undulating colors and chattering of various languages to the first place I wanted to go: St. Peter's Square.

I roamed around St. Peter's Square, again with the creeping sensation that I was being watched. I tried to keep calm, to swallow the paranoia that skittered up my back like spider's legs. I was one of thousands of people there. How could anyone but another Scintilla spot me?

Silver had become as elusive to me as those first days of seeing auras and wondering why mine was so different.

I missed Giovanni more in those lonely moments, missed the intimacy of having someone *like me* by my side. How could I not wonder if he was right about Scintilla's fate to be together? Our fate?

And why did I feel that tug of fate from the first moment I'd met Finn?

It doesn't matter.

Every step closer to the imposing statue of St. Peter made my breaths come shorter. I don't know what I expected, that his hand would still be gone, that the church would leave the keeper of the keys standing there with just a stump like Ultana Lennon's?

Instead, St. Peter pointed his large marble finger toward me as if to accuse, "There she is. She's the one who has my hidden key." Reflexively, I touched the key my grandmother had stolen from him to make sure it was concealed beneath my shirt.

For the longest time, I stood in the sun on the gray square pavers, staring at the imposing statue from every angle. St. Peter had been hiding a secret in his hand, right above the adoring heads of Catholics from all over the world. *Someone* had to know that his famous keys hid a secret key within them. Someone had to know *why*.

Willing an answer from the curly-haired stone, I asked over and over again, what were his secrets?

After an amber-saturated evening of walking amid the humming noise of Rome past the timeworn buildings and fountains, and slurping down pasta slick with sauce, and then a tart *limone* gelato on my way to my hotel, I woke to another bright day in Rome. *Signore* Salamone was to meet me in St. Peter's Basilica to begin our tour in front of Michelangelo's famous sculpture, *La Pietà.*

I'd arrived a bit early and found myself staring in still rapture at the impossibly alive statue of the young Virgin Mary, who cradled her dead son across her lap. It was so breathtakingly lifelike and gave the impression a wand had been waved over them and had frozen the devastating scene for all eternity. I was mesmerized.

Agony froze my chest so that it was hard to breathe and pity washed over me for their suffering. I'd watched both of my parents die at the uncaring hands of others. My hands squeezed into hard knots. I could not feel as placidly resigned as the sweet face of Mary looked in Michelangelo's interpretation, though her upturned left hand seemed to ask, *why?* I'd wondered why he'd chosen to make her so. Maybe Michelangelo believed it was beneath Mary to feel wrathful anger.

I was not so good.

"It's the only sculptural piece the artist ever signed." I spun around to face the kindly looking elderly man who'd spoken. As I assessed his aura, he extended his hand. "You are Miss Sandoval, I hope?"

"Yes," I said, afraid to offer my own hand but not wanting to offend. My hands felt like weapons against myself. He perceptively dropped his own while I debated. "Where is his signature?" I asked, hoping to see the circular monogram with my own eyes.

Instead of pointing to the base of the sculpture, where I'd guess an artist would place a small, modest claim, Piero gestured upward, right at the Virgin Mary. "See her cloak strap there?" he said, pointing to the middle of Mary's chest where a sash ran from her waist upward between her breasts and over her left shoulder. A series of Latin capital letters were engraved into the strap.

"It doesn't look like his name," I said, trying to make out the bold engraving. I stepped closer and peered at the letters. Not only was it some kind of Latin version of his name, but I noticed that within the words, random letters were oddly engraved smaller than all the others, and set in circles. Three circles, in fact.

My heart flopped in my chest as I identified the random letters one by one:

T- R - I.

Every hair on my arms stood on end. My silver aura leaped from my skin in excited spikes. The only piece he ever signed, and done so audaciously it was almost arrogant. He'd stamped his name on a sash, a freaking banner to the world, and on it he'd placed three letters in three circles. A Latin derivative—for *three*.

Instantly, I thought of Dante and his structure of *The Divine Comedy* and its full-on reliance on threes—three parts, thirty-three stanzas, each with thirty-three lines, all written in third rhyme.

"Moving, isn't it?" Piero asked.

I could hardly utter my agreement. I was totally moved, like whoa. I concentrated on calming myself as we walked away from *La Pieta* and through a long, narrow room toward an altar. Behind the altar and covering the entire wall was Michelangelo's famous painting, *The Last Judgment.*

The image was enormous, violent and dark in a way that surprised me. Piero explained that Michelangelo had originally painted the figures nude, but the church found it obscene and had the masterpiece altered. It would have taken me weeks to discover many of the hidden messages within the painting on my own, but within minutes, I was given intimate details of the work as if Piero had known the artist himself.

Piero showed me Michelangelo's self-portrait in the flayed skin of Saint Bartholomew *and* the face of—no way!—Dante Alghieri, which the painter had included along with figures from Dante's *Inferno*—a direct nod to *The Divine Comedy*.

"Moved" was becoming an understatement. I had to remind myself to close my open mouth.

I noted auras painted around Jesus and his mother, and the eerily familiar way Mary had her arms crossed over her chest self-protectively as I'd had when my aura was attacked for the first time in the hospital and in the many times since.

St. Peter, a burly figure to Christ's left in the painting, seemed to be offering one gold and one silver key to Christ. *Follow your instincts* was what my grandmother told me, so I asked the only question I truly sought. "*Signore*, I'm fascinated by the symbolism of keys. Is there anything special about the keys in this painting? Or in any other art in the Vatican?"

Piero looked at me quizzically before answering. "Keys are quite important in Christian art. There are the keys in St. Peter's hand, of course. They are the keys to the Kingdom of Heaven bestowed to him by Jesus. But many don't realize that there is another set of keys painted within *The Last Judgment*..." We craned our heads up, and he gave me a small pair of binoculars through which to better see. "Over on the right, there is a man dangling upside down over the fires of hell."

It took me a moment to pick out the man, but it helped that he was upside down as Piero described. The hulking naked figure was being shoved down toward hell by angels. "I see him." Then something else caught my eye. "He has keys," I said, "two of them. There's also a small pouch."

"Yes. Some say it's a moneybag of gold, meant to show that someone from the church was going to hell for avarice, for being corruptible. Some say the bag held something else, but we don't know what. Only the artist knew for certain."

"Dante's ashes?" I whispered to myself. That's what the pouch reminded me of.

"Pardon?" His hand was suddenly on my shoulder, and I stepped out of his reach. "My, but you do know how to impress an old art professor, Miss Sandoval. Not many people know of the pouches from Dante's remains."

I could've been right or it could have been money. In Michelangelo's adoring eyes, someone should've gone to hell for ordering Dante's death. Did Michelangelo know about that? But how could he? Gold *or* ashes, it was a condemnation of someone within the church, the two keys made that clear.

If Dante's *Paradiso* was a message to Scintilla, then it might take another Scintilla to recognize it. Was Michelangelo Buonarotti, like his beloved Dante, using his art to send messages of his own? One last look through the binoculars set my heart quickening.

One of the keys of the damned man being shoved into hell looked startlingly similar to the key around my neck.

Chapter Eleven

Finn

Saoirse texted twice more, asking where I was and leaving me no idea how much she knew about Newgrange. If Lorcan had been ignorant of his mother's fate, perhaps Saoirse was as well. I couldn't imagine that if Saoirse or Lorcan knew I'd been present when their mother died, that I'd be getting a text as innocuous as "Where are you?"

I texted back: *On biz with me mum*

I need to see you

Is everything okay?

You left me hanging! Last I heard you needed to help your ex-girlfriend and wanted me to run interference between Lorcan and my mother. What happened?

I sighed. Okay, so she *was* in the dark, for the moment. I thought about whether to type my answer, realizing that to keep Saoirse's trust, the news about the Arrazi battle at Newgrange should come from me and not her brother. It was only a matter of time before he told her what he'd stumbled upon, and I wanted to admit to her myself that I'd killed my own uncle, and why.

I'd not, however, tell her what I knew about her mother's death. The last thing I wanted was to endanger Cora further. What if Saoirse and her brother, Lorcan, somehow blamed Cora and the Scintilla for their mother's death? Cora had enough enemies breathing down her neck—she didn't need more.

We've had a death in the family. I could use a friend. Can I come by later?

After Cora departed through security and texted her arrival at the gate, my mother and I walked to the car, whispering worries and scenarios. I wondered how Clancy had gotten out of that tomb. Had anyone helped him? Had they found Ultana?

"I could go and check the tomb," I said to my mother. "See if Clancy left her body there. Maybe lock it up again?"

"Don't be ridiculous. You can't go anywhere near that place. Newgrange is closed because of the deaths, and the entire area is on high alert. Ultana's dead—a bloody relief, if you ask me. Maybe now all this nonsense will stop. You don't need to be connected with it."

"I'm already connected. Lorcan saw me at Newgrange." I swallowed hard. "With his mother's dagger. If they find her body, they'll see she was run through with a blade as well."

"Let's pray he's too stupid to put two and two together."

"I didn't kill Ultana, mother."

"You think anyone will believe she drove the blade into her *own* stomach? Who does that?"

"Someone who believed she couldn't die."

"Why on earth would Lorcan Lennon protect you when the news is out that Clancy was killed with a dagger? When they find Ultana, every *eejit* Arrazi for miles will assume you killed both of them."

I swallowed hard. Lorcan found me, the only Arrazi alive in a sea of dead bodies. We'd been attacked. I'd attacked in return to defend the Scintilla. "You love who you love, man," I'd said to Lorcan by way of desperate explanation. "And I fell in love with a Scintilla. Clancy was trying to take them for himself when he found out your mother wanted them. He was betraying her orders."

Lorcan's face had been a mix of astonishment and confusion. "Weren't you betraying orders?" he'd asked.

"I don't take orders."

I'd defended for love and defended all of us against my ruthless uncle. Pray Lorcan would leave it at that. I needed to stay in the Lennons' inner circle. Surely, Saoirse and Lorcan would have some idea what the Arrazi were up to. Hopefully, they were a rudderless ship without Ultana as their captain.

"I'm going to go over to the Lennons," I told my mother.

"Wait until everything settles, Finn. You have no idea what the fallout will be. With any luck, this mission of hers will die with her."

Despite my mum's warnings, I couldn't just sit and wait for the fallout. If Ultana no longer gave instructions to the Arrazi, what would happen? Would they abandon their mission to hunt and kill the Scintilla?

If Ultana's instructions came to her from any religious order, who specifically issued those instructions and with what bait? Would they simply find another Arrazi to take on the job? My gut clenched. Too many people would be happy to replace Ultana as the most powerful Arrazi in the world. Didn't matter if we were an unknown breed of humans; power is power and a breed of human with superpowers is even more formidable.

Made me wonder why the Arrazi needed to take orders from anyone at all.

When I arrived at the Lennons' house Saoirse flung open the front door and pitched herself into my chest, slight arms clutched around my neck. She abruptly withdrew and blushed. "Jaysus, what is it with you? I seem unable to stifle my stupid impulses around you, Finn. Forgive me. You did scare me, though, with that call of yours. What happened, for Christ's sake?"

I gave her a tight smile. "Is everyone home?" I asked, trying to sound casual, like I didn't have a block of freezing dread melting at my core, especially when we walked past Ultana's collection of ancient weaponry hanging on the wall. One of her deadly blades was now hidden in our kitchen, high up on a shelf.

"Just us," Saoirse said, leading me into their kitchen. "I haven't heard from my mother in two days. Typical," she added, pulling biscuits from a cupboard and a wedge of cheddar from the fridge and setting them on the white marble countertop. "Strange, though, two different Arrazi have shown up at my door today, asking about her."

I took her arm. "I reckon they want to talk to her about Newgrange," I said, affecting a dramatic tone. "You knew about it, 'ey? Lorcan said you'd caught wind of something going down there. You'll not want to have much to do with me after I tell you what happened."

Soairse's ginger brows pinched together as I proceeded to tell her about the battle at Newgrange, or as much of it as I could so she'd know I'd been caught in a hopeless situation against my uncle.

"How *did* you know that something was brewing there?" I asked her.

"Clancy—he called here looking for my mother, and when I told him she wasn't here, he said to give her a message to meet him there."

That set me back. Why would he call for Ultana when he knew damn well she was dead? Maybe he wanted to know if *they* knew it...

"When did he call?"

"I can't right remember exactly," Saoirse said, nibbling the edge of a thin cracker. "Why?"

"You once told me that your mum told Clancy she wanted nothing more than to find three Scintilla. Well, Clancy set his sights on three Scintilla, to be sure, and was racing to capture them for himself before your mother found them. That's why I don't understand why he called her. He wouldn't have wanted her to know..." It made no sense.

If Clancy just wanted to know if they knew something had happened to their mother, why would he then tell Saoirse that he was going to Newgrange? Maybe he was trying to worm himself into the *vacated* leadership position through Ultana's children. "They cornered us at *Brú na Bóinne*. I had to help the Scintilla. I had to stand against them for—"

"For her," she said with a knowing look.

I nodded. "I wish I knew where she is now, or that she'll be okay." I bowed my head for effect, but my words were so true. Cora was on my mind constantly, and my heart ached with a persistent need to know if she was safe.

"Cora has the Scintilla guy to look out for her now, right?" Saoirse said. Sympathy filled her eyes as she gripped my forearm. "Let her go, Finn. It's tragically obvious, isn't it? You can *never* be together. You did what you could, you let them—helped them—escape."

I pulled away from her grasp, anger punching rhythmically at my temples. "Nothing is obvious when the world tries to tell you who you're allowed to love."

"Finn, this isn't prejudice. It's biology. We are genetically designed to kill the silver ones. She has to know she'll never truly be safe with you."

Her words were a kick in the gut, an echo of Cora's words at the airport.

"Maybe she could be. My uncle was able to keep a Scintilla captive, behind everyone's back, including your mother's," I added stubbornly, hoping it would make his duplicity even more rank, "and he didn't kill her. For twelve years, he didn't kill her. I think there might be more to the story of why we were made this way, if only we could find it."

"You're a romantic," Saoirse said, with a tart splash of condescension. "It's sweet. But how much are you willing to risk for love?"

Everything.

"Surely your brother will tell your mother that I killed fellow Arrazi," I said, doing my best to hold her gaze through my deceit, "and once she knows, I doubt she'll be so keen to have me around anymore."

"Are you kidding?" Saoirse laughed in a lighthearted way that made me feel sorry for her loss, and her ignorance. "You'll never get away from my mother."

The doorbell clanged and my nerves with it.

"Are you bleedin' kidding me?" she said. I stayed in the kitchen while Saoirse ran to answer it but listened as best I could to the unfamiliar voice in the foyer.

"All the world is talking about the mysterious deaths at Newgrange," the man said in his southwestern Irish dialect. I was glad I'd beaten this stranger to Saoirse's door. "But all the *Arrazi* are talking about now is why some of ours were dead among them. Arrazi know that it's been all too easy to nip a few here and a few there to take advantage of the drop-deads. Hell, I'm sure our kind killed those folks. But who killed *them*? Everyone is terrified your mother had a hand in it, bein' as she's threatened every Arrazi under the sun. And if it wasn't her, then who?"

"You came here to accuse her mother?" I asked, stepping into the foyer and putting my arm around Saoirse's small waist.

"No, no," the man said, eyeing me from top to toe with a squint. "I came to see if Ultana Lennon knows the truth, to settle the talk."

Saoirse's back went rigid under my hand. "You came like a common gossip to my door. People ought to worry more about how my mother will react to the talk. She's been occupied on business, and this idle chatter of her possible involvement with those deaths is insulting. Perhaps the Arrazi are just as vulnerable to the sickness that is claiming the lives of people all over the world. Talk about *that*." She slammed the door in his face.

"Saoirse, you're wrong," I said. "The Arrazi *weren't* vulnerable to the sickness. I saw with my own eyes. Those people began to fall, began to die, before any Arrazi hooked their claws into the auras of the few who were still standing."

What I didn't tell her was that something uncanny happened out there… A sense that the battle outside that monument had rippled outward and somehow brought on the deaths.

Saoirse sagged against me. "I don't know the answers. I just wanted him off my back."

"You handled him like a teacher to a schoolchild," I told her. "I like how you surprise me sometimes."

"My mother had better get home soon," she said, pursing her bow lips. "She'll put them all in their places."

Cruelly, I yearned to scoff. Ultana had been put in her place by her own hand. "And what place is that?" I asked.

Saoirse didn't look at me. Her eyes fixed resolutely out the window. "In the ground, if they continue to turn on us."

Chapter Twelve

Giovanni

"Where did they come from?" I asked Mami Tulke as we walked through what I now saw was a community, a kind of utopian Scintilla enclave, which she named *Rancho Estrella*. Star Ranch.

We passed a communal garden where they grew their own food, including papayas for sale to local markets. They had stables for goats, pens for chickens, hens, and roosters, and a kitchen where each person served on rotation. As artisans, they made money selling pottery, tiles, paintings, and even managed a thriving pisco vineyard.

"They've come to me from everywhere," she said. "Washing up from all over the world like silver flecks in a stream."

"How do they know to come here?"

"Most feel a magnetic pull to the energy of this place. I believe that was true for Cora's mother. Her search for spirals led her to the *El Molle* petroglyphs at *Valle de Encanto*, but soon she found her way to my doorstep. Then there are those," she said, leaning against a shaded wall in a bent way that made me consider her advanced age, "who find us by other means—an underground system of word of mouth. The internet has helped that way, but I fear it might be a danger to us as well. If the Arrazi find us hiding here, they will be able to wipe out the remaining Scintilla in one swoop."

"How do you hide when you aren't sure who your enemies are?"

"I'm sure one enemy is someone somehow involved with the most powerful religion on earth," she said. "But even they aren't the *true* enemy."

The surety in her statement made me stop observing the various Scintilla around me and the curious stares I was getting as some strolled past. "Who is the *true* enemy? And if you know, why is Cora traipsing around Italy by herself at this very moment?"

Mami Tulke had a way of smiling that made me feel the very unfamiliar sensation of ignorance or stupidity. "The true enemy is everywhere, Giovanni. Not just in Italy. The Scintilla's true enemy is fear."

I shook my head. "They want to kill us because they fear us?"

"Of course. Fear would make us a pest, a bug they believe they must squash. Fear is this world's most destructive force; it erodes our connection to one another. Where humans might learn from those who are different, instead they turn their faces away as if we aren't all mirrors."

"Mirrors? But Scintilla are obviously vastly different, or they wouldn't be afraid of us."

"Every person, no matter how different, reflects ourselves back onto us. Both sides should ask themselves who they want to be when they look into the face of *the other*."

"I don't want to look into the face of *the other*, I want—" Before the words "to kill them" could come out of my mouth, I saw two Scintilla—a couple—pointing excitedly at me. With their hands clasped, they approached us. Their expressions were friendly, open, as were their silver auras. The young woman was a bit unsure of me. Her aura hooked into her companion's for reassurance.

Mami Tulke introduced me to Will, an American—a Texan, which I understood to be a whole different breed of American—and his wife, Maya. They were a study in contrasts—his gleaming, freckled skin next to the sheen of her black skin—but the same in the only way that counted, the sparks that surrounded their bodies. It lit my own aura with the effervescent thrill of being around people like me. Maya smiled as my aura betrayed my longing to connect with them. It was an embarrassing show. Instantly, I was a boy of ten.

Will shook my hand heartily, and Maya did the same. "Welcome to paradise, newcomer," he said with a genuine smile.

"It's great to have you here. A relief. Enough time goes by without new arrivals and we get to thinking we're going extinct." Maya said. Her accent was American-Southern, as well, but different from Will's. Hers was like dark rum cake or peaches soaked in syrup, which she confirmed by stating that she was from Arkansas. Maya had found herself in South America researching the spirals first in Nazca in Peru, and then in Tiwanaku in Bolivia. She and Will met there on the hills of a mysterious civilization, which I had to admit reminded me of the story of Newgrange.

When I inquired about Maya's research into spirals, she launched into her theory that spirals all around the world were connected and were intended as a clear message about celestial beings coming to earth to help mankind. I could see that Will wasn't entirely on board with her ideas by the way he raised his eyebrow at me at certain points.

"This place certainly gets its share of E.T. fanatics," he said, causing her to suck in her cheeks and scowl at him.

To ease Mami Tulke's burden of standing in the afternoon heat, we moved to a patio area outside the communal eating and meeting building and sat together at a wooden picnic bench to talk more.

Maya was animated when she talked, her hands undulating and moving as much as her silver aura did. "Spirals are especially important everywhere on earth. In plants, weather, and our own bodies. The spiral is the world's oldest known symbol, used by peoples all over the world at a time when they had no way to communicate with one another. From the outer reaches of the universe to our own planet, the spiral is everywhere. They are clues, and we need to find out what they're telling us because I believe, as many here believe," Maya said with a quick shushing glance at her man, "that the spirals have everything to do with the Scintilla."

"And what do you all believe about the Arrazi? Do you believe the spirals have anything to do with them?" I asked. I appreciated how Will's eyes narrowed in disgust at the mention of their name.

"I don't see how," he said. "Altogether different creatures, my friend. Those parasites are our polar opposite."

"Everything has an opposite, hon," Maya said with a temperate tone. "I don't think we can say either way. Wouldn't it be arrogant to assume the signals were just for us? They could be a message to the whole of humanity, of which we are all a part."

Will cocked his head at her in a way that told me they'd had this particular discussion many times over and it was at a friendly stalemate.

When Maya offered to take a wilting Mami Tulke back to her house, I wasted no time in telling him how severe the situation had become for Scintilla everywhere. "They are hunting us." I held up my hand when Will gave a look like what I'd said was obvious. "Like animals, methodically, and at the direction of someone else. It is their sole purpose to eradicate us all. There will not be another Scintilla left on this earth if they succeed."

It didn't seem possible for someone so fair to pale even further, but the color drained from Will's face. "You're sure?"

"Without a doubt."

I told him of Ultana Lennon and her secret society, Xepa, and of her dogged aim to find and kill us all. "She's dead, but according to an Arrazi who seems to be sympathetic to the Scintilla," I said, begrudgingly thankful for Finn's help, "she corralled many an Arrazi to do her work. I had no idea of your existence until Mami Tulke brought me to the ranch. They seemingly know nothing of you all hiding here."

"We're not just hiding. This is our home now. This is a community. They *can't* find out about us. Dozens of people will have no place to go." Will's voice was desperate, his eyes round with fear.

"They *will* find us," I said. "They already kidnapped Mami Tulke. That's where she's been. She was lucky to escape."

"Shit."

"Xepa had power, bestowed by someone with even more power. We're trying to find out exactly who. Whoever it is wants us all dead. They know Mami Tulke lives in the Elqui Valley. I'd say it's a matter of certainty that the days of peace here are numbered. Everyone should prepare."

Will stood abruptly. "Excuse me. I want to think about this. Please, don't say anything to anyone else just yet. I don't want the place to erupt in panic. I don't want Maya to panic."

"I'm—I'm sorry, Will," I said, standing and clasping his shoulder. "I know I don't bring good news. But I'd rather we all be prepared than hide our heads in the sand, hoping they won't find us. The war is coming, and if we want to survive, the Scintilla will have to do battle."

Chapter Thirteen

Cora

The floor of the Sistine Chapel was elaborately tiled, and I couldn't help but notice the many spirals and triangles placed within the layout of the tiles.

Piero Salamone studied me as he spoke. "I'm quite intrigued by you, Cora. Not many people your age have such an ardent interest in the specifics of Michelangelo's work. You already seem to be aware that he had a fascination with Dante. Do you mind if I ask what fuels your interest?"

"I'm intrigued by the hidden messages in art," I said, knowing it was both an answer and a question. I was hoping Piero would elaborate on any hidden messages the Vatican might have. "I mean," I said, suddenly squirming under his scrutinizing eyes, "that all artists probably have their own agendas and ways of making their personal opinions known." I pointed to Minos, the donkey-eared god of the underworld sporting the face of one of the artist's critics. Minos was also depicted with a snake biting his penis. Piero had told me the history of that figure in the painting. "Michelangelo definitely had a rebellious agenda there."

"Indeed he did," Piero said, laughing. "You must have very strong beliefs about hidden messages to tattoo them on your body. If you don't mind me asking, why did you choose to permanently mark yourself with the three circles? Did you mean them to be the Borromean Rings? Or is it Michelangelo's *tre giri*? What is your take on its meaning, then?"

"It's very personal to me," I said, resisting the urge to cover the mark with my hand and wishing I'd stopped to buy makeup. "I believe as he did, that contemplating the three circles—"

"Raises one's thoughts to heaven," interrupted a baritone voice behind me. I spun around. I didn't know enough about Catholicism to say if the man was a cardinal, or bishop, or a freaking Red Knight of the High Church of Whatever, but he wore a red robe and looked like he stepped right out of history. His aura wasn't the white I'd come to fear, nor did I feel Arrazi energy from him. He had a fair amount of dark purple in his aura, which I'd learned could mean a sense of superiority, but it was tinged with black as if the edges of his aura had been burned. I'd seen black before, which could indicate illness or anger that's been held in. It could also signal dark intention and lies. I wasn't experienced enough yet to know for sure, but I knew enough to be guarded.

His white hair was closely cropped around the ears beneath his cap. As he stepped forward, my gaze fell to the folds of his red garment. It reminded me of something. My mind raced to place it.

He greeted Piero warmly. "*Buongiorno, Professore* Salamone. And who is this young lady?"

Piero's aura jiggled with aqua-colored nervousness. The robed man was obviously important. "This is Cora Sandoval, Your Eminence. I'm pleased to introduce you to Cardinal Báthory. Cora is a young art student on holiday before school begins."

"And a searcher of truth," I interjected, trying to smile but feeling my cheeks freeze up. When both men snapped curious eyes at me I added with an awkward, weak laugh, "In that...I believe great truths are often revealed in the art of great masters."

"If your search for truth has brought you to the house of the Lord, you are on the right path. Pilgrims the world over come to Vatican City because they feel in their hearts that the truth is here." Cardinal Báthory delivered this in such a high-handed tone I wanted to argue just for the sake of challenging him. People and their "truths." Seemed to me that "truth" was the most subjective word on the planet.

"Exactly why I'm here." It took everything I had not to scowl at the cardinal. I wondered why such an official had approached us, of all people, especially among so many other sightseers milling around, and desperately hoped the man was specifically drawn to speak to Piero Salamone and not drawn to me by *extrasensory* means.

"Perhaps you gentlemen can help me with something," I said, smiling at the two men as amiably as I could but fearing I'd already attracted the wrong kind of attention. The world was a maze of tripwires, and I was barreling through them all. "I read online that some years ago you had an outrageous theft. The hand of St. Peter was stolen. Why do you suppose someone would do such a shocking thing?"

The cardinal looked affronted. "Is logic to be applied to the actions of fanatical lunatics? There can be no reason, just as there was no reason for a raving man to hack away at Michelangelo's *La Pieta* years ago and desecrate a priceless masterpiece."

"I mean," I pressed, "of all the things to steal, why take the hand of St. Peter?" I ventured further out on a precarious ledge. Anger and desperation compelled me to ask. His aura might say more than his answer. I delivered one of my two most pressing questions. "I read somewhere on the internet that something might have been *hidden* in St. Peter's hand."

There was a flash of consternation in the cardinal's eyes, and his aura turned the muddy red of anger. "The internet is hardly a source of reliable information."

His answer reminded me of my father's when I'd been searching for information on silver auras. "Which is why I'm asking *you*. As you said, the truth is here."

"I'd never seen that mentioned in the investigations of the theft," the cardinal answered with a puff of black curling around his lips, exposing his lie. I damn near smirked. "Child, what St. Peter holds in his hands are the very keys to the Kingdom of Heaven bestowed upon him by Jesus Christ, our Lord and Savior. It's likely the thief was simply after the notoriety."

"But there is no notoriety if the identity of the thief remains unknown."

The corners of his lips turned up in a smile like a puppeteer pulled strings on each side of his mouth. His eyes computed as he assessed me. "You presume that the Vatican doesn't know the identity of the thief."

My heart jammed somewhere around my belly button. "Really?" I asked in a near-whisper, trying to look impressed rather than scared. "You *know* who stole it?"

Cardinal Báthory lowered his chin and gave another of his impressively joyless smiles, but he didn't confirm or deny. He absentmindedly spun a ring on his right hand. The movement forced the sudden recognition from me. Someone dressed just like this man had given Ultana Lennon her ring. I'd seen the flash of thick red fabric in the vision when she and I struggled in the tomb and her memories flew into my mind. At the time, I had erroneously mistaken the red fabric for a skirt. "My dear," he said, "one must never underestimate the reach of the holy church."

"I don't." I breathed, forcing myself not to back away when I spotted the triangular symbol on the ring as he spun it over the hill of his fat finger and back under again.

Chapter Fourteen

Finn

I left Saoirse with lightness of relief followed by heavy doom that rattled my chest like a bird flinging itself against its bloody cage. She hadn't vilified me for killing my uncle while protecting the Scintilla, but there was something unsettling about the spite in her eyes and her harsh words after she scolded that man. I dreaded the moment when Saoirse and Lorcan realized their mother was never coming home. If her body was ever found, the dagger wound would be obvious. Lorcan would assume I'd killed his mother, being as he'd caught me with the bloody—literally—thing at Newgrange.

I felt like a dry piece of *shite*. I knew the truth about what happened to Ultana, and Saoirse was in the dark. But having them blame Cora, or even cut me from their circle, wasn't an option. I kissed her cheek in my own secretive apology and left for home, hoping that if, as Ultana had said, there was no one above her in Xepa, then God willing, her agenda would wither on the vine and fade to nothing.

All that had gone down at Newgrange and at the tomb where Ultana died had me thinking hard about what Saoirse revealed when we first met: that Newgrange was a base for the supernatural races. My uncle tried to sacrifice the three Scintilla *there* for a reason. Were the chambers within the megalithic monuments always used to kill Scintilla? More than ever, I longed to know the unknowable history of that place.

I stood shirtless in front of the mirror and stared at my own tattoo—an exact replica of the triple spiral, but made of stars. Was the true meaning of the symbol lost forever? Bollocks. I refused to believe that. Cora believed there would be a message in the stone. She almost died trying to retrieve it.

Online, there was much about spirals in ancient art, especially in Ireland and the rest of the U.K, also in South America. I looked for anything to tie the spirals to religion, to either support or refute Ultana's claims. Truthfully, I'd do anything to disprove it and get Cora out of her obstinate solo trip. Even dead, I didn't trust that Ultana wouldn't play Cora into the hands of danger.

A webpage directed me to one of Ireland's finest national treasures, the *Book of Kells*, an ancient manuscript housed in the library at Trinity College. Spirals and triskelions were used liberally in the artwork in the book, most notably and extensively on the *Chi Rho* page translated to "This is how Christ came to be born." The oldest western depiction of the Virgin Mary was also in the *Book of Kells*. I stared long and hard at her tunic in the drawing, which was adorned with dozens of dots in triplicate, triangular patterns, which looked to my bleary eyes like the form of the triple spiral.

"That's the problem with what you're doing," my mother commented later when I went downstairs for supper and showed her the printouts of the two folios from the *Book of Kells*. "You're looking for connections in things that may very well be unrelated. Seriously, dots? You will fritter away your life trying to solve this unsolvable puzzle." Her eyes darkened and went to another place for just a moment.

The heat of aggravation rose from my chest to my tensed jaw. "Is there a reason you don't want it solved? Why didn't you tell me that Newgrange was where we all originated?"

My mother's chin pulled back incredulously. "Dammit, Finn, because we don't *know* for sure! Why would I fill your head with superstition?"

"But you always said that the triple spiral was important to our family."

Her sigh was heavy as she dropped her soup spoon down with a clang. "Because I suspect something does not make it so. And how will it help save Cora to know where we come from? Seems to me that saving the Scintilla is your only real concern. My little brother," she said, crossing herself, "dragged us into a war, and now you're keeping us in it."

"So you'd rather the Scintilla all be killed?"

"I'd rather—" My mother's voice faltered and lowered as did her eyes. "I'd rather you forget about Cora Sandoval and move on with your life before you're killed trying to save hers."

"I. Can. Not. Forget."

My mother sighed. "I know. But I lost you once, Finn.

Don't make me go through that again. A mother should never have to go through that—" Her hands shook, and she placed them in her lap.

Beats of uncomfortable silence bounced between us until I ventured another question. "Saoirse said that her mother was eager to pull me close because I was from one of the oldest Arrazi families around, specifically *your* side of the family. Why would that matter to Ultana?"

"I assumed it was some kind of antediluvian notion about bloodlines. Ultana Lennon thought herself superior, even among Arrazi. The only thing that makes our family special is that, to my knowledge, there has never been a union that wasn't between two pure Arrazi."

Was it bloodlines or something else Ultana wanted?

"The woman's dead, and she still has secrets," I said. "She was a thief. So much so that the mark on her face was branded there hundreds of years ago, a thief's brand. She had stolen ashes from Dante's tomb inside the heart—stolen, too, by the way—from Christ Church, right there in her office! I saw her collect souvenirs from a kill," I said, recalling how Ultana snipped off a clutch of hair from Mari's friend, Teruko, and added a coin from her pocket to her collection plates. If there was a coin for every life she took, then she was a prolific murderer over her many centuries. "I'm glad that *moldy* bitch is finally dead."

My mother shot me a stern look for my language, but to hell with that. "Maybe she had more than one goal," I said. "She might have been after me for her daughter, like you say, but I wonder if she was after something else."

Those words had an odd effect on my mother. She stared at me, but I could see her thoughts were racing. Her forehead creased as she thought. "Do you know what she might have been after?" I asked, hoping my sortilege would make her explain her odd reaction.

Abruptly, she stood and said, "Yes. Come."

We left the dining room and entered the hall outside the library. I thought she meant to go into the library, possibly after a book, but she stopped in front of *The Scintillating Host of Heaven*.

Bizarrely, my mother reached and pulled the art open like a door. Behind it was a small panel in the wall, which she slid down, revealing a keypad. "Three, twenty-six, seven," she said aloud as she entered the numbers. The display flashed green, I heard a loud *click*, and an entire door-sized section of the wall slid open.

"Feckin' Jaysus!"

My mother shot me a tired look and opened the door.

"No more secrets," she said. "The existence of this vault and its contents has been passed to every eldest child in the Mulcarr family. Even my brother was ignorant of its existence. You'd have been notified upon my death, but I'm giving you access now to every item I possess from our family's history." Mum placed her hand on my cheek and left it there long enough to warm my heart. "If there is anything here that will give you answers"—her eyes glossed with sadness—"or peace, then I entrust it to you."

The sharp inhale of surprise from my mother when I pulled her into a tight hug made me sad. We'd never been touchy-feely, but this gesture of trust from her was enormous. I'd always felt the inflexible rope of her protectiveness, always sensed secrecy in her, and it kept us from being truly close. I knew what it took for her to release ultimate control and finally trust me, and I loved her more for it.

She flipped a light switch and a short corridor illuminat-ed an old wooden door. The door groaned when she pushed it open for us to enter into a single room about the size of my parents' walk-in closet. It contained a large rectangular desk at one end. The walls on either side were lined with filing cabinets that were both deep and wide, the kind that might be used by artists or architects to house large papers flat without folding.

"Under the staircase?" It was laughable that I'd never even wondered what might lie below the wide staircase. "Wicked. Have you spent much time in here?" I asked, trac-ing a triangle in the thick dust on top of one of the wooden cabinets. It seemed no one had been inside in years. I sud-denly foresaw hours of my future in this dank room.

"After my father died, I spent quite a bit of time perus-ing the contents of various drawers," she said, pulling one drawer open and lifting the corner of a stack of old papers, sending motes dancing in the shafts of light. "But there's so much here, so much history, literally hundreds and hundreds of years, and when one doesn't have a specific thing to look for, nothing leaps out.

"If there was anything in this room that could help us, don't you think the information would have been passed down and spread to other Arrazi? Eventually, we had you, and the current of life rushed forward in its winding, swift way. I accepted what I was and closed the door on the past."

"Thank you for this—for not keeping any more secrets from me, Mum. For trusting me."

Her eyes shone with appreciation, and she wrapped her hand behind my neck and pulled me to her. "Oh, darlin',

I love you." Then she pushed me at arm's length, and her face turned sardonic. "There's another secret, to be sure. It's another reason I brought you in here. The Mulcarr family hasn't exactly been stock full of saints, I'm afraid."

Chapter Fifteen

Giovanni

I walked back to Mami Tulke's house on the same dusty road we drove up in her golf cart, all the while looking down on the community of Scintilla she'd hidden in the Elqui Valley. How strange that these inhospitable-looking mountains with cactus and goats and dirt would cradle the world's most rare species of human.

From talking to Will, it seemed they were totally unaware of the menace that was bearing down on all Scintilla. Clancy knew Cora's grandmother was a Scintilla; surely he'd have told someone. At the very least, they'd come to Chile looking for more family members.

They'd stumble upon a damn diamond mine.

And crush every single one.

Sweat trickled down my back as I came upon Mami Tulke's small house. Claire was outside with Yolanda picking strawberries from raised beds. My steps stuttered when I saw my daughter, and I shaded my eyes so I could more clearly observe her. Never had I seen such a brazen aura on someone, as if she wanted to color the whole sky with her brilliant rainbow. Even back at Dr. M's, when we could see and feel her strength, it wasn't this big. It was as though by freeing her from his facility, her spirit had been freed.

I didn't like the way it rolled over Yolanda like feelers. I reminded myself that Claire was a child and had little to no experience with the outside world. It was up to me to teach her about her own energy. How was I going to do that when I barely knew how to untangle her hair? I supposed, though, that I knew more about auras than grooming a kid. When she saw me watching, she bounded over and handed me a plump red strawberry. "We came outside to listen to the buzzing," she said through stained lips, "and I found some strawberries."

"Buzzing?"

"You don't hear it? Yolanda says she can't hear it, either. It's loud, though. It's this place," she said, glancing at the trees and foliage around us.

I listened harder but didn't hear anything but the screech and hum of nature, which I figured she was hearing, and the occasional clang of someone in Mami Tulke's kitchen banging around a little too loudly. It kicked up a childhood memory of my mother, who cooked louder when she was mad. "Hungry?" I asked her as she stuffed another strawberry into her mouth. "We'd better get you fed, *topolina*. And a bath. It's bad that I can't recall your last bath, no?"

It took some getting used to, but I was catching on to the most basic routines of fatherhood. Well, Mami Tulke did have to remind me about the bath thing that morning. Having never cared for anyone's basic needs but my own, I was proud for adjusting so quickly. Proud of Claire, too. Her phantom buzzing concerned me, though. Perhaps she should have her ears checked? I trusted my ability to detect illness in a person's aura. It usually showed up as a noticeably dark area over the affected body part. The space over Claire's ears looked fine.

"The whipped cream is ready," Mami Tulke said to Claire from the doorway. "You have enough berries to bring me, or are you eating them as fast as you can pick them?" Mami Tulke's voice sounded happy, but her eyes dragged over me with a weary glint as we went inside.

After dinner of roast pork and fresh green salad, and the bowl of summer that was berries and cream, Claire trounced off to take a bath. Mami Tulke blocked me with her squat little body as I tried to leave the kitchen. "Will called," she said, hands firmly planted on her apron-clad hips. "Wants to meet with me. It's *urgent,* he says. What in the name of Christ on the Cross did you say to him?"

I felt the slap of defensiveness on my back. "Mami Tulke, you've done a good thing by hiding them here, but they have a right to know the truth and to do what they can to prepare themselves for the arrival of the Arrazi."

"We need to be strong, not panicked. I told you, fear is our enemy. Fear weakens everyone here."

"*Ignorance* weakens everyone here."

We glared at each other. "Giovanni, if people panic and

scatter to the winds, they will be out in the world, defenseless. There is always strength in numbers."

"Defenseless is defenseless, no matter how many we number. We have *no* defense against an Arrazi's power."

"You are young—the young are always so impulsive—and your own fear has you jumpy and stirring up trouble. Do not be so arrogant as to assume there are no protections in place." Her aura jabbed at me as much as her words did. God, the women of this family…

Young. Impulsive. I bristled at her condescension. I'd lost my parents, been attacked by the Arrazi, and nearly lost the most important person in my life. Yes, I was afraid. But fear was hot coal burning in my gut, and it would burn until the threat was gone. "What, are they going to protect themselves with Qigong? Positive energy? Positive energy didn't save Gráinne when it mattered most. It's war! If I have fear, it's because I now understand what we're up against."

I thought of Cora, and my chest ached with missing and worrying about her even though she'd already checked in with Mami Tulke twice. I thought of Claire, splashing in the bathtub, who deserved to live a life of freedom and a life without losing everyone she loved. I thought of the surprising community of Scintilla living in Chile, who might be the very last of a supernatural race.

I even thought of Cora's father, Benito, and what he said the night he was murdered. He spoke about energy and the mysterious deaths and planetary instability. Even the crazy Dr. M thought innocent people all over the world might face destruction if the Arrazi won.

Too much depended upon destroying the Arrazi.

A strange sound rumbled outside, and my initial thought

was "thunder." I felt a hulking jerk beneath my feet, and the world rattled and heaved.

Mami Tulke's aura flared in alarm as she yelled, "*Terremoto!*"

Earthquake.

Adrenaline burst through my body. The entire house shook like a snow globe in a careless child's hand. Amid the sounds of falling objects and breaking glass, I staggered to the bathroom. Claire's hands gripped the sides of the tub, her face warped in fear. I struggled to keep my balance as I yanked a towel from a rod and wrapped it around her little body, pulling her from the water. The ground pitched and jolted, knocking my feet out from under me. We fell together against the wall. Her head burrowed into my chest as I curled around her like a shell with my arms shielding her head and waited for the earth to end its tantrum.

Chapter Sixteen

Cora

Cardinal Báthory didn't *feel* like an Arrazi. But the ring confirmed his connection with an Arrazi, a ruthless one who'd murdered Dante Alighieri and whose job it was to hunt down and kill every last Scintilla.

That made him my enemy.

No amount of will was strong enough to stop my knees from shaking.

When Ultana had said, "as long as there is a god upon their altar, they will never stop hunting you," was it the altar I now stood before? Had I finally found the top of the pyramid? Who *was* this guy? Was he working alone, or on orders from someone another step up? My legs itched to run. Self-preservation in the immediate warred with my desire to stop this craziness forever. There were still unanswered questions.

Most importantly—I didn't know *why*.

A well-dressed man in a suit approached the three of

us with rushed steps and leaned in to the cardinal's ear. A troubled expression blanketed his face, and he crossed himself. Piero and I exchanged curious glances. "Check in again with the archbishop in La Serena, Chile."

Cardinal Báthory excused himself and strode away without a look back, but the mention of my grandmother's country sent bursts of anxiety through me. "What did he say? He said something about Chile," I said, and realized I'd grabbed Piero's arm. The cardinal had hinted that they knew who stole the hand. Would they go after my grandmother? If so, they'd stumble on the last Scintilla: Mami Tulke and Giovanni. As soon as I was away from Piero I had to call and warn them.

"I'm sorry. I couldn't hear, but it seemed urgent, no?" Piero said.

"What is that man's role here?" I asked, clueless about the hierarchy of the Roman Catholic Church.

"He works in the Congregation for the Doctrine of the Faith. Used to be known as the Supreme Sacred Congregation of the Roman and Universal Inquisition."

That word was cold water in my face, and my mouth went dry. Piero noticed my reaction, and one side of his mouth lifted into a knowing smile. "The Inquisition? Like witch hunts and burnings at the stake? *That* Inquisition?"

"Yes," he said. "There will always be an aftertaste to that word. No wonder they changed the name of the office, eh?" he added with a chuckle. "I've enjoyed our time, but I must be going soon. I have a group tour at half past. Do you have any last questions for me?"

I tried to act nonchalant despite the reasons to be anything but: the cardinal and his Xepa ring, his alarmed mention of

Chile after our unnerving conversation, and the fact that he headed the church office that was once known for violently routing out anyone they deemed a heretic. My hands drummed anxiously against my thighs.

"I really appreciate your time. Thank you. I've learned a lot." I meant it. I now felt sure that Michelangelo and Dante were similar in one deep respect: they both tried to plant messages within their art about threes and the corruption they saw in the church. I also knew that the man who headed the new office of what was once known as the Inquisition had a Xepa ring. My brain was a spinning top, and my aura was dropping silver flecks of dread around me. I had to get out of this place, call Chile, and then do what I could to learn about Cardinal Báthory.

Piero Salamone gave a little nod and walked away. Another question sprang to mind and I rushed across the spiraled tiles to tap his shoulder. "Um, I do have a last question... Did Michelangelo Buonarotti ever *live* here at the Vatican?"

"Many have speculated for centuries over that very question. Funny you should ask because rather recently, in 2007, there was a significant finding that proves Michelangelo did, in fact, reside here at St. Peter's at one point."

"Oh?" I yearned to see his room, to touch his memories. "What was the significant finding?"

"A ledger entry for a 450-year-old receipt was discovered with a notation that Michelangelo had a very expensive key made for a chest in his room. It said, '*10 scudi*'—much money in that time—'*to make a key for a chest in the room in St. Peter's where Master Michelangelo retires to.*'"

Piero's entire aura buzzed with the kind of excitement

that a discovery of that magnitude would give an art geek. My own aura responded, alighting with hot and nervous excitement at the word *key*.

"Can I visit the room? Do they have the key?" I asked eagerly. Impatient fervor threaded through my blood and, though I needed to call Mami Tulke, there was no way I could leave before trying to touch Michelangelo's room.

"Neither, I'm afraid," Piero said, bursting my hope. "It's believed he lived in a small room inside a wing called the *Fabricca*, while working on *The Last Judgment*. He was the Pope's chief architect during that time. No one knows why he would have ordered such an expensive key. Odd, as he was quite the miser, known to keep a wooden chest of gold under his bed. That may very well be what the key was for. If they have found either the room or the key, it has not been made public knowledge."

"A valuable key would have to unlock a valuable secret," I said to emphatic nodding from Piero. I was less interested in the key itself than the lock.

The key around my neck suddenly weighed a billion pounds, and every thump of my heart felt like the key had a heartbeat. The guileful artist could easily have found a way to hide a key within the hand of St. Peter.

Piero must have taken my contemplation as an indication to leave because he shook my hand and said good-bye, leaving me standing alone with my racing thoughts.

If I couldn't see Michelangelo's room, where else could I look for clues as to why the church would include the Scintilla in its witch hunt? I couldn't very well come straight out and ask Báthory if there was a modern-day witch hunt and why, though I suddenly wanted to know where the office was located and if there was any way to get in.

I made my way outside so I could call Mami Tulke to tell her about the developments and that the man I'd met had mentioned South America. Paranoid or not, I had to assume everything was a threat and keep them posted.

Ramp-like steps led down to the pavers of St. Peter's Square. I scanned the tourists' auras for anything peculiar or dangerous. Nothing obvious, but I continued to feel the prickling sensation of eyes on my back. To my right, St. Peter stood watch over his square as I dialed Mami Tulke's number. Busy signal. I tried to call Giovanni's number, and it went straight to voicemail. How many flaming-fresh-hell-hoops was I going to have to jump through?

I kept walking, approaching the obelisk straight in front of me. People were taking pictures in front of the tiered fountains that flanked the obelisk, lying on the ground to take upward pictures of the obelisk itself, and darting in all different directions. My eyes darted just as quickly. A troop of uniformed school kids marched past me in two lines. Each child had a buddy whose hand he or she clasped, creating a bubble of colorful light around their joined hands. Lovely, seeing the openhearted auras among children who hadn't yet learned to separate their energy. It made me suddenly wonder: if we were born with no sense or reason to separate our energy, wouldn't that mean that the most natural state to be in was one of connection with one another? It reminded me of Giovanni and the *oneness* conversation we had at Dr. M's. It also made me think of Finn and the sense of inexplicable connectedness we had.

I kept moving, kept dialing South America, growing more frightened every time I redialed and was unable to get through. I stood scanning the crowd and waited a couple of minutes before dialing Mami Tulke again, getting yet another strange-sounding busy signal. "Damn," I said, punching the end-call button on the phone. Of all times not to be able to get ahold of them...

Again, I felt like I was being watched and spun around toward the Sistine Chapel. Nothing caught my eye except the stately giant statue of St. Peter with his gold keys and his pointing finger. The more I stood there and stared at St. Peter, the odder it seemed that he wasn't just holding the sacred keys to heaven but using his finger to point. And not up at heaven either, as one would think, but straight ahead of him, like he was pointing the way to something...*earthly*.

I turned and looked in the direction in which he pointed but saw nothing but a long street leading straight from the middle of the oval of St. Peter's Square. Severely agitated by my inability to contact my grandmother or Giovanni and not sure what to do with myself, I let St. Peter lead the way.

Via della Concilazione was an incredibly straight and long street, but there didn't seem to be anything special about it except that a great number of tourists with maps in hands and cameras around their necks headed in both directions. There had to be some kind of tourist attraction. I walked far enough that St. Peter could no longer be seen when I turned around. Following close behind four elderly women who chatted in English and cackled continuously at one another's jokes, I soon realized what it was that drew the crowds. A sign said, CASTEL SANT'ANGELO.

It was a castle all right, topped with a statue of an angel like a cake topper. I overheard one of the women say that the bridge, the *Ponte Sant'Angelo,* which spanned the Tiber

River and led from the castle out to the city, used to be called *Pons Sancti Petri—The Bridge of St. Peter.*

Intrigued, I paid the fee to enter, took a pamphlet, and began a self-guided tour of the castle, searching for any sign that would indicate a reason I should be wandering through the ancient building, a reason for St. Peter to point to this place.

Twists and turns led inside old corridors to the atrium and a spiral ramp. I toured rooms with frescoed chambers, a theater courtyard with a door leading to the prison, and learned that Galileo had a trial at the castle once. It was fascinating to discover that there was an elevated passage leading from *Castel Sant'Angelo* to St. Peter's Basilica. I spent quite a bit of time in what's known as the Angel Courtyard, which was designed by Michelangelo, but could find nothing clue-ish. I left the courtyard frustrated and headed to the last part of the museum I hadn't seen, the Room of the Treasuries/Room of the Library where the most secret archives and treasures of the papacy were once kept.

I entered the library first. Off the library was the Treasury Room. Nothing prepared me for what I saw there. The room was small and circular and paneled with dark wood with one small window high to my left. The floor looked like brick and was patterned in a spiral. Iron candelabras stood off to the sides. What took my breath away were the four treasure chests taking up most of the floor space in the room. One was enormous, easily seven feet tall. In front of that were two chests that reached my waist, and in front of those, the smallest chest at knee height.

My father would have been in heaven at the sight of these treasure chests. A pang of missing him, of missing our

California home filled with his collection of treasure chests hit me so hard I bit my lip to keep from crying. He'd hidden the truth about my mother in one of his treasure chests. It's where I'd found my mother's letter to him and had cried onto the scribbled sheets, realizing for the first time ever that she hadn't abandoned us, me. She loved me. My fingers touched her Celtic mark on my forehead, and I kissed them. It had become my way of remembering her.

No longer able to stave off the tears, I silently cried as I thought about my parents and relived their last moments, their deaths by ruthless Arrazi. Tears trickled down my cheeks, my neck, and met the chain holding the key.

Oh my God, the key! Michelangelo had a key made for a chest, and I was staring at four chests that belonged to the church. Was it possible that one of them was his?

I stepped forward with my hand outstretched.

Chapter Seventeen

Finn

"We had thieves in our family, too," my mother said, pulling two pairs of medical gloves from a box and handing me a pair before slipping her hands into the other. What looked like a small fridge sat on top of one chest, and my mother used the same combination as the outer door to access it and pull out a large black box.

"What's that?"

"An acid-free archival box. The outer box is temperature controlled to minimize damage to the artifact."

"Artifact?" I said, stifling a smirk, though my curiosity was peaked. That entire room had me buzzing. Mum lifted the lid of the box and I—I couldn't help it—I literally stepped back with my hand on my chest. "No…"

"Yes, son."

"You realize what you have here?"

"If it is not the original cover and missing first pages from the *Book of Kells*, then it's a copy. A very convincing one."

"It's Ireland's national treasure, for Christ's sake. Why? Why have you kept it? Why did someone from our family take it to begin with? I thought it had been stolen during the raids on Kells."

"I have no answers for you. I'm showing this to you, all of this, that you might find answers that will bring peace to you. I don't know how this came to be in our family. All but one jewel are in place, so I don't believe it was for the value of the gems."

"Why haven't you turned it in?"

"What do you suggest? I leave it in a pram on the steps of Trinity College with a note? Good God, no. I haven't relinquished it for one simple reason: I believe it was taken and kept in our family for a purpose, and that it should remain in the family until that reason is discovered."

"Stolen artifacts… Can we call ourselves different from Ultana Lennon, then?"

My mum was the Queen of Derisive Looks, but this look won out. "In this respect, we can't." She waved her arm toward the desk. "There's a computer here as well, in case you want to look something up. I know it's come in handy for me a fair few times. Have your time with the book, but mind your handling of it, and put it back the way we found it."

"Aye, Mummy. Can you pat me on the head and bring me my bottle like a wee lad while you're at it? Only put some whiskey in it, aye? It's the water of life, after all."

Her eyebrow arched at me. "Mind the security cameras

before leaving so you're not seen by your father or Mary."
With no other words, my mother left me in that secret Mulcarr family vault, and my search began. I started with the
book, of course. I'd read that some stolen pages were recovered under sod but that the cover and a few pages were
never found. This cover either was never buried under soil,
or had been meticulously cleaned if it was. It was in impec-
cable condition.

The cover was rigid, with weight to it, possibly a thin
cutting of wood. It was probably the most beautiful thing
I'd ever had my hands on besides Cora. The design stunned
me, drove me nearly mad with the desire to understand its
significance.

Gold metalwork decorated the cover, and a series of
tacks held the metal in place along the sides of the wood.
The gold was embossed with intricate designs. Three of the
corners had a lovely Celtic knot with a different delicate
jewel. Only one corner was missing its gem. There were
triskele spirals linked together in threes around the entire
border. Emeralds, sapphires, rubies, and even small pearls
decorated the cover. The jewels glittered in the light as if
they'd been lonely for it.

The largest gilded relief was in the middle of the cover.

The triple spiral.

Each of the three spirals had a large jewel encased in the
center. I wished so badly that Cora was with me to see it. *To
touch it.* I wondered how on earth I could get it to her. She
could see more with her hands than I could with my eyes.

One thing was certain: the spiral was a very old and important symbol, and now I understood why it was so significant to my mum and to our family. Cora and her mother

thought they were an important clue to our shared past. I believed that to be true, now more than ever.

The fact that the spirals were so often clustered in threes, especially on a document like the *Book of Kells*, could signify the trinity. But I kept reminding myself that spirals were around long before people sat around and decided what would go into their holy books.

With a delicate touch, I turned the cover.

The ornate inscription on the first page of vellum, the title page, was written in Latin and said: *Nere Ponentus Tenebras Lucem.*

I gently lifted that page and turned it over. More surprising than the triple spiral being on the front of the *Book of Kells* was the illustration on the first page. Drawn on a background of saturated hues of deep reds and rich blues, and taking up nearly the whole page, was a hexagram, beautifully sketched with one triangle facing upward in gold, the other facing down in silver.

My brain whirred with questions, trying to make connections. Recently, the symbol had come up a lot. The rock my father gave me after I returned home from attempting to die on my boat was painted with the *shatkona* upon it—an ancient Indian symbol for the union of opposites—that phrase again—also fire and water in alchemy, or male and female. It represented *Sefirah Tifaret*...perfection. Also, divine union.

Maybe it was bloody ignorant of me, but I was surprised to see it in this book. After staring into space for a few minutes, I rolled my chair over to the computer and logged on to educate myself about the design that I'd always assumed was a symbol of Judaism.

I was wrong. The hexagram was one of the most universal spiritual symbols in all of recorded time. Pictures of engravings from the oldest known civilization in Sumeria had star clusters believed to be the hexagram. It was everywhere: Japanese shrines from the fifth century BCE and ancient sites and artifacts from countries as varied as Sri Lanka, India, Greece, Egypt, Mexico, and Rome. It was all over Rome, in actual fact, including St. Peter's Basilica. An aerial view of Vatican City showed that the property of the Vatican museum called the *Castel Sant' Angelo* was in the *exact* shape of the six-pointed star.

It had been employed by the Freemasons and was even on the Seal of the United States. Surprisingly, I learned that it wasn't until the seventeenth century that it was adopted as a Jewish icon, a relatively new incarnation of the ancient symbol.

In the lost pages of this famous book, the hexagram joined hands with the spiral and stood together, two of the most enduring symbols in all of mankind. I had to find out what they had in common.

Being as careful as I could, I put the manuscript back in the black box and tucked it safely away in its controlled environment, but not without first looking up the Latin inscription on the title page.

It translated as: Spinning…or turning…darkness into light.

I hadn't opened a single cabinet drawer and yet I felt I'd touched on something vital. Only I couldn't say exactly what, and that was the most maddening part.

"It's been over two hours," my mother said, setting a sandwich and a halfer of whiskey on the desk in front of me. I looked up at her in surprise. "Your water of life, luv."

Her brows lifted in an uncharacteristic show of humor. But it was her words that set me to deeper pondering. I thanked her and left the room momentarily to find a sketchpad and a pencil. I felt like my head might explode from holding too much random information at one time. I needed to purge it. I needed to make connections.

I pulled out a paper and began to diagram some of the findings in all of my searching and to frantically draw arrows to see how the scraps of information connected.

When I was done, I slumped back in the chair and closed my tired eyes. The thrum of excitement and discovery was too potent. My feet tapped like they did before a gig. I might have just stumbled upon the mother of all family secrets and a vital hint to the Arrazi's past. I *had* to get the jeweled cover into Cora's hands.

Chapter Eighteen

Giovanni

The quake had been wicked and destructive.

Inside Mami Tulke's house, the floors were strewn with broken shards of fallen pottery, frames lying face down after having fallen from the walls, and toppled lamps. La Serena had been hardest hit. According to the only radio station we could access after searching for batteries to fit an ancient radio Mami Tulke unearthed from a closet, tsunami warnings were in effect along the coast. Boulders from the mountains above were scattered across the road like chess pieces swiped to the floor by the arm of an angry giant. None of us slept after the first one hit, and we'd spent the morning cleaning up debris inside the house—in between aftershocks.

Just as Benito Sandoval had predicted, natural disasters

were striking harder and more often.

Claire sat in my lap as we drove toward Mami Tulke's secret community disguised as a New Age commune. In the early morning quiet, the sound of the river that quenched the farms and vineyards of the valley was much more noticeable. My daughter looked up at me often for reassurance, her eyes crackling with questions. Since the major quake the night before, a series of aftershocks kept all of us rattled, and Claire hadn't wanted to leave my side. Mami Tulke said that aftershocks could continue for a few weeks after a quake. Claire lay her palm atop my open palm. My little girl's hand was so tiny inside mine. A swell of love surprised me. Sad to be surprised to ever trust someone and then to ever love anyone again.

Cora cracked me open, and Claire snuck in behind her.

When the golf cart could go no farther because of a fallen tree clawing at the ground from both ends, Mami Tulke parked, donned a wide hat, and we set off to walk the rest of the way. I hoped the restless earth had settled enough for it to be safe outside with Claire. Mami Tulke was her typical unflappable self, announcing that in Chile, earthquakes were as common as pisco drinkers, though her eyes said that this quake wasn't so common.

I was uneasy. It seemed strange that at the moment I was pondering Cora's father's theories about earth's natural disasters, one of the largest earthquakes in recorded history struck Chile. The phone lines were still down. If Cora heard about it, she'd have to be worried sick. Maybe it would be enough to lure her home to us.

Claire grew agitated as we approached the houses and buildings of "the ranch." She shook her head in a way that reminded me of a blind person seemingly feeling for frequencies. I didn't know what to do for her. Mami Tulke noticed, too, and told me there was someone at the ranch who used their sortilege as a healer who might be able to help.

The savory smell of roasting meat wafted up the path and teased us the rest of the way to the village. Claire's hand was damp in mine, but honestly, I didn't know if it was her or me. I had mild trepidation at seeing Will again. He'd obviously been shaken up by our conversation, enough so to call Mami Tulke and whine about it. I still couldn't regret telling him the truth, but some lobsters need the heat to be turned up slowly.

From our elevated path, I saw that someone had created a large labyrinth out of rocks in the shape of the triple spiral, and a lone figure was winding her way through it. The path took us past the large vegetable and fruit plots and onto the main, wider dirt path through the community. Small piles of broken things and rubble sat outside each home, and two teen boys, twins, loaded pile after pile into a wagon. They looked up at us as we approached and started whispering to each other with sideways glances.

Word had spread.

It was obvious from the looks from the people—the upward tilts of chins giving me props, or the sideways glances of the fearful and guarded. I'd lived my life reading expressions and auras. I could line them up by supporters and dissenters just by their auras. Mami Tulke obviously saw it, too. She slanted her eyes at me from under her straw hat.

Will stepped out of a pack of onlookers and greeted me with his arm outstretched, perhaps a bit too soon. It looked like it hung out there for an unnaturally long time. We shook hands, and he patted my back. "Giovanni."

"Will."

Will's aura arced over his wife, Maya, who stepped forward. "Nice to see you again," she said, less enthusiastically than yesterday. I blinked at her aura. I don't know why I didn't see it before. It explained Will's protective energy and his fear. Maya was pregnant.

"Congratulations," I said, and Claire looked up at me curiously. "She's having a baby," I explained. "Will, Maya, this is Claire. My daughter." Claire stepped forward and reached her hands to Maya's belly. Maya flinched and her eyes rounded at Will. I saw Will's hand jerk with the urge to slap Claire's hand away.

They were scared of her.

Claire didn't seem to pick up on their fear, but her aura drank it up in a way that set my hairs at attention. "Claire, honey, you should ask before you touch people." *Or their energy.* Our lessons in that regard would have to start immediately.

Claire rejoined me, and Will cleared his throat and asked how Mami Tulke had fared in the earthquake. Apparently, the death toll in Chile was near a thousand, and they were barely beginning to unearth the missing people from the rubble.

Will then invited us to sit with them in the dining hall. Mami Tulke introduced us to the crowd of Scintilla that had gathered inside. I knew it was commonplace for them, but the sight of their mercury auras filling the air and the room left me winded. They were beautiful. They *felt* beautiful. I wished the distrust in some of their eyes would fade because when I looked at them, I only saw extended family. People

I longed to protect. To save. I tried to expose the energy around my chest to display my openness. We could not fight together without trust.

A man stood and pointed his finger at me. "You, tell us what we need to know. Many of us are in hiding because of rumors of attack or loved ones who've disappeared. But we've lived so long here in peace that it feels like the threat is gone. You come here and suddenly we're in danger?"

I opened my mouth to respond but Mami Tulke, surprisingly, spoke on my behalf. "Giovanni does not bring the danger with him."

"Oh yeah? What's up with his little girl? What's wrong with her eyes?" one anonymous person asked. "Is she dangerous?" another asked. *What in the hell?* How could they say such things in front of her?

Mami Tulke placed a hand on Claire's head. "She is in my home. Her life was like something you cannot know. Do not fear her. Have compassion."

"Hey," I said with a warning tone, curling Claire under my wing. She wasn't like other children, obliviously letting chatter roll over them. She was too smart for that.

"Why are they afraid of me?" she asked, proving my point.

"It's not you, *bella*. They are afraid of anything that shakes up their way of life," I said into her hair.

Mami Tulke placed both hands on the table in front of her and took a few disquieting moments before speaking again. "Giovanni did not *bring* the threat," she repeated. "I did." Confused glances went around the room. "The threat follows every Scintilla. You'd not be hiding here if there were no threat. I consider it a job well done if you've lived happy and free from fear the past few years."

"Should we be afraid now?" Maya asked, her black eyes shining at Mami Tulke, her hand on her not yet rounded belly. I felt for her, and for her baby. What a foolishly optimistic thing it was to bring another Scintilla into this world.

Mami Tulke took too long to answer. She didn't want to incite fear, but she couldn't mislead them.

"Yes," I cut in. "You should be afraid." The glare I got from Cora's grandmother told me that was not the answer she'd intended to give. But this was a moment of choice, and the audience was present and listening. "You trust Mami Tulke, and you're right to. She's hidden you away like the precious gems you are. But there are"—I looked at Claire and realized I needed to temper my language—"gem hunters."

"G?" she said, pulling my shirt. "Metaphor?"

I sighed. She might as well know. "The Arrazi are coming. Soon. Hiding here, keeping away from the outside world, that was wise, but that is over. The time to fight has come."

"We can run!" someone shouted. "That's another option!"

Mami Tulke's fists clenched on the table. That, she was correct about. Some would choose to run. "You run and you'll be picked like easy fruit," I said. "Choose your end-game. Do you want a life of fear or a life of freedom?"

The communal dining hall erupted in shouting and sparks. Claire clapped her hands over her ears. Mami Tulke picked her up, slung her on her thick hip like a sack of potatoes, and walked out into the Chilean evening. I followed. Let them hash it out. They needed to. Change was its own kind of earthquake. I reached for Claire, but Mami Tulke shrugged me off and set Claire's feet to the ground. "I'll take her back," she said. "You, stay." Her nut-brown eyes slashed at me as she said, "This is the war you wanted. Go lead it."

I watched her walk with my daughter between two buildings and through the trees just as the sun left the valley in shadow. Already, even in the half-light, stars dotted the sky. I'd heard that people came from all over the world to stargaze here. The community made a fair bit off the tourists who were attracted by the astronomy domes, the stargazing tours, and the "magnetic feel" of the place. Outsiders had no idea why it felt so good to be here. The stars were magnificent, yes. But the people…the Scintilla gave the Elqui Valley its magic.

Footsteps crunched in the gravel behind me. Will and Maya approached. Her arms were crossed, her aura self-protective. "My husband and I do not agree on the best course of action," she said to me. "But I want to thank you for warning us. We came to find you because we don't want you to feel alone or unwelcome."

Will rocked back on his cowboy boots. "I just want to protect my wife and protect our baby. I don't want a life on the run, and I don't want to live here in fear. Hell, I don't know what to do." He sounded defensive. He looked at me hopefully, like I might say something to change her mind.

"Arrazi came and took my parents when I was a boy. My mom was pregnant," I admitted in a rush that constricted my chest. "I—I never saw them again." Cora had been the only person I'd ever told that story to. I told it now to convince this woman, with another precious Scintilla in her belly, that alternatives had run out.

Will watched Maya's face distort with horror as she listened. He looked back to me with worry in his eyes. "What will they do to us? We've all heard the rumors… Scintilla being sold, held prisoner for years, killed by having their auras drained completely."

"They are no longer interested in selling or keeping us. They've been directed to kill us all." I let those words seep in before speaking again. "I was in a battle very recently, at Newgrange." Maya's gaze snapped to Will's and back to me. "The Arrazi's attack is supernatural—swift and deadly. Each Arrazi can take from multiple people at once, from at least thirty feet away. And that's their power without using the sortileges some of them have gained."

Maya's hand flew to her mouth, and the other reached for Will's hand. "How did you escape?" she asked.

I credited Cora, and I had to credit Finn. "I was attacked first and was uselessly weakened," I said, swallowing a stone of shame in my throat. I'd make up for my failure this time around. I was cursed against saving Cora's life, but I could save these people's. "We'd not have escaped were it not for the dagger." I'd run that battle through my mind over and over again from the moment we escaped Newgrange. The conclusion was always the same. "In order to win against the Arrazi, we need weapons."

"This is unbelievable," Maya said. "I am against this, Will." She turned and grabbed his hands. "You know I am."

A large group of Scintilla exited the dining hall and spotted us. I had an audience and could not let the moment pass. I wanted everyone to be ready. When Cora arrived, she'd see the vital role I played in protecting us, in protecting her. I wouldn't be useless again.

"With all due respect," I said louder, pulling more Scintilla out with my voice, "what is it you are against? Defending yourselves? Fighting against those who would see you lifeless on the ground and use their powers to terrorize the rest of humanity?"

"Hey..." Will cautioned at my increasing temper, but I would not be daunted. The world was literally falling apart around us.

"Offer yourselves up, if you will. Lay down and die at their feet. Be sacrificial lambs if that makes you feel more saintly. The Arrazi will come, and you will have no choice but to decide. I, however, will not be unprepared. I will fight for you if you're too timid to fight for yourselves. The Arrazi don't fight fair, and neither should we. We need weapons. God willing, we'll never have to use them. But God didn't save my parents. God didn't save Mami Tulke's son or his wife."

Murmurs and gasps arose from the group. "So this is serious?" someone asked.

"It doesn't give me pleasure to come here and give you this news. I've spent my life flying under the radar, and I feel lucky to have lived this long. Some are searching for answers as we speak, but I don't believe in my heart that there is any answer that will stop the Arrazi. If there were, wouldn't it have been found by now? I don't judge anyone who hopes for a peaceful resolution. I can only say that I have no such hope. This is serious, yes. This is life or death."

I surveyed the crowd, young and old, and felt the weight of the moment press upon me. No doubt existed within me. I'd meet might with might.

"Who's with me?"

Chapter Nineteen

Cora

"*Perdono*, miss. It is not permissible to touch the historic artifacts."

I snatched my hand back and turned around to face the museum guard who filled the doorway. He had the most horizontal face I'd ever seen: eyebrows in a straight line above eyes that flattened into slits and a scowling mouth with no hint of an upward curve. I wondered if he'd ever smiled in his life.

"I'm sorry, I—" How could I explain? Touching these chests was the most driving need I had in the world just then. My palm tingled with need. I had to know the memories of the treasure chests. I had to know if the key around my neck fit one of the locks. I had to know whether my instincts were spot-on or numb and useless. It felt eerily like I was directed to that place, and my dad was a sudden presence. I grew up surrounded by treasure boxes. Crazy as it sounds, I felt like I was meant to find these treasure boxes in this room at this exact moment. "Please, sir," I begged. "I simply—"

"No."

Desperate, I did the only thing I could think of. I funneled light, sparks, positive energy, every good feeling I had in me directly into the man. It was enough to bring Giovanni back from the brink of death after Clancy and Griffin beat him; perhaps it would be enough of a hit of feel-good that this man would give me license to touch the boxes.

His eyebrows shot up, arched in a way that seemed impossible moments ago. His mouth followed. But more than the outward signs of his attitude morphing in front of my eyes was his aura. It expanded and puffed in waves of golden light. He was feeling it, that much I could see.

I gave more.

Just like with Giovanni, it didn't drain me to give the way it drained me when the Arrazi stole from me. Strange…

The man's stance relaxed. His arms hung limp at his sides, and he gazed at me with the goofiest grin. "I'll just be a moment," I said, testing the waters.

"*Si*, just a moment," he murmured. I felt very Obi-Wan for a second but wasted no time. I ran over to the first box and touched it. Memories flashed, yes. But like the triple spiral, I could detect nothing but many hands over many centuries. I touched the next box and the next, finally pressing my hand flat against the enormous eight-foot-tall box at the back. Nothing but fragmented images of the box being moved, its various contents, a torrid quickie inside.

Disappointment was a heavy lid, slamming down on my

hopes. I continued to shoot beams of light at the guard who watched me with a pleasant, curious expression. I smiled. I'd touched the treasure boxes and learned nothing. The only other question was whether this key I possessed would fit one of the locks.

I tugged the chain on my neck, whipped they key from under my shirt, and pulled it over my head. The enormous box had a place that once held a locking mechanism, but you could see it had been removed. There was nowhere to insert the key but a gaping, key-shaped hole. No good.

I skipped one of the medium boxes, determining just by looking at it that they key was too small for the lock. The third box didn't even have a built-in lock, just a half circle of metal, which would have been used for some kind of padlock.

"You can't possibly think your key there—"

"Shhh, and feel good," I snapped. "Aren't you happy just watching me bumble around?"

"In fact, yes," he said amiably.

I wanted to kick the boxes to the Roman Colosseum after I bent over the last, smallest chest and realized the box would never accept the key. I leaned over it, near tears. "What a waste of ti—"

Just below my chin, on the backside of the box, wasn't a keyhole but a key-shaped indentation: a place to rest a key flat in the surface of the box, as if for ornamentation. I looked at the outline of the space in the wood, looked at my key, and shoved it in. A cracking sound split the air.

"I really must insist you remove your body from the box," the guard said, though there was no conviction in his voice. I looked over his shoulder and smiled, giving him one last hit of energy before turning back to the box and prying open the back section that had inexplicably come apart, like a page in a book.

A spider ambled out as I pressed the secret compartment away from me to see inside. I had to tilt my head sideways to see the yellowed and crackled painting affixed to the wood of the trunk.

Every bit of air whooshed out of me.

Beneath my fingers was an exquisite rendering of Madonna and Jesus; a youthful Jesus, not quite a child, not quite a man. A teen like…like me. He and his mother gazed lovingly at each other. I bit my bottom lip and became aware that my head was shaking "no" involuntarily. It couldn't be…

It wasn't the finding of a hidden painting, or the most tender and loving expressions between mother and son, or seeing Jesus Christ as a teenager that affected me so deeply. It was the crowd behind them. All had blurred faces but with auras as polychromatic as a rainbow. It was the *tiri gondi* adorning the hems of Mary's robe and the hexagram, like on the church in the Basilica of Santa Croce, where the great men were buried, which was on the four corners of the painting.

Above all, it was the luminous pure silver auras depicted around the bodies and heads of Mary and Jesus, which spiraled out from them and flowed toward each other to connect in the space between them like a sacred rope.

It was a piece of the puzzle.

It was a message, if I was reading it right. One that would shock the world.

Jesus and his mother were Scintilla.

A drawing of the key, my key, was in the upper middle

with these words, sadly in Italian:

San Pietro è la chiave che registra le malefatte di coloro che hanno il coraggio di rivendicare il dominio sui regni al di là delle porte della Terra.

There was no way to peel the painting from the wood, and while I'd voodoo'd the guard into letting me touch the trunks, I doubted he'd let me do much more. He was already shuffling nervously behind me. I snapped a picture of the painting with my cell phone, eased the compartment shut, and yanked the key from its hold just as he leaned forward.

"Thank you," I said sincerely, while scooting around him and running from the room. "Have a *happy* day!"

I bolted out of the Room of Treasures and walked-ran through the *Castel Sant'Angelo* toward the nearest exit. Once my feet hit the pavement outside, I tried to call Giovanni to show him and have him translate the words on the painting, but my call still would not go through. Giovanni could verify the words, but who could authenticate the painter? I ran full out toward the Sistine Chapel. I needed to see Piero Salamone immediately. I had to show him the picture and get his take on it. What if it *had* been painted by the hand of Michelangelo? Piero could probably tell. If it was, Michelangelo took great pains to hide it, even hiding the only key that could open it.

My breath was choppy at the halfway point down the *Via della Concilazione*. The great round top of the Sistine Chapel rose in front of me like a beacon. All I could think as I ran was, *could Jesus have really been a Scintilla? Is that the* truth, *the great secret that people killed to keep?*

Chapter Twenty

Finn

"The Lennon girl is here."

I stood quickly and followed my mother from the secret room. "I've asked her to wait in the library," Mum whispered, closing the door behind us and shutting the painting on its hinge. Her voice turned sour. "You two are quick friends…"

"Don't forget why I started up with the Lennon clan to begin with."

"Careful there."

"The worst of their lot is gone, though her children may not know it yet." I wiped my palms on my jeans and entered the library, choking on the same repulsive memory of nearly killing Cora that always assaulted me when I entered that room. Saoirse was kneeling in front of the bookshelves, tilting out books and pushing them back again. "My mom doesn't keep books like these around," she said, standing up abruptly when she heard me walk in. "Doesn't think we should worry ourselves about the common human's flawed take on energy."

"Your mom and I disagree on that," I said, swallowing hard. It was difficult to use the present tense when speaking of Ultana.

"I still haven't heard from her…"

"Hmm."

Her brows cinched over her tiny, lightly freckled nose. "Is it a bad time?"

"No. No, sorry. It's fine," I said, wishing I were still tucked away in that burrow of a room, investigating. I wanted so badly to be able to talk to Saoirse about it. She might know something that could glue the fragments together, but I couldn't fully trust her. Not yet. "You're worried about your mom. Understandable after what's gone on."

She wearily rubbed the back of her neck. "People keep coming 'round looking for her. All they want is to talk about the deaths at Newgrange. My thick-headed brother could tell them more than I, as could you. But like my mother, he's never home. Everyone else who was there is inconveniently dead. What am I supposed to tell the Arrazi? I wasn't even there and my mother's missing. What if something awful happened to her?"

"I'm sure she's fine," I said, wishing for the thousandth time that her body would never be found. "You said yourself that while she was very open about her views on being an Arrazi, that her business dealings weren't as transparent. She's likely in the middle of something very important, especially after what's gone on, and as you and Lorcan are old enough, she's trusting you to handle yourselves until she returns."

Her head dropped forward like a prayer. "I have a bad feeling."

My pulse was hammering so hard at my throat I was sure she'd see my obvious nervousness. I spun away from her and walked to the window where Cora and I once stood, looking out at the full moon and talking about her favorite author who curtseyed to it. I'd started doing that, in Cora's honor. It felt like a secret pact between the moon and me.

"It's no secret that your mother wants all Scintilla dead," I found myself saying. "She said it at dinner the night I first met you." I turned to look in Saoirse's eyes, tried to focus my sortilege on her. She'd never see her mother again, and I had to know if I had a true ally. Maybe together we could influence the Arrazi her mother once controlled. My parents would help, as well. "I'm sorry, but I have to ask… If anything *has* happened, where will you and your brother stand?"

Her chin trembled. "Why are you asking me this?"

"Because I—I think it's time to pick sides."

Her blue-green eyes did not waver. She crossed the room, took my hand, and squeezed it. "On the side of *right*, of course, Finn. It's bad enough we have to do what we have to do in order to survive. The Arrazi don't need to make sport of it." She waved her hand. "I can't speak for my beast of a brother, though. He's always bowed to our mum."

"And you haven't?" I asked, thinking of every time she jumped when Ultana said jump, thinking of how readily she killed Teruko that first time, and the submissive fear I saw in her eyes whenever her mother looked at her.

Saoirse knocked me with her elbow. "Hey. That's rude." Her eyes squinted apprehensively.

"Sorry."

"My mom *is* frightening, yes." Her smile faded and her eyes darkened. "You have *no idea*. But I've disagreed with her on many things. It was just easier to make her believe what she wanted to believe."

It was hard to imagine anyone *making* Ultana believe something. Our hands remained clasped as we stared at each other. "I'm damn relieved to hear you say that," I said. "After what I saw at Newgrange, after what I was forced to do—to have to kill my own uncle—my focus is and will always be the search for the truth about our races, why we were created the way we are."

"What if there is no why?"

"You sound like my mother."

Saoirse let go of my hand and raised it to my cheek. "You have a good heart, Finn."

"I just want to end this. Can you help me put out a call to the Arrazi, schedule a gathering?"

A burst of scandalized laughter came from her. "What? Usurp my mother's authority while she's MIA and call a town-hall meeting of all Arrazi we know? You've lost it, Finn. She'll kill me."

I gritted my teeth and looked back out the window. I'd have to be patient and wait for her and Lorcan to realize that their mother was never coming home. Or...

"What's to stop *my* family from calling a meeting?"

"Simple—you'd be an immediate enemy."

My head jerked to look at her.

"I don't make the rules, Finn. My mother does. She and whoever is powerful enough to give *her* orders. They threaten to kill all Arrazi who don't fall in line, and you want to draw a new line? Just because you want to end it doesn't mean you *can* end it. You're powerless, Finn." She almost sounded smug.

Burning anger ripped through my limbs. I turned away from Saoirse so she wouldn't see the intensity of the fire. I needed her, with her Lennon name, to help me shift the tide. Otherwise, what was I doing in Ireland? I could be on my way to Chile with the long-lost cover to the *Book of Kells*. Maybe I should be, regardless. Maybe standing alongside the Scintilla was a better gamble than trying to change the fixed minds of their enemies.

Saoirse placed her hand on my back. "You okay?"

"Grand, yeah. Just a lot on my mind."

"The girl."

"Of course."

"Do you know where she is? How she's doing?"

Saoirse's phone rang, and she crossed the room to get it from her bag. While I was busy thinking of ways to cut our visit short, she startled me with a gasp. Her hand covered her heart, and a stricken expression twisted her fine features. "Impossible," she said into the phone. "There must be some mistake." Then she looked to me and muttered, "My mother has been found. She's…dead."

Chapter Twenty-One

Giovanni

The ground shook beneath us so hard it seemed as though the stars might fall from the sky and drop around us like bombs. Another aftershock.

Some people scattered, some clutched the nearest person with their eyes squeezed shut. Will and I both leaped for Maya, a primal instinct to protect mother and child. She cowered beneath us, our arms wrapped over and around her like a human shield. As we clutched each other's shoulders over Maya's bowed head, Will's fearful eyes met mine, but I saw something else in them, too—gratitude. He nodded. A silent pact made in a moment of fear. He would stand with me.

When the shaking stopped and everyone was accounted for and safe, Will and two other men pulled me aside. A black-haired burly man introduced himself as Ehsan. His hands were as rough as his voice, but he had kind eyes and a temperate aura. "You don't have to tell me twice. I've known this day was coming. I nearly died in Kabul when a white-one attacked me at mosque. It was because of a nearby bomb detonating that I got away. Many died from the explosion, and yet I was spared. I'll never understand…"

The other man, young, pale, as tall as me but wiry, had an aura that drew close around him and was as slivered as he was skinny. He pounded on his chest with one tattoo-covered hand. "I will fight with you," he said. "My family is these people. I will fight anyone."

His accent had a similar twang as Will's but with a Latin overtone. His name was Adrian. I smiled at his bravado and was glad for it, but felt a pinch of apprehension. I hated to think of his boldness snuffed out by the ruthlessness I'd encountered in the likes of Clancy Mulcarr and Ultana Lennon. Did he have any idea, did any of them *really* comprehend what we were up against?

Will, Ehsan, and Adrian led me inside one of the octagonal huts.

Being inside was altogether different than I imagined. The huts were small and reminded me a little too much of the cavern in which Gráinne was killed. This was Ehsan's home, I guessed, by the way he began rummaging through the small fridge on the kitchen floor. The fabric had been pulled back from a round section in the ceiling to expose the sky over two reclined chairs. I stared up and marveled at the stars. The chairs were covered with shards of glass that had fallen from the shelf behind them.

"Here," I said to Ehsan, stooping to pick up a framed

photograph that had tumbled to the floor. It was a group photo of a bunch of browned young people, my age I'd guess, standing next to a river. Men wearing *shalwar kameez* and wide smiles. Ehsan shook the frame against his jeans, causing the broken glass to fall to the floor in tiny pieces. He blew on the photo. "Good times," he said, looking at the picture with softness.

In the light of the room I got a better look at Adrian, though he was too skittish to look me in the eyes. He bounced from window to window as if the Arrazi were outside in the trees at that very moment, watching us, ready to strike. Bumps rose on my arms.

"Gang?" I asked, noting the various tattoos on his neck, arms, and hands.

"So?" His chin tilted up defiantly.

"*Va bene.* I don't care," I said with a smile, and I honestly didn't. "You'll be a scrapper."

"Fighting with guns and knives is one thing; people sucking your soul out of you is another, man." His aura shuddered with the memory.

"So you've seen it?"

"Yeah, I've seen it. First started seein' auras one night after me and my boys jumped a dude who stole from us." He snickered. "Thought it was a bad trip, you know, laced drugs or something. But yo, this was a trip that never ended. After a few months, I spotted a girl in my town, silver like me, and we started hanging." His eyes took on a faraway look.

"She introduced me to her grandmother, who was Scintilla, too. We were thick as thieves, the three of us, but I had to keep it from my boys. The girl and her grandmother, well, we didn't run in the same circles. The three of us were out together one day, at the fair where her grandma made bank running an aura-reading booth. Two women came in together—a mother and a daughter—and killed her grandma, right there. Never even touched her. Scariest shit I ever seen, bro."

"How'd you get away?" Ehsan asked.

Adrian shook his hands like he was flicking water off them—a nervous habit, I guessed. By doing that, he was dispelling more energy than he kept, and I wondered if he knew that. I wondered if that's why his aura was so drawn in—that, and his barely masked insecurity.

"We'd been watching her do readings from behind the curtain. When Grams slumped over and one woman's aura exploded in white, my friend and I ran out, but they turned on us. I choked the older one. The younger woman ran, but not without killing my girl first. I threw my knife at her," he said, laying his hand on the hilt of a knife sheathed at his waist. His eyes turned prideful. "She made the mistake of looking back. Stuck her right in her eye." We all absorbed that story, seeing the horror in our minds. "Brown," he added.

"Pardon?"

"Her eyes were brown. Anyway, the cops, they thought I killed them all. There was a manhunt. I went to Mexico, and then someone helped me get here."

"How'd you know about this place?" I asked.

"A dude in Mexico City, one of *us*, said he'd heard there was an old woman hiding people in South America. I wandered around Santiago for almost a year before someone spotted me."

"You mean spotted your aura," Ehsan said.

"Shut up, Ehsan. Literal bastard."

"One thing I do know," Adrian said, his voice lowering conspiratorially, "is that there's a woman in Santiago who sells a helluva lot more than empanadas, if you catch me."

"Weapons? Guns?"

For the first time since we'd begun talking, Adrian lit up. "Everything we need, man."

I shook hands with Ehsan and Adrian and Will, and I went to the door. "Can we go see her?" I asked.

Everyone nodded, but it was Adrian who answered. "The roads are nasty 'cause of the quakes. We'll give it a couple of days and go. Good?"

"Good," Will said, looking at his watch. "I gotta run 'n' check on Maya."

Outside, I inhaled the fresh air. Will started to walk away, but I stopped him. "I know Maya disagrees with the idea of fighting. What made you decide to join me?" I asked.

"I figure if your first instinct was to protect my pregnant wife when the earthquake struck, then your genuine aim is to protect us all." He kicked a rock with his boot. "My job is to protect her and my baby, even if she disagrees with my methods. My pop taught me never to back down from what I think is right, even in the face of opposition, especially then, I s'pose. I've gotta follow my gut on this." He smiled. "Since when do women think we know what we're doing, anyway?"

"Thank you, Will. Perhaps more will follow after your lead."

"I do hope Maya comes around. She's got a deadly sortilege. My woman can kill with a touch." When I opened my mouth to ask about it, he added, "Don't mention it to her, though. It's a really sensitive topic."

"Why?" My mind was already forming battle plans. If

we could just get Maya close enough… "We could really use a power like that against the Arrazi." I made a mental note to take stock of each Scintilla's sortilege, excited about the idea that some of us might just *be* a weapon against the Arrazi. I'd certainly used mine to help when those men attacked from under Gráinne's cottage. That was before the damned *geis* was put upon me. My fingers twitched with the desire to use my sortilege to throw Lorcan Lennon's head against the nearest rock. Let him come for me now.

Will looked up into the star-strewn sky before his gaze landed on me. "Maya will never use her sortilege. Never. When she was a teenager, she accidentally killed her mother with it."

Chapter Twenty-Two

Cora

Again, I felt the presence of someone behind me as I ran toward St. Peter's Basilica. This time, I heard footsteps padding along in cadence with mine. I abruptly stopped and spun around.

"No freaking way!" I yelled at a very hangdog, flush-faced Dun staring at me with eyes that morphed quickly from guilty to daring me to challenge him.

"I had to," he said, tossing up his arms. "I tried to stay out of the way, just keep an eye on you, but you're running like a damn bat out of hell and I thought someone was after you." He approached until he stood before me, close enough for me to feel the aura I could recognize blindfolded. "I thought you were in trouble, girl."

"I *am* in trouble! You should be in California, a million

miles away from me. You should be safe. Not here. Not here with me. I came alone because I can't watch anyone else die, don't you get that? You have no idea what—"

Dun gripped my shoulders and pulled me into a tight hug. "Shut up."

I breathed him in, reveled in his hug. Surrendered. "Shutting up." After I allowed myself a moment to soak up the love and surprising relief at seeing my best friend, I told Dun why I was running. "We have to get to St. Peter's. There's a man there, a professor who guided me through the Basilica today. I have to show him a picture of something I just found. Come on!" I dragged his hand, and we ran toward St. Peter's Square and then the entrance gates.

"What'd you find that you're in such a big-ass hurry to show this professor?"

Our feet plodded on the sidewalk. "I found what this key opens."

"Yeah?"

"Yeah. I think Jesus was a Scintilla."

His steps stuttered, but we kept running. His response was a gasped, "Holy. Shit."

"Right?" Pigeons took flight as we crashed through their cliques and sprinted through the square. All senses were on high alert. My brain registered the streaked clouds behind the dome, the laughter of children, the splash of the fountains, the din of conversations in many languages, and the anguished screams of panic.

Panic?

"What the…?" Dun said, grabbing my arm. I looked to where he was looking, at the pack of schoolchildren I'd seen earlier. Two had fallen to the ground in messy tangles of arms and legs. Their hands were still clasped, but their auras were as colorless as the majestic statues that looked down on them from the colonnade.

Their lights were out.

The adults with them were kneeling down, frantically feeling their necks for pulses, crying out.

I ran toward them and watched in horror as two more fell, and another pair after that. The teachers were screaming for someone to call an ambulance, that the children had no pulses, no life. The other children were backing away or frozen in terror at the open but sightless eyes of their classmates. Rather than rush forward to help, many adults backed away as well.

The kids had dropped dead.

"No!" Not the children. Not those innocent, beautiful kids. I scanned the crowd for white auras but saw none at all. An Arrazi hadn't done this.

The crowd was a swirling mass of outcry and horror and people dropped to their knees in droves to pray. Dun shouted my name as I left his side, ran across the cobblestones, and slid down next to the nearest child.

A boy, blue-black hair as curled as a cherub's. Lashes just as dark as his hair. I touched his pale skin below his eyes. He had one freckle on his lower lip. The sticker nametag on his shirt said "Caleb Matan." "Caleb," I cried, slipping my hand under his collar, feeling the cool dampness of kid sweat against my palm and curls brushing my wrist. "Sweetie?"

There was no response to his name, or any responses at all from the small bodies lying around me. "Why?" I cried. All of the drop-dead deaths were a tragedy, but these children, these beautiful beings… Why was this happening?

My soul cracked under the heavy unfairness of it.

I bent over Caleb, stared into his sweet, innocent face, and did the only resuscitation I could think to do. I poured myself over him. I marshaled every bit of love I had for my father, my mother, Mari, Dun, Finn, and Giovanni. Panoramic visions of the beauty of the earth scrolled through my mind: sunsets, mountains, sprays of wildflowers, water in all its incarnations. I was transported to another place, as though my body were just a small vessel for the vastness that was the universe, that was the vastness of me, love, pouring through it.

I swelled with a surge of beauty, appreciation, gratitude, pure love, and light and directed it at the little boy whose head was cradled in my hand. My energy felt like a bottomless well of pure spirit, and I'd gladly have dredged up every drop for this one boy, for all of them.

I knew without a doubt...I'd die for them.

When I most wanted to scream in anguish, Caleb's eyes closed, then fluttered open again, deep blue and bright. He smiled up at me. I gasped and turned to the girl whose hand Caleb still gripped. She was a field of strawberries, this one...all reddish-blond hair, plump lips, and creamed skin. Her name was Thea.

"Please," I whispered a prayer of my own as I wrapped her in silver light. *Let me have enough light to give.* Then I tried what I'd seen my enemy do, but in reverse. I gave to all of them at once. I cocooned all of us in silver light and watched it thread around them, into them. I was a conduit of pure, divine, loving energy, the focus of which was only one thing. Save them. Do not let them die.

Don't let the light go out. Not on my watch.

One by one, their eyes opened. Some began to cry and reach for teachers. Some just lay and stared up at the sunset, their eyes calm, brimming with feeling.

"*Miracolo*!"

"She brought them back to life!"

Dun was suddenly at my side, pulling me up from the children. I was mildly aware of resisting him at first. My mind had such tunnel vision in that moment that the rest of the world had fallen away. Protectiveness for these kids flared fresh as Dun tugged on me. Would they be okay? Did I do enough?

"Cora, look," Dun hissed in my ear.

Bewildered, I glanced around me and saw that a vast crowd of people surrounded us, some staring, some holding their cell phones up at me like this was some kind of spectacle. "Why—why are they filming me?"

"Are you effing kidding me?" Dun said. "What's your next trick? Walking on water?"

Whistles blew and a thunderous footfall approached. Through the crowd, I saw the uniformed security of Vatican City running toward us. With them, Cardinal Báthory, his red robe flying behind him. His eyes were intent and entirely focused on me. Not the children, not the turbulent crowd of onlookers...*me*.

Dun grabbed my hand and yanked me away. Would we be able to outrun them? I should feel weak, right? I should be depleted to my core. But my legs had the strength of a hundred horses as we ran toward the gates and through them as fast as we could, heading in who knew what direction.

"Where the hell can we go?" I asked, just starting to register the magnitude of what had happened. Cold fear replaced the euphoria I'd felt when giving to those children. It was the most beautiful thing I'd ever done, but for a girl on the run and trying to stay out of sight, the most stupid. I groaned. "And I thought the airport video was a nightmare."

A middle-aged man ran up alongside us. "Hey. Hey, excuse me," he panted. "I want to help you. Hey!" When the man reached for me, Dun shoved me behind him, ready to fight. "My car is right over there," the guy said, motioning toward a parking lot. "I saw what happened. Man! You need wheels. I'll get you away from here, I swear it. I just want to talk to you."

"Dude. Thanks, but no. You don't want any part of this crazy."

"I do, actually. I excel at crazy," he insisted with a tilted grin. "Some would say I'm an expert on crazy." I peered around Dun's arm at the man whose voice registered a ping of recollection in me. I immediately recognized the wild-haired guy with his suit and his trademark alien tie. He had an enormous camera dangling from his arm. I'd seen him enough times to know him anywhere.

The prolific New Age author and television personality, Edmund Nustber.

"It's okay," I said to Dun. "I know who he is." Just when I thought my world couldn't get more surreal. "My dad used to watch his show on TV," I said stupidly, as if that was the criteria for trustworthiness. There was commotion down the street. Sirens blared, broadcasting their approach, people ran in our direction, their eyes fixed on me. I snapped to attention. "Yes. Fine. Let's go."

We piled into Edmund Nustber's small car and screeched out of the parking lot, jumped the curb with a thud that threw us forward, and fishtailed our way up the street until Edmund gained control of the wheel and sped away.

"Thank God the Italians are a bunch of lunatic drivers. We'll blend right in," Dun said.

"I can't believe what I just saw back there." Edmund raked his hand through the front of his hair, pushing it into even higher crazy-peaks. "Incredible. A bona fide miracle."

I looked out the window behind us to see if anyone was following. "It was a miracle to me, too, believe me."

"Amazing. I got it on film. All of it." He was breathless, his lemon yellow aura—indicative of his logical, exploratory inquisitiveness—jumping with excitement.

"You can't show that film. I don't want it shown," I insisted, acutely aware that for the Arrazi who were looking for me, it would point right to my location.

Edmund Nustber gave me the biggest *are you freaking kidding me* eyes and said, "Honey, hundreds of people just saw you bring children back from the dead in the middle of St. Peter's Square, the doorstep of the Vatican. You'll be all over the world in hours. It's probably on YouTube already." He laughed in an adrenaline-coated way and slapped the steering wheel. "Awww, man! I can't *believe* this!" His tone abruptly changed from delight to analytical. "Watch the church try to take credit for it," he said. He shot a glance at me and his face turned serious, studying me. "There's obviously something very special about you."

A laugh came out of me, unbidden. "You have *no* idea."

"Tell me. Tell me how you did it. It looked like you went into some sort of trance or something. Have you always been a healer?"

"Look, I could tell you the whole story, but I doubt

you'd believe me. I'm just trying to fully understand what I am. Honestly, it would blow your mind to know what I am."

"Angel? Alien? Higher being from another realm?" Edmund rattled these things off like an everyday grocery list.

I rolled my eyes.

"Well," he said, looking in the rearview mirror. "You just healed the dead. No matter what you are, right now, I'd say you're a target."

Chapter Twenty-Three

Finn

Despite my secret knowledge about her mother, I had empathy for Saoirse's loss. She dissolved into tears after news of her mother's death. The strength of my compassion for her surprised me, but even as I doubted it, I pulled her to me and wrapped my arms around her trembling body. It felt criminal to comfort her, wrong to deceive her when I knew more about what happened to her mother than she ever would. It was an accident of fate that I was present when it happened. We were after Clancy, after saving Cora. How could I know that Ultana would show up?

The overriding feeling, though, was that I needed to stand by Saoirse and see her through the death of her mother. If I stood by her when it counted, would she stand by me?

"What are we going to do, Finn?"

"We" was she and Lorcan, but from what I'd seen, Saoirse and her brother weren't tight. He was a couple of years older. Would he immediately step in and try to rule over Ultana's deviant kingdom? I rubbed Saoirse's back, feeling both the weight of her head on my shoulder and the weight of my two-faced agenda. "I'm here for you. You're not alone."

"Lorcan is with her—her body." She sniffed. "He wants to know if I will come to the crematorium and sign papers and meet with our family lawyer. I don't understand how this could happen. I thought my mother would *never* die."

What an odd thing to say, unless she knew what I did; that her mother believed herself to be someone called the White Queen and immortal. "You said 'never.' Was that just disbelief, or—?"

"Or did I mean it literally? I don't suppose it matters to tell you this now... Secrets of the dead are less guarded. My mother dying was impossible, or so I was led to believe. I thought her sortilege was immortality." I jerked my head back like what she was saying was pure bollocks. "Or so she told me," she continued. "But who knows? My mother will forever be a mystery to me." She began to cry in earnest.

Cold dread spread down my limbs as I asked, "How did she die?" That damn dagger was my nemesis. If Lorcan had never seen me with it, I'd have nothing to worry about. So deep were my thoughts, I hadn't noticed that Saoirse had lifted her head and was staring at me quizzically through teary eyes. I kept my voice steady, my eyes concerned rather than fearful. "What happened to her? Did he say?"

Her answer was just a whisper. "No. You'll come with me, Finn?"

Shite. Of all the things she could ask... "Aye. If that's what you need, of course. We'll go now."

My mom burst into the library, creased her brows at me in an embrace with Saoirse, and swiping tears from her cheeks. The alarm on Mum's face, the way her fingers twirled the cross on her neck, made me immediately think something bad had happened to my father. "Darling," she said, crossing the room to the television. "There's something incredible on the news."

"Can't it wait?" I said. "Saoirse just got news of her own." An enormous beat of quiet passed between us as I tried to convey the seriousness with my eyes, but hers were just as grim and meaningful. "Her mother's passed on."

For another heavy moment, my mother looked at me as if I were daft, but she already knew the truth. Had she missed what I'd said? She flicked on the television despite my announcement, leaving me to puzzle what in the hell was wrong with her. She let the TV blare behind her as she approached us, put her hands on Saoirse's upper arms, and looked deep into her eyes. "I'm very sorry for your loss."

Saoirse blinked, thanked her, then looked away.

Commercials trilled in the background as I wondered what secret my mother might unearth from Saoirse's eyes, if any. But then the sensationalized voice of the newscaster filled the room, and like sound tunneling right into my brain, I heard the words: "MIRACLE AT VATICAN CITY!"

One after the other, different shots filled the screen. First, of little children dropping dead on the stones of St. Peter's Square. Then, of Cora...my sweet Cora, sliding into view as she ran to the children and dropped to her knees with an expression that could only be described as utter anguish.

Bowing over a black-haired little boy in a blue school uniform, her entire body was a prayer, and though no one could see it onscreen, or even in real life, I knew what they'd see if they had the ability—her luminous silver aura, her light, pouring through that wee lad. She pulled them back from the clutch of death.

"Finn?" Saoirse's voice questioned from behind me, but I was busy switching channels, seeing if there were more or different versions of the story, desperately trying to find out information as to where Cora was now.

Hoax... Miracle on hallowed ground... Sign from God... Devil... Savior...

News crews poured into St. Peter's Square, competing for space with the masses of people, well and sick, who'd quickly streamed into Vatican City. People were kissing the ground where she'd knelt. Others were chanting about devil's work.

Inwardly, I groaned. Cora needed anonymity to stay hidden, to stay safe. She needed to remain out of the Arrazi's vast scope and suddenly she was the most famous and sought-after mystery-girl miracle-worker on the planet.

"Jaysus Fecking Christ."

"That's incredible," Saoirse said, standing next to me. "If it's real, how do you think she did—" Her mouth hung open. "Is that *her?* Is that your Scintilla?"

"We'd better go," I said, taking Saoirse's hand and leading her to her car in the drive. I mumbled apologies and something about her being upset about her mother. "I think I should drive," I said, "under the circumstances."

She handed me the keys. "All right. Though, I'd say you look as though you've lost someone as well."

My teeth ground. "Of course I have."

We drove in silence to the crematorium. I assumed it was the same one the Lennon family used to dispose of their victims. The building was thoroughly modern, though a very old brick smokestack pointed like a finger into the sky. Pointing the way for the souls, I mused. I thought of Teruko and Mari and lifted a silent prayer up for their souls as we walked into the building.

Glossy white marble was used for the floors and the walls except for a large wall of windows with a lovely reflection pond outside. At the far end of the main lobby was a wall of ebony, and in front of it sat a hollowed-out stone basin very similar to the stone basins used to burn bodies in the tomb at Newgrange. How fitting. "Your family doesn't by any chance own this crematorium, does it?"

Saoirse looked surprised. "Yes, in actual fact."

How that woman acquired the things she did was a mystery to me. I guess when you've been a thief for hundreds of years you can amass quite a treasury. Saoirse led me from the naturally lit lobby toward a door with a large circular carving over it with the three hares, their ears forming a triangle. Within that triangle was the Xepa symbol.

We entered an adjacent room with a desk and plush wingback chairs, where I presumed the business of death was conducted. Lights were dimmed in the room, as if brightness was an insult to the dead. Maybe it was meant to be soothing to the deceased's loved ones, but it seemed to me it was a reminder of death, that someone's light had gone out. It was impossible to imagine Ultana as a soul with light. Her unnaturally long life meant she'd snuffed out countless others.

It had been just a couple of days since I took that man's

life at Newgrange. Sitting in that place made me nauseated, because all I could imagine was the families of my victims coming into places like this to say good-bye forever.

Saoirse sent a text to Lorcan that we'd arrived. Moments later, he stepped through the door looking slack and drawn, like air had gone out of him. He hugged his sister, which surprised me. I didn't have siblings, so really, what did I know of the complexities of their taut banter? Maybe the complicated love between siblings was an inhospitable country I'd never be able to visit or understand. I was thinking that it was nice to see softness from him toward his little sister when he cut his dark eyes to me and nudged her away from him.

"Let's talk a moment," he said to me.

"Lorcan, *really*. Not now. Can I see her?" Saoirse asked, perturbed.

What other reason did he have to want to talk to me if not his mother's weapon? I wanted to back out the door, be free of the soot of this family that made me feel grimier than I already felt just being an Arrazi.

I wanted to find Cora and suddenly had the desperate inkling that my prospects for helping her in Ireland were doomed. How was *I* going to convince potentially dozens, if not more, Arrazi in Ireland to abandon the exaltation and power they'd been promised and to ignore threats of death if they didn't comply?

I stuffed my hands into my pockets and kept my eyes steady on Lorcan's when I replied, "I came to support your sister. We can talk later."

Lorcan's jaw shifted back and forth like he was gnawing on his thoughts. He seemed to reach some kind of frustrated determination as he cocked his head. "Im'a be straight with you, Doyle. Our mother was found dead in a tomb on private land near Newgrange. She had a wound in her stomach from a sizeable blade." Saoirse gasped. "Clean through," he added.

My hands shot up in a gesture of supplication. "I know where you're going with this. You saw me at Newgrange with your mother's blade. Are you actually asking if I killed her?"

Saoirse was staring hard at me; I could see that without meeting her eyes. I could feel the heat of her aura. "I am asking, aye," Lorcan answered.

"I did not kill your mother." It was true. I hadn't. And I could state this without reservation. *She killed herself!* I wanted to yell, but I held my tongue.

"Do you know what happened? Was there more to the story than you told me?" Saoirse asked.

Of course. So much more, but how could I tell her what I knew without exposing myself or fostering hatred against Cora? I'd divulged everything about the fight at Newgrange, including killing my uncle. Pretending not to know anything about her mother while she fretted about it would cost me everything I was fighting to achieve. I simply shook my head, yet a new question was forming for me. How did Ultana know to go to the tomb in the first place? I suspected that git human, the driver. He was the only one who seemed connected to both Clancy *and* Ultana.

"Had to ask, you know," Lorcan said, with unsaid thoughts swimming in his eyes.

"Are police involved?" I asked. "They have their fill of unsolved deaths right now, don't they?"

"Of course not," Lorcan snapped. "We don't involve them in the deaths we cause. We certainly don't involve them in our own if we can help it. Papers will say she died at home under natural causes and was cremated. Her lawyer is already on her way here."

Saoirse bowed her head behind thin and shaking hands. "I can't believe this is happening. Can I see her before she's cremated?"

"It's already done," Lorcan said to her, cold, matter-of-fact.

The shocked incredulity that passed over Saoirse's face was understandable. "How could you?" she gasped.

"We were lucky it was an Arrazi who found her and not someone else or her body'd have been kept in a morgue for just anyone to gawk at and paw over. It had to be done quickly. You know that."

"You want me to take you home?" I asked her, but Lorcan refused me, saying that this was a private family matter and they had further business to attend to. His tone irked me, but I half smiled supportively to Saoirse before they disappeared through a door. I sat in the wingback chair in the dim room and waited.

Moments later, a woman who looked every part the crisp lawyer strode in with a briefcase. I reached out with my energy to feel her aura, detecting her doing the same to me like two strangers brushing against each other on the street. We both nodded, silently acknowledging our shared lineage. She strode through the door where Lorcan and Saoirse had gone, no doubt to stamp the paperwork, making official the demise of her very rich, very powerful, and very dead client.

Glad for the privacy, I used my phone to scroll through media newsfeeds. To add to my worries, I saw that Chile had suffered a major earthquake and a series of devastating aftershocks. All I could do was hope that Cora's grandmother was unaffected. What was happening to the world? Weather was freaky. Disasters were rampant. It felt like the world was crumbling around my ears.

The news of the quake was eclipsed by the media storm surrounding the "Miracle at the Vatican!" My body iced over; worry and dread were a thick elixir pushing their way through my veins. The connection had already been made between the Dublin Airport video and the Vatican videos, and a tearful family appeared on television and wanted to know why Cora didn't save *their* loved ones who'd died at her feet in Dublin. I wanted to chuck my phone at the wall when the word "lawsuit" was mentioned. People could be such opportunistic *arses*.

Even those who now crammed St. Peter's Square were hoping to benefit by their proximity to the miracle, like if they stood downwind of one, holiness would stick to their skin. Bounty hunters were offering their services in the "hunt" for the new *savior*. Churches around the globe were reporting record numbers at impromptu services and record contributions to the church in the mere hours since.

Cora's offering of herself to those children was the best thing that happened to the business of religion.

She'd tithed her soul, and the world wanted more.

Did the church, to which Ultana pointed, and whose garish robes Cora had trampled, know *what* she was? I could only pray not. Ironic that we'd pray to the same God for different outcomes, as if God cared a whit who won football games and got certain jobs, or which breed of human annihilated another. Humans had been annihilating each other since we could grunt.

Segue from grunt; Lorcan burst through the door, made

a barely audible sound as he passed, and shoved his way outside. It wasn't grief I saw on his face. He was pissed off. Saoirse and the woman with the briefcase followed his exit a few minutes later. The woman whispered something in Saoirse's ear before leaving.

"Are you okay?" I asked, rising to stand. "Lorcan looked sorta distraught when he left."

"He's distraught, but not for the obvious reason. He's fit to be tied because our mother bucked tradition in a way he can't stomach." Saoirse made eyes indicating that was nothing new, then said, "My mother left control of everything to me."

Everything.

Without further explanation, Saoirse started for the door. It begged so many questions, but asking them would be insensitive and intrusive. She let me drive her home, saying I could use her car to go home, and we'd figure out the logistics of getting it back to her tomorrow. The radio blasted nothing but the news in Rome, and I could feel the weight of both our unasked questions in the air between us.

"Thank you for your friendship today," Saoirse said when we arrived at her house. She leaned in and gave my cheek a peck. Her body inclined against my arm, and her mouth lingered over my skin as she whispered, "I intend to do things differently than my mother did." Hope lit in me that my need for an Arrazi ally might be realized. "It's a new era. I hope that answers your earlier question, Finn. The Two of Cups," she said against my cheek, reminding me of the tarot reading she once gave me and the card that spoke of union, before pulling my chin to face her. "I think that card was about us. I think it was about *this* moment."

Chapter Twenty-Four

Giovanni

No war should commence without an accounting of the assets. With the mention of Maya's sortilege to kill with a touch, it was all I could think about aside from the ever-present concern about Cora. Right away, I'd compile a list of everyone in the village and their abilities. Gráinne had mentioned a clairvoyant in her journal. That could obviously come in handy. Was the woman still around after seventeen years? I couldn't wait to find out what the people here were capable of.

I rolled up and put my feet to the floor, expecting the cold linoleum, but instead I felt a lump of a girl under my toes. Claire had apparently crept into my room during the night and decided to camp out on the floor next to my bed. The tremors had her very nervous, and more than once she'd asked to return to Ireland *where the ground didn't shake and the air didn't buzz.*

We hadn't heard from Cora in a couple of days. This had both Mami Tulke and me on edge. She called on her way from Florence to Rome. The impression was that it was a less than revelatory trip so far.

Mami Tulke served breakfast in a sullen mood, barely speaking with me. Only Claire could produce a smile from her. Her chatter fluctuated between eerily intelligent savant to girlish ramblings about how she would like to decorate her room in "bohemian colors" and twinkle lights like the ones in the garden at Dr. M's.

Only then did her blue eyes turn sad and her aura wilted.

Lured with promises of learning Qigong—which was my way of introducing Claire to the skill of controlling her energy—Claire, Mami Tulke, and I set out to *Rancho Estrella.* Mami Tulke said she had ranch business to attend to, and we walked with her to the "main lobby," which was just a large building with a front desk and seating area and a big, spalike vat of cucumber water and soft, chiming music playing. "Run along," Mami Tulke said. "They'll be starting soon."

Claire skipped ahead, her blond curls bouncing in the sunlight. Mami Tulke told me to contact someone named Monica about getting Claire back into her schooling. I hadn't even thought of that, my own life being devoid of traditional education. My cheeks flushed at having to be told what a parent should do. Here I was, in charge of a little human, and I was clueless. A virgin. Having a child without the bonus of sex was a complete shaft. *Not* the way it's supposed to go.

Claire's incredible IQ meant that she'd likely learn with much older children than herself. Though, I'd only seen the teenage twins so far, Mami Tulke told me there were about ten Scintilla children on the grounds.

It only took sideways glances from a couple of the adults on the grass field where they practiced their martial arts to remind me that the kids were likely to be hard on Claire. Kids were brutal. Everyone was going to have to get over the subtle undercurrent of bias. So she had really strange eyes...so she was unschooled in how to control her reaching energy...those things didn't make her scary—just different.

I told Claire to go ahead and practice with the group. I intended to hang back and watch, curious to see if there was a collective change in their energy since that was their intention in practicing the ancient art. Their movements were slow, rhythmic, and I had to admit that with each passing moment, the more they worked together in unison, the larger the field of silver grew around them and above them until finally their auras all joined in a bubble of intense energy that I could see and feel from the sidelines.

Claire's was the only rainbow-hued aura on the field. From what Mami Tulke told me, the most fundamental difference between Scintilla and Arrazi was that we were born seeing auras while they can only feel them, sense them. Scintilla are born with our silver auras, and it's only our sortilege that comes when we're older. Cora told me on the day we met that she remembered seeing auras as a child. Since Claire never spoke about seeing colors and since the only silver that showed in her aura were quick flashes, it was unlikely she was Scintilla, despite my hope. That must have been why Dr. M called her—his experiment—his "great failure." I wondered what he was really trying to achieve.

The bubble of silver from the people rippled toward

me, hitting me in the chest. My own aura surged like I had been plugged in. The few times in my life I'd allowed myself to open up to a performance—usually singing and always in a crowd—I found that emotion became so intense that tears would easily come. It unnerved me to the point that I stopped going to concerts until I learned to better ground myself and not let the crowd's energy in. This swelling of Scintilla energy was a million times more potent and felt just like—love.

The group stopped moving, and Claire suddenly flopped to the grass like a snow angel. I ran to her, my heart careening with both good energy and fear that something was wrong. But when I reached her, her arms were outstretched, her eyes were closed, and her face tilted up to the sun and the cloud of energy. "It just feels so good." She sighed.

"I know it does, sweetheart," I said, looking down on her. "I'm going to start teaching you to better feel the energy around you and to control your own." I kept my voice light, made it sound gamelike and fun, but it was essential she learn. Regular humans were capable of being aware of energy. Claire was already aware of it, so much so that she was currently ecstatically bathing in it. It was subtle or non-existent only to those who sleepwalked through their lives.

"Yes, please," Claire squealed, sitting upright. "Can we start *now*?"

I laughed and pulled her up by her hand. "How about we let this good burst of energy fade so you'll be as close to normal as possible, okay? Like a baseline."

"Okay," she said with a down-note of disappointment. I squeezed her hand, and we walked to a bench in the shade under the portico of the large common room.

"I bet they'd love a helper in the kitchen," I said to Claire. "Everyone's supposed to lend a hand around here."

"How are you lending a hand?" she asked.

"I'm going to meet with people and ask them if they have any special abilities."

"Like how you can move things?" she asked, her eerie eyes lighting up.

"Exactly like that," I said, floating a leaf up in front of her to land on her head.

Claire giggled and skipped off toward the kitchen, and I pulled out a pen and paper, ready to chronicle the abilities of the people at the ranch. I figured going door to door was too forceful, but if it came to that, I would. No ability was inconsequential, and if we were smart, we'd devise a plan of defense that took advantage of every supernatural ability in the compound.

After two hours I'd compiled quite a list. The sortileges were as varied as the countries from which the people came:

Maya – kill by touch

Ehsan – shadow manipulation

Will – telekinesis

Sydney – morph to look like someone she's met

Cooper – elemental (water)

Gavin – elemental (fire)

Samantha – telepathic cozening

Sierra – shape-shifting "mimicry"

Sage – telekinesis

Hannah – the power to control or morph an aura

Suey — resident computer expert/ sortilege: telepathy

When more people passed me by than stopped, I stood to leave and stuffed the notepad in my pocket.

"*Buon pomeriggio.*" The greeting of "good afternoon" in my home language was enough to halt me and besides, the rotund man in suspenders was already sitting and looking up at me expectantly.

"*Come sta?*" I asked, but he waved me off.

"English is fine. When you move around as much as I have, you learn many tongues."

"How did you know I am Italian?" I asked, sitting across from him. Most people took my fair looks for the Nordic in my lineage, as my mother was Danish, though Cora insisted my Italian accent was fairly pronounced.

"Come, how many of us are there? The world is a small place for our band of misfits, and you look very much like your father," he said.

Nothing could have prepared me for that statement or for the rush of blood to my face when he said it. My family was a deserted island. My family was a bomb that went off and nobody noticed. "You—you knew my parents?"

"*Si,* I often wondered what happened. The rumors were gruesome. The truth worse, I'm afraid. You and your parents were assumed dead these many years. How did you escape? Where are they now?"

I was utterly confused. Dumbfounded to the point of mute. "I—they—I wasn't taken. They hid me, and I've been alone." Tears choked me. How readily my heart wrung out when someone who actually knew my family sat himself across from me. I cleared my throat, looked anywhere but at his penetrating eyes.

"Extraordinary," he said, nodding at a distant memory

that shone in his eyes. "I warned them, you know? I am a seer. I told them I saw two men and white, all white, and them falling to the ground."

"Yes," I whispered, seeing the scene fresh in my mind. The only person I'd ever revealed the story to was Cora until I told the abbreviated version to Will and Maya, and here this man knew. He'd warned them. He'd warned them and what did they do about it? "How much time did they have?"

The man leaned back in his chair and rested his arms on his ample belly. "Does it matter, son?"

"Hell yes, it matters! Why didn't they prepare?" My hand stung from slapping it on the table. Passersby stopped and stared. "Why didn't they ru—" I snapped my mouth shut. How could I even ask that when I was asking these people *not* to run? One side of the man's lip curved up in a half smile, and I knew he was thinking the same thing. I felt tricked.

He just chewed on the inside of his lip and studied me before answering. "I can see why you're so motivated to be ready. You were young, caught off guard. You think you might have done differently, changed things?"

My throat tightened with emotion.

"Warnings are what you're giving these people, and you don't have the gift of *sight,* do you, boy? Yet you see how you're disregarded? Dismissed?" A tinge of anger flooded his voice. "Lead the horses to water... I know these feelings well."

Stunned, stinging, I tried to wall myself off, focus on the task at hand. "So, you're clairvoyant?"

"Yes. But sometimes things don't go exactly as I see them. You were supposed to die, yet you did not. Many will die here." He cocked an eyebrow at me. "I see it."

Claire ran up and threw herself on my lap. The man, whose name I still didn't know, scrunched his eyes at her. His chest lifted and fell with a heavy sigh. His expression was troubled in a way that made me wonder if he was seeing something right then.

"You could be wrong again," I said, hearing the truculent tone in my voice.

"Every sortilege has its weak spot. Anything can happen." With effort, he hefted himself from his seat and shuffled a few steps before turning to look at me again. "After all, you're alive when you should not be."

Chapter Twenty-Five

Cora

"I'm already a target," I told Edmund as he jerked the steering wheel to the side and careened around another corner, barely missing a street lamp.

"If they bust out helicopters, we're screwed," Dun said from the back.

That comment caused both Edmund and me to simultaneously peer up through the windshield at the sky. The streaks of clouds had morphed from white to deep rose with the setting sun. None of us were sure where to go. We seemed to have lost the trail of pursuers, but for how long? How many traps were being set? I had the sensation of being a Godzilla-like giant, plodding over the earth and unable to hide or rest because everyone's eyes were on me. I was too big. The more I relived the last hour, the more I knew Edmund Nustber was right; I had to stay off every grid known to man 'cause my face was about to become fully recognizable.

I turned on the radio to see if the news was out but soon realized that finding an English-speaking radio station was a challenge. "You can use my phone to check the major news sites," Edmund said, fishing it out of his pocket. "Bet you a tank of gas that you're already on there. You'll be bigger news than that massive earthquake in Chile."

"What?" I shrieked. "How bad was it? Where?" That had to be why I couldn't get through on the phone. I tried again and got the same busy signal. My stomach was sick with nerves.

Edmund eyed me curiously. "Near Santiago, I think. A ton of structural damage, and the death toll is nearing eighteen hundred. It was *bad*."

"How am I ever going to get out of this country?" I said, thinking of Chile and the people I loved. I looked back at Dun. "I should be there with them."

Edmund loosened his tie with a tug. "I have some thoughts on getting you hidden, but I have conditions, too."

"*Dude...*" Dun's voice was a warning.

"Look, this is what I do. This is what I'm about—chasing down the supernatural and separating wheat from chaff, so to speak. You recognized me," he said, motioning to me, "so you know who I am. There's obviously something supernatural about what occurred back there, and you said I wouldn't believe you if you told me. Try me. I have some contacts, and if we act fast and keep out of sight, I think I can get you away from here until you're ready."

"Ready for what?" I asked. I needed help, obviously, but

I wasn't sure what he wanted from me or supposed I was ready for. Who could ever be ready for the things that had happened to me since I started seeing auras?

"Ready to tell the truth about who or *what* you are. Give me an exclusive interview."

Dun actually laughed. "I don't know whether you are the most opportunistic bastard ever or—"

"Your new best friend?" Edmund said. "I know an opportunity when I see one, yes. That doesn't make me a bastard. I consider myself a seeker of truth, and I'm not afraid of what others might see as terrifying. I imagine that you terrify some select people, Cora Sandoval. You're a threat to the system."

It made sense. Why else would the Scintilla be a target if they weren't a threat? My throat tightened so that my words came out low and angry. "I terrify them enough to hunt me down and kill me—and everyone like me."

Edmund's eyes rounded. "There's *more* like you?"

I sighed. "Not very many. Maybe just three of us now." Dun and I met eyes, and I knew we were both thinking of the loss of my mother. I fingered the scrap of tartan tied around my wrist that Finn gave me from Mom's grave and my heart gave a lurch—both for my mother and for Finn. "Guess I should start at the beginning…"

Edmund drove on as I recounted my story. He'd been one of the resources I'd consulted to learn about energy, and my father obviously watched his show for more than entertainment value. Edmund might have knowledge that could help me. I kept scanning the roads and skies while I talked, and he listened intently, occasionally jerking his face toward me with a look of incredulity. "For a guy who believes in aliens and crop circles, you're looking mighty shocked by some of this."

"I think this is the biggest conspiracy ever perpetrated in our world, particularly the part about Jesus. I'm over the moon that you thought to snap a picture of the hidden painting. From what you're telling me, though, this goes further back than Jesus. Some of the ancient carvings are thousands of years before his time. I've covered some of those mysteries on my show. If you can finally answer questions that have been posed for millennia, you could wake up the whole of civilization to a new truth."

We pulled over at a roadside petrol station and convenience store, and Edmund ran in while we waited in the car. We were parked right in front and watched him closely through the windows for any sign that he was texting or calling someone. How could I truly know he'd not sell me out? I did believe he wanted my story for himself, but his words were ringing in my ears. I didn't want to be some kind of New Age prophet. It was hard to believe the truth would end the carnage. I had the sinking feeling it would be a starting gun for more.

"Think we can trust him?" Dun asked, breaking the silence.

"I'm not sure we have a choice," I said, reaching over the seat for the reassurance of his hand. He gave mine a squeeze. "My allies keep dying on me, and within hours the whole world will be talking about what happened, stalking the girl who brought children back from the dead." I hung my head in my hands and massaged my aching temples. "I can't hide."

"Even if they're not behind the conspiracy as a whole, the

church has a lot of reasons to be terrified of you," Edmund said, sliding back into the car and into the conversation. He had three bags of food and drinks and set them in the backseat. Dun rifled through and handed me a sandwich. "I wouldn't be surprised if they were happy to see you dead," Edmund added.

"Why do you say that?" "Why" had been the elusive cog in the mystery. With the key and the clues I'd pieced together, I felt sure I was closing in on my "who," but the cardinal's reasons were unknown.

"Think about it. The church would never want the public to know that Jesus was a Scintilla, but worse, that he wasn't the only one. You said you think his mother was one, too. They wouldn't want that truth out because that would mean there are many saviors among us. And if there are, why go to religious organizations at all?"

"They could lose everything—influence, power, money. Lots of money," Dun astutely stated.

Edmund seemed lost in thought, but then he said, "'*These things I do, you can do also.*'"

"I always wondered about that line," Dun said. "I wonder how many dumbasses in history have tried to walk on water because of it."

Dun got a small grin out of me. "But they're not trying to kill the Arrazi, and the Arrazi also have powers if they've taken from a Scintilla. They're seemingly working hand in hand with each other. Why? Why aren't they threatened by the Arrazi? Seems to me the Arrazi don't need to take threats from anybody."

"Maybe it's not what's being held over the Arrazi's head," Edmund said. "Maybe it's what's being dangled in front of them. Maybe it's what's being promised."

Dun tapped my shoulder and handed me a bag of candy like a proper best friend. "Seems to me they got them some supernatural henchmen," he said.

I nodded. "Of course. Use the Arrazi to exterminate us and then," I bit my lip. "God, the awful things someone could do with an Arrazi army." Horrific acts, worse than the ones I'd seen in the visions from the key, that's what awaited humanity if Arrazi had free reign.

"If this goes back as far and as deep as you say," Edmund said, "then those who control the masses have always been threatened by the Scintilla."

"The images I got from the key were gruesome: people burned at the stake or hung, mothers with babies in their arms, shot and left on the ground. Whole villages destroyed." The car was quiet as the images floated around us. "I met a man today in St. Peter's Basilica—Cardinal Báthory. He is connected somehow with Xepa. Whether he's just a member of the secret society or in charge of it, I don't know. But interestingly, he works for an office that used to be known as The Inquisition."

I'd wanted to look it up when Professor Salamone had first said it, so I used Edmund's phone to search the Inquisition. I read aloud what Wikipedia had to say:

"… many persons of both sexes, heedless of their own salvation and forsaking the Catholic faith, give themselves over to devils male and female, and by their incantations, charms, and conjurings, and by other abominable superstitions and sortileges…"

"Sortileges. That's what we call our abilities. It's unreal to think they might have been hunting for us plain as day back then."

"And calling you witches," Dun said. "Nice spin."

Edmund became very animated, waving one hand while he spoke, like I'd seen him do on TV when my father watched his show. It was weird to see it in person. "It's how they discredit. Slap a label on what's different. Call anyone with an extraordinary ability a witch, a heretic, a nutcase. Except, oddly enough, *one* man in history who clearly had extraordinary abilities. Perhaps Jesus's fame outgrew their capacity to contain it. Even in my arena, the New Age community has been discredited, ridiculed, and shamed because we dare to investigate the extraordinary in the universe. Make it wrong or crazy or a sin to ask questions so people won't believe something other than *their* dogma. The Inquisition even had their mitts on Galileo at one point for doing that very thing: questioning their layout of the universe. And he was right!"

"Galileo's tomb is with Dante's and Michelangelo's," I said. "Makes sense that he'd be on their list if he knew about the Scintilla and Arrazi. Galileo gave them the finger, though. Well, three fingers to be exact. The number three has been a huge part of this saga, I just don't know exactly what its meaning is."

"*Three is the mystery come from the Great One, hear and light on thee will dawn.*"

My jaw dropped. "My mother said that once."

He nodded. "From the Emerald Tablets written between the sixth and eight centuries. Alchemists, including Newton, revered it. Three is a very mystical number, and not just in the Emerald Tablets. Some say it's the *perfect* number as it gives rise to all others. The number three is supposed to represent the soul, and is thought to symbolize overcoming or transcending duality."

"Duality?"

"Yeah. I think we're walking now in the garden of good and evil. Eve didn't fall because of knowledge. She fell because she bought into the duality. She fell because she believed in our separateness. The knowledge of good and evil are an example of dualism. We've forgotten our oneness."

Edmund had been driving on the twisted highways of Italy, though I had no idea what direction we were headed as the sun had already set when we were leaving Rome. He seemed to be looking for something out the windows as we drove and soon pulled the car over when he spotted a gothic church.

"Why?" I asked, anxiety riding up my spine. "I don't think this is the safest—"

"I want to go in and get a bible. Be right back," Edmund said.

Dun opened the back door. "Oh no you don't. How do we know you're not contacting the Vatican?" he asked him.

Edmund leaned forward with an irritated sigh. "If you watched my show at all, or read *any* of my many books, you'd know that organized religion and I—particularly the Vatican—don't exactly see eye to eye. Come with me if you like, but your mug was filmed at that scene, too, and you're not the most inconspicuous guy around. Look at you, all *Dances with Wolves*. Neither of you should be seen." He cocked his head and smiled. "That's just my opinion. Here, keep the keys if you're worried," he said, tossing the keys to me through the window. "Be right back."

We watched him spring up the stairs and enter the

church. Both Dun and I stared at the large double doors, waiting for Edmund to come out. He did, just moments later, carrying a red bible with gold-leaf pages. He handed it to me and buckled up. "There're some passages niggling at me. I wanted to take a look since cell coverage has been so spotty. There are things I want to look up in the noncanonical gospels as well."

"What's on your mind?" I asked, remembering the moment in Christ Church when Giovanni showed me a bible passage saying there "was a natural body and a spiritual body." "My friend Giovanni showed me a passage from Ezekiel," I said, suddenly feeling a fresh wave of wishing he were with us. "It spoke of light over the living, shining like awe-inspiring crystal, spread out above their heads."

Edmund had recited the last part with me. "I'm familiar with it. Quoted it in one of my books about auras. Sometimes the truth is hiding in plain sight. The more I think about it, the more I believe there are passages, particularly about Jesus Christ, that support what you've told me."

"You've already got your worldwide exclusive special spinning in your head, don't you?" Dun said with a smile. "Complete with bible quotes and everything."

"Help me get safely to my grandmother's house in Chile," I said, venturing to trust him further. "And then we'll talk. I'll do your interview. It's high time for the world to hear my truth. Even if it's the last thing I do."

"I'll do everything I can to make that happen. Hope you have some thick skin," Edmund said, patting my arm. "The world loves to exalt people before they shoot them down."

"Or nail them to a cross," Dun said, oh so helpfully.

"They may take me down. In fact, I think it's likely. My

being alive right now is a freaking miracle." Steely resolve hardened my core. "But they won't take me down without a fight. First, I will sling some arrows of my own. I have a right to exist. I have a right to be who I am without fear. They *should* be afraid of me. Truth can be a sharp spear."

Chapter Twenty-Six

Finn

My da greeted me when I arrived. "Whose car is that?" he asked, holding the door open and peering past me at Saoirse's wheels. "Saoirse Lennon's," I answered with a glance at the sopping clouds that looked soon to bust open all over her gleaming Mercedes.

"I heard about her mother," he said, one brow rising in a way that suggested relief, like hearing that the rabid neighborhood dog had been dutifully put down. "Do they suspect you were there when she died?"

We walked inside, and I followed my nose to the dining room. "I think Lorcan does, and now he's planted that seed in his sister's mind. I hope I've deflected their suspicion."

"You know about Rome, I reckon. I've been watching the news since."

"Aye." I collapsed in a chair at the dining room table. My father poured two halfers of whiskey and handed me one. "*Sláinte*," he said, raising the glass to his lips and downing it in one gulp. It was good to see him and felt good to be treated like an adult, an equal.

"Damn glad to have you back, Da."

"*Uisce beatha*," he said as a toast.

Water of Life.

"Suppose that phrase actually meant water originally?" I asked, lifting the amber liquid to my lips.

"Why not?" he asked. "The world is wholly made up of it, as are our bodies."

I tapped my fingers on the table in a familiar guitar series. "For us, it's not water. It's souls."

He looked down and pursed his lips together. "I see your point."

Time wore on, smoothed out in the way it often did when I sat with my father. He excelled at warm silence. It allowed me to voice what could only bubble up if given enough space. "I'm scared for her." Just saying that made my throat swell uncomfortably.

"I don't blame you," he said. "It changes everything. It won't do to question why she did it. Speaks to the kind of person she is."

I nodded. "Aye, it does."

"But that lass is in more peril now than she ever was. The world is fit to tear shreds of her for keepsakes."

A groan pushed from me. Mary entered with plates. The smell of her delectable beef stew wafted around us, and I was hit with the remembrance of the night I spotted Cora in Ireland after I thought I might never see her again. We had enjoyed beef stew with Clancy. My chest tightened with the memory. The bastard had known who and what she was all along.

No longer able to eat, I pushed my plate away. "Sorry, Mary…I…"

Their gazes pressed on my back as I left supper and went to bed.

Before sunup, I was back in the hidden room. Since I could hardly sleep, I began a fresh round on the flow chart I'd drawn and had left lying on the table before Saoirse had arrived yesterday. What she'd whispered in the car ate at me. Halfway home, I was convinced she was right. It was time for us to ally and do things differently. Wasn't this what I'd been after? She was playing right into my plans.

But the farther away from Saoirse I got, the less convinced I became. I was sure I was right about the Two of Cups, and when my father mentioned "water of life" I couldn't deny the surety settling on my bones. That card dropped for me because it truly meant the "reconciliation of opposites," and when I connected the dots I felt certain that the "water of life" was a metaphor and that, in every historical sense, meant something much more vital than water. I was developing a crude theory that likely couldn't be proved, but it was more than I'd had at the start.

Our soul's energy was the water of life.

By midday, I was neck deep in family records. The history of my family was interesting, to be sure, but there was no history that would quench my need if it didn't have to do with *what* we were. I came across a captivating diary from an ancestor named Gillian Mulcarr in the 1880s titled: *A True and Faithful Account, by Gillian Mulcarr*. My throat constricted as I read her anguished story of turning, of the horror of what she was, and how God would never forgive her. At the back of the book were odd tally marks I could only assume were her kills.

I carefully put the papers and Gillian's diary back in the drawer and shut it with a force born of frustration, my fists clenching on top of the wooden cabinet. Cora's face shone in my mind. Helping her was my only redemption. She was all I could think about.

My phone rang with an unfamiliar number. "Hello?"

"Finn, it's Cora."

"Jaysus, luv! Are you all right?" My heart went from zero to warp speed in one second. "I saw the news. Where the devil are—"

"I can't tell you where I am, only that I'm trying to…to get to…"

"I know." I understood why she didn't want to say it aloud. Even now, she wanted to protect others. God, it was good to hear her voice, to know she was safe. "I'll come to you, if you need me." The words tumbled out unsolicited. True.

"Dun is with me."

So, he'd found her. I was glad. When he came to me with the notion of secretly following her, I was 100 percent on board, funded it in fact. "Grand," I said. "I'm glad you're not alone."

"I just wanted you to know I'm okay. And I have a favor to ask… Get ahold of them for me, if you can. I left the number and address in the top drawer in the tower. Please, tell them I'm all right."

"I will. Listen, I have something really important to show you."

"I don't see how *that's* gonna happen."

The sarcastic point to her voice sent shockwaves of longing through me. I missed everything about her, including her edges. "This is big, Cora. *Fookin'* major." I lowered my voice to a whisper. "I have something you need to—to get your *hands* on."

"How major?" Before I answered, she said, "You know it's unlikely I'll ever step foot on Irish soil again."

I closed my eyes and willed myself to take a breath and then another. What she was saying was more than she might never come back to Ireland, might never have a reason; she was saying she might not live to return. "I'll—I'll find you. I'll bring it to you." Even as I said it, I had no earthly clue how I'd be able to conceal the cover of the *Book of Kells* and smuggle it out of Ireland to Chile. Plus, I'd not want to lead anyone to her if—*if* she made it safely there. *Dear Lord, let her make it safely there.*

"We both know you shouldn't do that."

As we hung in the space between heartbeats, I noticed the triangle I'd drawn in the dust atop the bureau when my mom first brought me in the room. A radical notion overtook me and I drew a hexagram next to that, and the Xepa symbol—two triangles joined at their tips—next to that. A realization so potent struck the air from me. "Of course!" I whispered and opened my mouth to explain.

"Finn, I have to go."

"Push the Xepa triangles together, luv." I was certain I

was absolutely right. An inner joint snapped into place, the cogs slid together. But before I could explain my idea, she was gone, and miles of dead air stood between us.

Chapter Twenty-Seven

Giovanni

I'd had all afternoon and night to catch my breath from meeting the Italian clairvoyant. I'd learned his name, Raimondo, and intended to speak further with him about what he foresaw with the Arrazi but more specifically why he'd looked upon my daughter with such troubled eyes.

My heart clenched with anxiety. Would I ever leave all of these people to protect her? There was enough fairness in me to understand by asking that one question of myself, that I had no idea the choices my parents faced. I couldn't condemn them, though the questions kept me up the entire night. He said he'd foreseen the death of my entire family, including me. Yet, I survived. Destiny must be a fluid thing, if it existed at all. I wondered who'd made the one choice that changed mine.

Before I could speak to Raimondo about Claire, I received the call that it was time for the long trek back to Santiago with Will, Ehsan, and Adrian to visit this mysterious street food vendor who sold empanadas with a side of hand grenades.

Mami Tulke didn't know exactly why I was going on a group excursion to the city, or if she did, she didn't let on. But her aura was as cold as her shoulder when I told her I'd be leaving with the men as soon as they arrived. She didn't balk at having my daughter with her for the day, and for that I was grateful. How *did* parents get anything done in their lives? Grateful for Claire as I was, I'd suddenly grown a new appendage and was learning to walk again.

Claire had crept into my room and made camp on my floor for the second night in a row. She rustled in her sleep when I stirred. I pushed a hit of happy her way, which settled her again. I longed to touch her curls but feared I'd wake her. Loving energy would have to do.

The arrival of the car skidding in the dirt outside rushed me to the door. I said good-bye to Mami Tulke, who just replied, "Yah, yah," as she stuffed a supplies list in my hand along with a wad of bills.

I climbed in the SUV. Everyone was accounted for with an additional, unexpected extra, Will's wife, Maya. "I need to get some things I can't find in La Serena and get away for a day. You all are my captive audience," she announced, crossing her arms over her chest. "I intend to use this time well."

"Will this one *sorry* cover it, guys?" Will teased. "I don't want to keep repeating it. And for the record, opinions of the Maya do not necessarily reflect those of the management."

"Confusing," Maya demurred. "Since I don't recall pro-moting *you* to management."

We all laughed and set off on the journey.

"Gentlemen," Maya began, and the men surrendered to the inevitable fact that we were indeed captives and would have to listen to what she had to say. Maya's charisma and strength commanded attention. Respect for Will demanded we give it, even if he was the most captive of us all and had likely heard her opinions many times over.

"With the exception of Giovanni, you all know me to be frank and fair in my views."

"Mostly frank," Ehsan goaded.

Maya ignored the teasing and pressed on. "I want you to know that I do not agree with what y'all are planning."

Will pinched the bridge of his nose. "Maya…"

"No, Will. I love you, but before you boys get all war-games on me and destroy our peaceful way of life, I *will* be heard." She smoothed her hand over her black hair, which had been pulled tight away from her face and ended in a ball of pouf at the back of her head with a colorful scarf tied around it. Maya looked to me like an exotic black cat, earthy but sleek. The determined set of her mouth said she was not one to be trifled with.

"My heart tells me that Giovanni truly wants to protect us, save us even." She held up her hand to quiet me when I opened my mouth. "But my heart also tells me that by charging into a mindset of war, killing, and fear, it will only *attract* those things to us. This is basic Law of Attraction."

"Those things are coming," I promised. "Uninvited by us and inescapable — they are coming. We did not create this, we are only reacting to it, doing what we must to survive. Is there not energy in *that*?"

The excitement in her aura told me she had been eagerly anticipating this debate. "Every human on this planet is a being of energy. Thoughts have energy, they're creative, they're the roots of our reality. The world is the way it is because of the way we collectively think."

I struggled to stay calm. "If my thoughts and words are creative, then I create survival. I will not be passive about being exterminated."

Ehsan nodded affirmatively. "It's not too hard to recall many, too many, historical instances in this world where one 'kind' of human exterminated another," he said, stroking his black goatee. "Rwanda, Bosnia, Cambodia, natives in the Americas, Serbs, Jews, Romani. In the Middle East, jihadists hunt and kill minorities they deem infidels. It's heartbreaking and ungodly. In many cases, might was met with might to end the atrocities. Sadly, I think that war is sometimes justifiable."

The auras in the car settled into graven pools reflecting our dark thoughts. How did we become a world where one clan of human got to decide that another clan of human didn't deserve to live?

When Maya spoke again, her voice was soft. "All this talk of killing 'the other.' How does that make us any different than them?"

Will put his hand on Maya's leg. "Honey, we're talking about defending ourselves. It's not the same thing."

"But what if we could talk to them? If we—"

"What would you possibly talk to them about? '*Pretty please…please don't do this thing you're hell-bent on doing and that you're likely being rewarded for doing.*'"

Maya's head tilted, and she shot me a stern look at my sarcasm. "We are givers of energy. And our mortal enemy is our polar opposite—takers of energy. Doesn't that strike you as perfectly odd? Haven't any of you ever wondered why we were created as the two extremes of each other? Might there be a reason, a divine purpose and beauty in that symmetry?"

"Beauty in murder? Beauty in your loved ones disappearing forever? Beauty in extinguishing an entire race of human?" My patience was waning.

"Beauty in the duality," Maya answered simply. "Don't you see it?"

"No," Adrian said, throwing up his inked hands. "Girl, I don't even know what you're talking about."

"I'm suggesting that there must be a higher purpose for the design of us," she said. "I'm talking about *duality*. Opposites. Relativity. Light dark, up down, on off, yin yang, good bad. We exalt the lighter or more positive aspects of duality simply because they are more...*pleasant*. But it doesn't make the light *better* than the dark. It is not inherently evil to take. It is the relative opposite of giving. You must have one to have the other. In this world, choice is possible only because we have opposites.

"Joseph Campbell wrote, '*I and you, this and that, true and untrue—every one of them has its opposite. But mythology suggests that behind that duality there is a singularity over which this plays like a shadow game.*'"

One by one, Maya looked deep into our eyes; she'd reach into our souls with her eyes if she could. "Think about that. *Really think* about that before you launch into this battle you're preparing for. What is the shadow game we're playing?"

If Maya's strategy was to plant a seed that would sprout into guilt, it seemed to work on the other men. Each was silent, staring out of the windows for a long stretch of time.

Duality was thought-provoking but seemed too existential to matter. Surely Scintilla and Arrazi had endeavored for as long as they'd existed to find the "reason." What if there were no reason? What if it was simple biology? Predator and prey?

S antiago was bustling in the afternoon sun, frenetic in a way the city hadn't been when we'd first arrived from Dublin. "The earthquakes must have shaken people up," Will said, navigating the SUV through throngs of people in the streets near the *Plaza De Armas* at the city's center.

"Ha," Adrian laughed a beat too late.

Looking closer, it seemed this was something more. "Is there a political demonstration? A religious holiday?" I asked, curious as to how this many people could be out in droves in the middle of a weekday. I got shrugs in answer. "The earthquake must have hit harder here," I guessed. We'd been unable to get news deep in the valley for a couple of days since the big quake hit. Telephone lines were still dead. Cell phones were spotty in the best of circumstances.

"I hope there weren't too many deaths," Maya murmured. "Tragedies have a way of filling churches."

I followed her gaze to see a large church, the Metropolitan Cathedral, which bulged with people spilling out of its large triple doors, down the steps, and into the street. People were openly praying. Many looked like they were camping out in the square in front of the church. Vendors walked back and forth selling rosaries, which swung like pendulums off their arms or off their street carts as they rolled them up and down the avenue. This had to be about the earthquakes. Maya was right, natural disasters had a way of bringing people together, and fear had a way of bringing people to church.

The opportunists were out in droves with the worshipers. Everything you needed could be had at a price: rosaries, food, water, and merchandise. A universal truth was understood by all people: when there's an epic calamity or disaster, you sell T-shirts.

Will pulled the car over on a side street because we couldn't find parking anywhere else. A man sat in his cracked driveway in a frayed beach chair with a cooler full of *cerveza* and a radio and charged us thirty thousand *pesos* to park there. "We'll be out here forever, if we don't," Will complained. Adrian fanned himself with a dusty Texas Rangers baseball cap as we walked through the people to find our contact.

"Always be on the lookout for an all-white aura," I warned them, scanning the thick crowds for any sign of an Arrazi. The crowds made me tense. "I can recognize them by feel now, but not unless they're close."

Ehsan muttered "And if they're that close —"

"Then it'll be too late."

Nothing should have surprised me at that point, but Gerda did. I didn't expect an elderly, female, German arms dealer in the heart of Chile. Ehsan explained that there was quite a large German population in Chile from immigration in the late nineteenth and early twentieth centuries. Gerda ushered us through a makeshift door made of two car trunks suspended by hinges in the doorframe. Will said he didn't know her personal story, but her age and the mezuzah outside her trunk-doors gave me a hint. "I half thought you'd not come," she said. "Too crazy out there."

Will wasted no time. "We had to come. It's very important. We're looking for weapons."

"When? What kind? How many?" she spat, but sounded distracted, half interested. "Why?"

Will looked to me, and so I stepped forward to answer. "Any moment. Anything you've got. As much as you've got. And assume we're fighting an army."

Her white brows shot up. "I've seen armies, young man. You five are no army."

"I'm willing to bet you've seen genocide as well. *That* is what we're up against."

That is when her eyes squinted at us and she seemed to regard us for the first time. Three white men, an Afghani man, and one black woman. The question was written all over her face: how could this tapestry of humans be a target for eradication? What could we possibly have in common? Flies buzzed, horns honked outside, the world hummed.

"I'm no longer in the business," she said, abruptly shooing us out.

"What?"

"I think you bugged her out, man," Adrian whispered. "We're for real," he said to her in a placating tone. "We really need your help."

"Go to God for help. Everyone else is," she said, waving her arms toward the two bell towers of the church. "The end times are coming. You were my test. I passed. My sin is behind me. I passed and I shall stand on the right side of the Lord."

"What is she on about?" Ehsan whispered to me.

"I couldn't begin to tell you," I said, infuriated. "Why'd we come here at all?"

The woman perched herself in front of my chest and looked up at me. "Your visit was either an answer to your prayers or an answer to mine. Or both."

Adrian's high-pitched voice cut through the dusty air. "What the—"

"Guys," called Maya from outside the trunk-door doors. "C'mere. I don't think this is earthquake hysteria at all." We found her on the sidewalk, inspecting a row of cheap T-shirts for sale from a crusty old man wearing a hat that was more holes than straw.

I ripped a shirt from its hanger, ignoring his curses in Spanish. On the front of the shirt was a quote in Spanish, "*Porque se levantarán falsos Cristos, y falsos profetas se levantarán, y harán grandes señales y prodigios, de tal manera que engañarán...Mathew 24:24.*"

Underneath the quote, a picture of a girl on her knees at the feet of St. Peter, her hands over the heart of a child, her picture the very face of angelic torment and sorrow.

My body went cold.

Cora.

Nothing on earth could explain why her face was plastered all over cheap T-shirts next to cheaply made pocket bibles. "What is this?" I asked, thrusting the shirt at the vendor. "What does this mean?"

Maya's voice funneled to me the literal translation:

"*False Christs and false prophets will arise and perform great signs and wonders, so as to deceive...*" But the words meant nothing—they weren't the explanation I needed. My body iced over as I stared at the black and white picture of Cora's stricken face. I spun on the sidewalk and saw others like it, all variations on the same beautiful and familiar face in the same unreal scene.

I stumbled down the street in a bleary daze, finding more carnival funhouse versions of the mysterious event. What in the hell had happened in Rome? Was she okay? Alive? I'd been hiding in a remote seam of mountains in South America, waiting for the girl I loved to come home to us, and now her face was plastered everywhere I looked with bible quotes that ranged from claiming Cora was the incarnation of Jesus, or that the "Daughter of Man" came at an hour we did not expect, to bold red letters over her picture proclaiming she was the Antichrist.

Will and Maya's energies and hands reached for me. "I need to know what happened to her," I cried, shaking the T-shirt in their faces. "This is Mami Tulke's granddaughter." Everyone's eyes widened and their mouths dropped open. "Whatever happened to her," I said, meeting Maya's eyes, "it means that we are no longer in a shadow game. We are out in the open."

Chapter Twenty-Eight

Cora

Divulging to Edmund that I intended to go to Chile was a big leap of faith on my part. What choice did I have, though? He dangled resources that I didn't have. I needed him, and since he seemed to need something from me, the deal *felt* right.

Edmund's aura was as clear and crystalline as Faye's, the owner of Say Chi's, the first time I met her. I came to trust that clarity because it coincided with clarity of thought, clarity of purpose. The texture of his aura was soft, nonaggressive. He *felt* nonthreatening.

I used his phone to call Mami Tulke's house again but got that same annoying out-of-service signal. Taking a deep breath and another leap of faith, I had called Finn.

God, to hear his voice… He'd never know how deeply

it strummed my heart. It probably always would. It hadn't seemed to surprise him that Dun was with me. I knew then that he'd helped Dun follow me. If Giovanni didn't have Claire to look after, he'd have done the same. When Finn and I hung up, I had to swallow more tears that threatened like they did in the airport. I never knew which good-bye would be our last. Forever.

"What's up, Cora? Did Captain Kilt say something freaky?"

"He said he found something important but wouldn't say what. He wants to get it to me somehow so I can see what imprint it holds. But that's not the weirdest part. His last words were, *push the triangles together*." I turned my palm up and looked at the Xepa symbol on the ring. I could envision what he meant mentally, but I blew hot breath on the car window and traced one upside-down triangle with my finger. I then traced the other triangle over the top of it.

I'd seen the symbol—the hexagram—in surprising places, like the church at the tomb of Dante, Michelangelo, and Galileo, and then on the four corners of the painting of Jesus and Mary.

"Jewish thingy?" Dun asked.

"The hexagram," Edmund corrected. "It was an important symbol *long* before it was adopted by the Jews. Unification of opposites; that's what the six-pointed star *really* means. It's a divine symbol of unity."

Realization struck. "So, symbolically speaking, to pull them apart would mean to separate what should be unified."

Dun hung his arms over the seat and spoke into the leather. "More explanation would be helpful," he said, sounding like he did when I used to tutor him on his math homework.

"If I'm coming to the right conclusion, then Xepa's whole agenda is to remain disconnected—that goal is symbolized by the *disunion* of opposites. If that's what Xepa stands for," I said, my brain barely accepting the idea that was forming, "then it would mean that the Scintilla and Arrazi are somehow supposed to be...*united*?"

It was the most preposterous, the most impossible theory ever. That couldn't be what Finn was suggesting. I immediately called him back. "Okay, one symbol means unity. One, separation. What do *you* think it means?"

"I think it means that we're supposed to be together."

Fear, disbelief, impossibility, and beneath all that, a wild sprig of hope. All those emotions stemmed my words while my heart ticked off the seconds until I could finally speak. "You mean the Scintilla and Arrazi?"

I heard his sigh through the phone. "You know what I mean." When I didn't answer, couldn't answer, he said, "We've come to the same conclusion. The trouble is—proving it."

"That's what I need you to do. First off, can you find out for sure why *this* is their symbol?"

"I'm on it. Ultana's daughter has inherited control of all of Ultana's business. Her brother's ticked about it. But I'm getting closer with Saoirse. I'll learn what I can. I hope she'll come round to our way of thinking."

Closer...

I shook off the rogue dart of jealousy. "Let me know what you find out. With luck, I'll get myself to my grandmother's. Were you able to get ahold of them?"

"No. But I won't stop trying."

"Thank you, Finn. I'm worried."

"You're welcome." His voice softened. I felt like he was whispering in my ear. I could feel the memory of his breath on my skin. "Every time I talk to you I'm afraid—"

"It'll be the last time."

"Aye. You must know that I love you. No matter what."

My ragged breathing made my words rickety and weak. "'No matter what' is something people say before they know *what*."

"I'll poke around and see if I can verify if our theory is right. What we do with that theory is another mystery."

"Someone is helping us," I said, knowing Edmund was listening intently. "His name is Edmund Nustber."

"The author?" Finn's voice was surprised, but I was just as surprised that he immediately knew the name.

"The very one."

"I hope he's trustworthy."

"Well, if he's not, you know his name."

I hung up.

"Who was that?" Edmund asked.

"An Arrazi."

I hoped Edmund understood the implied threat. If he hurt me, if he threw me to the wolves, there was one Arrazi on this planet who I knew would eat his soul for it.

Familiar conflicted feelings came like a tidal wave. Love for Finn. Abhorrence for what he was, though I knew that wasn't his fault. Still, I hated what he'd done. I couldn't imagine ever truly believing he didn't have a choice but to kill Mari. Whether it was the most merciful thing to do, or the most evil, I wasn't able to decide. I only knew that the reason my heart felt so fractured was that he was the first boy I'd given my heart to before I took it back so I could move on. Giovanni also had a piece. I loved his mind and his loyalty but suspected he was loyal to himself above all. Multiple fragments of my heart had dissolved like ice in red wine with the deaths of my father, mother, and Mari. The only time that pain went away was when I gave my light to those children.

I'd felt whole in those moments in a way I never had before.

Each one of us was a disaster in crumpled clothing, yawning and drifting into moody silences as we drove through the Italian countryside. We needed somewhere to stop for the night. A sign on the side of the road said we were in Chianti, and we soon found an old cluster of farmhouses from as far back as 1497 turned hotel. Edmund went in to reserve a room while we waited. A bed. A bed and a shower. My needs were pretty basic at that point. Survival came down to what was next. Immediate needs.

Luckily, procuring a room turned out to be no problem. He drove around one of the old stone buildings and parked in front of our door. We entered as fast as we could and fell into beds. I could hear Edmund on his laptop, typing away, but even that faded to nothing as I slipped under.

Sounds of near-rabid television newscasters woke me in the morning. Edmund and Dun were watching the news on the hotel's TV.

Couldn't reality wait?

I rolled over and pulled the pillow over my head.

"Hey, sleeping beauty." I glanced out the window. The sun was definitely screaming midmorning. Edmund stood in my doorway. "I have a plan in place. It's not foolproof, but it's the best I've got. Come on out here so we can talk about it."

I scratched my nails through my tangled hair and brushed my teeth, then went to the main room and sat on an ottoman, putting my back to the TV and the news that proclaimed to the world that I'd worked a miracle. Astutely, Dun turned off the volume, but his eyes kept roving back to the coverage.

Edmund handed me a cup of bitter coffee. "My man, Rodney, is on crew for a movie being shot on location in Venice right now. They are due to fly to Costa Rica. He thinks he can help us get on one of the chartered private jets. Cora, you'll have to act as flight crew. Dun, whip that long hair in a ponytail and act like film crew. Because Cora has already been identified by name—" I gasped but Dun just raised his brows and confirmed with a slow nod. "I will use my production company to pay off a female crew member to use her ID under the auspices that she's a confidential source for a story I'm doing. Cora will have to impersonate her and hope we get to Costa Rica, and from there, south to Chile, without anyone recognizing her or worse, organizing a media ambush when we land.

It sucked, but it was better odds than any plan I could have devised. "I was about to dye my hair blond or pay Italian godfathers to get me fake papers. I like your plan better," I told him. "So tell me without the infomercial voice. What's the news saying? What's going on out there?"

Edmund and Dun cast sideways glances at each other.

"What?" I asked.

Dun propped his feet on my lap. "Okay, like, imagine if Jesus, Jimmy Hoffa, Elvis, Amelia Earhart, and JFK announced they were actually alive and having a dinner party for the press to answer all their questions—"

"All right, all right," I said, closing my eyes as if that would turn off my ears. "I get it."

"That's how bad they want you," Edmund said. His face blushed scarlet, as did his aura. "Holy shit, the ratings I'm going to have. I will be forever thankful to you, Cora."

"I'll take your thanks. And seventy percent of all advertising, sponsors, and distribution monies received."

Dun grinned at me.

"If I manage to live through this," I said, all business, "I'm not going to end up with nothing while you traipse off into super-stardom off my story."

"You're changing our deal," Edmund pouted. "You have no idea the money that's exchanging hands just to pull this off. Even Rod is being paid off."

"*No*. I'm not changing the deal. It's the fine print," I said with a smile and stood to go to the shower. "And I want it in writing." What was he going to say? *No*? Edmund "Nutball" as my stepmom, Janelle, used to call him, was salivating to get me on camera. His life was about to be made even if my life was over.

"This is totally unfair!" he yelled at my back.

"We need each other, Eddie. This is business."

"Only my brother calls me Eddie!" he yelled as I shut the bathroom door.

I actually thought of cutting my hair as I looked at myself in the mirror. I was unrecognizable to myself anyway. A shadow girl. I hoped the attendant on the private jet wasn't some 4'1" blonde. I saw Mari in my mind and said to my reflection, "She'd better have dark hair and a fully realized butt."

Chapter Twenty-Nine

Finn

Cora's second call came while I was in my room putting another shirt over my T-shirt and hoping the chill I felt was from the rain rather than hunger. I'd know soon enough if the cold on the surface of my skin burrowed underneath to my blood and then wormed into a vague feeling of doom, followed by pure need. It was coming. My last kill was the man at Newgrange.

Her call invigorated me. She saw the same thing I did when she looked at the triangles, and she hadn't even seen the *Book of Kells* cover and pages with the triple spiral *and* the hexagram. She *had* to touch the remnant. How would I possibly get it to her? I didn't want to ship it and risk it being stolen or lost. I couldn't fathom carrying it through security at the airport in Ireland. It was the equivalent of an American trying to fly out of New York concealing the stolen Declaration of Independence!

Saoirse texted me and asked me to drive her car back and have lunch at her house, promising that she'd make sure I made it home. She lured me with an "idea" she wanted to discuss. I was eager to hear it but sensed I was stepping into muddy territory.

I thought of our good-bye yesterday. Her lips against my ear had been unsettling, but her whispered words lit a small victory fire within me. It was the promise of everything I was after. It could get very complicated if she wanted more than my friendship. The kiss in her house the day of her first kill told me how she *really* felt despite her declarations when we first met that she wanted nothing to do with me romantically. She'd been resisting her mother's machinations to get us together because she hadn't wanted to turn. I had to admit the possibility that her feelings for me might have instigated her transformation.

Her take on the tarot card reading was entirely different than mine, but that could work to my advantage. I didn't want to deceive her or use her. We'd formed an exploratory friendship and it was that friendship I hoped would make us great allies.

The cards couldn't have meant Saoirse and I, though I had to admit that with her mother's death came a new opportunity to work together. But Cora and I hit on something with the triangles. The Two of Cups had more meaning to me since discovering the ancient *shatkona* within the *Book of Kells* pages. It symbolized the joining of opposites and made me surer than ever that Cora and I *were* those opposites.

For the first time in weeks, I experienced a hope so

foreign it felt forbidden. Hope was a tightrope, and I was teetering in the middle. No going back, only forward, unable to see what waited for me on the other side. Surely, my sins could not be forgiven so that Cora could ever love me again. The most I could hope for was that maybe, like the picture of the tarot card, we'd pour our opposite realities together and make a new reality. Together, we'd find a way to end this and bring peace.

Peace between Arrazi and Scintilla was a delicate golden chain. Whether Saoirse wanted to be a vital link was up to her.

If the two races were united, could we stop the person directing the Arrazi toward genocide? In our hasty conversations, I'd neglected to ask Cora what she'd found out in Rome, if anything. I hoped her trip yielded more than pulling to herself the hugest spotlight in recent news history. Even a tornado the size of Nevada, which dragged its nail across the southwest hours ago and killed hundreds, couldn't unseat the *miracle* she'd performed. The upsurge in natural disasters, the increasing mysterious deaths, and now Cora's "resurrection" of those children was adding fuel to the apocalyptic fire.

Her home in Santa Cruz had a legion of news crews around it. I wondered how Cora's stepmother, Janelle, was faring. It was only a matter of time before they discovered who Dun was and stalked his family, too. *Jaysus*, I realized with a start, it was only a matter of time before they traced the family tree and found Mami Tulke.

My hope was a shrinking balloon when I let myself wonder how the world would respond to knowing the truth about the different races of man. Humans didn't seem to excel at *different*. We categorized, labeled, and *tribalized*: us and *them*, the *other*.

"Other" was too often another name for "enemy."

It was the Arrazi lawyer who opened the door to the Lennon home.

"Makenzie," she said, holding out her hand, though I wasn't sure if that was her first name or her last. We shook, and she let me inside.

Saoirse met us in the hall, wearing more formal clothes than I'd seen on her before. "Makenzie is here to reset the security pads for my mother's office so I can familiarize myself with, well, with everything." Her shoulders slumped faintly. "It's a lot to take in."

I put my hand on her arm. "I reckon it is. I'm sorry."

"Lorcan still hasn't come home," she said, turning and leading us toward the dining room where lunch was already set out. Makenzie disappeared to another room. "I don't know if he'll ever accept our mother's decision."

"So it surprised him?" I asked, waiting for Saoirse to sit before I did. If Lorcan was so put out, I worried that he'd rebel against any change for good that Saoirse might attempt.

"It shouldn't have. My mother was a consummate feminist."

"Oh? Like how she tried to arrange your romantic life for you rather than letting you choose for yourself?" I teased.

Saoirse gave a smirk full of challenge. "You were the pawn on that move. Not me." She picked up her fork and pushed food around but didn't take a bite. "My mother was patently against patriarchal dominance in society. I assume that to have a man—even her own son—take over her affairs went against her beliefs. Wonder if she'd have made the same decision if she knew that I didn't agree with her *politics*." Waving one hand dismissively in the air, she added, "Well, it's mine now to do with what I will."

Her statement fed my avidity for an Arrazi cease-fire. The Lorcan name and the influence that came with it would be a major coup. "What *will* you do with it?" I asked with an excited but tremulous snag to my voice.

"Run a benevolent empire, of course." Her face broke into a sly smile, and she tilted her head coyly. "I told you yesterday, Finn, my choice would be to do things differently than my mother. Now I have the chance to do something really important," she said, her voice rising. "To *be* important." I had no idea Saoirse had ambition in her but understood it when she added, "I grew up feeling insignificant in my mother's world and consequently my own life."

"Your mother took up a lot of room."

"She did, yes." There was a pause that was heavy with the words, "not any more," but I couldn't be sure if it was just I who was thinking it. "I have an idea that kept me up all last night, and you're a vital part of it. You're the only Arrazi I know who is connected with any Scintilla. You're a link between us and them."

Mention of my connection with Scintilla sat wrong with me. I gritted my teeth. "I don't know where they are."

"Are you trying to tell me that girl all over every news outlet in the world isn't a Scintilla? *The* Scintilla? Or do we believe in angels now?"

I returned her cunning smile. "I already believe in angels—*and* demons."

"My mother was in charge of Xepa," she continued. "What I don't know, yet, is who my mother took orders from. It has been extremely quiet since her death. No more visitors. No calls. Little to go on. But once I have access to everything, I will find out who we're up against and why we need to be following anyone's orders. We're Arrazi, after all."

That messed with my mind. It sounded a little too much like something Clancy or Ultana would say. "That first night at dinner with my family, your mother said the Arrazi were promised 'a seat at the table.' I assume that someone dangled a *shite*-ton of power, something huge, or she wouldn't have threatened fellow Arrazi lives for it."

"She's gone now." Impatience flared in her words. She looked down and softened. "We can do everything our way. I can make the Arrazi believe that I wield the same power my mother did. I don't think it's wise to do too abrupt of an about-face. At first, we'll have to act like nothing's changed so they don't turn from us. It'll be an uphill battle anyway, because I'm so young and a woman and the world is still filled with Neanderthals. My hope is that, over time, if they followed my mother into war, perhaps they'll follow *us* into peace."

"We don't have time."

"We have position. Think of it, Finn… The Scintilla and the Arrazi can help each other. We can work to convince the Arrazi that it would be folly to let the Scintilla die out. And I've thought of a way to negate any threat we might face. My idea is that if we meet peaceably with the remaining Scintilla, and the Scintilla let us take from them—"

My fist hit the table. "Absolutely not!"

"Hear me out," she urged, leaning forward with sincerity emanating from her eyes. "My mother was already a very powerful woman. Someone with a scary amount of influence motivated her to do what she did. You? Me? The ragtag bunch of Arrazi around here have nothing, *are* nothing against influence like that. We have to be able to offer them something better."

"We're killers," I said.

"They knew that, and yet, according to my mother, they still threatened us."

"Maybe no one is threatening us. What if your mother was acting alone? What if there is no one holding a knife to our throats?" I cringed for mentioning a knife in light of her mother's death. "She could have been lying to create fear and make us do what she wanted."

"And if you're wrong?"

"If I am, what if we refuse to do their dirty work? What can they possibly do to us? We'll turn the tables on them, expose them. Or kill them," I said, knowing I'd not hesitate if it would eliminate the threat to Cora.

"Expose them? C'mon. Look at what's happening to that poor girl—and she *saved* lives! Imagine what people will do if they expose *us*. Killers. Murderers. Soul stealers. They've got their angel. How will the world see *us*? The biggest threat against the Arrazi is the truth, and if there's someone out there who knows the truth, then they are a threat to us."

Rain pattered against the windows as we lost ourselves in braided thoughts. I couldn't stop thinking about what she'd just said. She just handed me the bullet against the

Arrazi. How could I expose us?

"We need sortileges. We need to be as strong as we can be and also as unpredictable. We need our enemies to be terrified of our powers and how we might use them. It's a good idea. You know it is," she said.

I looked deep into her eyes, using the full strength of my own sortilege on her. I had nothing else up my sleeve but the hope that Saoirse and I could yank the Arrazi collar and pull them off the Scintilla's throats. "Saoirse, can I trust you?"

Her hand reached across the table and rested softly atop mine. "Trust me. Believe what I say."

I felt myself soften, and strangely, I was suddenly pondering her idea. If the Arrazi all had sortileges, we *would* be more formidable to anyone who tried to control us. Our inherent ability was a weapon. But *supernatural* abilities—that was another level of lethal. There was a war inside of me: remove the threat over the Arrazi heads while not posing a threat to Cora. "We're already dangerous," I murmured, desperate for any solution that wouldn't endanger Cora further.

Saoirse squeezed my hand. "Not. Dangerous. Enough."

Chapter Thirty

Giovanni

The men and Maya all gawked at me after I told them who the girl was on the T-shirts.

"You're sure that's her?" Ehsan finally asked.

"*Manache*! I'm in love with her. Of course I'm sure!" I paced like a caged animal, my hands scraping roughly at my hair. My mind had already processed the hundred ways this was the most disastrous thing that could happen. "How is she going to get out of Italy? How will she come here, without leading the world straight to us?"

Despite my admonition not to ever call her, to only wait for her to contact us in case she was in a dangerous situation, I pulled out my cell phone and dialed the number of the phone Finn had given her. I had to try. I prayed the phone would work at all.

"G." That whispered call of my nickname triggered paroxysms of relief so profound, I thought I could cry.

I tucked my head to my chest and turned my back from the others. "You're alive."

"Amazing, right?"

"I saw your picture…"

"So you've seen the news." She sighed. "Is everyone okay, from the earthquakes I mean?"

"Yes. We're all okay. I haven't seen news," I explained. "The churches, they are like madhouses. Your face is plastered all over T-shirts on the street. This is crazy."

"I know." Her voice was so small. Defeated.

"How can I get to you? I'll come to you. I don't want you to be alone."

"I'm not alone."

My fists clenched. "He went to you?" I asked. "Or has he been with you all along?" It was petty jealousy. I should be with her, not Finn. True to her stubborn nature, she didn't answer.

"Someone is helping us get to you. If all goes as planned, we'll arrive first in Costa Rica and then make our way to you."

"When?"

"Soon. Hopefully. A couple of days."

"I knew you should not have gone to Italy," I said. Dread had nested low in my stomach from the moment she had the idea to go there. "It was for nothing and look what happened."

"It wasn't for nothing. I found out what the key opens. It's *big*. Bigger than what I did in that square."

Despite myself, I laughed. "I don't see how that's

possible."

"Trust me. I'm going to text you a picture, and I'm hoping you can translate the Italian painted on it. I'm sending it right now because...mostly because I'm afraid...if anything happens to me..." her voice choked. "I don't want it to stay hidden like it has for so long. I don't want it to die with me."

"*Bella,* shhh. I love you."

Soft crying filtered to my ears, funneled straight to my heart. "I know, G. But loving me is not a good bet."

We said good-bye and the lightness at hearing her alive dimmed to a faint glow and was soon replaced by a worry so absolute, I'd give anything to have her in my arms, to protect her. If...when...people found out where her family lived, we'd have a lot more trouble on our hands than just the Arrazi.

I pulled Adrian aside. "If that old woman won't help us, there's got to be someone in this city who can."

His lips pushed out, a bit of bravado. "I told you, man, I kicked around these streets for a year." He gave me a chin lift. "I might know some people." Then he looked me up and down. "You're a little squeaky for them, bro. You look like a damn underwear model. I don't know if they'll trust you."

"They trust *you*. Should be good enough. Look, since I was ten I lived my life on the streets in more cities than you have fingers and toes. I can mix with anyone."

Adrian thought the whole crew might make his friends nervous, so a plan was hatched that he and I would go find them and put out feelers for weapons, and Will, Maya, and Ehsan would go for supplies and meet us in front of this church at sundown. I gave them Mami Tulke's list of provisions, and we set off.

I called Mami Tulke and was able to get through. I told her that I'd spoken to Cora and that she was on her way—hopefully in a few days. Mami Tulke didn't seem to know yet about what happened to Cora in Rome, but I wanted her to know that Cora was alive and running. For now. I continued to check my phone for Cora's text.

Every city, without exception, has its seedy section. The part you hope not to find yourself in when you look up after wandering aimlessly, tired, looking for food, for shelter, for opportunity. "Honestly," I told Adrian as we ducked through the cut in a chain link fence and crossed a trash-strewn field, "I've received more help and kindness in my life from people on this side of the tracks."

Adrian didn't answer but cupped his hands around his mouth and made a whoop-whistle type of sound. His eyes were on the apartments above, with open squares in the cinderblock for windows. He called again, stopped, and listened.

I whirled around before the voice said, "No move!" I'd felt the aggressive energy laced with adrenaline. Fear tinged his aura in mustard yellow. "How the hell did you know I was behind you?" he asked.

I shrugged, trying to push as much calming, positive energy I could at him. I'd drown him in it, if it would get that small black pistol pointing in another direction. He gave me the sideways eyes, then turned his scrutiny on Adrian who was smiling like an idiot.

"You're still ugly," Adrian said to the young man.

They guy looked fit to pull the trigger until his eyes widened in recognition. "Heeeyyyy!" They did that man-bro hug that I never understood, and Adrian introduced me.

Jose instantly relaxed and smiled like a little boy. *He's getting a double dose,* I thought, realizing that Adrian had also thought to use his aura on Jose. "It's so damn good to see you, Texas!" Jose said, tapping the bill of Adrian's cap.

We walked through the brush, careful not to step on the fallen fences or get bitten by the barbed wire that curled like spiked waves beneath our feet. I followed them silently, ducking around a hanging sheet that stood for a door. It took a few breaths to adjust my eyes, and I sent my silver aura out as a preemptive strike, just in case. If anyone attacked, they were going to be feeling real good when they did it. I was but one of the good vibes in the room. From the hazy cloud of stink, they were already feeling good long before we'd arrived.

Instead of attack or even wariness, the men in the room barely took notice of us; so complete was their focus on the TV and the video game blaring in front of them. These guys had a sheet for a door but a complete gaming setup. Well, everyone had their priorities.

Jose offered us a beer, and we each took one gladly. "Where you been hiding?" Jose asked Adrian. "You vanished, *pendejo*."

"Nah," Adrian said. "I just found my family."

"Good, good," Jose said. "I got my family right here."

Adrian took a big swig and swallowed hard. "Mine's in trouble though, man."

There's a valor among men that I'd witnessed many times. I'd never experienced it myself because since my parents were killed I never let myself get close to anyone enough to call them "family." Until recently. From the concern in Jose's eyes and the fight in his face, Adrian had brothers here, and they'd help him, no matter what.

"What kind of trouble?"

Adrian shuffled on his feet, looked to me, unsure of what to say. "Nothing you want to be involved in. I think we might be ambushed, dude. We need weapons, just in case, to defend ourselves."

"Borrow or buy?" Jose asked.

"If borrowing's an option, all the better," I said. They both raised their brows at me. But this was my money. I hadn't asked any of the Scintilla to contribute. It was enough of an uphill battle just convincing them that we should have weapons. "I'll give you a thousand, just for your trouble. Consider it a safety deposit that you never have to return."

With that, the game paused. Every pair of eyes in the room landed on me. I plastered a smile on my face. "Maybe you can buy yourselves a door?"

Laughter filled the room, and I took a relieved breath.

Jose clapped me on my back. "We'd help our man here for free. But you're good in my book for throwing down cash in good faith." We leaned around a table where Jose drew a crude map, explaining the location where his uncle in the Elqui Valley had a hidden cache of weaponry. "If you're in deep shit, here's my number. Call us if you need backup."

"If all goes well," I said, handing ten folded bills to Jose, "we'll return the weapons to your hiding place."

"And if it don't?"

"Then you'll hear about it on the news."

"That big, huh?"

One of the other guys chimed in. "Big enough to replace the angel on the news who's saving drop-dead people?" he joked.

Another guy fell backward on the couch with his hand over his heart. "Man, I'd *fake* dead just to have her on her knees, looking down on me."

"Bet I can turn that angel into a little devil," another joked.

Adrian whirled his energy on me and smacked my back. "Ready to go?" he screeched.

I unclenched my fists and nodded. "Ready."

More man-hugs and handshakes and we left the apartment, making our way to the city center to meet the others. "Sorry about that," Adrian whispered. "They're not bad, really."

"Really? Would Cora have been safe here with us?" I knew my perspective was skewed. I knew what he meant, but my blood was still boiling. "I just can't help but think, if a couple of random men in a Santiago slum are talking about her that way, how many other people in the world are?"

"Aw, Giovanni," he crooned in his border accent. "The bigger the hero, the bigger the bull's-eye."

My phone vibrated in my pocket and I whipped it out— Cora's text. I tapped on the image and waited impatiently for it to download. When the image appeared on the screen, I froze. Silver light around a woman and a boy—barely a man. No...not just a young man and a woman—Jesus and his mother. The *tiri gondi* in the painting was more than co-incidence. My eyes followed the auras of people in the background, up to the very key that Cora wore around her neck. The inscription in Italian said:

St. Peter holds the key that records the misdeeds of those who have the audacity to claim dominion over the kingdoms beyond the gates of Earth.

My face snapped up to meet Adrian's curious eyes. There was no other interpretation. The key was actually *made* to record the heinous deeds that Cora saw when she touched it. A Scintilla must have had the sortilege to create the key and a Scintilla alone would have the power to receive its stored impressions, and Michelangelo...he knew that.

I immediately texted my translation back to Cora.

"What's up?" Adrian asked.

"What truth would the church do anything to keep secret?" I asked, though not for Adrian's benefit. I was processing aloud. Would saying it aloud make it more plausible, more conceivable?

"Thaaaat sex before marriage is a virtue?" he joked.

"How about that they knew what Jesus really was and created an elaborate story to explain him?" I said. I looked at the painting again. Certainty as sure and solid as the ground under my feet settled over me. "Jesus and his mother—they were Scintilla."

Chapter Thirty-One

Cora

Turns out, Italy is a very small boot and it took just three hours to reach the airport in Venice where we abandoned Edmund's rental car in the lot. It also turns out that Venice was created by magic fairies that once envisioned a city of serenity, water, and golden light.

We boarded a water taxi in the dark, when the ocean was rolling softly in its sleep and the moon was our lamplight. I hung my head out the window of the boat and marveled at how much of the world I'd seen in such a short time. I'd never have known, when I ran away to Ireland, that my hunger for freedom would be fed while on the run for my life.

The taxi driver peered at me as he helped me disembark near the Piazza San Marco where the film crew was wrapping up their last day of shooting. It had been a huge challenge to keep me out of sight and that was punctuated by the challenge of keeping my very visible markings hidden. Already, I was stuffing my recognizably thick, curly black hair into a cheap "I love Italy" cap Edmund bought at the convenience store and, despite it being midsummer, I wore a light scarf around my neck—trying to obscure the three black circles—and leather fingerless gloves to hide my hands. In an effort to stay anonymous, I was sure I stuck out more than ever. I'd fix that very soon.

We stepped onto cobblestone pavers and made our way to a gondola to take us closer to our hotel. The night belonged to lovers, who strode arm in arm under the lamps and kissed in passing gondolas with singing gondoliers. The water quietly lapped against door fronts on the first floors of buildings that had long ago sunk past their doorknobs due to rising water and sinking land. I must have still been love-high from Rome, because all I wanted was to have everyone I cared about in the history of my life with me at that moment to see the beauty and magic of Venice. Chills snaked up my arms and spine. Was it some kind of life-flashing-before-your-eyes instinct? Was my death imminent and making me crave my loved ones around me? Making me want to share beauty with the only people who mattered, before I died?

I tucked my knees to my chest and rubbed my gloved hands over my arms. Everyone dies, right? I just didn't think death would feel like an open door that followed me everywhere. I was sixteen…too young to…wait… "What's the date?" I asked the guys.

"Third of August, I believe," Edmund said, pinching a button on his watch to verify. "Yes."

"I forgot to make a wish," I said, sinking lower on the

wooden seat. "I turned seventeen a few days ago."

Dun scooted over and pulled me into his side.

"I want cake," I whined softly. "Chocolate cake. Heavy on the frosting."

He kissed my temple. "Done."

"I want cake and ice cream."

"Done."

"And a foot massage."

"Greedy wench."

We chuckled as the gondola passed under a familiar-looking bridge I was sure I was supposed to know the name of.

I let out a long sigh and stared up at the stars.

Edmund booked a room in a hotel adjacent to the movie crew's hotel so we could depart with them the next morning in a large, boisterous group and hopefully blend in. "What about the people on the crew?" I asked. "There's too many people to contain this information if I'm recognized or caught."

Edmund, who had been pulling clothes from his duffel, halted and looked at me with an exasperated expression only partially hidden by his floppy hair. "I didn't tell them who you are, but these people aren't blind or stupid. It's fortunate they're used to being around celebrities. Best we can hope is that they don't recognize you."

Dun came up behind me and put his hands on my shoulders. "I think we've bypassed Celebrity Road and are cruising fast down Worst Case Scenario Street. The whole world is looking for her. How do we know someone won't try to take advantage of that?"

"We don't!"

I startled, and Dun gripped harder on my shoulders.

"Sorry," Edmund said. "I'm tired. One thing at a time, okay? Priority one is getting her out of Italy, away from the immediate danger of the damn modern-day Inquisition. I've already lied and said she was an informant who'd run into some trouble and needed to get out of Italy. With luck, they'll think she had some trouble with the mafia and keep a wide berth."

Dun affected a godfather voice. "Ask questions, my friend, and it's your tongue on a kebab."

Edmund carried his clothes to the bathroom for a shower.

"I know this is a girly question, but do either of you have a spare razor? I need a pair of scissors, too."

"I can go get them," Dun said.

Edmund stopped at the bathroom door. "I'll go," he said with a sigh, pointing to Dun. "The less you're out in public, the better." The door clicked behind him, and we scrambled for the TV to get the latest news.

Apparently, I'd been spotted in California, Mexico, and Disney World. That was the only part of the "Miracle" story that made me smile. Seeing an aerial view of my house in Santa Cruz surrounded by news vans made me sick. Poor Janelle. She'd apparently handled this ordeal by burrowing in the house and leaving no clue if or when she'd come out. The news reporters had an air of hound dogs on the hunt — they'd bark and bay relentlessly until they snuffed her out of her hole. Papers for a search warrant were already on a judge's desk. "How can they do that?" I said, anger making me want to punch something, someone. "I didn't commit a crime!"

Dun looked at me with sad eyes. "The crime is being different. A mystery. Problem with people is that they think they're entitled to know you. Sweet cheeks, it's a *privilege* to know you."

"I met you because people attacked you for being different," I said, tucking a strand of his long black hair behind his ear and remembering the little Indian boy with the braid, and how a brutish kid had tried to cut it off. "I love you, Dun."

"Duh."

"Thank you for being a dogged ass and following me."

"Did you seriously just call me a dog's ass?"

We turned back to the TV. The Vatican had yet to make an official statement to the world. Hordes of people filled their city, and the world perched on the edge of their La-Z-Boys for an explanation. Who among us should be capable of miracles? What could they possibly say, I thought cynically. *Yeah, we knew that people like her existed, but we didn't think you could handle that, and we kinda wanted a monopoly on miracles, so we've been trying to kill them all.*

Many tried to dismiss the "miracle" because *We don't really know that these children were dead. They could have simply fallen down, lost consciousness... This could have been a misunderstanding brought on by the hysteria of the very real deaths occurring around the world.*

There would be no convincing the masses who couldn't see auras that those kids *were* dead, their pulses were still, their lights extinguished. And whether or not their glow had dimmed so that only the heat of life remained somewhere deep inside, before I blew it into flame again, could never be proven.

But for every voice of dissent, for every naysayer, there was another voice of someone who needed to believe in me. Why? I had no idea. Maybe a lifetime of faith—faith in the truest sense—had finally paid off when proof fell at their feet. The families of the children certainly believed I'd brought them back to life. All of the children reported having some kind of afterlife experience. They'd spoken of seeing lights: gold-blue spirals that beckoned them like winding roads to heaven.

"Spirals…" I whispered, astonished.

The lock sprang free on the door, and then Edmund dropped a small bag on my lap. "Ladies first," he said, gesturing to the bathroom.

"You sure? I might be a while."

I locked myself in the bathroom and took deep, bracing breaths. This was a wild notion that too much thought would depress. I stared long and hard at my reflection. If there was anything the last few weeks had taught me, it was impermanence. Everything changes. I lifted the scissors and took another strengthening breath.

Rather than fear, every snap of the scissors shot a rebellious jolt of power through my body. Another strip of long curly hair fell from my head. I didn't mourn the hair that pooled around my feet. I was proud.

I had a sudden flash of memory, of telling Giovanni when I first met him that I pitched my tent in the "low maintenance camp." Vanity was never my vice. This was survival. I had to make it to Chile, and if looking like Betty Boop upped my chances of survival, then fine. Hair would grow back, if I survived long enough.

Permanent though, were the markings that felt like a punishment for my sortilege. Evidence of memories forced their way onto my body, much like Arrazi forced their way into my soul. I resented the intrusion. Though my marks were a badge of what I'd lived through. Battle scars.

It took forever to cut my hair. I showered and futzed with it for about a minute, tripping out on the way the curls arched every which way all over my head. I wondered what Mari would say and mourned her all over again. I didn't know what the reaction would be when the guys saw me, and I'd kinda run out of give-a-*fooks*. Without preamble, I opened the door and stepped out of the bathroom.

"Surprise!" Dun yelled, but his voice did this funny little squeak on the "ise" part of the word, like a balloon whizzing overhead and falling to the floor, empty.

Edmund snored on the couch and only twitched with Dun's shout. A room-service slice of chocolate cake and a bowl of half-melted ice cream sat on a table in front of the TV. One lone candle blinked in the dim room.

"Um, happy birth-to-a-badass day?" Dun said.

Perfect. Tears filled my eyes as I tentatively crossed the room, bending forward to blow out the candle. "I wish…" I said in a rush of breath. But the wishes were too many, too complicated, and were for more than just myself. If my wishes had power, the whole world would be different. "I wish Mari were here," I whispered. "She'd tell me how to use black eyeliner and red lipstick to complete my look."

"True that," Dun said, clearing his throat. He had enormous silent wishes, too. I could see them in his eyes.

"Let's wish together," I said, holding his big puppy-dog paws in mine. We clinked forks and ate cake by candlelight, neither of us needing to say anything. Some moments carry more weight without words. Some moments are perfection in the horror, reminding us of what's worth fighting for.

We climbed into bed, and the best birthday gift Dun could give me, far surpassing sprays of chocolate frosting, was to run his hand over my shorn hair as I drifted off, like it was the softest downy treasure, and remind me that I was still and would always be...me.

Chapter Thirty-Two

Finn

"Your office is ready for you," Makenzie said to Saoirse, ducking her head into the doorway of the dining room. No longer Ultana's office—Saoirse's office. That fact was driven home when Saoirse motioned for me to go with her into a place I'd only been in before by breaking and entering.

In the hallway, Makenzie put a restraining hand on Saoirse's shoulder. "Wouldn't you rather first acquaint yourself privately?" she asked, her eyes pointedly saying it was a breach to take me into the office.

Saoirse shrugged from her grasp. "I trust Finn. Did you question everyone my mother trusted?"

Makenzie's deep breath bordered on condescending, as if Saoirse just didn't know any better. "Your mother trusted no one."

"Did my mother have the trust of others?" Saoirse asked, cheeks flaring red.

"I trusted her judgment."

"And her judgment was to appoint *me* as her successor."

"I'm sorry, Ms. Lennon. It wasn't my intention to offend. If you need anything further, don't hesitate to contact me." Makenzie spun on her high heels with her briefcase in hand and left us.

"I think you're already being tested," I said. "You handled her well." I nearly put my palm to her flaming cheek to reassure her. She was a little thing but tough. This couldn't be easy on her.

"Come on in," she said, putting her delicate hands onto the triple spiral carved into the wooden door and pushing it open. I gazed around the room as if it were the first time I'd seen it, luxuriating in the freedom to look at things with more leisure and less fear. The ashes of Dante I'd taken from the wooden heart were still in my room, concealed inside my guitar. I planned to take them to the hidden room and chronicle how they came to be there for some future descendant to find—if there were future descendants.

The wooden devil looked down over the desk where Saoirse now sat. "The night of the party at Christ Church, you told me of Dublin's neighborhood, Hell, and the devil who guarded its gates—"

"I *could* have been talking about my mother," she joked, riffling through a stack of mail, which she dropped on the desk. Her face turned serious, self-reproaching. "I shouldn't have said that. Are you asking if that's *the* devil?" she said, gesturing above her.

"Yes."

"My mother was a collector and took great pride in acquiring things that no one else could. The more important the artifact, the more she wanted it. There's one artifact that eluded her, however, one thing she'd have given all her collection to possess—her personal holy grail."

My mouth went dry. "Oh?"

"Oh yes. She spoke of it many times. She actually thought she could find the missing cover of the *Book of Kells*."

The tinny laugh that came from me sounded bogus even to my ears. I prayed my face didn't turn scarlet. "Wasn't it stolen for its gems and tossed in a bog somewhere by Viking raiders?" I said, still keeping humor in my voice despite my racing heart. So, Ultana wanted the book. Did she have *any* inkling that the Mulcarr clan possessed it? Her interest in me made more sense if she did. I might have simply been her means of getting to it.

"I don't think she cared a whit about the gems. I heard her say that the gems were nothing compared to the value of the secrets it was rumored to hold."

I turned my back on Saoirse, pretending to interest myself in the books on the shelf so she couldn't read my face. "What would be the point of possessing a treasure like that only to hide it away in her private collection?"

"Oh. She didn't mean to hide it. She meant to destroy it."

I spun around. "That's nuts!" There'd be nothing to gain from destroying those pages of the illuminated manuscript unless it contained something that threatened Ultana. Saoirse didn't reply or even look at me. She was absorbed in what she was doing, pressing her palm to the scanner. The computer on the desk flared to life.

"Let's see your secrets, Mother."

There was no way I was leaving that room, unless Saoirse asked me to. I wanted to hear anything she might tell me. Her trust in me was flattering but felt like a gift wrapped in too many layers and that peeling them back might reveal it wasn't such a gift after all.

After nearly an hour of me reading a book plucked from Ultana's shelf, and Saoirse tapping away at her mother's secrets, she sighed loudly. When I looked up, she was biting her lip and frowning. "If I'm right…" she said, but before she could finish her sentence, Lorcan burst through the door and stumbled toward the desk.

He tipped forward and pointed at Saoirse, his bloodshot eyes radiating anger. I jumped to my feet. "It's not right," he slurred, totally ossified. "Mother told me things. Certain things for safe keepin' in case she ever disappeared. She said they had the power to make her disappear."

Saoirse tapped a key and the computer blinked to black. "Who, Lorcan?"

"Wouldn't you like to know?" he roared. I put a hand on his chest, which he slapped away. "The reason you don't know is that you weren't meant to. I was meant to! You did this, little sister. Somehow, *you* did this. You're not supposed to be behind that desk. I am."

Slowly, Saoirse stood, pressed her tiny hands on the wood, and leaned forward. "You're supposed to be behind this desk? Look at you, you drunk bastard. Control of Xepa was supposed to go to someone with absolutely *no* self-control? That's rich." Her voice was so measured, so level, it was eerie. Like with the man at her doorstep, asking about her mother, she sounded like there lived a cold beast in her who snarled in spite of its cage. "You're pathetic. No doubt she told you things. She told me things, too. It was insurance to tell each of us *things*. Day One and we're going to stop this nonsense now. I cannot allow you to undermine everything because your ego is butt-sore. Respect our mother's wishes or you will be out. Give me a reason and you'll be gone."

"Gone?" he spat.

Even I wondered at her use of the word "gone." Their glares were rancid enough to tell me that each felt justified and neither was backing down. Nothing like the death of a powerful and wealthy person to make the family members bare their teeth over the carrion of money and/or power she left behind. They were both threatening. The difference between them was that he was piss drunk and, therefore, threatening *and* volatile.

My body hummed with adrenaline. "Look," I said. "It's fresh. You saw your mother's body just yesterday. I'm sure this is a shock to both of you."

"Notice how *I* didn't see the body?" Saoirse reminded with a hostile glare at her brother.

He rolled his head my way, almost as though he'd forgotten my presence. His thick finger shook as he pointed at her again. "You trust this bogtrotter more than your own family?"

Saoirse didn't answer, but the reply was in her body language, her eyes, in the fact that I was in the inner sanctum of Ultana's—now Saoirse's—empire.

Lorcan swayed and spit as he said, "He cares about one thing—his precious Scintilla. He killed his own uncle for her, you know."

"Hey!" I yelled. "She already knows what I was forced to do that day. I trusted *her* enough to tell her! And you will not say another word about it. To anyone," I warned him. Saoirse was right, the secrets of the dead are less guarded, and I found I no longer needed to keep silent. "You don't know what he did behind your mother's back—or maybe you do," I added. "He kept a Scintilla woman prisoner for over a decade. He preyed on her daughter and kidnapped her as well and, when he had a third Scintilla in his grasp, he worked to keep that a secret from Ultana so that he wouldn't have to share the power of what he had—what your mother wanted. He was a traitor to Xepa, and a ruthless, conniving bastard." I was gasping from the purge.

He rolled his head away from me with a sneer on his lips and focused again on Saoirse. "She's the one on the news, you know. His pretty Scintilla...the one from the party." Saoirse's eye twitched. She'd suspected it when we saw the news, but I wouldn't confirm it. "Did he trust you enough to tell you that?"

Her eyes flitted to me and back to him.

"If he killed his own uncle to protect her, what makes you think he won't kill any of us to protect her?"

"Christ, Lorcan. How did this become about me, or the Scintilla? You're bent because your dear mum didn't trust you enough to run her massive network, and you then stray in here, bellowing about trust? Evidently, you don't trust your sister's ability to do what she's been asked to do."

"Exactly," Saoirse said. Lorcan had rattled her. She folded her arms protectively over herself.

"I *don't* trust you," he bold-facedly admitted. His body swayed again. His nose flared. He was a bull, pawing at the ground. "Somehow you manipulated your way into my position, and I'ma promise you something, luv, you will run *all* of our affairs with me as your equal partner, or—"

Or!

That word was the curse of a *geis*. I reared back and punched him full-out in the mouth to stop the careless words from tumbling out. He fell to the floor, devil eyes boring into me as he swiped blood from his lips and finished his sentence. "Or you, sister, will die."

Chapter Thirty-Three

Giovanni

"Just because someone painted a picture of people with auras and imagined that Jesus and his mother had silver auras does not make it true," Will said after my phone was passed around for everyone to see. "It really only tells me that whoever painted it was Scintilla or knew about us."

"Would you still doubt it if I said the painting was done by Michelangelo?" I said, pointing out the *tiri gondi* monogram.

Maya gasped. "*The* Michelangelo?"

"It's not as though he knew Jesus personally," Ehsan said, doubt lacing his words.

"He left a trail of crumbs, picking up from a trail left by Dante Alighieri and with a key that Mami Tulke swiped from the statue of St. Peter. It's why Cora went to Italy. And *this* is what she found."

After Adrian and I had secured the map to the stash of weapons, we met up with the others. Our group congregated near the cathedral, trying to get more news to take back to the Elqui Valley in case we still didn't have access. The crowds were thicker in the *Plaza De Armas* than they'd been earlier, and an extended line formed well beyond the palm trees of the square, stretching at least two city blocks long, leading into the church. "What's that about?" I asked.

"Emergency baptisms," Maya said. "People here are convinced that *she* was a sign that the end is near and that her miracle was a reminder to the faithful. Some guy is even performing baptisms in Simon Bolivar's fountain."

"Funny how faith is a ladder some people only want to climb at the last minute," I said, stopping to stare down in shock at an exquisite chalk drawing of Cora's face someone had done on the sidewalk. They'd drawn the glow of a saint's light over her head. If they only knew…

Will gestured to the eager initiates. "Well, maybe *seeing* is believing. Would these people be here if they hadn't seen proof of a miracle on TV?"

A derisive grunt came from Adrian. "Opposite of *faith*, ain't it?"

The supplies were loaded into the truck. We'd intended to stay overnight in the city to avoid the long drive back to Mami Tulke's on the same day, but there were no rooms to be found. It would be nearly sunrise before we got back.

I didn't know how I was going to break news of this magnitude to Mami Tulke when we did get there, but I knew it'd be better coming from me than the radio or television. The only good news I had given her earlier was that I'd spoken to Cora and that we might soon have her back with us. Whatever the world brought next, at least we'd be together.

If she made it.

I'd look into her expressive eyes, as faceted and as deeply hued as a dark emerald. I'd once again smile at the stubborn jut of her jaw when she challenged me. With luck, I'd someday hold her body against mine and let our sparks collide in a rage of silver and taste the sweet flame on her skin.

Flushing when I realized Ehsan was waiting for me to reply to an unheard question, I cleared my throat. "Pardon, what?"

"I suggest we begin weapons training in the village immediately," he said in his calm, thoughtful sandpaper voice. Even so, Maya made a disapproving huff. "I don't like it, either. But this business with Mami Tulke's granddaughter has me on edge. Very on edge. They know her name now. They know where she lived with her father in California. If we are days away from the media descending on us here, isn't it safe to say that we're days away from our enemies coming as well?"

Maya sighed. "I never thought I'd say this, but maybe the media coming will be helpful. The Arrazi can't kill us with cameras in their faces."

"You don't think so? The Arrazi can kill live on CNN and the world would just think that we dropped dead like all the other drop-dead people. No one could prove they murdered us, and they'd walk away with superpowers to boot. The whole world will have a front seat to a race war, and they won't even know it."

"So negative."

"Realistic."

Will turned on the radio, more to shut us up, I think, than to hear the news—a regurgitation of the same information over and over. No one knew where the dark-haired enigma might be. It didn't seem likely she'd return to California, where legions of media waited, ready to pounce with their cameras and their questions. They'd tracked down the company where her father worked, which claimed that he'd requested an emergency leave of absence and hadn't been heard from since. A report had surfaced that Benito Sandoval had been one of a team of scientists studying the mysterious deaths and that records of his experiments were being requested by the CDC and other agencies.

"What a damn mess," I grumbled, my soul twitching with the need to have Cora in my presence.

The rest of the drive was quiet as we journeyed along the pleat of the valley to the village nestled within. We'd taken turns sleeping and driving through the night. Concentrated stars shone down on me as I climbed from the car in front of Mami Tulke's house. I told Adrian we'd go to the hiding spot for the weapons later after more sleep, though I suspected sleep might elude me. The bottom dropped out of my heart as I turned toward the house and saw the blue-white flickering of the television through Mami Tulke's living room window.

"It was my son, Eduardo, who told me," she said, not taking her eyes off the images of Cora leaning over the dead children. "He finally got through on the phone lines after the earthquake." I pulled her up into a hug, and she sagged against me, her wiry gray head barely reaching my chest. "I had to tell him that Mari was dead." The groan that came from her gripped my emotions like a fist. "His brother, his daughter. I had to break my last child's heart."

"I'm so sorry," I said, rubbing her back. I let her sag into the threadbare chair.

"He told me to turn on the news. You don't seem surprised."

"I saw. It's all over Santiago."

"It's all over the entire world. She'll be lost to us now. The vultures will tear her apart."

"Don't forget that I spoke to her and that she's okay, for now, and she's doing everything she can to get here."

Mami Tulke's palms pressed together, and she rocked back and forth with her eyes closed, pressing tears out of their corners. "It's all I want," she said, opening her eyes. "My granddaughter safe and home with us."

"We both want that."

"The one person in this world I would shield from harm, and I can't. I try every day, but my connection to Cora is lost. My granddaughter is pursued and hunted, and my sortilege can't help her at all."

"I will use every power within me, both natural and supernatural, to protect her. I swear it." She patted my face with her hand and nodded. There was no more to say about Cora. Our hearts would chug and churn, clotted by worry, until she was with us again.

"Claire is sleeping in your room again," Mami Tulke told me. "She tells me you are going to teach her how to be more aware of her energy and the energy of people around her. I think that's wise," she said, not waiting for me to answer, and she offered no explanation. It made me wonder if anything had happened while I was gone.

I pulled my phone out and showed her the texted photograph from Cora. "Your key did unlock something," I said with an encouraging smile. Mami Tulke's face stretched into astonishment as she looked from the picture to me. "It's the most beautiful painting I've ever seen," she whispered. Her eyes pierced mine. "And the most frightening."

"Yes. This is the kind of painting that can unhinge society."

If anyone in the church ever knew Jesus was a different breed of human, a Scintilla, then they've distorted it and covered it up and used their falsehood to control millions upon millions of people. How would those people react to knowing the truth? Would any heart be open to the knowledge that there were descendants of his race among them now, that they themselves might carry faint traces of the light?

If not, then the givers of light would have *no* allies in this world. They wouldn't even need the Arrazi to kill us all. Fired up by the religious authorities who could easily declare that we are some manifestation of devilry, would armies of humans turn on us—would they crucify us?

My morning belonged to Claire. She delighted me. I could have deeper conversations with her than most adults. If Dr. M could be credited with anything, it was that he'd obviously taken care to challenge Claire's considerable intellect. I burned to know who her mother was, but I supposed it didn't really matter. She wasn't Scintilla.

Claire grabbed a fistful of grass and tossed it aside. "I

wanted to do Qigong again yesterday, but they wouldn't let me."

"Did they say why?" I asked, feeling the noose of parental overprotection slip around me and squeeze my stomach.

"No. I think it's because I'm not Scintilla," she said.

"How would you know who is and who isn't?" I asked, amused.

Her eyes—blue like mine but with the triple dots of black that marked her for abnormality—looked at me with absolute certainty. "Because you told me to pay attention to energy and I did. You all feel different to me than regular people do. You feel like Abraham did."

"Clever girl." She had the ability to so easily detect the nuances of people's energy with little to no instruction. She'd grown up very close to Abraham, Teruko's Scintilla grandfather, who lived with her at Dr. M's. She'd discovered how to recognize the same essence of aura when she felt it again. "That's very good, Claire. Let's work on your ability to be less spongy when it comes to the energies of others. It's rather like hands. You wouldn't want people to come up and touch you without your permission, right?"

"Certainly not!" she said emphatically.

I nodded. "Our energies do that, too. It's like invisible hands. I want to teach you to be more considerate not to touch people's energy with your own, and possibly how to make a bubble around yourself so other people can't touch yours."

For two hours, we worked on teaching Claire to create a protective bubble of light around her astral body. I could see when it worked; despite how large her aura was, she was able to ground herself quite well when I thrust energy at her. I had to remind her multiple times that while I knew it was a good feeling when a Scintilla gave of their energy, she shouldn't let her aura get greedy as she had a tendency to do.

When she grew bored or tired of our game, her aura released like air from a balloon and she hopped up, ready to move her physical body and let her energetic body be free for a while.

Initially it made me happy to see, until I realized that though I couldn't see her after she rounded the house, her aura was still attached to mine. Was it normal for a child to be so psychically attached to their parent? I knew parents often latched unknowingly onto their children's auras, tethering their energies together, but Claire's aura roped around me tightly and didn't let go.

Chapter Thirty-Four

Cora

"I like the way you think." The first words I heard as Edmund shook me awake.

"Thanks," I said, squinting at the unnatural glaring light in the room and rubbing my hand over my head as if all of my hair might have sprouted back overnight. I hadn't slept well because I was too aware of my head as it brushed the pillow like a live wire every time I rolled over. I sat up and swayed my neck. My head felt twenty pounds lighter.

From Edmund's frenetic energy, I figured that we should get up, get ready, and do it in a hurry. "The movie crew's departure time is five a.m. A boat will take us to the airport where the chartered planes are waiting. We're to meet the girl who is going to get you on the plane as flight crew."

I quickly showered because who knew when I'd be

able to again? Edmund made another run to the lobby for makeup to cover my forehead and neck markings and for black eyeliner to complete my "look."

Before we left the hotel, I texted both Finn and Giovanni, telling them that I'd be out of service for a day and that, with luck, I'd find my way "home." Not playing nice, my head repeated something I'd said to my mother once.

There is no home for the hunted.

I needn't have worried about fitting in.

The movie crew was the most varied, scrubby, tattooed bunch of people I'd seen in a while. Edmund greeted his friend, Rod, while Dun and I stood around shuffling our feet, exchanging stupid glances. Honestly, Dun got more curious stares than I did, a nerve-wracking reminder that I wasn't the only one on that video. The world wanted to know more about the "heavenly hunk" who whisked me away from St. Peter's Square. The media loved to point out that twice now I'd been pulled away from a scene by dashing young men. After hearing that on the news this morning, Dun and I had laughed, and I threatened to call him "heavenly hunk" as much as possible.

What made us want to puke was Serena Tate, queen of the VIPs at our school, affecting a tragic demeanor as she spoke of how close we all were and how badly she missed her besties. "Is it bad to hope an Arrazi finds her deliciously irresistible?" I said to Dun.

My head felt like a heat-releasing orb outside in the chill of the Venice early morning. My body shook, but that was more from nerves than cold. In the small terminal for private commercial aircraft, I met Angelica. Her eyes smiled, which I liked, as she gave me a uniform to put on. "You won't need to actually do any work," she said. "You're faking as a crewmember who's using what we call the jump seat. It's how we bum rides off each other to places we want to go."

"I appreciate it," I said, feeling shy all of a sudden and very grateful that a stranger would put herself out for me— someone she didn't know—just because she'd been told I was a girl who needed help. I think I'd started to lose my faith in humanity.

"Don't know what you're running from, but I hope you get far enough away from it to feel safe."

"It'd have to be pretty far," I said, going into the stall to change. I slipped the badge around my neck and repeated the information over and over to memorize it. I remember Mari telling me how she used a friend's fake ID once, and the bouncer grilled her on her address, birthdate, and even her astrological sign. The girl whose ID I'd borrowed was an Aquarius, like my dad.

To my utter surprise, the boarding process was quick and easy. Angelica checked me in with a sly grin. Edmund, Dun, and I sat in a row together near the back of the plane. My heart could have powered the jet engines until we were airborne, climbing into the clouds, no longer on Italian soil.

The many hours en route on our first leg gave me ample time to retrace my steps through Italy and clutch the information I'd gathered like tiny crystals in my palm. Dante and Michelangelo: one had tried to tell the truth in rhyme, one had tried to tell the truth—and keep the truth safe—by dropping visual clues in his art. Michelangelo's key unlocked his secret painting revealing Jesus and his mother as Scintilla. Xepa had a personal connection within the Vatican in Cardinal Báthory, who just happened to run the office that once ran the Inquisition. I knew that didn't indict the whole church, but it sure wasn't a good sign. There was power and money behind that office and a history of misdeeds recorded by the key *and* by the history books.

The key solved one mystery—why the church would want to keep us a secret—but didn't solve why the Scintilla were known as The Light Keys to Heaven. I'd felt nothing but defenseless and utter powerlessness since this all began, and as I stared down at the world outside the window, I wondered, what power did we have that could so scare the church?

Dante embedded the number three in nearly every way in his work. Michelangelo's only signed work, *The Pieta*, had a hidden *tri* and he was known to use three interlocked circles as his signature. The painting of Mary and Jesus had silver auras and showed the colored auras of humanity behind them, it had triple spirals, and it had a drawing of my key with a very cryptic sentence about the key's ability to store the church's misdeeds. It also had the hexagram.

If the hexagram stood for reconciliation of opposites, as Arrazi and Scintilla were so clearly opposites, then Xepa's insignia pointed to their agenda, their mission to divide the two races. It begged the question: what was so threatening about *uniting* the two races?

I don't need you. I need you dead. When every last Scintilla dies, then the truth dies with you. Ultana's words. She said that she was tired of her tedious job of ridding the world of our kind. There had to be something the Scintilla were capable of, something threatening to the Arrazi, threatening to existing power structures. My mother told me once that she'd tried to bring a bird back to life. *But it stayed dead.* I'd saved lives. Could all Scintilla do what I did? Or was it a sortilege? Could I have more than one?

Edmund snapped closed his laptop and grinned at his own notes. He'd been reading and scribbling, and every so often, thumbing through the bible. His hair stood on end like I'd always made fun of when I'd seen him on TV. I'd thought that was just his way of being showy, but no, he looked just as nutty in real life.

It was obvious Edmund wanted to talk to me, especially in the way his aura practically tapped my shoulder for attention. "I have some great stuff here. Great stuff. Listen to this... In Matthew 5:14-16 Jesus said, 'You are the light of the world. A town built on a hill cannot be hidden. Neither do people light a lamp and put it under a bowl. Instead they put it on its stand, and it gives light to everyone in the house. In the same way, let your light shine before others, that they may see your good deeds and glorify your Father in heaven.'"

I opened my mouth to respond, but Edmund very excitedly pointed to another note. "This one's even better." His voice lowered as he realized his volume was matching his excitement. "In Luke 8:46 Jesus said, 'Someone touched me. I could feel the power go out of me.'"

"No way."

Edmund's head tipped sideways and his eyebrows reached far up as if to say, "WAY!" "Uncanny, in the context of everything you've told me."

Uncanny was right. If I let myself imagine Jesus as a

Scintilla, it wasn't hard to imagine him strolling through a dusty market busy with crowds of people who congregated around his energy and reputation. I could easily imagine an Arrazi following close behind and slyly taking from him. The hair on my arms stood on end just thinking about it. How else could anyone have the capability to pull *power* from Jesus Christ? Who but an Arrazi could do that?

"Is there more?" I asked, peeking at his crazy scribbles.

"I'm going to keep looking. And I want to check into the noncanonical gospels, as well. Many weren't included because of verbiage that was deemed heretical by the officials who decided which books would be included in the official canon. If there were allusions to anything that would support Jesus being like you at—" Edmund looked past me and made eyes to alert me that a few people were waiting for the lavatory and standing in the aisle right next to us. It'd have to wait.

As the flight progressed, I felt more at ease. It had something to do with leaving the Vatican behind but also because we were ignored for the most part by everyone around us. There were a few curious glances, but no more curious than could be explained away by the fact that we weren't part of their film crew.

My brain kept stirring the pot of what Edmund had found. I was no bible expert by any stretch, but what else could Jesus have meant? Just as when he said, "These things I can do, you can do also," why wasn't anyone talking about what he *really* meant by that? It was thrilling to think there were needles of truth in the proverbial haystack. Even though Edmund couldn't speak freely while the people were standing so close, the hairs on my arms still hadn't let down.

At first, I'd figured it for excitement, but I realized that my body was on high alert, and when I tuned in to what it was telling me, it was screaming that my enemy was near.

I was thirty thousand feet in the air, trapped in a metal can with wings—with an Arrazi.

Chapter Thirty-Five

Finn

"Y ou'd curse your own sister?"

My foot kicked and connected with Lorcan's ribs before I even thought to wonder how he might put another *geis* on me again in retaliation. It wasn't Saoirse's fault her mother "gifted" her with running Xepa. He'd lashed out at his sister when his dead mother wasn't an option. There might have been many legitimate revenue sources, investments, and ventures to manage, but Ultana also had Xepa, and it was the business of extermination. As far as I was concerned, Ultana's decision to place her daughter at the head was the *first* curse to be placed on Saoirse.

Saoirse hadn't moved from behind the desk. She looked at her brother in stupefied horror, her petite frame shaking with either fear, or rage, or both. Another emotion glinted in her eyes and was the closest approximation to hatred I'd seen on Saoirse's delicate face. "Learn how to use your sortilege, really," she said, almost derisively, as if she was unconcerned with her own death. "How can you possibly quantify half?" she asked him. It was an unexpected question. "How about I take the important half and give you the grunt work you deserve?"

That girl constantly threw me. I was impressed but also worried she was right. Would she drop dead in one moment of decision where her brother wasn't consulted? "Intention," I pondered aloud. Her eyes snapped to me and I clarified. "You'd have to know what he intended when he put the *geis* on you in order to play by his rules."

A slow smile spread across her face. "Exactly. See, Finn," she said. "We do make a good team." She turned to her brother, who was clutching his ribs with one hand and his bloody lip with the other as he stood. "Tell me what you expect, Lorcan. I will not die because you throw your sortilege around as sloppily as your pints."

"Not now," he said, looking a scary shade of gray-green.

"Now!" we both shouted at him, knowing that what his thoughts were at that moment dictated the terms of her *geis*. I'd block the damn door if I had to.

Lorcan practically looked regretful. It was so easy to throw out threatening words, but now he had to work to justify them with a cognitive explanation. "We have equal access to all information. I will have access to the computer and files. Decisions are made together." He took a breath. "But what I was really thinking was that when it comes to this Scintilla business and Xepa, it's absolutely transparent. You do not get to do whatever you want with them. I want in on it all. You do not run the show. *We* run the show."

Shite. Fookin' shite.

Lorcan Lennon was going to be the stub in our wheel of change.

Evidently, Saoirse had the same thought. The apology on her face when she looked at me sent waves of frustration through my body. If she was hog-tied by her brother, how was I going to influence the Arrazi to abandon their mission of hunting and killing the remaining Scintilla?

As Lorcan wordlessly left the room, he also left the door open. I didn't want to give the lub more credit than was due, but it seemed to me that his leaving the office door open was a metaphor and a message: no locks.

When I heard his door slam upstairs, I had two questions for Saoirse, the first of which she anticipated before I asked it. "I need to think about this, Finn. I'm still on your side, but I need to think about *how*. How would it even be possible to work behind his back? I know you're"—she bit her lip—"I know what this means to *you*—but I'm not willing to die for the Scintilla."

"There must be a way. Maybe we can convince Lorcan—"

She laughed. "Are you joking? His rotten core fell straight from our mother's tree. He's ruthless. He won't change."

If this was the abrupt end of our plans together, if this was my last visit to the inner circle, I wanted to know something. "What were you about to tell me before he came in? You sounded as though you'd found something surprising."

A slow nod showed she now deliberated whether she should tell me what it was. She came around the desk to stand in front of me, slipping her hands into mine. She looked up at me with her red brows creased in worry. "Instructions have been given to Arrazi worldwide." She looked down at her feet, and I found myself staring at the shades of red in her hair like one would a leaf, waiting with a knot in my stomach for the rest of what she would tell me. It was bad, this news. I could feel the dread rolling off her. Her face tilted up again to look into my eyes. "Arrazi have been directed to take advantage of the sudden deaths all over the world—the drop-dead people—and to kill openly and indiscriminately."

I literally staggered back. "Directed by whom?"

"I don't know yet. I saw a document in my mother's computer files. She said it was 'only the beginning.'"

"Of what? Widespread murder and panic?"

"Of the Arrazi stepping out of the shadows of shame and into power."

"Worldwide…" My mind was reeling at the enormity of an edict like that. This was so much larger a dark horse than I'd hoped to rein in. "We've got to find out who issued that order. We've got to…" What? My flailing fists were laughable on the chest of a giant like this. A ball of sickening dread grew in my stomach. "How can we possibly stop this?"

Saoirse placed her small hand on my cheek and looked at me with compassion and, worse, resignation. "I don't know that we can."

My parents' reaction was equally as shocked as mine had been. "You'd think we'd have heard rumblings of this," my father said to my mother. "You especially, Ina, with the Mulcarr family being so prominent."

"We lost our *prominence* when it was clear we weren't going to cooperate with Ultana. My brother can hardly confirm or deny the plans," she said. It was only in moments like that that I felt any pang of remorse at all for killing him.

"Is it too much to hope that the edict hadn't gone out yet?" Dad wondered.

I forced myself to take another bite of roast chicken. Food wasn't what my body craved, and I felt increasingly miserable. "I think the order must have gone out," I said. "Clancy and the other Arrazi at Newgrange killed every last person there when the first people dropped dead. They were all in on it. When Clancy gave the signal, they all knew what to do. It was gruesome."

"But imagining it happening all over the world is another matter. The world will fret about pandemics, and there may very well be one, but in the midst of it, silent killers will take more lives. Panic—that's what they'll cause—widespread panic, rioting, lawlessness."

"And the rest of them will go to church." I'd said it in half jest but as soon as I did, a missing rung slid into place. Of course! "Ask yourselves who would benefit."

My mother's hand flew to the crucifix she always wore. "You can't be suggesting…" Then her eyes rounded. "That's why she went to Rome?"

"Aye. It was something Ultana said along with other clues, but with this latest news, doesn't it make you wonder who in the world would want the Arrazi to so openly and blatantly kill?"

"Ultana wanted it," my father said. "She sat at this very table and spoke of the Arrazi finally being accepted."

"Exalted was her word," my mother said with a liberal

sip of wine.

He shrugged. "Maybe it goes no further up than her?"

"You didn't hear Ultana in that tomb, Da. When she knew she was actually going to die, she seemed happy to taunt Cora about formidable enemies still to face down. Ultana's the one who pointed her finger at the church."

I wondered what Cora had learned in Rome. She knew I'd found something I wanted to show her, but we didn't speak about what *she'd* found. I only knew she was en route to Chile, and I hoped to God she'd make it, but a sour dread coated my spirit. If Arrazi had been instructed to kill in this manner, no matter where Cora landed in this world, she wasn't safe.

"How far gone are you?" my father asked with concern, probably noticing my pallor and trembling hand as I half-heartedly lifted my fork. I needed to kill.

"I might have a couple days," I admitted. "Saoirse and I spoke about going together."

My mother looked to him and a silent communication passed between them. "I don't trust her, Finn."

I dropped my fork. "If she's willing to help me, then she's the only Arrazi who might be able to counteract her mother's evil. Though her brother poses a problem."

"I do know that feeling well," Mum responded. "If she's truly good, then I feel for her. But I saw something in her eyes…" She took a deep breath and another sip of wine. "Secrets change, sometimes moment to moment, depending upon who the person is speaking to or what they most want to hide in a situation. I'm learning much about my sortilege since I acquired it," she said. "I had a moment with Saoirse in the library when I came in to show you the news of Cora.

A secret flickered by in her eyes as fast as a changing channel. It was as if the picture she showed, the secret, changed as her eyes shifted from you to me. I can't be sure—"

"What was it you saw?"

"Saoirse Lennon feels responsible for her mother's death."

Chapter Thirty-Six

Giovanni

A rental car pulled up outside of Mami Tulke's house as I sat pondering the mysteries of my daughter's unique energy. Two middle-aged women got out, one white, one black, looking very disheveled and tired. Their auras looked similarly weary. The black woman had gray dreads that defied gravity. Probably more visitors to the "ranch" as guests called it. Their auras were benign enough, though the white lady was going through something rough. Her aura was thin, flimsy, and the deep gray-almost-black color of grief.

One couldn't be too sure, though, so I got up to greet them and get a better feel for their energy. Just then, Mami Tulke opened the door and gave a surprised gasp. She walked to the women with her hands over her mouth and then pulled the sorrowful woman into a tight embrace. The woman immediately dissolved into tears on Mami Tulke's shoulder. These were no mere guests of the ranch.

It was an intimate moment, and neither the woman's companion nor I knew what to do with ourselves as it played out in front of us. We smiled awkwardly at each other.

"I had to come," the woman said to Mami Tulke. "I've been totally in the dark. No one has explained what's happened, and I can't get ahold of Cora. Then I saw her on the news, and I knew I had to come here."

Cora. That's when Mami Tulke gestured me closer and introduced me to Janelle Sandoval, Cora's widowed stepmother. I immediately understood the grief. "This is Faye," Janelle said, introducing us to her friend. "Faye's been a godsend. She's the only reason I was able to skirt the media before they landed on my doorstep."

"I met your granddaughter," Faye said to Mami Tulke, her bluish aura undulating like smooth waves. "She came into my bookstore in California when she first began seeing auras." Her aura paused, like a held breath for just a moment. "I told her what I could, but in the end…" Faye shook her head. "I let her down. When I saw her on the news, I immediately contacted her house and spoke to Janelle."

"Faye offered to let me hide out at her home," Janelle said. "But I realized I had to get here right away before they figured out my name and stopped me at the airports. I think we were lucky to get here."

Mami Tulke and I shared a look of dismay. Janelle's travels would be traced. It was only a matter of time. Who was I kidding? It was only a matter of time before the whole damn world landed in the Elqui Valley.

Faye touched Mami Tulke's shoulder. "Not a day's gone

by that I haven't thought of Cora and wondered about her. I shut the door in her face. I was scared, but I'm sure it was nothing to how scared she must've been. If I can help, in any way, I want to try. Never too late for redemption, right?" She gave a nervous but throaty laugh.

"Why did she come to you for help?" I asked, fascinated by this account.

"I own a spiritual bookstore in Santa Cruz. She was so sweet and bewildered and looking for answers. Didn't know an aura from an abacus, that girl. But she was eager to learn. I knew she was special. She detected my cancer within minutes. That's a gift," Faye said, pressing her palms together. "It wasn't until she mentioned that her aura was pure silver that I suspected *how* special she was. I started looking into it, but then someone vandalized my shop and left a threatening note."

These two women fascinated me, but perhaps only because of their connection to Cora before I knew her. One thing stuck out, though. "You said you knew silver auras were special?"

"Like I told Cora, it was a scrap of something I'd either read or heard. To this day, I don't know where. I only recall that pure silver auras were rare and that there were people in this world who sought them like a prize. I told her as much, that there might be people who want nothing more than to get their hands on her."

Grim feelings settled over me when I thought of Cora. "She knows that now, I assure you."

"She's on her way to us, I hope," Mami Tulke said as we walked toward the front door where Claire skipped up and met them, too. Mami Tulke ushered the women inside, saying, "You came here to get away from the storm, but I'm afraid we are the epicenter of much more than earthquakes."

A car horn stopped me in the drive. I turned around. Adrian waved from the SUV. I'd nearly forgotten about my plans with him.

Adrian's buddies had drawn the crudest map in all of treasure hunting. More time was wasted trying to decipher whether descriptions of the indentation in the hill fit the one we spotted from the side of the winding river, and once we were upon the hill, it looked completely different, causing us to question ourselves. It wasn't until we found a pile of rocks in the shape of a cross that we knew we were on the right track.

"That's why they used it as a marker. What asshole disturbs graves?" Adrian explained.

We worked together to move big boulders aside and then used the shovels Adrian brought to dig around the bottoms of the largest ones so we could use a long piece of steel as leverage to move them. It was sweaty, grueling work, and we both cursed ourselves for not bringing more help. Once the last enormous rock was moved aside, the opening to the cave was revealed.

I stuck my head through the hole. "Got a flashlight?" I called out.

He ran to the truck and returned not with a flashlight but a lighter. "Here, man. It's all I got."

With light, it became evident that we scored fairly well on this deal. The Scintilla might have little defense or power. Our sortileges were a mix of potentially useful ESPs to sugary sweet abilities. But in this cave of boxes, which presumably were filled with guns and ammunition, we had the makings of an army.

Defenseless no more.

I fished my buzzing phone from my pocket. It was a text from Cora—a miracle it had gotten through to me in the remote section of the valley.

Just landed for layover. Worried. I think there's "one of them" on this flight.

Adrian, the weapons, the sun on my neck, the sounds of the wilderness around me—they all faded to nothing as I responded with two texts, praying they would go through. A while later she responded with one word: *bye*.

Deflated, I kept working. It took two hours to count the guns, knives, grenades, and boxes of ammunition. We restacked them in the crates, realizing we'd need more help if we were to move them down to the ranch. Adrian and I took what we could easily carry, leaving the rest for when we returned. The work kept me from obsessing about Cora and the possible Arrazi on the plane with her. *Please let her come back to me.*

When we were done, we drank syrupy warm sodas and watched the sun dip below the mountains before setting off again toward the ranch. I had battle plans to make and training to start.

Adrian drove me back to Mami Tulke's. Without going inside I could see that the house was abuzz with activity. Claire's voice carried to me like birdsong. Someone laughed—Faye, I guessed, from the richness I'd heard earlier. There was a man's voice, too. One I didn't recognize. My chest lurched when I wondered if it was possible in any way that Cora could have arrived already. I ran to the door and burst through it, causing everyone to momentarily look up, startled.

Claire was at the kitchen table, cutting out shapes in a large round of dough. The adults hovered around a computer, their faces lit blue-white by the light of it. A man named Suey with a crisp silver aura, whom I'd met down at the ranch, smiled at me when I walked in. He was the resident computer guru. "This almost looks celebratory," I said.

"A small victory," Mami Tulke answered, patting the man on the back. "Janelle brought Benito's computer. Suey just hacked it."

"Everyone's after Benito's research," Janelle said. "We need to know what he knew."

People wanted Cora's blood, figuratively *and* literally.

Janelle elaborated. "On his home computer he kept the information from the tests he did on Cora when he took her blood in the hospital. If we can find out exactly what he learned, maybe we can throw it like a bone to those vultures. Maybe they'll stop focusing on Cora and figure out how to save those poor people who are dying."

"What if they aren't mutually exclusive?" I asked. All eyes were on me, questioning. "What I mean is that—" I looked at Janelle apologetically. "I'm sorry. The night Benito died, he spoke about his experiments. He believed that Cora's cells brought the abnormal cell samples from the people who'd died back into normality. I don't have the expertise to express it the way he did. But he made it sound as though they were connected, that a severe energetic imbalance was causing both the increase in natural disasters in the world *and* causing the deaths. He spoke as though the Scintilla were an antidote."

"Do you believe that?" Faye asked, astonished. "You believe that the awful natural disasters are because of the energetic imbalance in the world?"

"I do," said Mami Tulke firmly.

"If there's an energetic imbalance," I said, "I think it's because the Arrazi have nearly wiped us all out. If you want to know the truth, I think that if they are removed, the world will be a better place."

Janelle's mouth hung open. "Removed? Are you talking about killing people?"

"I am."

"What. In. The. World?" Faye gasped.

"That's what's going on here. I don't know how much you know or what Cora's father told you, but that's what you've walked into. I'm sorry to scare you, but the people here might very well be the last Scintilla on earth, and we're fighting for our lives."

She took it in, swallowing hard. Her aura beat with resolve, the cranberry red of courage tinged with a bit of fear. "I knew *what* Cora was, yes. Honestly, I knew she was special from the moment I met her. When our relationship got serious, Benito was honest with me. He didn't want me to marry him, to be a mother to Cora, without knowing that someday there could be danger. I knew that Grace—Gráinne—had disappeared many years ago, probably because of what she was and that it could happen to Cora." Tears welled up in her eyes. "I walked into a future with them with my eyes open. My husband may be dead," Janelle's voice cracked, but she held her chin up and continued, "but my commitment to Cora, and to the vows I gave Benito, are very much alive."

Mami Tulke rubbed small circles on Janelle's back while simultaneously infusing her with loving energy and thanked her. Janelle's energy calmed, and the group turned back to Suey, who'd been typing away as we spoke.

"Everything Giovanni said is here in Benito's notes." Suey barely stopped pecking at the computer as he spoke. "When Benito writes about dark energy, it's in a way I've never heard applied to human cells before."

"So what...?" I said. "Are we supposed to donate blood to the entire human race?"

Suey shook his head and frowned at the screen. "His notes talk of dark energy on a macro and micro level, but I don't think he meant dark energy in a cosmological context. I think he means negative energy: collective negative energy in such an overwhelming amount that's affecting the earth and everyone on it. Not blood, Giovanni. I don't think that's what he meant. He seemed to be of the impression that somehow the Scintilla's *energy* can act as a counter to the negativity, and that we can *literally* save the world from destruction."

Chapter Thirty-Seven

Cora

Maybe I shouldn't have texted Giovanni. Everyone was already worried enough. But I couldn't shake the sensation that an Arrazi had been near me on that plane. It was like a scent carried on the breeze—something so fleeting, I wasn't sure if it was real or my imagination, and who else but Giovanni would understand?

Nobody really paid much attention to me or looked suspicious, but I was unable to relax from that point forward. We'd landed at a smaller commercial airport to refuel. Many disembarked from the plane to eat and stretch, but I was too afraid of not being able to get back on again. I needed to get as close as I could to my family. I'd freaking walk there if I had to.

While we sat on the tarmac, Giovanni texted me back: *Pull your own energy in. Do not reach out to feel for danger or they might detect it. Give nothing of yourself.*

There was a pause, and I waited to see if he'd write more.

Give nothing of yourself until you're here. Then I ask for you to consider giving your heart again. I hope you can forgive me. Life is too precious and tenuous. I'll love you for as many precious moments as I have.

I hadn't let myself think like a regular girl, like a girl who'd once had a conflicted heart—who maybe did still. Giovanni's text was a slow bullet to the chest, and I felt tears threaten as I stared at my phone and wondered how to respond. Passengers began filing back onto the plane. I had to be alert and aware so I simply said: *bye.*

It shamed me to realize that life had already proven how very precious it was and that I wasn't thinking about what made it so precious, as he was. How many opportunities would I have to use my beating heart or the vast and deep expanse of emotions it contained?

I pulled up his text and started typing: *If anything happens, please know I...*

"Excuse me, miss? Is anybody sitting here?" My fingers paused over the phone, and I looked up. My mouth went instantly dry. I could barely hear through the pounding in my head. The man, his aura flaring as white as snow around him, was pointing to the seat next to me and waiting with a polite smile for me to answer. It was all I could do to not scream. I dropped my phone on the floor, and he bent as I bent, and our hands touched. I heard his small intake of breath before Dun's voice, deep and safe, said, "Excuse me, man. That's my seat," and barreled his way into our aisle to block me. Edmund, who had left to talk to someone, came back moments later and saw me, clammy and shaking, in the window seat, peering through the glass and trying to make myself as small as could be. This was no time to puff up and act tough. The guy might not even know about Scintilla, and I could only hope he'd simply felt a bit of succulent energy and would then forget about it. He'd just killed, after all. His white aura confirmed it.

Trouble was, he sat in the row right in front of us. We'd be silenced the rest of the way to Santiago. It was too dangerous to speak of anything beyond the norm. The hardest part was overhearing the talk. The plane buzzed with news gathered from the layover. The Vatican had made a statement. They believed "the girl" was *chosen* as an instrument of God. That God worked through me, that God chose to save those children on the steps of the Holy Roman Church as a sign to the faithful.

Edmund acted as though he'd been personally taunted. "Can you freaking believe them? What'd I tell you? I knew they'd try to spin it to point their self-righteous fingers back at themselves."

"Shhhh."

"Hey, girl," Dun said, elbowing me lightly as I stared at the tops of clouds. "Go to sleep. I'll keep watch."

I wanted to protest, but my body was leaden, my heavy lids were barely staying open, and I felt fatigue so intense that I was nauseous. I could see the Arrazi's head still slumped to the side, and so I surrendered. Dun covered me with his hoodie and I drifted off, clutching his arm like a pillow.

He jiggled me awake after what felt like only minutes. "We're preparing to land. You might want to freshen up," he whispered, touching his neck to let me know I needed to cover up my marks again with fresh makeup.

"How often do people have to reapply this stuff? It felt like Spackle going on. I thought it would last for days."

"Depends on the girl," Dun said, like he was actually giving my question serious consideration.

"I don't really know how to *girl*."

"Well, right now you just want to be 'Scary Spice.' Put on some more eyeliner."

"What are you even talking about?" I said, moving my tongue over my dry lips. My mouth tasted like a cat had crapped in it. I clumsily dabbed foundation on my neck and forehead with my fingers.

Dun handed me a disposable toothbrush. "Yes, it stinks as bad as it tastes."

"Shut up."

"Yup. Shutting up."

With all the patience of a herd of wildebeests, the entire plane stood even before the doors were opened. The Arrazi in front of me had been asleep much of the trip, *likely full on his meal of human soul*, I thought wryly. He must've gotten off the plane and killed on the layover. I didn't like how many times he glanced at me, no matter how polite his smile was. Apparently Dun didn't, either, because he glared at the guy and said, "Turn around, will ya?" I pulled on the end of his sleeve and gave him the death stare. Even if by chance the guy didn't know about Scintilla, he still knew he could kill Dun without touching him. I could see it in his defiant stare and smirk back at Dun.

If I crawled under the seat, I didn't think I could make myself any smaller. It was the exact opposite of what I wanted to do. What I wanted was to kick the Arrazi in his teeth to rousing applause like a movie heroine. Some hero I was, meekly sitting behind Dun's ass as he blocked the guy from looking at me.

Luckily, the rows filed out and we shuffled forward with me at the very back. Through the plane, breathe, down the stairs, breathe, out of the airport, look around, breathe. That's what my life had become, a step-by-step endurance race.

"That guy was Arrazi," I hissed at Dun once we were clear of the crowds. "Do not *engage* people like that."

"What?" His face paled. "Why didn't you tell me?"

"Because he was right in front of us and telepathy isn't my sortilege. I also didn't want you emanating the fear and adrenaline like what's coming off your aura right now."

"I don't know how you slept with him there."

I shrugged. "Survival." I had to.

Customs was harrowing. I endured the scrutiny of the officer who looked from me to the "borrowed" passport and back. I shot energy at him in soft waves, and he eventually stamped me into South America. Edmund had rented us a car so we'd have privacy getting to my grandmother's. I had her address, and we used Edmund's phone for GPS. "Things are going smoother than I thought," Edmund said cheerfully.

I stretched my arms over my head and touched my toes. "That's what worries me." Like on cue, the guy from the airplane approached again. "Wonder if I could catch a ride with you to the city? I'm having trouble finding a taxi. Sorry about the misunderstanding earlier, bro," he said to Dun, who looked more cautious now. I nonchalantly slipped into the car with Edmund. "You looked familiar, and I thought maybe we'd worked together on another show."

"No man. We haven't," Dun said, opening the door and putting one foot inside. Edmund had the engine started. We couldn't be clearer or more unwelcoming.

"Let's go," I said, high unease hitting my limbs. This was weird. Arrazi or not, the guy was acting *off*. My *regular* human instincts were enough to tell me that.

"No ride," Dun said. "We're in a hurry. Sorry."

The man was typing in his phone. "I understand," he said and suddenly snapped a picture!

Dun jumped in the car as it was screeching away. Through the back window, we could see him taking photos of our license plate, too. "Dammit!" Edmund said, hitting the steering wheel.

"Okay, let's not panic," I said, trying hard to slow my pounding heart. "We don't know why he took those pictures. He's Arrazi but maybe clueless about what I am. So it's possible he just thinks he recognized us from the news?"

"Well I'm not cutting off all *my* pretty hair," Dun said, though his serious tone soiled the joke.

"The question is," Edmund said, "what's he going to *do* with that picture? Who's he going to share it with? I need to get control of this show."

"This is not a show. This is my life, my rad horror of a life. Let's just get to Mami Tulke's," I said, leaning my head on the window and watching La Serena roll by, showered with the pink and blue of a new dawn. "We can figure out what to do once we're there." With every moment, I regretted the decision to come to Chile. I'd only bring trouble on everyone. It was becoming clear that I'd be found no matter what. Either by the Arrazi or—everyone else.

"Your grandma's place is remote," Dun told us. "Away from pretty much all civilization, except the cosmic mystic hippies who live in this village near her. More like a commune. *They're* a trip, let me just tell you. Anyway, it's a good place to hide. If we're not followed, that is."

I sighed, thinking of the man and his camera, the worldwide news coverage, and the hounds who had already learned my identity. "We'll be followed."

It was a matter of time.

Chapter Thirty-Eight

Finn

How or why would Saoirse possibly feel responsible for her mother's death? Ultana drove the blade into her damn fool self. What kind of misplaced guilt was Saoirse carrying?

I thought back to the day I'd discovered Cora and the others at the research facility. After my confrontation with Cora, I'd walked out very angry, yes, but with nothing on my mind other than how I might protect her. I desperately hadn't wanted Lorcan to get in touch with his mother and tell her that three Scintilla were Dr. M's prisoners, so I'd called Saoirse and asked her to run interference in case Lorcan called. Maybe Saoirse had lied to her mother on my behalf. I never thought to ask. I had no idea how Ultana knew where Clancy had taken them.

I was the dolt who called my uncle to meet me at the facility. It was my foolish mistake to think I had something on him and could leverage it to help Cora.

My mother's warning bothered me. I believed Saoirse to be sincere. And though my uncle had circumvented my sortilege, Saoirse had answered my questions with candor from the beginning. If she would be prevented from being completely transparent with me now, it would be her brother's doing.

So, how did Ultana end up at that tomb if Clancy was double-crossing her? The questions were enough to make me want to riffle through my uncle's house, and so I said good-bye to my folks and left immediately.

Clancy's house was too far of a walk on our property from the main house. To drive around the property would be easier. I hoped that I might find something about that day, a paper trail or a clue that might give answers.

Just stepping up to his front door, one could feel the air of *gone. No one lives here anymore.* Mum hadn't had the heart yet to sort through Clancy's effects. After his body was recovered from Newgrange, it had been whisked away by some white-coated governmental agency for examination and autopsy with all of the other bodies. Since then, his house had remained untouched.

Inside the dark front room, I felt his loss for the first time. Not the loss of the heartless and cruel man I discovered him to be but the uncle I'd cherished as a boy. Clancy gave me my love of music. He fought my early battles alongside me as I yearned for more freedom. He trusted me with the pub. In a twisted way, I was grateful that he orchestrated my meeting Cora, though a part of me suspected our stars would have found a way to collide no matter what. Our fate was interwoven in a way I hoped to understand someday.

I walked around aimlessly, seeing random memories. Then I got more serious about the reason I was there. Secrets of the dead might be less guarded, but that didn't make them easier to find. Like his back office at the pub, his home was a bloody shambles. Papers were everywhere. Mail was stacked beneath magazines, or under pint glasses with brown crusted at their bases.

His closet was heaped with laundry, but when I kicked a pile aside, I saw something familiar that hit me like a punch. Cora's mother's journal. I'd last seen it the day he'd carried her out of our library when I was high from her energy and clawing the air for her like a monster. I swallowed hard. Just thinking about it sped my pulse and sharpened my increasing need.

I sat on the edge of the bed, remembering the sweeter part of that night. Her smell—that lovely scent of orange and a trace of vanilla, with warmth that was distinctively Cora. My throat tightened. Closing my eyes, I was sent back to a different night with her in California. We were in my car. My hands wound in her curls, my fingertips ran the ridge at the nape of her neck. My lips journeyed down the vanilla-scented trail of her collarbone. I remembered the soft sounds she made that drove me wild and how swiftly and madly I was falling.

I missed her with an ache that felt like a bruise.

With the thrill at finding the journal was the sick feeling of thinking of how Clancy had used it to find and lure Mami Tulke to Ireland and then abduct her. The only good thing I could say about my uncle at that moment was that he was greedy enough to want the Scintilla for himself. If he'd shared the information in this journal with Ultana, they'd probably all be dead.

It would mean so much for Cora to have it back, and my new resolve was to deliver two things to Chile: her mother's writing and the cover of the *Book of Kells*. I carried the journal with me back to the front room and tried to get on his computer, but it was password protected. I unplugged it and had someone in mind to help me get into it. I'd see if Clancy had any documents and emails stored that could be useful.

When I lifted the laptop, I saw pieces of mail underneath.

Most of the mail was rubbish but for a few utility bills. It occurred to me that the bill that would be the most illuminating would be his phone bill, and that was paid through the pub as a business expense—the pub that I now owned. I set the laptop and journal in the passenger's seat and set off.

Michael—we called him Tilt at school because he would screw with a piece of electronics until it fried—was an expert in computers. I dropped by his house and offered him two hundred euro if he'd bust through my uncle's passwords. I gave him one hour, mostly so he wouldn't have time to do any digging around. Tilt loved a challenge.

From there, I went straight to Mulcarr's Pub. The bartender, Rory, had kept the pub open since Clancy's death. The regulars lifted their glasses in salute and gave me sympathetic looks when I walked through to the back office. A stack of mail had grown, waiting for me to deal with it. I shuffled through the envelopes until I found the cell bill and ripped it open.

It didn't shock me to see Ultana's number. Clancy was in contact with her quite a lot, no surprise. There was a call from the Lennon's home on — I checked my phone history — the day Lorcan and I went to Dr. M's. Lorcan was with me, so it couldn't have been him. Ultana must have called from her office. Strange, though, it was moments after I'd spoken to Saoirse and asked her to run interference for me.

The sounds of the pub faded as I tried to run through the events of that day. Giovanni and I were arguing about who should run into the tomb when Ultana showed up. How *had* Ultana known Clancy was at the tomb with the Scintilla? The only person present that day who seemed connected to both Clancy *and* Ultana was that driver of hers. Was the man working both sides? If so, was he on his own, like a double-agent, or working for someone else entirely?

I locked up the office and slapped money on the bar for Rory, promising to be back in soon, though he looked at me like he knew I was lying. I'm sure they were all wondering why I'd disappeared from the pub until now. With a half-hearted wink, I pushed through the door to go outside.

From the corner of my eye, I spotted a dodgy black van a few cars back behind my car. For a moment I thought it might be Lorcan, but no one appeared to be inside. I got in my car and pulled into the after-work Dublin traffic, noticing that the van that moments ago appeared empty had pulled out in traffic behind me as well.

Black vans and I had history. At the stoplight, I texted Saoirse: *Where's your brother?*

Saoirse: *He said he was going to "tie up loose ends." I have no idea what that means.*

The light turned green but an additional text came in as

I drove: *I have good news and bad. Dinner tonight?*

I made a quick turn and the van followed. I was in no mood for this shite. I slowed down to a near crawl to get a look at the driver in my rearview mirror, recognizing him immediately. It was the man who'd worked for Ultana and Clancy both. Just moments ago, I'd been wondering about him. I should have killed him at Newgrange instead of leaving him unconscious, but now I had questions for him. A new one at the top of the list was *who was having him follow me?*

I clenched my teeth, shaking with need for another life. I couldn't keep putting it off if I hoped to get to Cora. A plan formulated as I drove. No longer would I dodge and weave this human bloke. If he wanted to follow me, it was at his own risk.

Within minutes, I was in the quieter city section of Dublin, the location of Dr. M's research facility. I didn't know what I'd find inside. Giovanni, Dun, and the little girl, Claire, had flown from the building like they'd been chewed up and spit out of its doors. Dun had a bloody ax, and I assumed the blood came from bodies inside. Bodies that were likely still there.

Let my stalker follow me. I had a message to send to whoever he worked for.

When Saoirse had said to me that the biggest threat to Arrazi was being outed, I suddenly had a wicked notion how I could threaten the Arrazi everywhere. Mari's rebellious voice rang in my head: *Soon the world will know about you. I bet they lock every last one of you up when that happens.*

Proof.

If I couldn't bring them to my side, maybe I could bring

them to their knees.

I had the master key Ultana gave to Lorcan and me the day we first came to this facility and found the Scintilla being kept prisoner. What I was about to do was ugly but wicked genius and would provide me with more than just answers from the driver. It'd be a threat in my pocket against the Arrazi. I had a plan and a ravenous soul that needed feeding.

Chapter Thirty-Nine

Giovanni

Two emotions that shouldn't go hand in hand: fear and peace. Yet they fused into a blend of agitation and excitement all day long after my text exchange with Cora earlier. Fear for her buzzed in my gut. Horrifying to be trapped on a plane with an Arrazi. If nothing happened to her, she should be getting close.

The small peace I felt was for telling her that I loved her. What if it was our last communication? I was sickened by that thought, but at least she'd know that I loved her and that I hoped to love her beyond this day, beyond our current circumstances.

I'd love her until the day I died.

Claire watched me from across the room with her strange and perceptive eyes, and I felt a pang of guilt. For necessary reasons, I'd had to leave her a lot. She'd handled the enormous changes and new people with maturity uncharacteristic for her age. I was proud of her. I joined her in the kitchen and helped her put cookies in the oven. "I want to take them to everyone tomorrow," she told me. "To make friends."

"That's nice of you, Claire."

Her small shoulders shrugged. "I don't know if it will make a difference."

Taken aback, I hugged her. "I'm sorry you feel their fear. I suppose they don't know what to make of such a smart, pretty little girl."

Claire pulled back and cocked her head sideways, grinning like she'd caught a politician in his spin. "That's not it and you know it. It's because they don't think I'm normal."

"The Scintilla are the ones who aren't normal. Anyway, standing out is always better than fitting in," I said, remembering overhearing a woman say that once to her daughter on a street corner in Barcelona. It was a sweet sentiment, meant to tell the girl not to want to be like everyone else. I liked the saying, but it wasn't how I felt most of my life. I'd only wanted to fit in, to not be so different, even if I was the only one who could see just how different I was. Standing out meant death.

This was a community of *my* kind. I belonged somewhere for the first time since my parents were taken from me. Now, my daughter was the outsider, and I just wanted her to be accepted.

We cleaned up the cookie mess, and I took extra time to settle Claire into her new sleeping place on the floor next to my bed. It was where she felt safe and it was just as well, as Mami Tulke's small home would have to accommodate, at least for tonight, the addition of Faye and Janelle. A new idea formed and I decided to ask Mami Tulke about it first thing in the morning. We should be down in the village with the other Scintilla. They needed to spend more time with us to accept us as family. With the group's acceptance would come their allegiance.

I pulled out the list and added more people and sortileges that Adrian had told me about while we were assessing the weapons. Tomorrow I'd also speak with the guys about retrieving those weapons and beginning training. Adrian said he'd schedule volunteers to keep watch at each end of the river gorge to alert us to suspicious arrivals. We couldn't police a public road or stop people from entering the valley, but we could do our best to be forewarned if danger was snaking its way toward us.

With Janelle's arrival, and hopefully Cora's, it surely wouldn't be too long before the rest of the world came knocking, including the Arrazi.

Mami Tulke was fine with my request for Claire and me to move to one of the empty huts in the village, though I felt nervous to solo parent without Mami Tulke's nudges. That must be what pilots feel like the first time they get to take the plane for a spin without an instructor. "It's good to join them," she said. "There is one of the rectangular buildings with a small loft for Claire to use for sleeping." She reminded me that it was also important to begin contributing to the varied communal duties of the group. "Side by side," she said, slapping her fist into rounds of dough she was preparing to bake.

"We have cookies…" I said, half joking.

"A bit of sweet to go with your bitter?" She gave me the number of the "hut" and the keys to the golf cart. "Take Claire. Go see."

Claire and I didn't have many belongings. Because the "cover" for the village was as a renowned stargazing locale and a New Age spirituality center, each hut was already supplied with hotel-like amenities. Beds, towels, blankets—basic needs. Claire and I had collected a patchwork of necessities from Ireland before we left, from my recent trip to Santiago, and from kind Scintilla who, despite their misgivings about us, had recognized we had little but the clothes on our backs.

The teenage twins, Cooper and Gavin, came by out of curiosity but offered good company while we settled in. They were a funny pair and entertaining, eager to show their Brazilian fighting dance, *capoeira*. They spun and kicked and swirled around each other in a dizzying display. Cooper made Claire squeal when, at the end of the dance, he poured water in his hand and created the illusion of two miniature bodies made of water, performing the very same martial art upon his palm. It was an impressive sortilege, which he obviously practiced a lot.

Moving had been a great distraction from my wound-up, hopeful anticipation of Cora's arrival. My body buzzed with nerves. It took every mental effort not to imagine an Arrazi attacking her, leaving her dead in an airplane seat, or outside of the airport, or following her here. I'd already placed a gun behind a potted plant on a high shelf in the hut.

Let one come. Let them all come.

I worked to stay calm. Not only could Cora see my every emotion reflected in my aura, but she had an advantage

many other Scintilla who'd always seen auras didn't have…
the subtle ways of sensing, because she'd grown up not
knowing what she was. I doubted that Cora missed a flicker
of the eye, the subtle variation of a voice, or even breaths.
She watched everything, and it had the effect of making me
feel incredibly exposed. And understood.

Only once had I deceived her. Every day, I regretted not
telling Cora about my arrangement with Dr. M. By keeping
anything from her, I broke the fragile trust she placed in
me. I think more than hating me for my omission, she hated
herself for not sensing it.

Our connection was real from the moment we'd met at
the airport. I swear I wanted to kiss her full, wet lips on that
bus. Certainly, we'd had beauty in our growing bond and
passion in those fleeting moments at Dr. M's, when magic
wound around us in the blissful cradle of time. Though it
began as a planned deception to fool Dr. M, all of that fell
away even before we kissed and touched. We became two
people allowing ourselves to reach for the other. She felt
love for me; I could see it and feel it. She carried a torch for
Finn, but in those moments with me, she had laid it down.

My blood ran hot with my runaway thoughts. I had to
get some air, but the air outside wasn't any cooler. Maya in-
tercepted me on the path to my door with a potted plant and
a wary smile. "There's a meeting tonight," she said. "Raimondo asked for a vote on fighting. He's against it."

"Majority rules?" I asked, incensed. What did I expect,
that just because Raimondo was Italian like me and knew
my parents, he'd be on my side? What had the clairvoyant
seen to make him oppose standing our ground and defending
ourselves?

She held out the plant. "That is generally how we settle big things."

"And what will happen if I refuse to play? I've lived my life alone, Maya. I don't play by others' rules." A man I hadn't yet met strolled up and inserted himself into our discussion.

"Some don't believe that trouble is coming. That maybe *you* are the trouble, with your talk of weapons and your strange…"

He didn't finish, but I wanted to hit him for what I knew he was about to say: my strange child.

"Maya," I implored, "you saw what was happening in Santiago. Madness. Mami Tulke's granddaughter is coming and—"

The man threw up his hands. "Maybe she *shouldn't* come."

"*What?*"

"If her coming is dangerous," he said, "then for the greater good, she should stay away."

My shoulders bunched up, my jaw tightened. "Her grandmother has sheltered *you* for how long? And you would turn away her family? Even if she didn't come, they know who she is and will find her grandmother, fool." I could barely contain my anger. The conversation was ridiculous. "They will find you. Cora is coming," I said, reassuring myself more than anything. "She deserves the same protection you've sat around on your asses enjoying all this time. After what she's been through, Cora deserves everything… good…and…everything…"

Uncharacteristically, I'd lost control. God, these people were in for a rude awakening. Maya and the man both looked at me like I was unstable. I barely registered the sound of footsteps approaching.

"G?"

Chapter Forty

Cora

Giovanni's head whipped toward me when I called to him.
I was full of nerves and self-consciousness and heard it
in my own trembling voice when I'd called out to him. One
slow blink from him made me wonder if he recognized me,
but I was swept from the ground as easily as a leaf is picked
up by the wind and propelled into his arms.

I heard the surprised gasp of the two people who'd been
standing with him and was totally shocked to realize both
were Scintilla. Giovanni's arms encircled my waist, and I'd
been lifted so high by his sortilege that mine curled around
his head, my fingers recalling the waves of his hair. I bent my
head down and cried into them. He walked us toward one
of the strange block houses I'd seen from the road. I don't
know who the Scintilla were who were there one moment

but gone the next. I only knew that I'd made it. I knew relief. And I knew tenderness.

When Giovanni slid me slowly down, my hands brushed his face, and his tears wetted my fingers. "I made it," I said, to reassure both of us that it was real.

The barest hint of a smile curved his lips as he brushed his palm over my cropped hair. I braced myself, but no snarky remark came, just gentle touch with light fingers over my cheekbones and my marked jaw. He traced each circle slowly, one by one, lighting my skin with sparks. Who can breathe when someone familiar, cherished, has your face in the palms of his hands and is looking at you like his lost treasure?

Closing in, lips parting like they were anticipating cake, I suddenly felt an unruly urge to bite his lip, to pull this free-floating desire over the hull of the boat and steer it. That flame of aggression surprised me. I thought that side of me only showed up with Finn, or that Finn somehow made me fiercer. For the first time, I recognized that what showed itself with Finn in the redwoods was my own strength. Mine. No man's gift to me.

Aggravated that I couldn't seem to divide thoughts of Finn from my experiences with Giovanni, I clutched his neck and looked deeply into his eyes. This strong me, the one who knew life was precious and could be too brief, wanted his lips on mine. Now.

"Cora?" a little voice squealed. Giovanni and I broke apart as Claire bounded into the room. She looked up at me and said, "I like your hair."

"Thanks," I said, laughing. "I'm so glad to see you again."

"It's a disguise, right?"

"Yes." A laugh fizzed up. "You're very clever. It is."

"*I* still knew who you were."

I looked at Giovanni, whose cheeks were flushed, making his blue eyes even brighter. He was saying a million things with them, things that would have to wait. "She is *so* your daughter," I said.

"Did you just get here? Where are the *others*?" he asked.

I knew he was still under the assumption that Finn was with me. Why hadn't I corrected him? "About an hour ago."

"Who else helped you get here?"

"Come with me up to the house, and I'll show you."

Giovanni didn't ask me too many questions on the way. *Everything* was a question, including us. Being in Chile was one big exhale. I'd made it this far. In a world where the ground was constantly shifting beneath my feet, I could only take things one step at a time.

"What are you doing?" I asked Edmund as we pulled the golf cart up to the front of the house. He had a camera with a large microphone attached to it, pointing at Giovanni and me. From the look on his face, Giovanni didn't appreciate the sudden appearance of someone who looked like paparazzi. "Giovanni, meet author and television personality and self-proclaimed expert on all things crazy, Edmund Nustber."

"You're Scintilla, too?" Edmund asked eagerly, to which Giovanni nodded. The glee on Edmund's face was almost cute. "Get used to the camera," Edmund said. "I'll be filming random bits to piece together for the documentary."

"How did our interview become a documentary?" I asked.

Giovanni touched my elbow. "Interview? Cora, what's going on?"

"Edmund helped us get out of Rome. He's the reason I was able to fly here. We made a deal."

"I actually like the idea," Giovanni said, surprising me. "We've got to get some kind of control of the media storm around you. You must realize what a worldwide phenomenon your story is right now."

"Spectacle is more like it. I'd like a chance to do the one thing they've tried to stop us from doing—telling the truth."

"You can tell it, but the question is, will anyone believe it? We have no proof."

"Giovanni, can you tell me how you know each other?" Edmund asked in his interview voice.

"I thought I might be one of the only ones left." He lifted my hand and kissed it. "Until I found her."

I rolled my eyes. "Cheeseball."

"You're the guy from the Dublin airport video!" Edmund exclaimed. His flip-out-o-meter was going to tilt.

We went inside where Mami Tulke, Janelle, and Faye were embroiled in an intense conversation. I'd been shocked to see my stepmom and Faye at my grandmother's. Shocked but so happy. Dun listened to them talk, looking interested but exhausted. He jumped up when he saw us walk in and gave Giovanni a slap on the back before pulling him into a man-hug. Giovanni was clearly surprised, and questions filled his eyes when he looked at me.

"They don't want humanity to believe in their own godliness," Faye was saying to Mami Tulke. "Organized religion tells humanity to believe that divinity is something that only they can dispense, like candy. Go to them, give them your money and the power that comes with that. In turn they, acting as interpreter for 'the voice of God,' will give you absolution."

Mami Tulke rested her chin on a temple of her fingers. "When people are afraid, they look to their governments and their churches for help. That's not a bad thing in and of itself. But neither institution can fathom or will admit that the Scintilla exist, let alone that we might be a source of healing for the mysterious deaths. To allow the world to know we have supernatural powers would be to share God's sandbox. They won't allow that."

"I couldn't agree more," Edmund said, camera still recording.

"Why is this relevant?" Giovanni asked.

I grabbed one of my grandmother's savory empanadas and put it on a plate. There was really only one answer to Giovanni's question. "Our existence is a threat to the world's systems."

Running underneath our conversation, an ever-constant current, was the television news, which Mami Tulke had kept on so that we might be forewarned when the media traced us here. Everyone shushed when breaking news came on. Dun turned up the sound.

A shocking new revelation in the Vatican Miracle. Two of the affected children's families have come forward claiming that their children were left with visible proof of the young woman's miracle healing. A picture flashed up of the sternum of the little boy, Caleb. *It appears to be spirals, three of them. Experts have compared this picture to photographs of the ancient megalithic site in Ireland and have concluded that the pattern is identical. While many contend that this is a hoax manufactured by two colluding families, others believe it to be a stigmata of some kind—evidence of their supernatural healing.*

We all exchanged glances. Stigmata? Could the news agency have picked a more inflammatory word? They might as well hang meat around my neck. I changed the subject. "I didn't get a chance to meet them, but I saw two Scintilla when I went down to find Giovanni," I said to Mami Tulke. "Why didn't you tell me? It's so exciting. There are five of us."

"Oh, there're many more than that," Giovanni said, his eyes glinting.

"Really? How dumb of me. I should have realized," I said. "In my mother's journal she wrote of discovering what we were called; she said it meant there were others like her. I thought she meant in the past. This is so much more than I'd ever hoped." Wonder filled me. We three weren't the only ones left. Wonder was soon replaced by dread. I didn't want them to be found.

"Your *abuela* has been a rescuer and protector of more than sixty Scintilla."

"Soon to be sixty-one," a voice said from the doorway. A young American man smiled at me. "My wife Maya here is expecting."

I stepped forward. "I saw you a while ago," I said, holding out my hand to Maya, but she wouldn't take it. I frowned. "Why be cold to me? I didn't expect to find my own kind here, and I'm so happy to know that we aren't the last."

"Please," she said, her deep brown eyes imploring. "Don't take it for rudeness. I—I try not to touch people."

"Ah." I nodded. "A sortilege issue. I *so* get that." I wondered what hers was. "I try not to touch *things*," I said, hoping to set her at ease. I pointed to my hands, neck, and forehead. "Does this to me." The couple smiled but with questions in their eyes. "Psychometry is my sortilege, but it leaves its trace."

"Maya told you about the meeting, Giovanni," Will said with a sideways look at Maya. "You know I'm already with you. I just wanted you to know that lots of others are, too. After dinner, we'll hold the vote."

"Vote?" I asked. "What, you going to elect Mayor of Scintilla-town?"

Mami Tulke harrumphed behind me as she slipped empanadas off cooling racks and onto platters. "Giovanni wasn't here a day before his talk of 'war' began. He has acquired weapons and wants the Scintilla to prepare to fight for their lives."

My eyes snapped to Giovanni, who wore a rebellious expression. Like most things he did, he was sure he was right. I could imagine that he'd been pretty domineering about it and that might not sit well with this established community of Scintilla. I still couldn't believe there were so many. It gave me hope and a desperate desire to protect them. I could see both sides of the war debate as I'd had the argument with myself. "Well then," I said, not meeting his eyes, "tonight we vote."

Chapter Forty-One

Finn

Premeditated murder.

The phrase washed over my mind like greasy residue. Guilt was oily. It coated your soul in sticky sludge that no amount of holy water would ever wash off.

I'd now gone from dreading the kill to anticipating it. This driver who followed me was up to his elbows in Ultana's evil and was apparently working multiple angles, as he'd been seen with my uncle as well. Both were dead, so it didn't take much to figure out who he was working for. If Lorcan thought he was going to use the man to spy on me and "tie up some loose ends," he was mistaken.

Ultana's master key worked on the underground garage gate, which slid open when I turned it. I drove through and parked in a spot near the inside doors. Better to stay out of sight of anyone who might pass by on the street. I waited a few minutes in my car and leaned my head back, humming Jonny Lang songs to myself. I wanted my pursuer to relax, lose focus, and become inattentive.

After a few impatient minutes, I snuck from the garage and crept up behind the van.

He was in the driver's seat, head low, probably on his phone. I latched on to his energy before he even saw me approach. Using him as a test, I began reaching for it long before I thought I could actually connect. I wanted to see from how far away I could take. As I walked up to the window and saw his slumped form, I wondered why the Arrazi would *ever* use regular humans to do their dirty work. They were too easy to take down.

I opened the door, pulled his head upright, and was gratified I'd identified him correctly. He was the bloke with the scarred lip. The one who had jabbed the needle in my arm not two blocks from here the day Clancy caught Cora and her mother. I yanked the car door open, and his phone fell to the ground. I snatched it up to verify my hunch about Lorcan and, sure enough, there were two calls that morning from the Lennon household. No texts, though. He must've deleted them. After making sure there were no cars approaching, I tossed the phone in the spare seat, pulled his limp body from the van, and dragged him down the ramp into the parking garage. My cells screamed for completion, for the concentrated ball of his soul to satiate mine. Just a bit longer…

His eyes opened and blinked as he tried to focus on me. One arm flailed toward me but didn't land. I hit him with another suck of his energy and pulled him along the concrete of the garage to an inner gate. Using the key again, I opened it, which caused the lights to flicker on. Ready to see something grisly from when Dun and Giovanni fought their way out, my senses were firing on high alert. I expected rank smells, decaying bodies, shattered glass, anything to show the fight I'd been told about. Nothing. To anyone walking in here, this was a posh but empty office building.

Ultana must have ordered the mess cleaned up before she went to the tomb. I was glad for it but prayed they hadn't yet removed *all* of the equipment or dismantled the one room I intended to use.

The guy was heavy and getting heavier as I pulled him through the corridors. I passed a room that looked familiar, though I couldn't say why, until I realized I'd seen it in a vision. Gráinne had given me a vision of a room full of gurneys with Cora and the others strapped down. In Gráinne's vision, I'd also seen Cora being led away at gunpoint.

The gurneys were still there, and next to that room was a smaller one that looked like a surveillance room with multiple computer monitors. I turned a main power source on, and the monitors flickered to life. The man lay at my feet as I tried to pull up video history within the facility, but it had been wiped. They'd scrubbed more than the floors.

Sweating and exhausted, I finally found the dining room with the sleek black walls and long table. Pressing the button that I remember Dr. M using, the walls came to life with my colorful pre-kill aura wafting around me. I grinned, and my aura lifted with faint streamers of gold. The man's aura was weak, faint. Imagining that Cora saw this way all the time was just as mind-blowing as it had been the first time I was in that room.

It was a small blessing that Arrazi couldn't see the beauty of the flowers they were picking; it would make killing that much harder.

I propped my phone against a flower vase on the table, sat the man in one of the dining chairs, and used the straps from the gurney to secure him upright in the chair. Bending to look into his face, I said, "I've seen you doing jobs for two different Arrazi—one working against the other. I know them both to be dead, and yet you're following me. Who do you work for?"

"I work for myself."

"You're not following me for your own amusement. Someone has hired you to follow me, and I think I know who it is."

His eyes pierced me with a challenging glare that bordered on a leer, as if I couldn't possibly know who he worked for. He shook his head, fighting my power. "I'll be killed." Laughter and spit sputtered from him. Maybe fear hit people differently, but laughing is not what I'd do if I were tied to a chair with an Arrazi in front of me. Mari's face flew to my mind, and I pushed the memory down.

He struggled with his own mind, which was commanding him to tell the truth against his will. "God in heaven, forgive me. I don't know why I'm telling you this! She'll—she'll kill me, and if she doesn't, the man will."

She? But Ultana was dead, *wasn't she?* A tempest of thoughts spun in my mind. She told Cora she couldn't be killed. She told her own daughter that she was immortal. And Lorcan hadn't let Saoirse see his mother's dead body...

"Name them."

"I would if I bloody well could! They are voices.

Phantoms. I never see who actually hires me. One is a woman. One is a man. I swear it. That's all I know!"

But the woman and the man I'd seen him serve were both dead. Lorcan had to be the man who'd called him from his house, and I was near to accepting that Ultana might have lived after all and was still playing puppets, her son the most strung up.

He was frantic, desperate, weakly flailing against the straps. "This is why, right? So I can't divulge their identities to scum like you."

I gave him a low, menacing promise. "You don't need to worry about them killing you because I'm going to kill you now."

"Kill me, then, if that's what you're about. That's what all of you Arrazi are about. Murder—murder of innocent people. I've seen more than you know."

"With bosses like yours, I bet you have."

His condemnation of the Arrazi was the perfect intro. I faced my phone, which had been recording the whole encounter, and readied myself to speak, surprised by the emotion building in my chest. It was the most important confessional of my life. I spoke to the invisible viewer, hoping for understanding, yes, but hoping for something more to come of the video. It was the only ammunition I could think of to use against the Arrazi who might be reluctant to join me. It was leverage.

I cleared my throat and began.

"I grew up like you, normal. Love of family, love of country, love of God, love of music." Cora's beautiful face rushed forward. "*Love* of a beautiful girl...my first love..." Emotion built and sat heavy on my chest. I had to man up, get through this.

"A few months ago, everything in my life changed. I found out that I am of a bloodline, or genetic breed..." I clenched my fists. It was harder to explain than I thought it would be. I imagined millions of faces staring at screens and asking themselves what in the hell I was talking about. "I am a different race of human, an ancient race, the existence of which has been kept secret for countless centuries."

It was impossible to speak with any sense of self beyond that I was a killer. I was hollowed out, barely hanging on to the young man I was before. Maybe he died when I took my first life on my boat. "I am an Arrazi," I managed to say. "This is not special. It's a bloody curse. My faith in my creator has been shattered because I do not understand why a human would exist who—who *must* kill other humans in order to survive. Your life energy is our sustenance."

My breathing sped, my heart churned with dread and guilt. Speaking the truth aloud, to the world, was not as liberating as I thought it might be. It was shameful. I hated what I was about to do and, yet, I felt like the world would never believe it if they didn't see it with their own eyes.

"The wall I'm standing in front of is based on technology that began with Kirlian photography. It allows you to see the energy fields around every human being."

"Don't do this," the man said, shaking. "You don't realize what you're doing."

I sent a sharp tendril of energy into him, which I'm sure the wall showed, and he was quiet again. "That girl you are chasing, the one who saved those children in Rome, she is a breed apart as well, known as Scintilla. The Scintilla are the counterparts to the Arrazi in every way." I found myself looking at the floor. "They give. We take."

Looking back at my phone, I said, "She is one of the most precious beings on this planet and deserves your protection, not your chase. You see, nearly all of the Scintilla are gone, wiped from the earth." I hadn't initially planned on saying what I knew I'd say next. Instinct reared up and forced the words from me.

"There is something precious in my possession, something I believe might answer so many questions about our two races. I have the missing cover to the *Book of Kells*, which I believe without doubt is a piece of the puzzle. I will not stop until I unravel its mysteries. It is a treasure, but even more so if it can illuminate this madness among men and stop it.

"There are people in power who want nothing more than to find every last Scintilla…and erase them from existence. Many Arrazi have joined them on this hunt. I am not one of them. While our races have been set up to be enemies, I believe there's more to the story. I'm trying desperately to learn it before it's too late.

"The world is understandably scared about the people who are dropping dead. I do not have the answer to that. But I can tell you that Arrazi all over the world are taking advantage of it. They are adding to the death toll by killing, out in the open, wherever people are dropping dead. I don't know why this is…but they've been directed to do this…by someone…"

Steeling myself with a deep breath, I continued, "It's my hope that the power the Arrazi expect to gain by their alliance with someone in command will be crushed if the world sees with their own eyes what we are."

I wanted to plead for understanding, grovel for forgiveness, explain and explain so that they might know and believe the torture of being a killer. Yet that's exactly what I needed them to see—me, the Arrazi killer. I was damning myself to damn the Arrazi.

I latched my energy onto the man tied to the chair, and his head arched back. He made a pathetic whimpering sound. Instead of watching him, I watched the wall. I was quick about it, my blood pumping harder with every strand of his pulsing life energy until that pop that I saw and also felt, that succulent burst, when his essence flew into my body and my own aura erupted with fullness and glowed on the screen in an enormous spray of white.

Chapter Forty-Two

Giovanni

Tension wove throughout the crowd of Scintilla as we ate, and it became so dense it choked off conversation. An anticipatory charge rippled in the air. I noticed that Will and Maya weren't eating together, and my guess was that their ongoing debate had reached a head after they left Mami Tulke's.

Cora handled the many stares with grace. Awe showed on her face as she took in the reality of the many Scintilla her grandmother had been hiding.

The Italian clairvoyant, Raimondo, rang a dinner bell to get everyone's attention. "You know why we're here. We've debated privately and with one another about Giovanni's plan. Our community of Scintilla will either fight our enemies or stand against them in peaceful resistance. But neither will be successful if we're divided. Show your vote by standing on either side of the room in rows of five. If you are for diplomacy and peaceful resistance, please come to my side of the room. If you favor fighting and discord, please cast your vote by standing over on that side of the room, with Giovanni."

I shoved away from the table and stood. "Before you make your choice based on Raimondo's words, know that I'm in favor of *defending ourselves*."

All at once, the people in the room stood and filed past each other like passengers in a metro station at rush hour. It was impossible at first to see which side of the room had more people. I was gratified to be clustered with three rows of five already, but we'd need at least twice that many for majority. Mami Tulke stood opposite me on the other side of the room, as I'd known she would. Maya held her head high, but her chin quivered when she looked across the room at Will standing next to me.

A few people lingered in the middle of the room with pained faces, trying make their final decision. The auras of some showed their decision before they consciously picked a side, arching toward the part of the large room where they'd eventually end up.

Cora stood among them.

I bit the inside of my cheek. How could she not be sure? She'd already had to fight to defend herself against the Arrazi. She'd killed a man. Or, was that *why* she was undecided? She could have killed Clancy when she had the chance — should have — and didn't. She didn't want to be a killer like the Arrazi, and I recalled her questioning how it would all end unless someone was willing to *not* strike back.

Hopefully, she'd feel like I did when she looked around this room…that this precious legacy had to be guarded, that we might be the last defenders against the loss of an entire race.

"And what about the rest of civilization?" I shouted above the din. "What if Cora's father and Dr. M were both right?" I felt Cora's limitless green eyes on me, but it was the rest of the crowd I hoped to convince. Her, I hoped to remind. The room hushed to hear me. "Cora's father, a scientist, believed that *we* are supposed to bring the energy of the world back into balance. He believed that the world and the people in it will face destruction if we don't and that the people who are dropping dead are but one sign, as are the violent natural disasters. These quakes aren't normal. Nor are the volcanoes, hurricanes, and tornadoes that have been happening over the last few weeks. This is about energy— the imbalance of positive and negative energy. We'll never be able to save the world if we're dead."

Tallying both sides, it was apparent the Scintilla were very evenly divided. As the number of undecided in the middle of the room dwindled, so the pressure increased. We all watched as eventually, Cora stood alone. Whispers flew around. Everyone's phones, radios, and televisions were operable again, and newspapers had been passed around. Not only did everyone know she was Mami Tulke's granddaughter, but they knew who she was—the girl who'd resurrected dead children. The girl the world was after.

Sixty Scintilla stared at her, waiting.

"This decision shouldn't be hard for me," she said, quieting the murmurs, "but it is." Her silver aura pulsed and grew, gaining confidence as she faced her moment of real introduction and her moment of decision. It rested on Cora. Her hand touched on her lips for an astonished moment as she looked around the room. "The only thing more beautiful than seeing this, seeing all of you together, would be if my parents could have lived to see it." She paused as her light flickered with sorrow. "But they were murdered. You met my cousin, Mari, when she stayed here recently. She…she was killed by the Arrazi, too.

"I was always a peaceful person. I *do* want peace," she said to Raimondo's side of the room, and I noticed a few sure, smug smiles on the faces over there. "I want freedom, too. No one is going to *give* us freedom. Like so many oppressed people in human history, we will have to fight for it. We have *no* allies. We are alone and outnumbered." Cora paused, her eyes lifting up, seeing a memory. "My father said I was a fighter. After he died, I remember thinking that if I wanted to stay alive, I'd better damn well fight."

Now the energy near me was shifting as people guessed where she might land.

"So where will you stand?" an impatient Scintilla asked.

Cora sighed. "With Mr. Nustber's help, I hope to tell the world the truth so that we might gain support."

"Or it'll backfire!" someone shouted. "And they'll be after all of us like they are you."

Cora's head jerked to look the dissenter in the eye. "They *are* after all of you. Our enemy said to me, 'Once every last Scintilla is dead, then the truth will die with you.' Don't you see? Their aim has been to deny our existence. I'm going to speak the truth and—"

"Speak the *truth*?" a catty voice called out. "Who do you think you are, Jesus?"

Cora nodded to Edmund, and he pressed a button on a projector I hadn't noticed. Michelangelo's secret painting burst onto the wall behind her.

Uproar. That's what the painting caused. She hadn't explained who had painted it, or how she'd come to have a picture of it. She just let them absorb the message. I didn't like the energy in the room. Even among Scintilla, there were diehard Christians who were obviously stunned, even angry, at her assertion.

I started to step forward, but Cora shot me a look that pinned me in my place. There was pain in that look—pain that she had to choose sides, that she had to defend herself after the trials she'd already endured. For some reason, she didn't want my backup.

"What I see in this room right now is that we're a microcosm of the world outside. You look on one another from your *place* across the room as if we aren't all the same."

A tendril of silver uncoiled from each of her hands as she looked from one side of the room to the other. Her face was impassive, and I wondered if she realized what she was doing. Her energy showed what she really wanted—for the Scintilla to be of one mind—but I didn't see that happening. Cora was going to have to choose.

She took a deep breath like she was surrendering. The discord that had strained her features relaxed. Serenity illuminated her face, and the crystalline silver light that came from her was the most beautiful thing I'd ever seen.

Suddenly, the silver strand of her energy that had been stretching from her toward both sides of the room hit me in the chest. The other went straight to Mami Tulke.

My aura ballooned. I was filled with pure, radiant love.

Somehow, this energy threaded into me and through me to the person next to me and continued from person to person around the room. Like flares going off, our auras clasped, connecting our astral bodies in every direction until the place was one swirling, spiraling mass of Scintilla energy.

Many cried, overwhelmed. Some swiped tears through laughter. Quite a few looked frightened and fixed Cora with eyes squinting with suspicion and trepidation. As for me, I'd never felt so connected to—to something so *big*. It was intimidating. I didn't know what she did. Or how. This was new magic.

Cora didn't cross over our lines to pick a side. She sought to erase the lines. The girl who was once so against influencing others using energy had just cast a spell with hers. I worried about those fearful glances. It was one thing to manipulate the ignorant, another to force-feed us our own medicine.

Chapter Forty-Three

Cora

"I don't know how," I said again, exasperated with Giovanni.

He'd asked me in three different ways what I had done that had united the auras of the Scintilla and connected all of us in some kind of cosmic love-bubble. "I was just thinking that when the world is after our kind, I wished we'd stop fighting each other and be…"

"What?"

"*One.*"

Giovanni smirked. "Ripples in the pond?" he asked, evoking our argument at Dr. M's about the concept of oneness.

"Unity consciousness," I said. That's what he'd called it. That's what it felt like, like submerging myself into a field of feeling and knowing and pure love.

"I've never experienced anything like it, and I'd venture to say none of them had, either. You didn't even have to give an Aragorn speech, and they're following you to the gates. Most of them, anyway. I'm scared for you, Cora."

Whatever I'd done had turned the tide and brought most of the Scintilla together, and I was grateful. I didn't have to choose. The people who crossed the room from one side to the other chose for us. "It was amazing, right? Everything *not* love fell away for just those few seconds. Did you notice that?" I asked him.

He only smiled.

"What?"

"I think you are a goddess."

I stepped on his toes. "And don't you forget it."

We walked together toward his lodge on a path lit by solar lights and stars. Claire had asked to go with Mami Tulke to help her bake for the next morning's breakfast and it was just as well; we had strategy to plan. Not something you want to do with a little one around.

"They have incredible wine here," Giovanni said. "Want?"

"What the hell? I'm on the 'life is short' plan." I thought he'd smile but he didn't, so then I flushed, thinking that he might wonder if that meant I'd say yes to *everything* because my sky was falling. "I've never planned a battle before," I quickly threw out, trying to look all business.

"There's two elements to discuss," he said, sitting on the couch with a pad of paper and a pen. "I've acquired weapons, but people will need to be trained in how to use them, and quickly."

"You've been a busy boy."

His eyebrow shot up. "We'll need a safe place for target

practice and knife throwing. I've made a list—though it's not complete—of people's sortileges."

"Do our sortileges really matter?"

"You'd be surprised, Cora. Maya can kill with a touch. My telekinesis has proven helpful before, and there's a girl, Sage, who can do it as well. Sierra can do mimicry, a sort of shape-shifting. One advantage is that many more of us have sortileges than the Arrazi because so few of them have ever taken from a Scintilla before."

"Right up until they start sipping from our auras like juice boxes. Then they'll be just as lethal."

His eyes were deadly serious. "With the weapons, perhaps they won't get the chance."

"No *bueno* on that plan. If we shoot first and are lucky enough to hit an Arrazi, then if we have any eyewitnesses from the outside world we look like we're murdering unarmed, innocent people. I don't think we want to live the rest of our *lucky* lives in jail."

Giovanni frowned. "Let's hope the outside world doesn't find us anytime soon."

"Yeah right."

"Tomorrow, we'll set up a meeting and discuss everyone's powers and how they might use them. The clairvoyants should do whatever it is they do to see danger coming."

"Giovanni, this is so much better than I thought when it was just us three." My heart darkened. "And so much worse if it all goes badly—all these people…" I flopped on the couch next to him and looked up through the large rectangular window in the ceiling. "Will you turn the light out for a second? I want to see the stars." The valley really was special. The stars were so clear, so seemingly close. "You could almost imagine we're out there, floating in space," I said, mesmerized.

When the wind scattered me to the stars...

Giovanni slipped his hand over mine. I thought he might move for more, but his aura was placid, his body motionless as his face tilted upward. We sat there together, stargazing, and letting the moments tumble into the nothingness.

"Quiet like this," he finally said, rolling his face sideways to look at me. "Sitting here with you like this, it teases me into imagining a different life." His eyes were starlit as he looked intently into mine. "With you."

I stood, though my hand was still holding his, and looked down at him. "It's probably best not to envision a future with me."

Giovanni lifted our entwined hands and pressed my fingers to his lips, slipping the tips of each one into his mouth like luscious slices of fruit. Did he know the fire that would build inside of me when he did that? He was blowing on the flames I'd tamped down when I told myself that my love life was frivolous in the face of what was ahead. When Giovanni tugged me onto his lap, it lit a fuse that raced from my fingers to every part of my body, striking my core.

His hands grasped both sides of my face, the pads of his fingers leaving tingling dots on my cheeks before he traced my bottom lip with one finger, adding a coiling trail of sparks across my skin. Slowly, he pulled my mouth to his.

Our kiss was softness and heat. Hunger and fear. Love and confusion. Inwardly I ran to him because this was *life*, then ran away because my life was messy, and I was making it messier. Outwardly, I took his lips and tasted them. I used my hands to know his shoulders, his chest, the strength in his arms. I clung to him like a life preserver because he *was* that, had been that since we met. Kisses were kindling, keeping me from icing over. Touch was bravery. Connection was *existence*.

It was a miracle I'd made it alive to Chile. With the powers against us, every additional minute was a miracle. So why at that moment did I think of Finn?

My phone trilled in the darkness. Our foreheads were pressed together amidst our panting breaths and beating hearts. I didn't want to answer it, but I had to. I fumbled for it on the table, and the screen lit up.

A text. From Finn.

Finn.

Finn: *Where are you?*

Um…straddling Giovanni's lap… I rolled off and sat with one leg curled under me. I could feel Giovanni's intense gaze on me.

Me: *I made it.*

He'd understand where and with whom. Finn never did need much explanation from me to understand.

Finn: *Please stay safe until I get there with the thing I found. Only you can tell us what it means, if anything. I have a strong feeling about this. Ultana wanted it and I have it.*

"Finn's coming," I said, feeling the bottom drop out of my heart and bounce against my ribs as I said it. Giovanni leaped up and raked his hands through his hair. I wanted to move clear of the aggravation he was projecting.

Finn: *There's something else…*

Another text followed. A video.

Finn: *I never wanted you to see me this way, but it was the only way I could think of to prove the Arrazi's existence, and the Arrazi's crimes. If this will help you, do with us what you will.*

I hit play. Finn's voice pierced Giovanni's starlit room. My heart lurched to hear it. Giovanni stood behind me to watch the video. We both recognized the room at Dr. M's.

"That man—" I started to say when I saw what Finn was doing to him.

"Yes. It's grotesque. We're watching the death of a poor innocent man—at the hands of your ex-boyfriend."

"He's not innocent."

"No shit. Finn is one of them no matter how he's helped—"

"I'm not talking about Finn!" I shoved the phone at Giovanni so he could see. "That man, the one he killed, I recognize him. He's one of the men who attacked us at my parents' house the night we dug up the ring."

Giovanni went silent as we watched Finn take the man's life in front of the walls that clearly showed what the Arrazi could do.

"I hate to say it," Giovanni said when it was over and enough stunned moments passed that we could speak again. "But it's excellent. It will condemn them forever."

"It condemns Finn," I said. He was sacrificing himself, outing his own kind—for me.

"He killed Mari, Cora. He's already condemned." Giovanni lifted my chin to look at him. "Isn't he? Please tell me that we're not back to that, that he won't come here and tear your heart in two. You can't possibly still love him."

I wrapped my hand around Giovanni's wrist and pushed it away. "Enough of this Team Finn versus Team Giovanni crap. How about Team Cora, huh? You are two different people whom I've loved *and* hated for very different reasons. He just signed his own death sentence with that video—to help *us*!"

"To help *you*, not us. You! Don't you see, you're the only reason he's ever helped."

"At least he's willing to do something for nothing."

Hurt spread through Giovanni's eyes and face.

"Finn can't possibly have hope for him and me." The words came out of my mouth, but I realized immediately that they weren't true. I saw Finn's hope at the airport. I heard his hope when we spoke on the phone about the hexagram and Xepa's symbol. I knew that underneath his question about why we would be so inexplicably drawn to each other was hope that the answer might bring us together.

It was me who'd given up hope.

I dug my nails into my palms in wadded fists. Kissing Giovanni was wrong. I'd thought of him like a life preserver, and he was that. From the first moment I'd met him, we'd bobbed together on the stormy sea. But if Giovanni was my buoy, then what was Finn?

Finn was the water. This substance that surrounded every part of me, that moved me, but that was also *in* me, part of me. Dangerous, too—a thing that could drown me. Most perplexing of all, it felt like we were made of the same stuff, and I'd never understand that at my most affecting moments with Giovanni, why waves of Finn crashed over me.

Chapter Forty-Four

Finn

The deed was done. I had no idea what Cora would do with the incriminating video. My fate was in her hands. She'd told me she was with Edmund Nustber. He was a platform, better than most, from which to hang my kind. If my actions took the wind out of the sails of her enemies, then it will have been worth it.

I had one goal left: to get the *Book of Kells* to her, and I'd better do it quick, because if she chose to show the video, the media—not to mention the police—would be after me as well.

As I drove to the crematorium with the body in my trunk, I kept thinking about what the man said. A woman and a man he couldn't identify had hired him. He'd previously worked for two people who acted like allies but truly weren't. Who *else* would have something to gain from knowing what those two vipers were up to? I was stuck in the middle of the Mulcarr versus Lennon families but—Christ... there *was* someone who'd want to keep very close tabs on Ultana and Clancy, someone for whom their war games were deeply personal...my mother.

My God. If Ultana *was* dead, what other woman would hire someone to keep tabs on me? My mother never could stand not knowing everything. The man had worked both sides before. It was possible he was taking jobs from both Lorcan and my mother now.

I wanted to knock my head against the steering wheel. What of the trust she recently gave by showing me my birthright, my history, in that room? For once, she'd treated me like a man instead of a cub she needed to handle by the scruff. If I was right about her using the man to keep tabs on me, then I was wrong about her trust.

Mr. Killian handled the body so efficiently it elevated my guilt to sickening proportions. Drive-through death. I left the crematorium with a drum in my stomach, beating out my remorse. From there, I went to Tilt's house to pick up Clancy's computer.

Rain—promised earlier in the day by heavy, low-hanging clouds—began to fall until it was pissing as I pulled into Tilt's neighborhood. Smoke rose from their chimney, and I sat in my car, watching it curl into the sky and wondering if Cora had seen the souls of those children leave their bodies like smoke of the living, proof of the fire in their souls, rising up and into the mist.

Burning within me were the fires of the souls I'd taken.

Sitting there, I realized I could vividly feel every one of them: the helpfulness and empathy of the fisherman, the ferocity of Mari's love and loyalty, the foul aftertaste of the man at Newgrange, and the bloke I'd just filmed at the facility whose soul was laced with disloyal ambition. They'd become a part of me. Perhaps my body was a scale that would tip in balance from one essence to another depending upon whom I killed.

I supposed it was true for regular humans, as well.

We were altered by the souls we let in.

I got out of the car and walked up to Tilt's door, realizing that it was ajar. I glanced at the dripping trees and felt the chill of the storm in the air and wondered why.

"How'ya," I called, pushing the door open and stepping inside. No one answered. "Tilt?" With each step of my boots on the plank floor, my apprehension rose. The untended fire burned low and smoky. It needed stirring. I went down the hall, past the pictures of my mate at every stage of his school years.

His parent's bedroom door was open, and his mum and pop lay draped across the bed as if they'd simply fallen asleep—but this was no sleep. His mother had her arms crossed over her chest. I ran to Tilt's room and found his slumped body over his desk. They were all dead. Gone.

Gone, too, was Clancy's laptop.

If they had simply dropped dead like so many others around the world, the laptop would still be there. It didn't bloody disappear into the ether! I backed out of the room and walked as calmly as I could to the car so as not to draw suspicion and drove away, my hands shaking on the wheel.

I'd caught the man following me, but this meant there were more. An Arrazi had done this evil thing. They'd obviously watched me drop off the computer, and while one followed me to the facility, another stayed behind to attack my mate and his family. Who? Who would have a reason to kill to keep anything incriminating from being seen?

Ultana, of course, but a dead woman can't give orders. I had doubt earlier but had dismissed it. She *had* to be dead—I saw her die. Yes, she told Cora she couldn't die, but Cora then confirmed that Ultana's light was gone. My stomach sank with the incongruous thought that we could have been wrong. Was it possible she was alive? Anything was possible in a world of magic powers and supernatural humans. Ultana's long life should have been impossible in itself, so was it too much of a stretch to believe in her immortality?

For this to be conceivable, Lorcan would have to be in on it. Lorcan had the body burned before Saoirse arrived. Could Ultana and her son be trying to fool us all? If he and his mother conspired to trick us all into believing she was dead, it would make sense that he placed a *geis* on his sister, so he could report back to Ultana what was going on with Xepa.

But then why would Ultana leave control to her daughter at all? If she wanted to fake her death yet remain in control, why not leave the control in her son's hands? Again and again, I felt I was putting together a puzzle without all the pieces, and the pieces I did have were void of any picture. I was blindly fumbling for the answers.

What the *fooking* hell was going on?

S aoirse called to see if I would be joining her for dinner. She said that she had good news. "I felt out some Arrazi, and there are more than a few who might be on our side. But I can't conduct a meeting with them without telling Lorcan." Her weighty sigh filled my ears. "Even telling you this scares me. I feel like I have a bomb strapped to my chest. One wrong move and...boom."

I agreed to go. There was the previous understanding that after dinner, we'd go and "feed" together. I'd have to tell her that I wouldn't be joining her for that portion of the evening. I'd had my fill.

"Is Lorcan not joining us?" I asked, hoping to see him, read his behavior, and try to sniff out what his involvement might be in Tilt's and his parents' deaths and the theft of my uncle's computer.

"I haven't seen him since this morning." A maid swooshed in with dinner on trays and Saoirse excused her politely. "What have you been up to all day?" she asked.

"I went to the facility where the Scintilla were being held for research."

Surprise creased her brows. "Why?"

"Your mother dangled what I want most when she sent me there. She said the facility was working on a manufactured way for us to have the energy we need so we wouldn't have to kill, and I wanted to see if there were records there that might indicate the extent of the research. It would solve everything, if it were true. The visit there with your brother hadn't gone"—I swallowed hard—"as planned. I went today because I wanted to poke around and see if I could find any files or documentation about the research."

"And you found nothing."

It wasn't a question in her voice but a surety. "Right. The place was completely cleaned out. It had to have been done very recently."

"Yes. I had the place cleaned yesterday. For *obvious* reasons. I had sensitive information there."

"*You* did?"

She smiled. "You know what I mean. My mother's sensitive information is now mine to contain. I had no idea that's what they were researching. If they were close,"—her eyes lit with excitement—"it could change our lives. I'll look at the records and let you know what I find."

Saoirse flattered me with appraising eyes. "Speaking of killing, you look *strong*."

Her comment reminded me of Cora's when we ran into each other at the masked ball in the crypt. It was slightly accusatory, but the truth was, Saoirse looked very well, also. "Yes, well, the opportunity presented itself."

"For me, as well. I think it's better," she said with a shy smile. "I'd rather we not think of each other that way."

There was a message in her tone that I couldn't be sure I was reading right. "How would you like us to think of each other?" I asked it because of her lingering stares, the way she touched her lips when looking at mine, and in the lean of her body when I was close.

Time had come to admit that Saoirse Lennon was "after me."

Her mother would be so pleased.

"Finn, I spent my life obeying my mother's dominating

will." Saoirse's eyes darkened as she looked at me, or rather, *through* me at her memories. "You have no idea how dominating," she said through a tightened jaw. Her eyes flicked back to mine. "She used to make us kill things, small things, animals and such, when we were children. Can you imagine? She wanted to harden us to what we'd become."

I shuddered. "Bloody hell."

"She used to tie us to chairs and plant herself against a wall and try, over and over, to be able to take from us without blowback. It never worked, but we felt it, physically and emotionally. It hurts to be attacked by your own mother."

"How do you feel about her death?" I tentatively asked, hoping to get an explanation for my mother's warning that Saoirse felt responsible for Ultana's death.

"I hated my mother. I guess—I guess I feel guilty because I wanted her to die, and I'm glad she did. She was wretched. My life with her was hell."

"Jaysus," I said, moving close and laying my hand atop hers. "I'm sorry. I had no idea."

"I was afraid of her. I had no choice but to play my part to appease her. Yet inside I seethed and resisted everything she wanted. She wanted you—for me—no... Let's be honest... I think she wanted you for her own reasons. Naturally, whatever my mother wanted, I resisted."

Her ginger brows curved over her fine nose as she struggled for words, fighting the truth that was pouring from her against her will. "Going to your house that first night was pure torment. To fight my mother, I had to fight my own initial response to you." Her voice shook. "I'll be God damned if you weren't the most intense and charismatic— this isn't coming out right." She looked so helpless it melted something in me. Her voice was soft, her eyes earnest and sweet, when she looked up at me. "I kissed you, Finn. Didn't that tell you everything you need to know about how I would like us to think of each other?"

She crushed her rose lips on mine before I could speak. This wasn't a girl who was having an internal battle or denying what she wanted. Confession had come hard, but now that it was said, she was free. It was in her unquenchable kisses, her soft hands against my face, the adoring and heated way she looked at me when I opened my eyes.

Her lips grazed my ear. "I accept you, Finn. For who you are. *What* you are. You never have to hide with me, or fight yourself." Her hands ran up my thighs as she kissed my neck. "Stop…fighting…yourself."

I held her by her upper arms and reluctantly, I admit, pulled away from her sweet mouth and her body, which curved into mine so delicately. "You've been so honest with me. You deserve honesty in return," I said, hoping she'd listen. "I will compare everyone on this earth…" Saoirse's eyes pleaded with me not to finish my sentence before she turned her cheek. "…to her."

Her seafoam eyes were bright with challenge and intensity. "I accept that. I do. Compare us, until you can't. Compare us, until you forget. We're the same. Meant to be together."

"If this is about that tarot card—"

Saoirse pressed my hand to her chest. "This is about my heart. Yours, too. I can feel it. Your heart wants something it can't have. But I offer something you haven't let yourself dream of because you're too busy wishing for things to be different."

Someday is a wish your heart makes when it wants things

to be different than they are.

"Damn," I whispered. Cora's words. She was right. Both girls were right.

"I offer you what *she* can't: total acceptance. I'm offering you my heart even though I know you might grasp it with only one hand while the other reaches for the past."

She was offering what everyone on this planet wants most: to be loved for exactly who and what they are. Why was my soul fighting it? Because it knew its place. "You're killing me, Saoirse," I whispered against the silk of her red hair.

"No, luv," she said. "Your memories are killing you. I can make you forget them."

If kisses were promises, then I'd made dozens to Saoirse Lennon before I inwardly cursed myself for being weak and wrong.

My excuse: I'd faced death and my future was grim as hell. What I hadn't imagined, ever, was the possibility of accepting what I was and trying to live a life in that paradigm. Saoirse offered me a glimpse of something that resembled normalcy. But to accept it would be wrong. I didn't want normal if it wasn't with Cora.

I stepped away from Saoirse, and the physical distance gave me clarity. I also owed it to Saoirse to tell her what I'd done. "I have to see my actions through. You want someone who's a condemned man?" I turned to face her. "I am condemned, Saoirse. The world just doesn't know it yet."

"What are you talking about?"

"The one thing your mother wanted—for the Arrazi to come out of the shadows, to be exalted, to finally have a seat at the table…I've done something to take that possibility away."

"What have you done, Finn?" She looked stricken, and I understood it. I threatened all Arrazi, of which she was one.

"I found a way to show how we kill." I pulled out my phone and showed her the video in all its disgusting glory.

"Good God, why?" she asked after it was over. Her face said it all: fear, disbelief, betrayal. She felt threatened.

"If the Arrazi don't abandon the genocide of the Scintilla, I will show the world what we are."

Saoirse slumped back in her chair, pale and shocked. Then she abruptly stood and went to the sidebar to pour a very liberal glass of whiskey. "*Uisca Beatha*," she murmured in Irish and downed a huge gulp. *Water of life.*

I was immediately reminded of the alchemical symbol for water of life, strikingly in between the Xepa symbol and the hexagram—*shatkona*—Seal of Solomon—whatever it was, whatever it meant, the triangles were everywhere. Tri—three—ever present in the mystery.

The alchemical symbol for water of life was two triangles pointing in opposite directions, just like the Xepa symbol; however, in the alchemical symbol, the tips were meshed together just enough to be called joined.

"What do you know about the Xepa symbol?" I asked.

"Nothing, really. Why?"

"What you just said reminded me of something, and I'd meant to ask you about the symbol anyway. The tarot card, the Two of Cups, has two people pouring water from their jugs into a single jug. See, it led me to do some research, and

I think the term 'Water of Life' is referring to energy. Not actual water, not blood, but our *life energy*."

"I don't see how the Xepa symbol has anything to do with that. I don't see how it matters," she said, tipping her glass up again. She was angry with me. Clearly, I'd shaken her up with my admission, and for that, I felt bad. She promised we'd be allies, yet I'd gone rogue and done something she would never sign off on. That, more than my admission about Cora, probably told Saoirse where I stood and with whom I'd always side.

"Maybe it doesn't matter," I conceded. "They're just symbols, right?" And I was just a boy whose every hope depended on it mattering.

Chapter Forty-Five

Giovanni

From another continent, Finn still managed to rattle Cora and insert himself between us.

If he was *gone*, she'd finally be free to love with her whole heart. Guilt pricked at my gut. He'd helped us, was still trying to help us, and having an Arrazi ally was potentially vital to our survival. So I swallowed down my pride and watched her leave. She said she wanted to "sleep on it", and while I was sure she meant his damning video, I couldn't help but wonder if she also meant us.

She stayed away most of the next day, killing me with her close distance. In the late afternoon she finally returned to me. She'd stayed up all night, she said, thinking about what to do about the video.

Cora texted Edmund, who was busy wiring the common

room for cameras to capture "a day in the life of the Scintilla," and told him to stay there; she had something to show him. She asked Mami Tulke to meet us at the common room, as well. Together, we walked over to Dun's hut.

"What, another Jesus painting?" Dun joked when we showed up and asked him to walk with us to meet up with Edmund. He'd kept to himself for the most part. Cora suggested that he probably just needed time alone to process— to grieve Mari and to grieve the life he'd once had. Everything had changed for all of us.

Edmund vibrated with anticipation, turquoise infusing his aura, as he climbed down from the ladder he was using to mount a camera from the corner of the ceiling. Mami Tulke had already shown up with Claire, Faye, and Janelle. A dozen or so Scintilla milled about or sat together, eating. "Should I ask the others to leave?" I asked Cora.

She stared at the Scintilla as she considered my question. "No. This affects them. For those who've never met an Arrazi in person, for those who still don't understand the threat, it will be *very* educational. Might convince any remaining dissenters. The more the merrier, as far as I'm concerned. In fact, can we get a runner to ask all adults to be here in ten minutes?"

"I'll do it." I ran from the room and went from hut to lodge asking everyone to please attend a meeting. The twins offered to split up and tell the rest, so I hurried back to stand beside Cora.

She was speaking with Edmund when I walked in. "My Arrazi friend sent me something," and then, meeting the eyes of everyone who'd gathered in the room, she said, "Something that proves the Arrazi's existence." She swallowed hard. "And proof of how they kill. I think he wants to use it to disarm the Arrazi, to strike them before they strike us. What I'm about to show you is graphic but might be something we can use, and it could take them off guard. It may be enough to send them into hiding."

The room snapped with anticipatory current. I gave Claire a kiss on the top of her head and sent her with a mom and a young toddler to watch a movie in the adjacent rec room. I had to protect her.

Edmund used a cord to connect Cora's phone to his laptop so we could all watch it more easily, though I noticed that she paced restlessly in the back once it started playing and didn't look at the video at all. It was all the more stunning on a larger screen, and when I looked at Edmund, he had an expression that was both fascinated and appalled, but he tapped a finger on his lips in a repetitive motion that told me he was thinking very hard about this as a journalist and how he was going to present it to the world. His aura showed ambition, but it was about knowledge and sharing it.

After watching Finn kill that man, the room was a vault of stunned silence. At first. With the first utterance of shock and horror, the room exploded into fearful chatter.

"This won't help anyone identify Arrazi on the street," Edmund said, quieting everyone down. "You'd have to reconstruct the whole world with walls like that."

"Right," I said, agreeing. "We could see auras and not be able to identify by sight an Arrazi who hasn't recently killed. But now the world will know the technology exists, and if the world knows about the Arrazi, it might scare them enough to lay low and abandon their mission to kill us and countless others."

Finn's action was brilliant, I had to concede that.

Cora unplugged her cell from the computer and started swiping at it. "I'm texting it to you, Edmund. There should be more than one copy, just in case."

"I can't wait to show this to the world," Edmund said. "It's big."

Cora's eyes were molten green fire, and her aura ticked with irritation. She spoke a muted but powerful warning, "You make a move without my approval and I will not co-operate with you any further."

Edmund fiddled with his phone to make sure the text came through and didn't meet her eyes. "I wasn't suggesting—"

"Sounded like you were," Dun said to him. "Cora didn't have to share this with any of us and, if you want to know the truth, I could live my whole life without seeing another murder," he said. I wondered if, when he watched Finn Doyle kill that man, he was thinking of how Mari had died so similarly. "Go off half-cocked with that video and I'll kick your ass."

Edmund laughed, but his nerves showed in his colors. "So now we're threatening each other? I'm merely saying that this is proof that someone's been party to the biggest conspiracy in history. The Arrazi and whoever is directing them might back down initially, but do you really think they're going to stop?"

Cora looked at me with her teeth pressing into her full bottom lip. Her eyes said what I was thinking. *They'll never stop… They'll never stop hunting you…*

"My ears hurt," Claire said, running in from the other room with her hands clasped over them and her eyes a mask of pain.

"I can do ear candling," Faye offered. "It helps earaches and congestion. I saw that they have the supplies in the medical room."

"You are actually offering to stick flaming candles in her ears?" Dun said, and Faye laughed. "And you're okay with this?" he asked me.

Faye said, "It's quite safe. I promise. I can do yours, too."

Dun waved her off. "I'm hot enough without fire shooting from my ears, thanks. I don't know if the ladies could handle that level of hot." It was the first genuine smile I'd seen on Cora's face in too long. I tried to remember the last time she smiled like that. "This, I want to see, though," he said, standing.

"Good with you, Claire?" I asked. She nodded, and the three of them left. Maybe Faye could get to the bottom of Claire's strange symptoms.

Raimondo grunted and tilted his head back. I thought he'd fallen asleep, because his mouth hung open. Then he said, "We're too late. No home. There is no home for the hunted."

Cora's eyes rounded in shock. "What did you—?"

Raimondo's head snapped up. He gasped. "We're found."

"What do you mean 'we're found'?" she asked, but he seemed to have slipped into a trancelike state, and she threw up her hands. "I *know* we'll be found. That's the worst part. Ugh, why can't people just live and let live," Cora said quietly. "We're not the ones hurting people, killing people. But we finally have something that might make our enemies submit."

The hairs on my arms stood on end. I met Cora's eyes, and they squinted into a question. *Something* had our hackles up. There was a sudden banging sound as a band of people, six or seven, stormed through the door into the common room. Four had guns. Most had regular auras, but two were deathly white and their energy filled the room like poisonous smoke.

As my heart pulsed wildly, I cursed myself for not already retrieving the weapons from the cave. We'd have them outnumbered if we had them, but we were too late. I prayed that Claire and the others wouldn't be found. With hope, Dun would have seen or heard something to alert him.

My arms and legs turned icy cold with fear. Whoever these people were, they'd found us, *all* of us, and they'd found Cora. Clearly that's who they were after, as more than one gun was trained on her alone.

A man in a tidy black suit strode in, his face plastered with an infuriating smirk, his focus on Cora. "Miss Sandoval, we do not submit. To man or"—he chuckled—"to *girl*. Only to God's will."

"Oh, *okay,* Cardinal Báthory," she said sarcastically, emphasizing his name. She knew who he was, and she wanted to make sure we did as well. "And I suppose it's God's will for you to come here and stick guns in the faces of innocent people?" Cora snipped at him with disgust in her words and in the look on her face.

This was the cardinal she'd met at the Vatican, the one with a Xepa ring, and presumably the one who gave orders to Ultana Lennon. The cardinal's gaze skimmed the rest of us, and recognition pinched his face as if he'd eaten spoiled food. "Mr. Nustber, I'm not surprised to find you here. Uncover a rat's nest and there's always more rats." He inclined his head to Cora. "I'd be more selective about whom you befriend, my dear."

Cora thrust her chin up, and I cringed for what might

come out of her mouth. "We were just debating who the big daddy rat was," she said with a jeering ring to her voice. "Then you come in here and confirm it. You threaten us, but I've got something on you. The world will know the truth about what the church has done, and it's about damn time."

The look he gave her was pure condescension. "You are too simple, child. Don't presume that my presence here implicates the holy Roman church."

"No, *Cardinal*?" she spat his condescension right back at him. "You're going to try and convince me this isn't just another Inquisition? History confirms the brutal actions of your office within the church."

"Incorrect. The Congregation for the Doctrine of the Faith has been in place since 1542, though that is simply when it was given an official title. It's had many names over the years, but our mission was in place *long* before that, long before there *was* a Vatican, long before there was a Rome! The hierarchy of the church is ignorant of my true mission and the true mission of every man who has ever held my position—to preserve the world's most volatile secret. I am one in a line of dauntless men who, over thousands of years, were tasked with this burden, and I take quite seriously the job of routing out and destroying the machinations of Satan. The sooner you devilish mutants are destroyed for good, the safer will be our world."

He was confirming that there was a society in place through history to hunt us down, to keep us a secret. I opened my mouth to rail at him, but Mami Tulke beat me to it.

"You think we were created by Satan?" Mami Tulke asked scornfully. "We who *give* life," she said, looking at Cora, "against those who…" Her eyes ran up and down the cardinal.

"Those who *take* life? Your machine is fed by fear. Fear divides us all, and people like you use that fear to make other creeds, other religions, other gods, wrong. It's the biggest divide among humans, it's poison, and you spoon-feed it to them."

"Are you suggesting the masses not come to the church to seek union with the Holy Spirit for their healing and salvation?" he asked Mami Tulke, disdain evident on his face.

Cora surged forward, facing off with the cardinal and putting herself between him and her grandmother. My body jerked to protect her. "Maybe we're *all* holy spirits, and if there's a God, he *or she* created us as such."

Cardinal Báthory and Cora stared hard into each other's eyes while all of us watched, our hearts thrashing. Her aura jabbed at him, belied her desire to attack him. He suddenly reached forward and plucked Cora's phone from her hands, causing her to reach to snag it away, but a gun barrel was thrust at her face, and she backed down. The cardinal pressed play.

Face white, jaw rigid, the man pulled out his own phone, took a picture of Cora's screen, and then dialed a call. "I've just sent you the photo of a young Irishman you need to find and deal with. Immediately. He's threatened to expose the Arrazi. Oh, and he also claims to have *the book*. Your life depends upon you eliminating him, getting that cover, and bringing it to me. Alert all Arrazi you can to immediately make way to *Rancho Estrella*, a hovel of a ranch in the Elqui Valley in Chile." His voice turned colder than before as his gaze swept over the Scintilla. "Do this and the Arrazi will get everything they've been promised and everything they deserve."

Chapter Forty-Six

Finn

My mother was the first person I sought out when I returned home, but she was in surgery. My questions about whether she hired that man to follow me would have to wait. Asking her in person was the only way I was sure to get the truth.

When I woke the next morning, I was thinking about my dinner with Saoirse. She had a way of getting inside my head and making me question myself. It was a classic head versus heart debate. My head knew that being close to Saoirse was smart if I wanted high-level information on what the Arrazi were up to. But my involvement with her had become more complicated than that. She played on my broken heart and made me wonder if a life with an Arrazi woman was possible; if I could have the semblance of a normal life, like my parents.

Admitting defeat to my heart felt like draping my head beneath the guillotine with my hands holding the rope. I'd never have the one person I truly wanted. I liked Saoirse, I had some attraction to her, but to pretend I felt more wouldn't be fair, to either of us. No one had ever struck lightning in my heart like Cora.

I had to be real. I had to stick with my higher reason and my strongest passion. So, after breakfast, I sat in the hidden room in my house and continued to research my theory about the water of life being a metaphor for energy. I'd also brought with me a shipping box, some random books from my mother's library, and the largest book I could find. That large book I intended to hollow out in order to conceal the cover of the *Book of Kells*. I'd then bundle it with the other books and pack it for shipping.

Hundreds of times, I pictured trying to get the artifact through customs on a plane, and I realized that the only way I was likely to get it to Chile was if I let go of it temporarily and shipped it hidden inside a box of books. It was an enormous risk, but if it worked, I could fly to Chile and pick up the box in Santiago, then take it to Cora.

There had to be a motive for Ultana to want to find the missing cover and destroy it. I was convinced Cora could charm the reason up out of the book when she touched it. With hope, our questions about our origins might be answered. If there was anything I wanted more than that, it was an answer for why we were created so hopelessly opposed.

Using a scalpel from some medical supplies my parents kept, I carefully cut away the inner pages of a large astrology book so that the illuminated manuscript would fit neatly within and not be damaged in transit. The book was placed in the middle of the haphazard pile of books, covered with packing materials, and then the box was sealed. I addressed it to a shipping store in Santiago, then carried the box to the trunk of my car before returning to the room and my fascination with the *water of life*. One simply had to type those words in a search to find intriguing examples to support my theory, and many of them came from arguably the most popular book in history.

Revelation 22:1 *And he showed me a river of water of life, bright as crystal, proceeding out of the throne of God and of the lamb.*

Revelation 21:6 *To the thirsty I will freely give from the fountain of the water of life.*

John 7:37 *Let anyone who is thirsty, come to me and drink.*

John 4:14 *But whoever drinks the water I give them will never thirst. Indeed, the water I give them will become in them a spring of water welling up to eternal life.*

Why would Jesus Christ talk in this manner? He was no aqua peddler. He was the savior, right? Who could argue that he was speaking metaphorically of anything *other* than *spirit*?

I'd been at it for hours and rolled my stiff neck left to right when movement from the security camera caught my eye. I watched Mary make her way past my concealed room to answer the door. I couldn't hear anything that was said, but two large figures stood in the doorway. There was something about Mary's posture that prickled my spine. She pushed the door closed, but they forced their way inside. Within seconds Mary fell to the floor. I leaped up. The men had dropped her without ever touching her.

Arrazi.

Disbelief and rage blazed through my body. Not in my *fookin'* house. I looked around the room for a weapon, but there was nothing but cabinets, a computer, and reams of our family's history. Nothing with which to defend my home or my… Jaysus, my parents!

Swiftly, like they knew the layout of the house, the men went straight down the hall toward the stairs that would lead to the bedrooms. I had no idea where my parents were, or even if they were in the house. I hadn't been paying attention. Last I saw of my father through the security camera was him heading down to the kitchen. I hadn't seen him go back up, but then, I'd been absorbed in what I was doing.

My mother appeared on the monitor at the top of the landing, and my body blasted with fear. Alarm showed in her eyes when she saw the men who'd taken the first few steps up the stairs toward her. Rather than run, she turned and looked directly in the security camera and held her finger up to her lips while shaking her head "no." I understood. She didn't want me to come out. She didn't want me, or this room, to be found. But it went against everything inside me. There was no way I'd stand by and watch while my family was attacked.

Never did my mother look so fiercely solid as she did at the top of those stairs, staring down the men who'd dared to enter her home. Dammit! This wasn't a time for bravado. Why wasn't she running? Before my hand even hit the handle of the door, one of the men drew a knife and plunged it into my mother's chest as he ran past her and straight toward my room across the hall. *My room?*

I yelled, and no one heard.

They were after *me*.

I slammed the lights off, carefully slid the door open, and stepped out into the hall, closing it behind me. I was absolutely torn about where to go first. I needed to check my mum, but I also needed a weapon to defend us when they came back out. Those men would not leave my house alive.

The closest weapon I could think of was Ultana's dagger in the kitchen. I ran full-out and found my father at the table, with the newspaper and leftovers. "Two Arrazi men are in the house, Da. They've killed Mary and stabbed—" I choked on the words. "My God, they've stabbed Mum."

The fork clattered to the plate, and he was on his feet and reaching for a biscuit tin over the fridge. *What the…* He turned around with a gun in his hand. "You stay here."

"No. If she's alive, she'll need *you* to help with the wound." I retrieved the dagger from its hiding place. "Either way, it's me they're looking for. She was simply in their way as they ran toward my room. Let's go."

He led the way out of the kitchen, flicking lights off as we went. My father was in battle mode. When we reached the stairs, we heard my mother moan, and both of us ran up the stairs to her. She leaned against the wall with her hand pressed firmly over the wound in her chest. Blood seeped between her fingers as she breathed in shallow puffs. Her eyes weren't panicked. I think I'd have felt better if they had been. They were resigned. "Out," she said to me through dusky lips. "Go."

"Ina, let me see," my father whispered, kneeling at her side. When he pulled her hand away, we knew. My hand curled around the knife, and I knelt to kiss my mother's forehead. *"Is breá liom tú."* I love you.

What else was there to say? Nothing else mattered. I shook with shock and rage.

As soon as I stood, one of the men rounded the corner and saw us. My father raised his hand, and the crack of the gunshot reverberated, making my ears ring. I leaped on the man with my knee on his bloody chest and my knife at his throat. "Who sent you? Why are you doing this?"

"If they want you dead," he sputtered, "you're already dead."

"They?" But the man's eyes closed forever.

"Finn!" my father yelled just as the other man grabbed me from behind with his forearm across my neck and a gun at my back. He spun me around to face my father, using me as a shield as he moved us toward the stairs.

My father stood and blocked the way. "You'll not take him."

The man fired at my father. It was too dark to see where he'd been hit or how badly, but he dropped to the floor over my mother and lay motionless. I struggled, but the man was too big and too strong and had the warm barrel pressed to my kidneys.

Why would someone want me dead?

"Where is it?" he hissed in my ear.

It? What, the book? I had nothing else of value to give him.

"Hidden," I said, unsure, desperate, and afraid. "In another house on the property."

He shoved me forward. "Take me." I dared a last frantic glance at my parents before he thrust me onto the stairs.

We trampled through the woods behind the manor and down the dirt lane that Clancy used to use with his beloved horse and buggy to get from house to house. I had no idea what I'd do when we got there. All I could hope for was an opening, any chance to fight. Instead of Clancy's house, I took him to the underground prison where he'd kept Cora's mother prisoner for over a decade and had kept Cora, as well. I tried to keep my hands steady as I recalled the code and pushed it in the keypad. The door slid open.

I led the man down the slanted walkway. "What the bloody hell is this place?" he barked.

"A place to hide things."

I stopped in front of the door where I'd first glimpsed Cora after my mother and I had found out where Clancy had taken her. The door was slightly ajar, and we stepped into the room with the ornate post bed, sheets still rumpled from use. Cora's grandmother, I reckoned. I scanned the room, looking for anything that I might use as a weapon. He had a gun. I had nothing. If I was fast enough, could I lock him in and get away without being shot? I needed to call an ambulance and the police and get back to my father.

If he was gone, dead—dead like my mother, then I had no one left in this world.

"Hurry it up!"

Next to the bed was a side table with nothing on it. If I could just grab it by a leg, I might be able to swing it at him before he got a clean shot, but I feared he'd fire at the first hint that I was reaching for the table. I knelt down next to the bed. For an absurd moment, I had a sudden memory of praying on my knees next to my bed as a child. Maybe those prayers would somehow coil through time and help me now.

I slipped my hand beneath the mattress and box spring, pretending to retrieve whatever it was he came for. My fingers lit on something hard, though, surprising me enough to yank it out.

"That there doesn't look so special," he said over my shoulder at the crude booklet that looked handmade. "No gold, no jewels." That's when I knew for sure what they were after.

I grasped the curved leg of the table and heaved it as hard as I could. He fell, the gun firing into the ceiling before skidding across the floor. I scrambled to pick it up and held it out with both hands. A slicing pain shot through my chest before the man blew backward across the floor. Having lost his weapon, he'd tried to attack my spirit.

I fired.

Bullet casings kicked onto the carved floor beneath my feet until the gun snapped open and stayed that way, rounds spent. I tossed the gun on the bed. The man was dead. His blood seeped into dozens of carved moons on the floor, and his eyes stared sightlessly at the small skylight in the ceiling. My body quivered with adrenaline. I had to get back to the house and find out if my father was okay. I turned to run, then saw the strange makeshift book on the floor. I scooped it up and ran as fast as I could, though my legs were rubber and my body shaking.

My father's frenzied voice called out to me in the trees.

"Da!" I yelled. "I'm coming!" Relief was a break in the onslaught of terror that had pumped through me since I saw Mary die at our front door. My mother was dead, I knew it; her last agenda wasn't to keep herself safe but to keep *me* safe, hidden. How could she possibly think I'd not run to defend her? Did she think I was a coward? That thought broke what was left of my heart.

Father and I called out back and forth through the trees and stumbled our way to each other, clasping into a tearful hug. "You're not hurt?" I asked.

"Superficially, yes. Bullet grazed my arm. I hoped he'd think I was dead so I could follow. Thank God you're all right, son." He sobbed into my hair, clutching me to his broad shoulder.

We made our way back to the house. "You've got to leave here," I told him. "Get away for a while. I don't think this will be the last of it."

"What do they want with us, Finn? The only person I'd thought capable of such evil is dead."

"Possibly," I answered with a pointed look. "When a woman tells you she can't die and believes it enough to run a blade through her own stomach, it might be wise to believe her."

"You can't mean…"

I nodded. "That's exactly what I mean. I killed a man who was following me. The man said the word 'she' when he spoke of a woman who'd hired him over the phone. I thought maybe it was Mum, but…"

My father shook his head, confused but somehow certain that I'd come to the wrong conclusion. "Your mother wasn't having you followed, son."

"The bloke I shot back there, he also said 'she.' That's why I now believe it could be Ultana. Can you really put it past her, Da? And Saoirse also told me that her mother was determined to obtain something very valuable, something—"

"Aye, the three Scintilla."

"No. Something that's been in the Mulcarr family for many generations." His head tilted questioningly. "The missing cover of the *Book of Kells*."

My father literally clutched his heart. "No…"

"I assure you, yes."

"Ina never told me," he said, as we stepped past my mother's body, and I choked down my emotions and continued to my room. My father sat on the edge of my bed, his body trembling. I picked up a blanket from the floor and wrapped it around his shoulders.

"I need to clean up quickly and get out of here. I have to go to Chile with the book. Cora's sortilege is to access information in objects by touching them. I have to get to her before it's too late."

"They came here looking for the book?" he asked, shock making his voice spongy. "How—how did they know we had it? Even I didn't know…"

My body froze. The only place I'd said anything about the book was in the video. How could anyone know of that video yet unless…?

Unless someone already had Cora.

My guess was that it was a woman we'd all believed to be dead. You don't watch for an enemy who's supposed to be rotting in hell.

Chapter Forty-Seven

Cora

This was shit.

From every angle.

We were surrounded by Arrazi, staring down the barrels of multiple guns, and a hit had just been ordered on Finn. He'd made that video to try to help, and this man wanted him dead for it. The jumps from enemy to enemy finally led me to the apex, the one person at the top who controlled everything. Arrazi, Xepa, and a literal Inquisitor from the Roman Catholic Church—those were the rungs of evil I'd scrabbled over only to end up here, having achieved nothing.

It freaking pissed me off.

"Theodore, come," Cardinal Báthory barked his order, and a young man, skinny, with a mouselike face scurried over. His aura was weak and tight around his body, but I recognized the Arrazi feel of it. "Theodore, I want you to identify the Scintilla in this room." He then inclined his head to another man at his right. "Go with him. You know what to do."

Theodore hesitated. "But sir, I can't be sure. I've never before met a silver—"

"Sniff them out like the dog you are!" Báthory roared, then pointed at me. "Start with that one. I suspect you'll find her quite different from anyone else you've ever tasted. Control yourself, though. I'm not ready for her to die just yet."

Rather than waiting for this mouse-boy to come to me, I marched up to him. "He calls you a dog yet he needs you to do his dirty work—and it is dirty," I hissed. "Without *you*, he is *just* a man."

"Silence!"

Theodore feared me. It was in his eyes, his shallow breaths. I was a wild thing to him, and he didn't know my capabilities. I vowed to myself not to show fear, not to cringe when he tasted my spirit. My chest split open. He took from me, puffing as he did so. His aura unfurled in white the way an Arrazi's did when they killed or when they took from a Scintilla.

"Good stuff, huh?" I gasped through gritted teeth. *Please let him stop in time.* My vision blurred and I felt light-headed. The attack abruptly stopped. He'd have a sortilege now, too. He was panting, clearly wanting more. The man at his side pulled something flat and square from his pocket with another item—a stamp? I flinched as he held me still by the back of my head and pressed the stamp firmly to my forehead over my mother's mark. "What the hell?"

Theodore walked toward Mami Tulke.

"Stop," I said. "Don't. I can point out the Scintilla in the room. You don't have to take from them."

Theodore didn't listen. Of course he didn't. He wanted more. "She is one," he said, standing in front of my grandmother. They also branded her with the stamp, which I now saw was two red triangles meeting at their tips—the Xepa symbol. It was inhumane, a God damned scarlet letter identifying us as Scintilla. The *other,* marked for being different.

He stepped in front of Janelle and I cried out as he took from her and she bent forward in agony. "She is not," he said, moving on to Edmund.

"I'm not Scintilla. You know I'm not!" he said with imploring eyes to the cardinal who simply nodded his permission for Theodore to take from Edmund's aura anyway. Edmund squared his shoulders, bravely, but when the attack started, it didn't stop him from clutching his chest and crying out. "Please," he begged and snapped back when the attack stopped.

"I am one," Giovanni said, squaring his shoulders and towering over Theodore with an intimidating glare downward. Theodore nodded his agreement, and the other man's arm rose to stamp Giovanni, but Giovanni shoved him away. He immediately bent forward, clutching his arms over his chest. The man with the stamp was Arrazi, too, and had no compunction about bringing Giovanni to his knees before he crushed the red stamp on his fair skin.

Cardinal Báthory seemed satisfied with the proceedings, and the sorting process continued. A Scintilla man I'd met earlier, Will, stood before the Arrazi with his nostrils flaring in anger.

"Search the premises," Báthory said after everyone in the room had been identified. His eyes practically gleamed with the reflection of the prize he'd found.

Will reached his arms out. "There's no one else!" Of course he was worried about Maya. No doubt she didn't come because of her objections, though many of the few who still opted for peaceful resistance had come to the common room anyway. Their curiosity earned them a red brand and the pain of having their aura attacked so that another Arrazi could obtain his supernatural gift.

A few of the Scintilla were not there. Adrian had already assigned watch at the road leading into the Elqui Valley. Ehsan was at the western end of the valley and Adrian at the eastern stretch of road a couple of miles from the ranch.

Cardinal Báthory dismissed Will with a nonchalant wave of his hand. "If there are no other Scintilla, then you needn't sound so panicked."

Two Arrazi men and an armed man led with his gun and they disappeared out the doors. We were all quiet, listening for screams or the sounds of struggle. My heart dropped to my feet when I heard the first scream.

Mami Tulke looked stricken and pale. They'd found the treasure my grandmother had kept hidden in this valley all these years.

The cardinal clasped his hands before him. "First order of business, now that we've got the riffraff sorted, is to return what you stole from the Vatican." He was speaking to Mami Tulke. She stared up at him with her hands planted defiantly on her round hips. "Let's not play games, madam," he said to her. "We have the video of the theft. We just couldn't trace you until your granddaughter landed herself all over the news. Once we tracked her family, we were able to identify you. Though, truth be told," he said, looking over his shoulder at me, "I should have known when you showed up at St. Peter's Basilica asking questions about the stolen hand. It was a news story that died quickly, yet you were sniffing around as if it were yesterday."

"Yes, I took the hand," Mami Tulke said. "The pieces are in a jar at my house."

"It's not the hand that I want," he said, condescendingly. "And you know it. Marble is so plentiful in Italy, it practically falls like fruit. You found what we've been searching centuries for. Michelangelo Buonarotti left mocking clues all over the premises. If you ask me, the mangy artist was given far too much freedom to run amok on Vatican grounds. In the last decade, it was found that he'd had a very expensive and rare key made. The maker was a man who was later imprisoned for necromancy. It was then we narrowed what we were looking for—a key rumored to have an hourglass made of rubies and enchanted so as to threaten the authority of the church." He moved closer to her and bent to eye level. "Where is the key?"

I lifted my sleeve and showed him my marking.

"What's your meaning?"

"Your key."

"What is your sortilege?"

"Psychometry." When I saw that he didn't know what that was, I rolled my eyes. "Object memory."

Perception bloomed in his eyes. "What did you see in the key?"

"Your. Bad. Deeds."

"Do *you* know what the key opens?" he asked in such a

way that I didn't know whether he knew himself.

"The key didn't open anything," I lied. "It simply record-ed what you've done to persecute people and corrupt what is supposed to represent a loving God. Michelangelo had a sense of humor, right?"

"Where is the key now?"

"Home. In Italy. Sunk to the bottom of a channel in Venice. Why don't you go and dredge it up like the bottom feeder you are."

The cardinal's eyes bulged like he wanted to slap me. The key I'd hidden in Mami Tulke's garden, at the base of a tree like I'd found it in California, wasn't the point anymore, but I didn't want him to know that. What *was* important was the painting it hid. Cardinal Báthory had my phone in his pocket. I had to assume it was a matter of time before he looked through my photos and texts with Michelangelo's painting of Jesus and Mary. Would it *matter* to him? Would his acidic hate for the Scintilla be diluted by knowing that Jesus was one also? Or maybe he already knew. Jesus *had* been murdered.

"You and you," Báthory said, pointing to two men. "Stay here and make sure no one leaves. Theodore and I shall take the young woman to a more private room where we might convince her to be more forthcoming."

"I've told you everything I know."

Giovanni dashed forward and was aurically attacked by Theodore. My heart wrenched to see him struggle to stay upright. Despite the ravaging of his aura, he managed to sputter a question. "How do I know you won't kill her?"

Cardinal Báthory ducked his chin with a grimacing smile. "You don't, son."

Edmund pulled his hands through his crazy hair. "Do you really expect us to believe that you're going to let *any* of us live after this?"

"Cora's *hope* that I will may make her very cooperative." He chucked me under the chin. "Hope is a good thing to have in a crumbling world, no?"

I was pushed from the building into the dark.

Chapter Forty-Eight

Giovanni

I watched, helpless, as Cora was led from the building. Where would they take her? What would they do to get information? My chest felt like it had been pounded by fists of ice. I had to find a way to help her.

Cora finally got her answer. Whether he was acting alone or not, a church official was in charge of the mission to eradicate us all. The sick feeling in my gut told me it was simply a matter of time before he did. I had to help her before it was too late. Not only were armed men guarding us, there was another on watch by the door. Scintilla sat motionless, wearing worried expressions, heads blazing with the red stamp.

Marked for death.

One hour ticked on in excruciating silence. Then another. At one point, Maya was shoved in through the doors by a gunman along with a few more hidden Scintilla. No sign yet of Dun, Faye, and Claire. I could only hope they were hiding and would stay hidden.

Will ran to Maya and clutched her against him. More time clicked slowly by, and my worry amplified until my body droned with tense static. I tried to imagine where Cora was, where Claire was. I tried to imagine getting out of the situation, living beyond it, because what else could I do? Hope wasn't something they'd suck from my body until they took my soul with it.

Meaningful glances passed around the room. I watched the two telepaths I knew of nod their heads every so often and wondered what they were saying. If only I could do the same. I'd give a signal to every Scintilla to use their sortileges in any way possible to take down our captors.

I made a steady and slow progression toward Will and Maya.

Will and I gave each other looks, but we had no way to communicate anything but distress and desperation with our eyes. He'd start to get up, but then Maya would pull him back down, her hand on her belly. Every time a guard turned his back, I moved another foot closer, ignoring Maya's steely glare and faint shake of her head. With my every covert move sideways, her hand gripped his tighter.

Maya thought I was moving toward her man, but *she* was my target.

I moved again, and the Arrazi's eyes snapped to me with a suspicious glance. He started to approach, but his phone went off, stopping him. Tense moments passed as he listened. "*Si*," he said into the phone with a visible swallow. He placed the phone in his pocket and glanced around the room as if he were surveying a pen of cattle. Heads dipped as his examining gaze passed over them.

An older man sat on the end of a bench and dozed against the wall. A resolute breath blew from our Arrazi guard as he approached the sleeping man with measured steps. We all watched in stupefied horror as he siphoned the life from the old man's body. Inwardly, while I was gutted by the act, I reveled in one thing: we were being punished for Cora's non-cooperation, which meant she was still alive.

Amidst the cries and movement of heads that had turned away from the killing, I pressed the final two feet through the crowd to Maya, praying my new location would not be noticed.

"Adrian and Ehsan are out there," Will whispered into my ear. "They'll help us if they can."

"*If*," I whispered. None of us had phones since we'd been searched and stamped. "In the meantime, we have to help ourselves. There are many Scintilla with powers in this room, but none so lethal as Maya's." I whispered to Maya. "You want to protect your unborn child?" I said urgently, glancing down at her fingers.

Maya jerked her eyes to me with a stabbing glare.

"You saw what just happened. They'll kill you and the rest of us before your child ever breathes." Will elbowed me, hard. I hated to say it and was breaking his confidence, but it might be the only thing to get Maya to do what needed to be done. She'd have to throw away her guilt and her pacifism and use her sortilege.

We needed Maya to take her gentle hands off her belly and her husband and use them on our enemy.

Chapter Forty-Nine

Finn

Sixteen hours.

That was my estimated travel time from Dublin to Chile *if* I made the flight. I booked it and ran to say good-bye to my father who, when I'd last seen him, was dragging the dead man from the stairs to "deal with the body." I found him in their bedroom where he'd placed Mum's body on the bed. He wasn't ready to say good-bye. Nor was I, but I had to.

Looking at her, I choked back a sob as I realized that life necessitated my moving forward. Why was it that, in those last moments of seeing her face, every negative trait that had irritated me about her instantly transformed to positives? My mother was a queen, and I kissed her fingers before lightly touching mine to her cheek.

I ran. As much *from* as *to*. I ran.

There was no time to ship the box of books. I'd have to risk getting the cover through security with me. My first hurdle. I packed it into my carry-on with Gráinne's journal and the strange handmade journal I'd found under the mattress at Clancy's. I had to assume it had been Cora's mother's as well, but I hadn't had time to investigate. I'd look on the plane. If I didn't make this flight, I'd not be able to depart until the next day, another twelve hours away. Twelve more hours to fret about Cora and who might have seen my video and ordered those men to my home. I wouldn't use my phone to check on her. I'd mentioned the *Book of Kells* in the video, and I'd sent her that video by text. If that's how they tracked me, then I hoped they'd think I was dead.

It was damn hard not to call Saoirse, but if my suspicions were correct and Lorcan was in cahoots with his mother to fool everyone about her death, then I needed them to be in the dark about what happened to me. I felt for Saoirse, bookended and threatened by her vile family members. I pictured her, tiny and flailing, in their giant clutching grasps.

Ultana wasn't going to get me *or* the book she coveted so much, if I had anything to say about it. I sped down the road toward the Dublin International Airport, making it there with enough time to go through security and catch the flight.

If I ran my ass off.

If I didn't get stopped in security.

Security was surprisingly light, and I overheard someone say it had been that way since the deaths and the natural disasters everywhere. International travel had plummeted. The world was becoming a scarier place, and when the world gets scary, people tend to batten the hatches and group together with those they know and love.

Tears filled my eyes when I thought of my mother—murdered. Did I have a right to grieve her when I'd been a murderer myself? I'd taken someone's loved ones. So had Mum. Were the gates of hell flung open for people like us when we died? Again, I questioned: how could God persecute us for doing what we were created to do?

Underneath my anguish and questions was a simple truth: she was my mother. I loved her. I'd never see her again, nor did I know if I'd ever see my father again. I was so alone. Even adrift on my boat, I knew people cared if I lived or died. Loneliness, true loneliness, is knowing you could disappear forever, and it would be as inconsequential as a star blinking out.

I shuffled in line, waiting to put my bag on the security belt. My heart beat hard and fast as I approached the scanner. I passed through, no problem, but my bag was somewhere in the hull of machinery being looked at by a bespectacled man with droopy lids and something spilled and crusted on his blue shirt. Even I could see my books outlined on the screen as he leaned forward slightly and peered. He opened his mouth to speak, and I did the only thing I could think to do. I hit him with a slicing surge of my energy. Enough to make him cough and gasp. A coworker asked if he was okay, looked at the line of people waiting behind me, and rolled the belt onward as his friend gasped and caught his breath.

I grabbed my bag from the belt and ran to the gate to find they were boarding the flight already. I was scanned through and fell back into my first-class seat moments before they closed the doors.

It occurred to me that an Arrazi must plan flights the way a smoker plans his fix. I was glad my need was satisfied or it would make an already tense flight much worse. Once we'd leveled off and I was free to get up, I pulled the homemade book from my duffel. It was a crudely made journal, cobbled together with two uneven pieces of board that looked like they had been one piece, broken in half. Sheets of paper simply lay inside, and the whole thing was bound with a black silk ribbon.

There was everything from scribbles and drawings to random notes about Gráinne's day. I had to assume it was Gráinne. She was the only captive he had for over twelve years until he took Cora there. And Gráinne had a history of journal keeping. It would make me happy to return both of her journals to her daughter. If she was alive.

Many of the book's pages were blank. I flipped through them and noticed writing in the back. Entries, like an appointment book, filled numerous pages. One heading said, "Estimated Date" and it saddened me. I couldn't imagine what it was like for Cora's mother, being ripped from her family, living underground for years with no sure sense of the passage of time, having an Arrazi attack her over and over again and…my God…and *other* people? Passed around like candy?

Entries showed numerous visits from a few select people. I realized that the limited Arrazi Clancy had "shared" Gráinne with must have obtained their sortilege. The same Arrazi had fed from her often, sometimes brutally, as one note indicated:

Clancy brought a female Arrazi today. My soul leaped to hear the gentleness of a feminine voice, as it had been so long. But she was just as ruthless as the worst man. It's a heartless woman who can see another woman in captivity and not be moved to help, to not see herself in the mirror of my suffering.

I am not another woman to her. I am the "other," a lesser being, succor for the stronger race.

She came back again—the brutal one who bites with no control, like a baby snake. Her voice is soft, but she rips my soul like her hunger is fueled by anger. Maybe it is. All hunger is a hole to be filled.

The records about the woman intrigued me. Ultana? But that wouldn't make sense. Clancy hadn't wanted Ultana to know what he possessed. There had been the Arrazi woman with him at Newgrange, the one I'd knocked out. Surely, Clancy was taking a risk by allowing other Arrazi in on his secret. What he'd done had given them their sortilege, yes, but how did he know he could trust them? Who would take from a rare Scintilla in secret and not tell the all-powerful Ultana Lennon?

While my body begged to sleep, my mind was on overdrive. I drifted but woke more than once with a panicked gasp from dreams of my mother looking down at her bloody robe, her face a mask of impassivity that she might have given a patient so as not to scare them. Was it habit? Was she doing it for me? In another dream, she wore the same remote expression, but her body had become Ultana's body, in the tomb, with the hilt of a blade jutting from her stomach.

She'd gotten up, pulled the knife from her gut, and walked from the tomb.

The attendant brought me whiskey, and I downed it in one gulp, finally slipping into a deeper sleep.

A s one of the first to deplane, I couldn't see everyone who was on board, but I felt an unnatural gust on my back—rank winds of Arrazi energy. I didn't want to look behind me and catch the eye of someone I might know, so I ducked into a novelty shop in the terminal and watched the passengers file by. I thought I recognized two Arrazi in the crowd. They'd been pointed out to me by Saoirse at the Xepa party, but we'd all been wearing masks, so I couldn't be sure. There was something about the way he guided her by her elbow that struck me. *Shite.* What were the odds that Arrazi suddenly needed to board a plane to South America? How many others, from how many countries, might also be converging on this place?

This was bad.

I clutched my bag handle with white knuckles as I went through customs and proceeded to rent a car. Having the cover of the most famous illuminated manuscript in history was bigger than possessing a priceless piece of Ireland's history—enough to make anyone nervous. But it was more than that; it was *our* history—the Arrazi and the Scintilla. Why else would my mother's family keep it for hundreds of years? Why else would it be Ultana's most coveted prize? Those men had tried to kill for it. If I could just get the gilded cover into Cora's hands to find out if I was right.

I looked behind me and saw the Arrazi couple from

earlier renting a car as well. If Ultana *was* dead, who would be summoning Arrazi to Chile? Then again, if Ultana was alive and her son was helping her, then she could still run things from behind a curtain.

I pulled up Mami Tulke's address. The radio blared as I drove through the hills of the Elqui Valley. The BBC reported that the hunt for the missing "miracle worker" was ongoing and that there were suspicions she might have headed to South America. They knew that Cora's stepmother, Janelle Sandoval, had flown to Santiago not two days ago. The whole world was closing in, including the media and the Arrazi. My fingers gripped the steering wheel.

My phone startled me when it buzzed with a text from Saoirse: *Hi. Been quiet over there. What are you up to? My brother is acting strange, and an email came to my mother from an undisclosed recipient that she should go to Santiago, Chile. I have no idea...*

Confirmation. The Arrazi were on their way.

I couldn't answer. Not because I wanted Saoirse to worry; I didn't trust her brother. I didn't know what to believe or who to trust. I could only listen to my gut and follow it to Cora.

I stopped at a roadside stand to buy snacks from a kind-faced Middle Eastern man who was sitting on his car with a sign that said: LAST STATION FOR FIFTY MILES. COLD WATER. FOOD. The closer I got, the more warily he eyed me. The closer I got, the more tantalizing his aura felt. My steps faltered.

This man was Scintilla.

What were the odds? Cora had thought perhaps she and her grandmother and Giovanni might be the last. He gave me my goods and my change without meeting my eyes when he said a perfunctory, "Good day." Did he know what I was? Was that why he feared to look at me?

"Everything good?" I asked, and his head jerked up, surprise written on his dark features. "You look nervous."

His nut-brown eyes scanned my face. "One can never be too careful," he finally answered. My head whipped to the side when I thought I saw the shadows of two men running toward me but, strangely, nothing was there.

"Yes, there're surely nutters in the world," I said. I took a step backward. "Not *all* of us are to be feared, brother," I added pointedly, hoping he'd hear the message beneath my words. It somehow seemed important that he know. He said nothing more, and I turned to walk back to my car, feeling his eyes on me. Pulling out, I saw him pick up and speak into a handheld radio. A warning? I'd like to think that if there were more Scintilla in this valley—a wonderful surprise if it were true—that there was a system of warning in place against the Arrazi.

Nights on the Irish Sea had nothing on the stars in this place. I tore my gaze from the sky to the map on my phone and raced on to find Cora. The closer I got, the harder it was to keep calm. My body pulsed with fear and agitation that made my breaths come fast and shallow, and my heart beat unevenly. The directions said I was approaching, just a thousand feet to my turn. An adobe house came into view in my headlights.

A light was on in the house, but when I knocked, nobody answered. I knocked again, louder. Where could everyone be? After sitting in my car for ten minutes, I noticed a wooden sign in the yard that said *Rancho Estrella* with an arrow pointing east. A few minutes later, I'd arrived. I parked in front of a strange polygonal-looking building, one of many. Some other similar buildings dotted the ranch—large tent-like structures—lit from inside like glowing igloos. The place had an air of abandonment that made my neck prickle. I walked through the grounds and came upon a large building with lights on inside and shadows of people moving about. I knocked. Shuffling and scurrying sounds came from inside before Mami Tulke answered the door, peering out at me through a narrow opening.

Her eyes rounded and she said, "Now is not a good time for visiting friends."

I cocked my head sideways. "Is it a good time for visiting enemies?" I asked with a teasing smile.

Her nostrils flared a touch and she said, "Plenty, I'd say," and shut the door in my face. Someone grabbed me by the scruff of my shirt and pulled me down and to the side. Dun had his finger over his lips, but I heard words, spoken as clear as if he were speaking them: *help us. Please help us.* I shook my head. Dun hadn't said a word, but someone inside was using telepathy to communicate with me.

As I'd feared, something bad was going down. Cora? Where was she?

We heard the click of the door. Dun pulled me around the side of the building and we peered beyond the wall. The barrel of a gun stuck out first and then a man's head. When he looked our way, he paused and we jerked back. Had he seen us? Slow footsteps approached, and when he rounded the corner of the building with his gun trained right on Dun and me, I did what came naturally.

I ripped his soul out and swallowed it like gristle.

Chapter Fifty

Cora

Death was a cliff they threw me over again and again only to be reeled back up before I plunged to the bottom.

The night had turned to day and night again. Hours of questions, torturous repeated attacks on my energy by Theodore, the cardinal's yelling until he became so frustrated, he'd called and ordered the first Scintilla to be killed. That was the moment I considered the cost of my defiance. I feared my death, but I feared causing the death of others much worse.

Cardinal Báthory would snip off the flowery heads of hope until no buds remained.

"I don't know what you want from me," I gasped, reaching toward Theodore with an outstretched beseeching hand, but he was powerless and submissive to his boss. It was the cardinal who answered.

"I want to know what you were looking for at Vatican City. What brought you there? Centuries of concealing the Scintilla's existence from the world and an unremarkable teenage girl gets close enough to rip the veil from everything. How?"

"Yeah, I'm so unremarkable that the entire world is looking for me because I brought those kids back from the dead."

He reared back and struck me with a stinging slap across the face. "Almighty God brought those children back to life!"

Blinks of light dotted my vision as my head recoiled. Rage rattled my chest and spread shaking hot fury through me so that I actually fantasized about being an Arrazi so I could kill him. "I *love* how you persecute those who can do extraordinary things. That's always been your office's M.O., right? Stomp out the pesky magic conjurers so you can keep the masses in the dark about their own magic. What ever happened to '*these things that I do, you can do also*'?"

His pasty face bunched into an incredulous knot. "You can't *possibly* be comparing yourself to our Lord and savior, Jesus Christ," he spat.

"I am," I snarled, low and serious, stepping purposely within his reach, pushing him to hit me again. I'd rather take his blows than the Arrazi, Theodore's. Theodore stared openmouthed at our exchange. My voice was low, nearly a whisper. "Isn't that what you're afraid the key will reveal?"

Buying time was what I'd hoped to do, hoping someone would get to the weapons stash and meet force with force. Maybe Dun, Adrian, or Ehsan? With every hour it seemed less likely, and I fretted endlessly, thinking about the Scintilla held in that room for so long. The cardinal pulled out his phone again and lifted his finger to make another call.

"Okay!" I said, wincing at the smug smirk that erupted on his face. "Enough, you freaking jerk. I lied. I hid the key. I know what it opens." I bit my lip and said, "I'll take you to it now."

He lowered his hand. "This is your last opportunity, Ms. Sandoval. If that key is not in my possession very soon, every single person at that ranch will pay for it with their lives."

"Yes. Okay." The snowy caps of the Andes glowed under the moonlight as we left the hut, got into a car, and I directed them up the road toward the cave. I didn't believe the cardinal knew what the key hid, but I did believe he knew that Jesus was Scintilla. Why else would his society have gone to such lengths to cover it up for so long? Their whole system would fall apart, of course. Can't have a bunch of miracle workers roaming the world, giving of themselves to help people, to save people. Not when the church is supposed to be the *only* door to salvation.

I figured Cardinal Báthory wanted the key so badly because he needed to know for sure that there wasn't some damning scrap of evidence that would come back to haunt him after the Scintilla were dead. There was evidence, but a fat lot of good it would do when it died with me.

I was going to die. That was clear.

So were the others.

I had no doubt we'd pay with our lives regardless of whether or not I gave him the key. He'd already ordered Arrazi to come. It was like inviting wolves to a sheep convention. The cardinal said my hope was what kept me compliant.

In that moment, hope became erroneous and *I* became dangerous. Cardinal Báthory neglected to consider that my sudden absence of optimism freed me to reach for more defiant emotions. When all hopefulness was lost, it was replaced with reckless desperation.

I might go down, but I was going down fighting.

Within minutes, we pulled over at the base of the hill where I best recollected the cave to be. Giovanni and I had marked the spot by tying the scrap of tartan Finn had given me to a tree branch on the road. It fluttered in the air as we climbed from the car. My body was sluggish from being attacked, but my heart still managed to chug faster as I thought about what I wanted to do once we reached the cave. If I could get my hands on a gun, the first bullet was headed straight for Theodore. If I managed to take the Arrazi out first, then it was Báthory and I. One human versus a very pissed-off Scintilla.

It was on.

I stumbled the last bit of the climb toward the entrance to the cave. "You'll each need to push the boulders aside," I said, my voice raspy. "I'm too weak to do it." They glanced dubiously at each other but moved to position their bodies against two large stones and began pushing. My fingers twitched against my thighs like a runner at the starting line. I stood as close as possible so that the moment the rocks were out of my way, I could dart in and grab the first gun within reach. It had to be a gun. It had to be fast.

Quickness and accuracy—well, luck—that's what I needed. Soon the rocks were rolled away and the cave opened like a giant eye, its center a black slit of a pupil staring me down. Daring me. As soon as I thought the eye was wide enough, I slipped sideways through the crack in the rocks and fumbled around in the blackness. My fingers hit nothing but the grit of dirt. Both men yelled amidst their scuffling and grunting as they pushed to get inside.

Their silhouetted forms in the entrance blocked out the sky behind them. I scrambled toward the back as the cardinal yelled for Theodore to kill me. "It's a cave. Just reach for her soul and take it." Crawling on my hands and knees, my hands finally hit a box. I ran my hands upward and felt the loaded handgun I knew was sitting on top. I grabbed it and rolled over, pointing it blindly at their shadows. I couldn't see who was who.

A light flashed on and lit the cardinal's face staring down at the phone he was using to light the cave. It also lit me, on my ass in the dirt, with two hands wrapped around the grip of a gun. I pulled the slide back and released it like Giovanni had showed me, and just as I felt the icy pull of Theodore's energy rip into me, I fired.

Chapter Fifty-One

Giovanni

Immediately after I tried to urge Maya to use her sortilege to kill one of our captors—preferably an Arrazi one—we all heard a knock at the door. There was a bit of arguing with the Arrazi and the armed men trying to decide what to do. Mami Tulke suddenly stood and said in a hushed voice that she should answer it and calmly send any innocents away. To whoever was at the door, she spoke clearly and loud enough for our captors to hear she wasn't giving furtive messages or seeking help. All of us wondered who was on the other side and hoped they'd somehow help us.

I noticed the telepath, Alejandro, sitting with his eyes closed like he was deep in meditation. Could I dare to hope he was using his sortilege to send a message? That was the kind of fighting back that we needed.

Apparently suspicious after she'd shut the door, one of the armed men, non-Arrazi, shoved past Mami Tulke, opened the door, and stepped outside. The only sound we heard was a faint thump, like a sack of potatoes being dropped to the ground, and then nothing. The door stood open with the sound of night and cool, fresh air pouring in.

"Who was out there, old woman?" the Arrazi asked.

Mami Tulke dismissed it with a hand wave. "A farmer from down the road. Nobody. You heard me send him away."

When the first gunman didn't return, the other men in the room with us exchanged worried glances, first at each other, then at the Scintilla. "I'll deal with it," the Arrazi said with barely masked bravado. "If anyone moves, shoot them."

"You're sure?"

"Very," he said, eyes roving the room. "But start with the non-Scintilla. The cardinal has plans for the others."

Plans?

One foot out the door, he yelled, "Hey!" The word flew from his mouth, and he flew backward through the air striking the wall hard enough to knock him out. The other man pointed his gun toward the door. I acted quickly, raising my hand to pull the gun from his grasp. It sailed into my outstretched palm as Dun rushed in the door, followed by... Finn.

"It's another Arrazi!" someone yelled.

"It's the killer from the video!"

"He's a friend," Dun shouted back, looking at Finn and clasping his shoulder. Finn's searching eyes frantically scanned the room for Cora. I swallowed down familiar exasperation at their connection.

He also looked thunderstruck, and I wondered if he

knew, and not just from the stamps they used to identify us, that nearly everyone in the room was Scintilla. He confirmed it when I ran over. "This room is buzzing with energy." His chest was heaving. "I had no idea there were so many left. Where's Cora?"

"She's not here. They took her, man. We don't know where."

"I have an idea where," Dun said. "Just before Finn arrived a couple of minutes ago, we heard a gunshot up on the ridge."

His meaningful glance told me it was probably near the weapons cave. Why? My stomach thudded to my feet. God, that girl... "Let's hope *she* lured them there." It killed me to imagine them taking her onto a hillside to shoot her. "Only one shot? You sure?"

"That's all I heard, but then things got kinda gnarly in here, so..."

"What do we do with this guy?" Will said, motioning to the unconscious Arrazi on the floor. "Tie him up?"

"That won't do you any good," Finn answered. "When he comes to he can literally kill you with his hands tied and blindfolded."

"So we know what we need to do then," Will boldly answered, looking Finn over with a mildly suspicious expression. "Go look for Cora," he said with a jerk of his head toward me. "We'll deal with the Arrazi." Will and Maya exchanged looks, and I was certain she'd had a change of heart about using her sortilege.

"Where's my daughter?" I asked Dun.

"I hid her with Janelle and Faye in the supply shed on the far side of the gardens. They should be all right there for a while," Dun said. "It was Claire who made us realize that something was up, man. She kept shaking her head and saying that something didn't feel right. That's when I snuck out and saw the men come in. That girl of yours has got some kind of hereditary mojo."

"You're the guy on the video." Edmund interrupted us with his hands on his hips, assessing Finn like a casting director considering an actor.

Finn's eyes narrowed curiously at Edmund before recognition widened them. "You're the guy from the back of all those books."

Edmund grinned. "I'm glad as hell you just showed up, but why are you here?"

"Only ever be one answer to that question, mate," Finn answered.

"We all saw that video you sent. It's why everyone is staring at you so fearfully right now. I'm just going to assume the guy you killed needed killing. I think it was a smart move and, truly, the only way I can show the world what the Arrazi are doing. With Cora's permission, I'm doing a documentary on everything." Edmund raked his hands through his wild hair. "There's light and dark in everyone, man. Even you. I really believe that. You wouldn't be here to help if that weren't true."

Finn shrugged. "Thanks."

Will and two others set about dragging the Arrazi outside as Dun, Finn, and I ran to Finn's rental car. Edmund yelled for us to wait for him and leaped in at the last minute with his camera. "You look at me like I'm annoying you now," he said defensively, "but I got everything that happened in that room tonight on film. If we make it out of this alive, it will be seriously incriminating for the cardinal."

One shot. One shot. Two men and one shot. *One girl.* My knees bounced as I directed Finn toward the cave. I'd left the Arrazi's gun with Will so he could defend the group should more Arrazi arrive. I was in the unbelievable position of being glad that Finn was with us. He was a deadly ally, though less so against another Arrazi. That little dog, Theodore, was with Cora and the cardinal.

"This might be a goose chase, man," Dun said, rubbing his brow with a thumb and forefinger. "Anyone could have shot off a round up in these hills. What if she's back at the village? We could be driving *away* from her."

Finn growled in frustration and sped up.

"There," I pointed as we came upon the spot with the tartan flapping from the branch. "Behind that car," I said with a sinking feeling. Finn got out and pulled three books from a carry-on bag in the trunk. "Why are you bringing that? This hardly seems like the time — " He shot me a shut-the-hell-up look. It had to be the book he'd mentioned on the video, the thing he'd told Cora he was bringing for her to touch. But why was it so urgent? We had to *save* her before she could use her power to access its memories.

Trying to be as quiet as possible, I led the group up the shadowy, uneven path. To my ears, we were the four horsemen of the apocalypse galloping up the hill. We dared not use a light, so we stumbled along until the mound of the cave came into view, reminding me of the mounds of Newgrange. A faint light moved around inside the cave like someone was using a phone or a very small flashlight or lighter. We snuck closer to the opening, and I saw the dark outline of a torso in the dirt. Someone small. All breath left my body as I rushed forward. Finn was also scrabbling next to me toward the motionless form. My phone buzzed in my pocket and everyone stopped moving, nearly stopped breathing, hoping whoever was inside hadn't heard it, or us.

Finn's eyes hadn't left the body on the ground, but he became very still and seemed to be reaching out with his energy to feel something from the body. He shook his head no, but I didn't understand if it was an indication that it was impossible for him to feel for a life that was already gone or if he was trying to say it wasn't Cora. I took a tentative step closer to the cave, my eyes shifting from the light inside to the body. A cloud drifted off the moon, shining just enough light to see that the face was not Cora's.

The Arrazi, Theodore, was dead. Pride roared through me. This had to be Cora's doing.

I tore my gaze away to quickly read the text. It was from Ehsan, whom we'd positioned as a lookout at the market fifty miles down the west end of the road.

Arrazi are coming!

Chapter Fifty-Two

Cora

Stabbing pain shot through my ears after I fired the gun in the cave.

Shaking, I moved to stand but never took the barrel off Cardinal Báthory. Blue-yellow light shone up on his face. He had pulled out a phone to light the cave, but it was my phone, and the astonishment on his face wasn't for his fallen Arrazi pet. It was for something on the screen. He actually seemed unconcerned that a gun was pointing at him.

"What is this?" he asked, flashing the picture of the painting at me.

"That's what your precious key was hiding."

"This means nothing," he said. "It's simply an artist's interpretation of Jesus and the Blessed Mother. Proves nothing to a world who knows nothing of you," though his quaking voice belied his fear that it did mean something. A whole hell of a lot.

"Oh, they know of me," I reminded him. "I'm big

news, or haven't you heard? You and I both know it means something, which would explain why you look like you're gonna piss yourself. Imagine for a sec, the whole world seeing that painting, and then the whole world seeing the Arrazi in front of the Kirlian wall on the video. Imagine showing the world a *Scintilla* in front of that wall. Proof. Your secret's out." I watched what little color he had drain from his face until blue smudges under his eyes were the most remarkable feature on his face. "What's the matter, Cardinal? Suddenly afraid your place in heaven isn't so secure?"

His chin thrust up pompously. "I am bound as prefect by oath of my office. I am bound by the duties entrusted to me from a long line of dedicated guardians in the Society. I am bound by the word of *God*." The way he slammed his fist on his palm with that last word reminded me of a little evil bully who once terrorized entire nations with his emphatic speeches. He was in the business of genocide, too.

"Do me a favor, count the number of races and creeds and people of diversity your *office* has persecuted. Can you do it on one hand? Your oath is to homogenize the entire world, and I don't believe God would create a world so varied so that one group could condemn His creations to death. You're killing Scintilla, and there is no *godly* reason to do so." My hand steadied on the gun. "But I'm just an unremarkable teenage girl, right? What do I know?"

A tumble of feet and bodies entered the cave, startling us both. I scrambled backward until my body hit the back wall, pointing it at the newcomers. The cardinal spun to shine the light on the intruders, and every cell in my body sighed with surprise, then relief.

Finn and Giovanni both looked at me warily. If his

camera didn't hide Edmund's eyes, I'm sure I'd see the same dubitable expression from him. "Why are you all looking at me like I'm a toddler with a gun? You saw the doormat previously known as Theodore, didn't you?"

"Put the gun down, luv," Finn said. "You're shaking like a leaf. It's okay now."

"You don't need to kill him for me. I can defend myself. I can defend the Scintilla." I didn't know where the petulance was coming from, but now that he so unhelpfully mentioned it, I became aware of my violent shivering. I took a breath and calmed my body with resolve. I was ready to eliminate this bully in an Italian suit. The top of the pyramid needed cutting off.

"You're about to get your chance," Giovanni said. "Ehsan says the Arrazi are on their way."

"I worried about that," Finn said. "It's sooner than I thought, but there were two on the plane with me, and Saoirse Lennon confirmed—"

The cardinal laughed, interrupting Finn. He opened his mouth to speak, and I lunged forward with the very real urge to stuff his open mouth with black steel. Both Finn and Giovanni held their arms in front of me, blocking me from getting too close. "What the hell?" I yelled, frustrated. "I'm the one with the gun! He's just...just...human..."

Human. That one word deflated me. I wanted to kill this ignorant human bastard and had spat the word like it was a lesser thing. What did that make me?

"Giovanni, will you take the gun and keep it trained on this man for a few minutes?" Finn asked. "Cora, I have something I need you to see, and I don't think it can wait. It might answer every question our two races have, and if there's a way to stop this, I want to know. If the Arrazi are coming, our time is up."

"What about Cardinal Báthory?" I asked. "He's the one Ultana took orders from. He's the one controlling the Arrazi and using them to kill innocent people."

Finn looked Cardinal Báthory up and down. "I think he deserves to die in the same manner he's condemned so many to death. Your soul won't belong to God," Finn said, stepping close to the cardinal and staring hard into his eyes. "Your filthy soul will belong to me."

Chapter Fifty-Three

Cora

Edmund's camera lit the cave like he'd invited in the sun. I blinked against the glare. Reluctantly, I gave Giovanni the handgun, which he pointed at the cardinal while muttering something to him in Italian that made the cardinal's eyes widen.

Finn held out three books. I recognized one immediately that made my heart soar—my mother's journal. "The other is your mother's as well. It's the big one I need you to open right now. It's the missing cover to the *Book of Kells*," he said, and the cardinal took tiny steps forward, eyes hungry.

"You," he gasped at Finn. "You were supposed to be dealt with."

Giovanni put a stop to that with a kick to the cardinal's stomach, sending him staggering backward.

I lifted the cover and found a jeweled book cover hidden within the cutout pages of the larger book. Back when Giovanni and I had been looking for my mother's journal at Trinity College, I remember seeing signs for the exhibit for the *Book of Kells: Turning Darkness to Light*. We didn't view the exhibit then, and I knew little else of the famous book. Through my mother's memory of those words, I'd known I was in the right place. How odd that she would hide her journal in the place that housed what might be *the* missing piece of our history. Did she have any idea?

The jewels reflected the light like colorful, otherworldly eyes. Every shade was represented in the gems, every basic tint of a human's aura. Astonishingly, the gold cover was emblazoned with the triple spiral. Without hesitation, I pressed my hand to it.

I flew backward in time, a vortex so strong that my stomach lurched. I might have screamed, or thought to scream. I was winded *and* I was the wind. Less a vision than a transportation back through memory and time to a further truth. I was thrust through centuries, beyond the creation of the cover, beyond the birth of countries and many religions and even the birth of Christ, until I came to a violent, tumbling stop. Instantly, I recognized where I stood.

Brú na Bóinne.

I was in the tomb at Newgrange, watching a person, neither man nor woman, but an epicene being of pure light, walk with outstretched hands toward the stone carving.

The triple spiral.

In the flickering torchlight the person placed both hands on the stone. Swirling white energy flowed from the being's hands into the rock, illuminating the labyrinthine spirals with liquid light. *White* light. Pure, luminous, beautiful. The white light didn't scare me.

The being turned and looked in my direction, maybe at me, or through me, like looking at a memory. I gasped in recognition. Though it wasn't something I recognized in the face—it was in the spirit—I realized that within this one being were two halves of a whole. Finn and I were in this body of light. At some point in history, we were *one*.

We were wholemates.

Alive and together in the most significant way two people can be. I cried out for the inexplicable beauty of it. This made no sense. The being looked at the stone and seemingly back to me with an expression like it wanted me to understand something vital now stored in the rock. But I'd already tried that. The truth had been worn away.

Pain tore through me as I witnessed their body suddenly split from the center—a great rending of the light being from one whole into two. I felt the searing rip of the soul in my cells. Thousands of voices cried out in agony so that I wanted to cover my ears.

It was the worst tragedy to witness. It was a separation more destructive than injury, more painful than missing a loved one.

More damaging than death.

Now, two irrevocably altered beings stood before me. Un-whole. One, a luminous silver, the other, pure white. They looked sadly at each other, turned to walk away, and somehow I knew that they would have many reincarnations, in different bodies, in different forms of being, and that spiritually they'd replay this split over many lifetimes. That they *had* done so. *We* had done so, would live and die over and over again, trying to find ways to "turn the darkness to light."

Their light faded into pinpricks, like fading stars, until I could no longer see them. "Wait!" I ran forward, tears blurring my eyes, but they were gone. I'd lost them again.

Wait...

Tingling energy ruffled outward from the stone next to me, caressing my aura, snagging my attention. Light still clung to its arched crevices and wafted from it like smoke from a lightning strike. The being had infused the object with thought and memory, leaving information that only I could retrieve. I knew it as my hand hovered over the spirals. *I* could unlock the secret.

Of course! Everything had led to this moment. I felt, *knew* how time coiled and wound, bringing souls within reach again and again until they fulfilled their soul's task. This moment was *my* task.

Not something without but something within. It wasn't a *literal* key or what it unlocked that would tell the absolute truth. I could know the truth with a touch. I could read the history.

I was the Light Key.

I pressed my hands against the stone and a voice rang out, so lovely and so full of truth—like the tolling of a bell, rain on trees, the howl of wind—that the sound of it choked me with tears. The voice sounded around me and within me, became part of me.

> *We've forgotten our wholeness in the wilderness of Earth.*
>
> *In this land of duality, one polarity cannot exist without its relative opposite. We have been the*

baby's first cry and the old man's last breath. Good and evil, pain and pleasure, fear and contentment, binding and loosing, trust and skepticism, the depths of despair and heights of ecstasy. We've known war and peace, and we've experienced hate and love.

Over time, the balance tipped toward the great, hungry darkness.

We came to heal, to demonstrate balance so that the spirits of Earth could rise in vibration, consciousness, and light. Our greatest task was our greatest failing. We were corrupted. Split. We've come to believe in our separateness and have forgotten our wholeness just as mankind has forgotten.

Join. That is your fate.

Fail again and you fail this world and all of its inhabitants.

Another image flew to my mind of two beings, facing each other—light coming from the heart center of one, willfully joining with the energy from the other. The meeting of their auras was cataclysmic beauty. Their energy expanded from two spirals of light, which fused together into a third spiral, a third energy, and exploded in one loving mass of light as incandescent as the sun.

I tore from the ecstatic vision, crying and aching, fearing the unknown, yet...*knowing.*

Everyone was silent. My ears rang with the quiet astonishment in the air. It was my vision; how could they look so moved? "What?"

"It was like a trance or something. You channeled a voice," Edmund said. He stood behind his camera and swiped his cheek on his forearm. "It was the most beautiful thing I've ever heard."

I sat back on one of the ammunition boxes and hugged my knees. I knew what had to be done. I saw it. It was such an impossible reality that I doubted it even as I'd seen and felt the overwhelming beauty and truth of it. Also, the end of life as I understood it.

"What did it mean?" Edmund asked. "I mean, we all heard it, but—"

"The Scintilla and the Arrazi were never supposed to be enemies. We—we were once one. We are *supposed* to be one."

Giovanni blew out a thin breath.

"Cora, what do you mean?" Finn asked, his voice soft, his eyes alight with an optimism I didn't feel. He may have heard what I heard, but he didn't see what I saw.

"Joining. I think—it might be hard to explain—I think I'm supposed to give freely of myself to an Arrazi."

It *had* to mean my death. Maybe our death. I didn't know. All I saw was light.

"It must be equal—consensual—done with openness, trust. Done in devotion to a higher purpose. As you reach, I give. We meet in the middle. All I can say is that it was terrifyingly beautiful." Tears welled in my eyes again. I teetered near hysterics. I felt like I'd just witnessed my own cataclysmic metamorphosis. There was peace in knowing the truth, but it was a big chasm to jump from knowing to doing.

"You want to know why I believe this could be true?"

Finn asked. He had everyone's attention. "Think back, Cora. You *gave* to me twice. Once, when I didn't realize you were doing it, and once to save my life. It was your choice. *Your* will. Done with..." His voice softened and he pierced me with his honeyed eyes. "...with love."

I sat with those words and realized the truth of them.

"It didn't hurt you or make you weak."

Remembering those moments with him, seeing them in this new light was a different kind of magic. He was right. It hadn't hurt me to *give* to an Arrazi. It hadn't hurt me to give to Giovanni when I brought him from the edge of death. It was bliss to give to those children.

Pain was in the taking. Pain was when it was against my will.

"The Arrazi and Scintilla are never to join!" the cardinal shouted. That one outburst, so very telling.

"It's what *you* don't want to happen," I said to him. "Right? Set us up as enemies on the opposite sides of your chessboard? Fight to the death so that the vision could never come true? But this isn't a game!"

The cardinal shrunk back.

"*Coniunctio*," Finn said in an awestruck voice. "I saw a tarot card—"

Giovanni rolled his head forward before looking up in exasperation at Finn. "Are you *kidding* me? Tarot cards? This conversation is making me angry."

"Go on," Edmund said to Finn. "I want to hear."

"The Two of Cups. The card I saw showed a man and woman pouring water from their own vessels into a joining stream. The card is supposed to signify—"

"Reconciliation of opposites," Edmund said, nodding.

"Yes. Every time I looked up reconciliation of opposites, it would always turn up alchemy. In alchemy, the metamorphosis necessary for true enlightenment is to recognize the duality and to join them, to take opposing forces and combine them. I kept thinking that it doesn't get more opposing than the Arrazi and Scintilla."

"Convenient theory when you're the one who'll benefit from Cora's light being sucked into your own," Giovanni said, clearly disgusted.

"You were right to be thinking along those lines," I said to Finn. "Right now, we are duality expressed in human form. But we didn't start that way. I saw them...us. We were once more evolved beings, the physical and spiritual embodiment of yin and yang, who came to demonstrate that we can unify duality and advance mankind, but we were corrupted.

"Arrazi, Scintilla—neither one is better than the other." Even as I said it, and met Giovanni's doubtful glare, it was hard to believe. The things we'd seen, experienced...

"We're both necessary if we want to end this. The truth about three is the union." I looked pointedly at Finn. "The reconciliation of opposites. We are supposed to bring the light and the dark into balance and demonstrate to the world that we are *one*. My dad was right. We can heal the planet of its imbalance. Our job was supposed to be to help the world see that they have both inside them and can save themselves with the balance of their disparate halves."

"Don't listen to her blasphemy," Cardinal Báthory hissed. "Like Eve, she seeks to poison you all."

I stood and pointed at him. "I want you to shut up. Quit pushing that tired crap."

I turned away from him, weary of the dogma and

hypocrisy. I faced a bigger challenge than him. Up until then, the biggest challenge of my life had been a quest for the truth, to discover the reason we were *what* we were. That paled in the face of the task of convincing two opposing races, enemies, of the unbelievable truth.

We literally had to be willing to join energies, unite, and die in order to save the world.

Chapter Fifty-Four

Finn

E veryone stepped out for a moment while I dealt with the wrinkled sack of self-righteous man in front of me.

The more I thought about it, the more dots he connected. Ultana had returned from a trip to Rome the night Saoirse started turning Arrazi. Xepa's party was held in Christ Church, and we'd entered the church through a hidden tunnel where Ultana was handed an invitation by a priest. Ultana herself had implicated the church. In fact, those were her last words.

As long as there is a God on their altar, they will never stop hunting you.

At the time of the party, I'd wondered how she'd garnered such privileges from the church. If this cardinal was the one Ultana reported to, then it was proof that someone deep inside the church was involved.

"Arrazi scum," he hissed. He dropped to his knees, closed his eyes, and began murmuring prayers in Latin. The show angered me enough to throw my energy at him like I was tossing an anchor into the black sea.

"Without me to stop them," he gasped, "your fellow Arrazi will act on my last order. They will kill every last Scintilla."

I halted my devouring of his aura long enough to consider what he was saying.

"And after they're dead, your kind will die as well. I'm the only one who can stop it."

What was he saying? He was going to use the Arrazi and then turn on them? Was that his plan all along? I pulled him to his feet, deciding on a different fate for him.

"Finn," Cora's frantic voice made me jump. "Ehsan texted again. He says a line of cars is snaking down the highway, headed this way. We have less than an hour. We have to go!" Her gaze slid over the cardinal, who was wheezing and holding his chest. "What about him?"

"I've got a new plan for him," I said, hoping Edmund had been taping our interaction moments before. That guy's camera was like another limb. But if the cardinal was the only one the Arrazi would listen to, then taking him back with us might prove valuable. I said to him, "If you say anything to the Arrazi other than what I tell you, that highly painful experience you just had will be magnified until you feel nothing ever again."

Giovanni skidded back into the cave. "The weapons..." he said, with a desperate slice to his words as he looked around. I didn't blame him. The Scintilla had no real defense against an onslaught of Arrazi. Judging from the stacked boxes and crates of guns and ammunition, however, we couldn't possibly move it all fast enough. The only gun we had was the one Cora had used.

Cora tilted her head back in thought. "Okay," she said to Giovanni, "Dun and Edmund, go back to warn the others. Take the cardinal's car. We'll get some of the weapons and be there as quickly as we can."

Giovanni stopped Dun as he started out of the cave's entrance. "Until we get there, all they'll have are their sortileges. Tell them to work together to use them."

"What about running away?" Dun asked. "Hell, I'm tempted."

"They will hunt us down. They've been given an order. We fight or we spend our lives running. And Dun," Giovanni said, his voice even more grave, "keep Claire hidden. No matter what."

"Part of me thinks the weapons are a bad idea," Cora said. "It's incredibly aggressive and threatening in the face of what we have to do."

Giovanni harrumphed in response.

"Didn't you hear anything I said back there?" she said. "We have to *join* with the Arrazi. We have to convince them to—"

Giovanni was already tugging on the lid of a box, trying to open it. "What, Cora, to *die*?"

"The only people who care about saving the world are fake ones in the movies. Most people care about what's personal to them, saving themselves and those they love. How do you think you're going to talk the Scintilla into abandoning their survival instincts? It's crazy. You know who'll be on board? The Arrazi. We offer ourselves up like sacrificial lambs, and they'll line up to devour us."

I listened quietly to their debate, but I had to admit, I saw Giovanni's point yet also wanted to refute it on a personal level. "*I'm* willing to die to end this," I said. "But I'm not willing to take your life, Cora. I can't do it. I can't kill you."

She blew out an exasperated breath, and her voice dropped low, sad. "I know what I saw. If I can't even convince you two, how am I supposed to convince everyone else? It's *why* we were created. We've been searching for a reason, and now we know that reason, and you two want to blow it off."

I squeezed her hand, ignoring the dart of Giovanni's tough stare. "I want to blow off any idea that involves your death."

Her crackling green eyes—full of sadness, despair, but also fierce determination—pierced mine. She was on the verge of crying. Her hands clutched the front of my shirt, and I was sure she could feel my heartbeat through the fabric. "You think I *want* to die?" That one desperate question hung in the air of the cave and pressed down on all of us.

"We do this, or *everyone* dies. Wrap your head around that. My father might not have had the whole picture, but he was totally on the right track. Everything in this world is falling apart, and it will get worse. Humans are destroying one another, and they're destroying the planet. But, Finn, you *have* to believe me, *we* can fix it."

"We just have to be willing to die together," I whispered. I'd do anything for her, anything. I'd die myself. But she was asking me to take all of her beautiful energy. Cora was essentially begging me to kill her. And what if it didn't *fookin'* work?

Her forehead dropped against my chest, and Giovanni turned away, busying himself with weapons. "You and I will have to be the first. With hope, the others…" She looked at Giovanni. "…will follow." Her face tilted up. "We have to be one. We're the example. For this to work, we have to join." A sardonic puff of a laugh slipped from her lips before she said, "Trust me enough to die with me?"

Chapter Fifty-Five

Giovanni

I'd give anything to have seen the vision for myself.

We'd all heard the words that flowed from Cora like she'd channeled a wraithlike entity—and the message *was* beautiful. Prophetic. And I fervently wished it to be untrue. Cora was so sure. Conviction hammered iron into her words, her voice, and her eyes as she looked up at Finn. That killed me. Partly because I knew what it was like to have her against my chest, looking up at me, and it wasn't me she was looking at now.

I unclenched my fists and moved some handguns into a box with a few rifles, wondering which box it was that I'd seen the knives and whether to even bother. Finn and I each lifted one side of the box to test the weight. It would be cumbersome getting it down the hill to the car, but we'd manage. "We have to hurry," I urged.

The cardinal kept his back to the cave, pinned there by Finn's reaching aura. Everyone startled when we heard what sounded like faraway explosions, but within seconds, the ground rumbled beneath our feet, tipping the cave like a snow globe and sending pellets and powder of dirt onto our heads. The shaking threw us all off balance, and I saw Cora grab for a large ammunitions box to steady herself but was tossed backward.

The quake was much worse than the previous. It felt like the entire world was splitting in two. "Out!" I yelled, sure that getting trapped in that cave was the worst thing that could happen to us then.

We all made for the opening. Cora pushed through first, and I followed. I turned to see one of the large boulders roll toward Finn, who had pushed Cardinal Báthory out and was slipping through the opening himself. The boulder was on target to crush him. Charged by instinct, I felt the power of my sortilege surge up my body and through my hand as I sent the rock on another trajectory. Finn watched the rock barreling toward him and saw it suddenly veer away. Our eyes met—gratitude—amidst the rumbling and cracking and another sound… Screaming?

I wheeled around. The absence of Cora was more startling than the fact that the earth was unceasingly tearing and ripping around us. I had a sudden flash of Claire and shuddered to imagine her huddled in a garden shed with Faye and Janelle. The women would do what they could to protect her, soothe her, I knew that. But would I ever see her again? I should be with her. That same protective flare also existed for Cora, and I had no idea where she was, but the yells for help were hers, and I had to find her.

It was still too dark to see. Everything around us was moving shadow and sound, a funnel of commotion and noise—and somewhere in the middle of it was the girl I loved. As quickly as it began, the shaking stopped and Cora's voice became the loudest thing around us. She was a bit farther down the hill, and as we scrambled toward her cries, I nearly fell into a split in the beige earth that started as a narrow seam and expanded into a gaping ravine. Finn grabbed my arm just in time, and we both realized that was where the shouting was coming from. Cora was down there.

"Help me!" she yelled, sounding so much younger and so frightened. "I'm—I'm down here." Both Finn and I used our phones to light the chasm and peer down, shocked at what we saw.

It was a narrow gap in the earth, ripped open in the quake. Cora was easily fifteen feet down, maybe more, and wedged between the walls of dirt with her hands pressed on either side of her and her scratched and dirt-caked face staring up at us with terrified eyes.

"Stay with her," Finn said. "I'll run down to the car to see if I can find a rope or any branches long enough. "*Shite*," he said, looking around. "Báthory's gone."

"We'll find him," I vowed but with a sinking, hollow feeling. "Don't bother looking for branches. No real trees up here. Just scrub," I said, to let him know not to waste time. "Go." I looked back down at Cora and called, "We're going to get you free. I promise."

"It's so deep, G…" Sounds of her struggling to climb up only to slip back down tore at my heart.

"I know, *bella*. I know. Finn's going to see if he can find a rope." Without the additional light of Finn's phone, I could barely see her moving. She was just a voice, speaking straight to my soul.

"I'm scared."

"Don't be. I'm with you. I'll never leave you, Cora."

Finn's footfall approached as he ran back up a few minutes later and slid onto his knees next to me, empty-handed. "Nothing." He sounded frantic. A full minute must have passed as we both tried to think of a solution.

"What? Tell me," Cora said, her voice shaking.

Finn leaned forward, his fingers gripping the edge. "Keep calm, luv. We're working on a way to get you out."

"What way? There is no way. I'm too deep."

Silence.

Finn slammed his palm on the ground. "Bloody Christ!" he yelled and looked at me with tormented eyes. "I'd trade places with her in a heartbeat."

Like a bird swooping over our heads and dropping the brick of an answer on my head, I suddenly knew what had to be done. I could get her out. I could save her. "Cora, I want you to put your hands tight at your sides if you can. Keep them there."

"Why? I don't underst—" But she did. She did understand, and that's why her words left her. "G, *no*! You can't. Lorcan's curse. You do this and you'll die!"

"There has to be another way," Finn said, also grasping my choiceless choice.

"I won't let you," she said through tears.

My own chin was trembling. "You can't stop me."

"You stubborn ass! Go with Finn. The unification can be the two of you." Her words were clipped and choppy through tears. "You can join. Do it. Please. Do it for me."

"Either way, I die, Cora. You said it yourself. And I'd rather die trading my life for yours."

I didn't wait for responses, or arguments, regrets, or fears. I couldn't. I pushed all of my strength and focused every ounce of energy within me to lift her body up. It was difficult. I could feel the tug on my energy, taking everything I had. Slowly. Carefully. I used all my power to pull her from the ravine, and when her face appeared she gasped the air and… no…not gasping…sobbing. Shaking her head no. Pleading with her green eyes. She hung in space, suspended there, biting that beautiful pad of bottom lip while tears made white tracks on her dirty skin.

Finn wrapped his arms around her waist and tugged her body onto the dirt where we knelt. As soon as her knees hit the dirt, I felt weak and winded. My body tilted, and my back hit the dirt with a thud that rattled my teeth.

"Giovanni," Cora whimpered, hovering over me. "Why didn't you listen?" she cried against my lips. Sweet. So sweet were her tears and her mouth and the unique spirit of herself, which she tried to gift me, but it was useless. Her energy was weak, scattered, and spinning off her ineffectually. "You told me once that nobody does something for nothing. You didn't have to die for me. Why?" Her question had such anguish in it. It was a guttural cry to the universe from someone who'd lost too many.

It took all the strength I had to lift my hand to her face and curl my fingers over the ridge of bone at the back of her head. I'd need the last of my strength to comprehend that this was the last kiss. This was time stopping. This was good-bye.

"Love is not nothing." Beyond the stars of her eyes, my eyes found the heavens above. "It's everything."

Chapter Fifty-Six

Cora

I was only aware that though Giovanni seemed to slip unconscious, he was still warm, and I didn't want to let go. I didn't want to leave him on that hill to grow cold. I didn't want to tell his daughter that he'd never come back and be her daddy.

How could I have a life without him in it? Giovanni taught me what I *was*. Beside him, I got to know my truer self. I sobbed into the crook of his neck and whispered a hundred apologies for the love I never fully gave.

I *never* gave him what he gave me.

"I'm so sorry," I heard Finn murmur from behind me. He pressed his hand to my back. That one touch was also a reminder. Time. Time was an enemy almost as ruthless as the Arrazi. *They're coming*, time whispered. *Hurry*.

I tried to stand but wobbled with shock and grief as I looked down at Giovanni's peaceful face, eyes forever closed. Finn steadied me. Led me silently down the hill, careful where we treaded lest the earth swallow us. It was still a hungry beast. We knew it by the weaker aftershock that hit before we reached the car.

"Let's just hope the quake slowed the Arrazi down, too," Finn said, opening the door for me. My mind wasn't entirely with my body as we drove. I was disassociated, detached, much like that time in the hospital when my limbs floated against the mooring weight of my head and trunk.

Of course I was split. Part of me was still on that hill.

"Nothing I say can make you hurt less," Finn said. "I know." The headlights split the darkness ahead of us. "I haven't been able to tell you—anyone—the Arrazi came to my house. They murdered my mum."

My mind rejoined my body like the snap of a rubber band and registered my physical grief, but also Finn's. "Oh my God. Finn, I'm sorry. Why? What happened?"

He shook his head like there was no explanation that would suffice. "At least Giovanni's death had purpose," he said, tilting his head in regret. "Hers was senseless. They were after me. After the book. What Giovanni did," Finn said, glancing at me with earnest eyes, "was the bravest and most noble thing I've ever seen." His jaw clenched. "He loved you."

My chest heaved with pain. "Yes."

The road followed the curve of the river, and we let silence have its palliative say before Finn spoke again. "I hope Nustber shows the Scintilla the video of you touching the book cover. They might be just as hard to convince,"

Finn said, pulling me more to the present and preparing me for what was ahead.

"I think some will be swayed. Some won't. Same with your kind." As soon as I said it, I regretted it. He was not apart from me. No longer could I think *us versus them*. We were supposed to be two halves of one coin. *Wholemates.* "Sorry." There was no crevasse deep enough for the well of guilt in my heart. One man had already died for me, and I was asking another to do the same. Possibly. I didn't know what we'd "be" afterward. But *I* didn't hand us our fates. This task was set before us thousands of years ago, and time was running out to complete it.

Finn's hand hovered over mine for a split second before he laid it softly down. "We'll convince them together."

Edmund greeted the car as we pulled up. His eyes scanned for Giovanni, but I couldn't say the words. Not yet. He slung his camera up to his face. "I have to ask just one question."

I held up my hand. "Not now, Edmund. This isn't the time. Is everyone okay?"

"Mostly, yes. Please Cora, I don't think there *is* another time," he said, desperate. "This could be your only chance to speak to the world the way you wanted. I can tell the story and have enough to show evidence. But the world will want to hear from *you*. I'm mad at myself for delaying."

I sighed. I'd keep my word to him and it *was* important. I wanted the world to hear the truth from me. "Go," I said, motioning impatiently for him to roll. "Quickly."

"Okay." Edmund slid into reporter mode. "Big question first. The world saw you save those children from the clutches of death. The church has said that it was an act of God, working *through* you. Do you think you are an instrument of God?"

"If we're all created in God's image, then I'd say I'm a reflection of God. And so are you. We all are."

Edmund looked moved by my answer, pulling his face away from his camera with an exhale toward the ground but quickly refocused and continued. "The tool of those in power is often secrecy. The existence of your kind—givers of light, the Scintilla, and the others, the takers known as Arrazi—has been shrouded in a vast conspiracy that has spanned thousands of years, at least. What would you say to those who might still wish to deny reality, who wish to deny that what we are revealing to the world isn't real?"

"I'd say ask yourselves, have you ever inexplicably felt your energy drain or lift depending upon who you're with? Then you've had your *own* taste of the lineage of the Scintilla and Arrazi. Beyond that, all I can say to the cynics is…" I squared my shoulders, blew out a breath. "I stand in my truth."

There was no simpler statement. Nothing more to say. Once I knew for certain what I was, what I was here to do, the cacophony of the messy world fell away. My intention was to save it, to give light so the darkness would retreat like a shadow under the sun's rays.

Finn, Edmund, and I walked toward the ranch. Not everyone was congregated in the big room where I'd expected them to be. There was a chaotic vibe running through *Rancho Estrella* and Scintilla milled around, unsure of what to do. "Do they know the Arrazi are coming?" Finn asked Edmund.

"Yes. Ehsan texted Adrian and Will, too. Adrian and

Will tried to set up a strategy based on their powers. No one was keen on sitting together in the common room like fish in a barrel, but there's a group still in there. We could really use Giovanni's leadership right now."

"He can't help us anymore. He's dead." I pushed the words out through the dam of my gritted teeth. I could barely say it to Edmund. How was I going to explain it to Claire? "And the cardinal is missing."

Edmund gave a shocked and apologetic look before his eyes tracked two Scintilla with packs on their backs, darting into the brush. They were running away. I had to step up. "I will lead now. Did you tell the Scintilla what needs to be done?" I asked. "Do they know about joining with the Arrazi?"

Edmund chuckled. "I did more than tell them. I showed them the video of your *episode* when you touched the book. Then, I did what any orator would do, I recited gospel— noncanonical but let's not split evangelical hairs." Edmund cleared his throat. "*He said to them, whoever has ears, let him hear. There is light within a man of light, and he lights up the whole world. If he does not shine, he is darkness.*"

"Who said that?" I asked. "It's beautiful."

"Jesus. Who else? When I saw they needed more, I read them this little ditty from the Gospel of Thomas. It's Jesus speaking again. *When you make the two into one, and when you make the inner like the outer and the outer like the inner, and the upper like the lower, and when you make male and female into a single one, so that the male will not be male nor the female be female, when you make eyes in place of an eye, a hand in place of a hand, a foot in place of a foot, an image in place of an image, then you will enter the Kingdom.*" Edmund waggled his brows at me when he finished. "Amazing, right?"

I was speechless. It was a nearly perfect description of my vision of the joining and of the being who left the truth in the spirals. "Thank you, Edmund. Running into you in Italy was a fate I'll always be glad for."

Edmund leaned and kissed my cheek. "It's been the biggest thrill and privilege of my life," he said. "Now let's go save the world."

The three of us set off. I needed to find Will and see what plan was in place so far. Convincing the Arrazi was paramount, but that would never happen if they killed us before the words even got out of our mouths. Just then, Will and Maya ran around the corner, and our eyes locked. They also had packs on their backs. They jogged over, both looking warily at Finn before exchanging glances.

"Where are you two going?" I asked, hearing the accusatory tone in my voice. I grabbed Finn's hand to show them they had no reason to fear him.

Much to my surprise, Maya leaned with her hands behind her back and kissed my cheek.

"I always knew this was about duality," Maya said. Her head jerked toward Will. "I told them in the car the other day, didn't I, Will?" Her deep brown eyes darkened with solemnity. "The Scintilla's role in the story is a much bigger part than I ever imagined."

"Tell her the rest," Will urged her.

"We can't do it. It sounds like the ultimate peace, right? Two enemies joining…but it also sounds like a suicide pact. *Will* is my other half—not some Arrazi I've never met who wants to kill me. We have a baby coming. We have to run, try to live our lives someplace else and give our baby a chance at life. We truly wish you luck and…light."

"You're telling me that you believe in the truth of what I saw, believe that we can save a world spiraling out of control, the world your baby will soon inhabit, and you're running away? Even if you refuse to join, can't you at least stay and help us?" I wanted to cry. If they ran, how many others would do the same?

In my deepest heart, I couldn't blame Maya, though. If I were pregnant, would I walk the plank with an Arrazi? "I'm sorry," I said, reaching for her hand, but she deftly held it out of reach. "I have no right to judge your choice. I wish you luck."

"Thank you," Will said. "Adrian's inside the hall, and he'll fill you in on the plan. Most Scintilla are going to be in a 'let me see it and *then* I'll believe it' mindset. None of us really knows what it means to join with an Arrazi, but it sounds like the end of life as we know it."

"Probably. I'm not going to lie." Will's eyes widened at that, or maybe not that, but something behind me.

Faster than if it had been a blade hurled through the air, Arrazi energy hit my back, slicing into the tender spot between my shoulders—right over my knife marking.

Chapter Fifty-Seven

Finn

Cora arched her back, gasping for breath, or air, and from the way she writhed, for relief from the pain. I spun around to confirm; she was under Arrazi attack. I let go of her hand to leap in front of her. Her agonized green eyes met mine, and for one sickening moment, I realized there was a shocked question in them. Did she think *I* attacked her? As soon as I blocked her, the clawing assault on her spirit hit my chest and seconds later, a surprised guttural yell came from the attacker as the man blew back and landed on the ground with the force of his own energy ricocheting off me.

Aside from the horrific scene at my house, this was the most terrifying moment of my life. Half a dozen Arrazi advanced toward us along the main road through the ranch, and more cars were arriving. Every beam of headlights and crunch of gravel under tires was a death knell. No telling how many would be upon us. Possibly much more Arrazi than Scintilla, and the Scintilla were already overpowered by nature. The Arrazi were on us, their leader, the cardinal, was missing, and we were so very unprepared.

The man who'd been flung to the ground didn't stay down long. He jumped paranormally fast to his feet and gave another Arrazi a sinister smile. "*Sortilege,*" he said. Like yelling "smorgasbord" to refugees, they hungrily attacked, wanting what only Scintilla energy could give them—supernatural powers. No doubt, after they obtained their power, they'd kill. More Arrazi energy whooshed our way, much more than I could hold off, though I tried. I stood my ground in front of Cora and yelled for them to stop. I blew some of them back, but I was taking multiple hits that were weakening me. I staggered backward into Cora.

Will and Maya whimpered behind us. I looked over my shoulder, and they were both crouched down, Will over the top of his wife, trying in vain to shield her. I worried what the attack could do to her unborn child. "Help!" I managed to scream out.

A soundless flash of red-orange fire shot out from between two of the domed huts and hit an Arrazi, igniting his clothes and hair. He screamed and flailed, and I swallowed down bile that rose as I watched him burn. The attack on our auras stopped as the Arrazi scrambled for cover and peered between the buildings to see where the threat came from.

"It's one of the twins," Cora said from behind me. "Gavin and Cooper. They're what Giovanni called 'elementals.' One wields fire, the other, water."

"Those twins just saved our *arses*," I said to Cora, and we both lifted Maya and Will by their arms. We rounded the corner of the hall, and Cora stopped to bang on one of the windows. "They're surrounding us!" someone yelled from within the ranch. Will and Maya exchanged petrified looks. Their window for escape had closed unless we could find an opening.

"We have to warn the people inside!" Cora said above more screaming. Behind us was the eerie glow of burning figures and black shadows. Someone's face appeared in the window. "Samantha, right?" Cora said to a young woman in an impressively calm tone. "Tell everyone that the Arrazi are here." The girl nodded, her large half-moon eyes showing fear but also resignation. "Everyone has to use their powers to stay alive until I can confront the Arrazi and convince them to stop attacking."

A big man pushed his way past Samantha. "She comes!" he said in a thick Italian accent. "I foresaw it. One most powerful is among us."

"Ultana," I murmured to Cora. Her gaze snapped to me. So much had happened that I hadn't the chance to tell her. "I don't think she's dead. I think her son Lorcan has helped her fool everyone."

"I saw her!" the man bellowed again. "Where is Giovanni? I must speak with him."

Cora didn't answer that question. It had to kill her every time someone asked it. "Does anyone know where my grandmother is?" Cora asked past the wild-eyed man to a new person at the window; a scrappy-looking young man with tattoos all over his neck and arms.

"I'm Adrian," the guy said. "She's in here, what's up?"

"Adrian," she said. "I know your name. Giovanni told me about you. Twin boys are out here being our only defense right now. *Everyone* needs to help. You can't hide in here and wait to be slaughtered."

Adrian gave a chin lift and steeled himself before turning to yell over his shoulder. "Yo, it's time! We have powers for a reason; let's go use 'em! We're sitting ducks in here! Out the back door!" We heard the stampeding feet and the scuffle of steps coming out the door just a few feet away from us. I didn't need to see auras to know they were afraid. Waves of fear rolled toward me and collided with my own. Their distinctive auras were honey, and the swarm was upon them.

"I need Mami Tulke," Cora said. Adrian bolted from the window. Mami Tulke was pushed through the crowd out the back door, and soon we had a group of Scintilla around us, waiting for instructions. "I have to speak to the Arrazi and convince them to join with us," Cora said to her. "I need you to shield me long enough to—"

"It can't be you," Mami Tulke said. "Remember, you are the *one* person I cannot shield."

Cora let her head fall back to the stone wall. "That's right..."

"Sydney and I will talk to them," Samantha said, motioning to a tall young woman with piercing gray eyes. "I can try to use my telepathic cozening to convince them to halt their attack so Sydney can mimic Cora's appearance for a short time. We can only pull it off for a few minutes, though."

"I can shield just *one* of the girls," Mami Tulke gravely reminded us.

"Shield Sydney," Samantha said, bravely. "She's the one

who has to do the talking." That was the first hint of fear I'd heard in her voice. For someone so young, she was incredibly self-assured.

"Are there others who can do telekinesis?" Cora asked, and Adrian nodded affirmatively. "Okay, tell them to position themselves by the debris piles from the earthquakes and use their sortilege to strike any Arrazi who threaten." Her voice lowered as she turned to her grandmother. "How many Scintilla have run?"

"Easily half." I couldn't tell from her tone what Mami Tulke thought of that fact, but it was clear as crystal what Cora thought. Her whole body seemed to droop for an instant as she mentally processed the implications.

"We were at a disadvantage anyway," Cora said. "This just makes it worse. Thirty some-odd Scintilla against who knows how many Arrazi who can take from and kill multiple people at once. We have to end this. For good."

"You've found a way," I reminded her. "We can do this."

No sooner had the words come from my mouth than a pack of Arrazi stepped from the shadows in the trees and charged the air with their hunger for the Scintilla. Everyone around me clutched their chests and bent forward like they were bowing to royalty. I moved to defend. Suddenly, chunks of cement and glass hurtled through the air in front of me, slamming into the Arrazi taking numerous bodies down. The Scintilla were fighting back, and it was clear that the Arrazi hadn't anticipated it.

From the ground a bloodied Arrazi focused all of her attention in the direction from where the objects had come, and moments later, a body fell to my right. A Scintilla was gone. The Arrazi who could stand did so, but before they could attack, a wall of water arced over the trees and the force of the wave knocked them down again.

"Cooper," one of the girls whispered as a teenage boy ran from the trees with his arms outstretched in front of him. His face contorted in effort as he balled the water around the Arrazi in an attempt to drown them. It was working, but for some reason his ability waned and the water splashed to the ground around their feet.

"Someone's taking from him!" Cora said. "His aura is pulling from his body to the left over there."

I ran out in front of the boy who fought to stay upright. He was so young, and he looked at me with terrified blue eyes until he realized that I intended not to attack him but to block him from the Arrazi man whose face I could now see a few feet away.

"Traitor," the man hissed at me. "You think you can stop this?"

"Aye. One Arrazi tool at a time."

The man walked calmly toward me, unconcerned about the Scintilla scattering around the compound and the intermittent yells around us. Three of the water-soaked and slightly injured Arrazi got to their hands and knees in the mud and then to their feet, their faces emanating total hate for me, the one Arrazi trying to defend these people. He unsheathed a knife from his belt, which glinted under the solar lights of the hall as the other Arrazi circled around me. Cooper was thankfully gone. He must have run when he could, and I was glad. Kid was too young to die. I was, too, come to think of it, and I had no defense from a blade.

The man raised the knife over his shoulder, poised to chuck it at me from only a few feet away.

"No!" Cora yelled, and I winced. She should be running, hiding. She shouldn't see this. Not only wasn't she running away, the blasted girl was running *toward* me until she was attacked so viciously that she was thrown from her feet and onto her back in the wet earth. Her body curled in on itself.

A loud popping crack split the air, and the man with the knife fell to the ground. I crouched as more shots rang out. Two Arrazi were hit and fell to the earth. The other two ran. Who among the Scintilla had a gun? We'd run for our lives from the cave when the earthquake struck, leaving everything behind. I crawled over to Cora, who was too weak to talk, and scooped her into my arms. Mami Tulke ran to us, and I felt the steam of Scintilla energy as she gave to Cora, helping her to regain her strength. My eyes searched the darkness for signs of the shooter, and I couldn't believe who ran from one of the small rectangular homes.

Giovanni.

Chapter Fifty-Eight

Giovanni

Alive.

It was a mystery to me how I woke on that quiet hillside next to the hole that had swallowed Cora. I'd saved her, used every ounce of strength I had to lift her gently from that chasm. I'd lost consciousness, and my last memory before I'd slipped away was the weight of her crying against my chest and her sweet words.

When my eyes opened and all I saw were stars, I thought, *how ironic…heaven isn't a place, a destination. Heaven really is above us and around us and the earth is just floating in it…*

I didn't know how long I lay there pondering heaven; I only knew that I had the sudden realization of gravity, and of the ground against my back, and the sound of crickets, and the kiss of a light breeze on my face. Earthly sensations.

Alive.

No explanation for why I wasn't dead, but the second I knew I was miraculously alive, I knew where I needed to be. I ran all the way back to *Rancho Estrella*, ducking behind trees every time a car passed. Too many cars were passing, every one shooting cold fear through me and propelling my spent body forward.

When I'd reached the compound, the sounds of fighting and struggle were all around. Scintilla lay dead on the ground near the entrance, strewn amidst debris from the quake. My heart twisted painfully, but there was no time to mourn. Arrazi moved like dogs in packs between the buildings and were searching them as they went. I had to stay out of sight, certain they could sense my energy by the way their heads veered in my direction, hound-like, when I passed too closely. I'd snuck into my house and found the one gun I'd hidden on the shelf and ran to find my people.

Ran to fight.

That's when I saw Cora flung to the mud by the Arrazi's attack and fired.

My hand still buzzed from the gun. I knelt over Cora and ran my hand along her jaw, sending her energy though I could see she didn't need it because of Mami Tulke's help. I just wanted her to feel it, to feel me.

Her eyes flew open, then wider still, and she rolled from Finn's arms and hugged me. "How — ?"

"I don't know, I really don't," I said through laugh-crying. Over her shoulder, Finn was smiling at me, and his gladness for me cemented a friendship I never thought was possible.

When she let go of me, Finn hugged me as well. "Thanks, mate. *Fookin'* hell I'm glad to see you right now."

The sounds of people running nearby made us jump to our feet. "Where's the garden supply shed?" I asked Mami Tulke. I had to find Claire and know she was all right. I'd seen the systematic way the Arrazi were searching buildings and killing those inside. Claire and the women would be helpless against them. Mami Tulke pointed the way, and we ran together toward the garden.

We spotted another small troop of Arrazi prowling the area and ducked behind a pungent compost pile hoping they hadn't seen us. The shed was just a few meters away, door closed. I prayed that was a good sign.

Rustling sounds whooshed over our head, and I craned my neck to see what it was, barely catching a glimpse of an Arrazi—who'd obviously gained his sortilege—whizzing over us and then landing between us and the shed. I lifted the gun to fire, but Cora shoved my arm down. "What if the bullet goes into the shed?"

"Keaton?" Finn said, recognizing the tall guy who blocked me from my daughter. Finn stood in front of us and started to say something else to the Arrazi, but within a blink, the man had teleported again and landed in front of Finn, nailing him with a punch that doubled Finn over. More Arrazi ran around each side of the compost heap, flanking us. Ripping pain tore through me. There were too many. I fired at one to my right but missed. Fired again, and the gun clicked ineffectually. Empty. I threw it to the ground.

A young Scintilla woman, Hannah, snatched it up as she fell forward next to me. I couldn't think why, unless she had spare bullets and a way to stop the attack. I tried to remember what her sortilege was.

Amidst the groans of the Scintilla around me, and the

gasping pleas from Finn, I heard another voice. A child's piercing scream, "Leave my papa alone!" and I quailed down to my aching soul. How could they let her run out of there? Stars dotted my vision as I watched my little girl bolt from the shed toward the deadly scene in front of her. She stopped in front of the man who was kicking Finn in the ribs. Finn rolled on the ground with his arms around his coughing body, trying to get up.

Claire's fists were balled at her sides as she stared up at the man. The ravaging of our auras stopped when the amused Arrazi became distracted by the brazen child in front of them. "What have we here?" I heard one of them say. "A stray? Maybe we can keep her."

"Oh God…" Cora moaned. "They can't take her. She's not one of us!" Cora yelled, hoping to deter them from thinking she was Scintilla or valuable as property. She wasn't special at all. They had to *feel* that.

With every bit of strength I had, I stumbled forward toward her, struck by the enormity of her aura and the ferociousness of her gaze. The Arrazi's energy whipped out like a tentacle, almost teasingly, like a cat that wants to remind of its claws. But before it struck her, her aura inexplicably reached around the man like giant squeezing vise grips and choked the life from him.

I saw his Arrazi energy leave his body before he dropped and I saw—even as my mind rejected the abhorrent possibility—Claire's aura explode in white.

Chapter Fifty-Nine

Finn

"It should be impossible," Mami Tulke gasped, her old face full of stunned astonishment. "She's just a child."

The Arrazi backed away with wary glances at Claire and then darted off through the buildings. No doubt they'd be back.

"Is it Claire's sortilege as a Scintilla?" I asked. It seemed the only explanation, though for all of us, sortileges were said to come during young-adulthood. What a terrifying thing to take a life at such a young age.

The Scintilla shook their heads at my question.

Cora squeezed my elbow and muttered. "Finn, her aura is glowing pure white right now," she said, still staring in awe across the vegetation at Claire. "And it's so big. I've never seen one so big. Claire's Arrazi."

Impossible.

"Arrazi don't change until much older. And she didn't blow back," I said. "Even if she *is* Arrazi, none of us are supposed to be able to attack another of our kind. I know," I said, remembering when Clancy tricked me into attacking him. "I've tried it, and it's how I've been blocking some of their attacks."

Claire stood alone in the garden, her chin trembling as she looked at her father—her *Scintilla* father, according to some mad scientist in Ireland—whose life she had just saved. Cora reached for Giovanni, but he shrugged away from her touch. When it became clear that he was paralyzed by shock or maybe even revulsion, Cora did the most beautiful and brave thing. She ran through the knee-high squash plants to where Claire stood frozen and scooped her in her arms. Claire wrapped her legs around Cora's waist and her arms around her neck.

So tiny, this little killer.

I marveled at Cora, shushing and comforting Claire while swaying softly as the child cried against Cora's neck. Cora's open and giving heart was evident in her actions; the walls between races were crumbling within her.

Mami Tulke pressed Giovanni's face with her hands, forcing him to look down at her. "Gather yourself up. Do not reject your own blood."

"I saw," the big Italian man, Raimondo, said. "I saw her kill. I told you she was among us."

"But how can she really be from me? Maybe her mother was Arrazi... She was an experiment, Dr. M's experiment..." Giovanni's voice was as small and shattered as I'd ever heard it. "She's a mutated version of *them*."

Mami Tulke scowled. "I'm not hearing that. You only have to look at her to see. Beyond that, ask your own heart. Once you throw off the black smoke of your prejudice, you'll see the truth. You're her family. Go to her."

I imagined the internal leap it must have taken Giovanni to move his feet forward. The Arrazi were the enemy. A battle still raged around the village as Arrazi indiscriminately hunted and killed, and it would only be moments before we were attacked again. A large group of Scintilla joined us in the garden, looking haggard and battle-damaged. They murmured fearful comments about Claire and some not so kind ones, too. Hindsight makes everyone a sudden prophetic genius.

Their whisperings also said that hope was fading that the Scintilla would survive the night. The fate of uniting the two races seemed more impossible than ever.

Giovanni reached for Claire, but the little girl didn't seem ready to let go of Cora, so he wrapped his arms around them both with Claire sandwiched between them. They stood entangled, looking every bit the family in a way that tore at my insides.

"Doyle!" yelled a familiar voice. The night and the dark clothes hid the face of the person who called out my name. The voice I recognized. Lorcan Lennon. Cora and Giovanni startled when he called out, and I saw the recognition shadow their faces as Lorcan got closer and the light from a building floodlit his features. "Christ," he yelled. "You're all standing around like a Goddamn beacon. Could you be any more daft?"

He was right that the cluster of Scintilla emitted an unbearably strong shockwave of energy, but what did he mean by sounding like he gave a damn? Giovanni's face twisted into one of vengeance, and he started to run toward Lorcan, but Cora stopped him with a fistful of his shirt.

"You cursed me!" Giovanni yelled with a finger pointing at Lorcan.

"You're obviously still alive, aren't you?" Lorcan said. "Or has the opportunity to save your fair maiden not come up?"

"He *did* save me," Cora said, suddenly looking at Giovanni. "And he... I thought he died. But..." None of us had had a chance to ask Giovanni if he knew what happened.

Lorcan touched a finger to his chest like this news both astonished and pleased him. "Then it worked."

"What worked?" I said.

Lorcan repeatedly looked behind him in a dodgy way that set my hairs to standing. Something was very off and clearly he was expecting someone to arrive.

He looked back at me. "I removed the *geis* off him, *eejit*."

"Why would you do that?" Cora asked.

"One would think you wished him dead with a question like that," Lorcan said, looking as confused as we did. He shrugged at me. "You were there that day, Doyle. How could anyone see the sight of the silver aura and not have it affect them? It was—I was *changed* by it."

I recalled his face at the facility when we'd seen the wall for the first time. Lorcan *had* looked visibly moved, as was I. "But you cursed him *after* we saw Gráinne's aura in the wall."

"Only because I knew *she'd* be watching everything I did. Then I had to learn how to undo it. It's not like we're born with a manual."

"Lorcan, I don't know what you're trying to pull. You've been—"

"I've been secretly *trying* to help. Shhh!" he hissed, spinning around. "Get the *fook* out of here, all of you," he said with a flap of his hands like he was shooing flies. "She's coming, and if you're still here when she gets here, you'll all be dead."

Lorcan's implausible warning fell like a bomb around us. If Ultana *was* coming, I had no doubt it would be lethal. The group of Scintilla and I scattered from the garden toward the trees that shielded the river beyond them. We'd have to cross the river, somehow. Cooper was already murmuring about how he'd part the water for us and get us through. At the edge of the garden, a group of Arrazi stepped from the trees, blocking our escape. We veered to the right, but another group formed a half-circle with their backs to the east—same on the west. Like the hub of a wheel, we all spun a quarter turn and saw the approach of another group of Arrazi behind Lorcan.

Their energy was a slow-moving wave that was as threatening as a knife to the throat when it hit. I recognized the Lennon's lawyer, Makenzie, among them. In the middle of the group was a figure that looked just as she did the first time I saw her. She pulled her hood back from her pale face. A braid of flaming red snaked over her shoulder.

Relief flooded me, but I'd feel much better if there weren't twenty other Arrazi surrounding us, and Lorcan's ploys were confusing. I needed to talk to Saoirse, but I was unwilling to leave Cora unprotected even though she held in her arms the most lethal Arrazi I'd ever known of aside from Ultana Lennon. Where was she, anyway?

Turned out I didn't need to approach Saoirse. She held up her hand to signal the Arrazi flanking her to stop and strode confidently past them and up to me. The smile she gave was a wilted flower. "I see we're late."

I grasped her arms and leaned in to kiss her cheek. "Better late than never. I'm glad you're here." When I pulled back, her seafoam eyes lingered on the Scintilla over my shoulder before darting back to me. "Are the Arrazi with you on our side? I have something huge to tell you. We found out how to end this. The Arrazi must stop their attack and hear us out. I can't believe they're not attacking now."

"They are waiting for the order."

"What's the whispering?" Lorcan said, suddenly at our side.

I shoved Lorcan's chest. "Leave us alone. You may have cursed your way into your sister's business, but you have no place in mine."

"What do you think that was back there?" he asked. "I warned you she was coming."

Saoirse glared at her brother.

"She—I thought you meant your mother."

Both Lennons looked at me like I'd lost my mind.

Lorcan threw up his hands. "Are you mad? What the hell are you talking about? My mother is *dead*, fool."

"Then why were you having me followed? The Arrazi who came to my house, who murdered my mother…" My chest heaved with anger. "They specifically said 'she' was looking for the cover to the *Book of Kells*." The words left my mouth and I knew instantly my error. I turned to Saoirse with a boulder of dread in my stomach. "Not *you*?"

"Don't look so surprised," Lorcan groaned. "I'm sure

she had something to do with my mother's death *and* the takeover of Xepa. Why do you think I put the *geis* on her? I was trying to keep tabs on what she was up to. My sister's a conniving snake."

You know about baby rattlesnakes, Finn? The baby ones… are the most…dangerous… They can't control their venom. Careful the baby ones.

Mari. She'd tried to warn me.

Saoirse acted as though Lorcan weren't standing there, leveling suspicion on her shoulders.

"It was you who beat up Mari and you hit me over the head when I had Ultana by the throat? *Jaysus.* My mother saw your secrets. She told me you felt responsible for the death of your mother and—"

"And now we're both motherless."

I lunged at Saoirse, knocking her onto her back. "Tell me the truth!" I roared. Her hand gripped the back of my neck, and she answered with a string of words that were more like a seductive incantation. "My mother killed herself, but it was me who convinced her she was immortal rather than having the sortilege for an unnaturally long life. I hoped she'd someday do something arrogant and stupid, and she did. The man who worked for me was in the cave—as you know, Finn. He told me what happened. She drove that knife into herself because she believed she wouldn't die." Saoirse chuckled at the thought. "She was a monster. You know that. She was wicked and *deserved* to die, and I took care of it. You don't want to hurt me, Finn. You want to be a team. Work together with me. I am not your enemy, the Scintilla are your enemy."

Confusion muddied my mind, pressing all previous thoughts under the silt. Her words felt like truth. Why was I fighting Saoirse?

"Don't listen to her, man!" *Eejit* Lorcan, why was he trying to protect me from Saoirse?

"That's right, Finn," she murmured. All that existed was her slender body underneath mine in this cloud of green. I could only watch her lips. "You and I belong together," she crooned. "Stand with me now. Let's finish the enemy and be together as we should be. The Arrazi are going to rule this world and you and I will lead them all. I told you before, we were meant to unite."

She rolled me onto my back and pressed a kiss to my lips like she was sealing an envelope of agreements with me. "Stand with me now," she said, holding out her hand. I grabbed it and, together, we faced the Scintilla.

Chapter Sixty

Giovanni

What in the hell was Finn doing rolling around with the red-headed Arrazi girl like splendor in the damn grass?

When he stood hand in hand with her and faced us, I said to Cora, "It's like she put a spell on him, isn't it?" His expression was blank, though he was entirely focused on us and his energy reached across the field like nerve gas.

Cora, stupid-stubborn-headstrong Cora, handed Claire over to me, broke our ranks, and marched up to them. "What's she done to you?" She clutched Finn by his shirt and shook him.

From next to me, Samantha yelled to her, "Cozening. It's her sortilege. Like mine. I know it when I hear it."

The redhead's glare at Samantha and then at Cora

standing in front of her, daring to challenge her, was evident even across the darkness. Cora cocked her head at the girl. "You have a *sortilege* to make him believe what you want him to believe?"

"Yes. A gift from your *sweet* mother," the girl said. "Finn's uncle was kind enough to share her with me. Numerous times."

She sounded so self-satisfied and smug, I wasn't at all surprised when Cora cracked her with a slap across the face. Saoirse's head snapped sideways. She slowly refocused on Cora and latched onto Cora's aura hard enough to yank her forward onto her knees, where Saoirse then took the opportunity to knee Cora in the face. Cora fell to the foliage.

All Finn had to do was step between them. He could stop the attack, but he was just standing there like a zombie.

Claire struggled against my grasp, her little voice saying, "Let me go. I can help Cora."

"No. I—" How could I give *permission* for my child to kill? I could barely handle the fact that she could. But someone had to. *I* had to. I set Claire down next to Dun and ran full-out toward them. Just as I reached Cora and screamed at Finn to snap the hell out of it and remember the truth, he ripped into my aura, pulling it from my body with agonizing swiftness. I fell back onto the grass next to Cora.

Our hands met. I rolled my head to the side to look at her, but her eyes sought her attacker's. She gasped out these words. "It's our belief in our separateness that causes all the pain on the earth. I know the truth about us. *Please,* Saoirse, listen to me…"

I pondered her words as I fought to stay conscious, then the strangest sound hit my ears—a tiny warrior yell coming toward us. I should know that sound, I thought, just as the blur of blond curls leaped over us, sending Finn and Saoirse soaring backward through the air and crashing into the fence bordering the garden. A group of Scintilla darted to us, surrounded us. I lost sight of Cora as they pushed me to sitting, infusing my aura with their life-affirming, numinous silver light.

As before, the Arrazi surrounding us exchanged fearful glances at my daughter and took a few steps back from her raging aura, which extended in an enormous circle to prick each and every Arrazi with the searing needle of their own acrid medicine.

"This looks like a battle between enemies," Cora said, gaining her strength and her voice, though both were shaky and slightly *off*. She looked sadly on Finn and Saoirse and then to the circle of deadly people around us. "We didn't start as enemies."

"What," gasped Saoirse, using the fence to pull herself up, "do you mean by that? We are natural enemies!"

Finn was coming to, and his eyes registered the clarity that had been gone minutes before. He looked confusedly at Saoirse, then limped toward us with his hands out. "I'm so sorry," he said. "I didn't have control." His eyes were fixed on Cora, pleading with her to understand.

"I know. She used her sortilege on you."

Finn wheeled around. "Sortilege? *You* were the one who took from Cora's mother. The brutal one she wrote about. You were Arrazi all along and used your sortilege to convince me, your family, everyone that you hadn't yet turned? *Fooking* hell...that night...you *let* yourself get weak so I'd believe it was the first time."

"Yes." Saoirse didn't look at him. Her focus was on Claire, the only person who'd been able to incite fear in all of the Arrazi. Cora spoke loud enough for everyone to hear, though her eyes didn't leave Saoirse. Clearly, Saoirse controlled the pack of Arrazi until Claire became the bigger threat.

Finn was still railing at Saoirse. "If he shared her with you, then you and my uncle Clancy worked together. What'd you promise him?"

"Everything," she said in a hollow voice. "He gave me the power to finally fight my mother. I promised him we'd oust her. I promised we'd rule our enemies, and we'd step out of mankind's shadow. That was the only thing my mother and I ever agreed on. Finn, you don't understand the power that's being handed to us."

"By who?" Cora asked. "Cardinal Báthory?"

"Saoirse, he's using the Arrazi and has been planning to—"

"Kill them now!" Báthory ordered the Arrazi as he strode up behind a line of them, using them as a shield. "You've had a taste of what's been promised you. Fulfill your duty to me, and I will fulfill mine to you."

"But sir, the girl..." the woman who'd arrived with Saoirse said.

Báthory misunderstood whom she meant. "Yes, Makenzie. The girl," he said, narrowing his eyes. "Cora Sandoval must be the first to die."

A leaf wafted down from one of the trees and mystifyingly suspended in mid-air.

My eyes moved to Finn and Cora, and they seemed just as suspended as the leaf, immobile, frozen, like the whole world and everyone in it was holding its breath. I tried to move but couldn't. No one moved. Nothing on earth moved, it seemed, but Makenzie, who strode toward Cora. She smiled as she plunged her white aura into Cora's chest and towed at the coiling string of silver.

Cora didn't even flinch.

Makenzie had dropped a sortilege that stopped time, or froze us, I had no idea... I commanded my body to move, tried to scream. Being in my head was like banging on thick, soundproof glass, shrieking, and no one could hear. Cora was being murdered, and we could only watch, frozen in horror.

As the last drop of Cora's soul floated like a nacreous and iridescent pearl from her chest, she fell to the ground and her body pulsed, seemed to flicker—flicker and morph into a lovely girl whose hair swept across her collarbone and whose gray-green eyes now stared forever at the stars.

The Arrazi woman's triumphant smile slid from her face as she realized...

It wasn't Cora she'd killed.

Sydney. They'd somehow switched, and Sydney had given her life to save Cora's.

The leaf fell to the ground.

Like a great button was pushed, Makenzie's sortilege broke. Cries rang out, and bodies rushed forward. Dun had his hands around the woman's throat. She tried to penetrate his aura with her powerful white energy, but it hit and rolled away from him like he had a force field surrounding him. A *shield*. I looked for Cora and saw Mami Tulke staring intently at him, keeping him safe from Makenzie as he killed her with his bare hands and threw her limp body to the ground.

"Why aren't you attacking?" Báthory raged. "Do as I—"

His words cut off as someone with a white aura pressed a gun to his temple. Hannah winked at us. She'd used her sortilege to alter her own aura and mix among the Arrazi. Brilliant. She'd gotten close enough to use my empty gun to silence the man who'd led this war. I wished it had a bullet and vowed I'd put one in his head before the day was done.

Cora stepped from behind the trees. I sucked in my breath. They had to have switched when the Scintilla surrounded us after Finn and Saoirse attacked us. She kissed Claire's cheek and whispered something in her ear. Claire nodded, and her white aura pressed harder on every Arrazi present. Even I could feel my daughter's chilling power. We all could.

When Cora reached Sydney's body, she knelt and pressed her hand over Sydney's heart and moved it in circles. "I'm so sorry you were hurt," she said through tears. "You are *so* brave." Like the Vatican video so many of us had seen, Cora's eyes closed and she focused a funnel of energy into Sydney until Sydney was surrounded by glowing silver light and her long dark lashes fluttered.

Cora gave one satisfied nod, smiled beatifically at the girl, then stood and cocked her head at Saoirse. Why focus on Saoirse in particular? Perhaps Cora thought hers was a heart she could touch. I seriously doubted it. Then Cora did something astonishing. She *gave* a most precious gift to her enemy—silver light. Saoirse's eyes widened before welling up with tears. Like Cora had in the common room the day of the vote, she lit a spark that passed from Saoirse Lennon to each Arrazi one by one, gifting them with her essence.

Some shook. Some cried openly.

"Stop! Don't give our enemies their powers!" I yelled to

her. "You're only making them more dangerous!"

"We aren't supposed to be enemies," Cora said loudly. "We were not created as predator and prey. We're made of the same stuff but were torn apart thousands of years ago." I could hear the emotion she fought to hold in check. This was her moment to convince everyone what must be done.

"Arrazi have forgotten what it is they *truly* hunger for. You mistake your need as need for the Scintilla's spirit. The truth is, the hunger you feel is a desperate desire for wholeness. You weren't created to kill us. You are meant to unite with us. To be one."

The Arrazi began whispering among them until one voice, Saoirse's, called out the big question. "You want to convince the powerful to unite with the powerless. Why would we *do* that?"

"Because we're more powerful *together*. We had one job. That was to be the living embodiment of balance, of reconciliation of opposites. Our two energies are supposed to fuse to make a third that will heal this world and save mankind. The greatest power we can achieve is to be one."

Finn spoke to the crowd of Arrazi. "I know you loathe what you are—what you're forced to do. You can make a different choice now. What felt toxic and inevitable isn't. Please believe us. The truth was hidden for so long, but this is it. *We* are it."

"Finn," Cora said softly. "Let's do this. *Someone* has to be the first."

Chapter Sixty-One

Cora

My mother once said to me, *Love is the strongest binding in this world. Love is the key.* I couldn't believe it then. Hate and fear had infected my heart.

Walking toward Finn with a fearful yet determined spirit and allowing him to take—no, not take—but *giving* him of my soul wasn't what I always dreamed of. Or wasn't it? There was a time, a time that seemed lifetimes ago, when I wanted that. I felt the surge of love and longing to connect with him from the moment we met. I'd felt like we just *fit* together. Magnets. It was inexplicable then. How could we have guessed at the enormous truth of us, the *reason* we'd always felt so drawn to each other? What looked like impetuous and hot-hearted love among teens was so much bigger. It was destiny and purpose.

We were meant to be together in the most literal and beautiful sense.

What we were doing was an act of faith. *Faith...* I didn't want it to be a dirty word after what Cardinal Báthory had done. But he was just one man, bent crooked by the weight of his own infected heart. Wasn't it faith that compelled me to do this now, faith that I might play a part in something so important as the reparation of the planet, as the advancement of humanity from the brink of disaster? Faith that my parents would be proud?

A helicopter crested the hills above the ranch and circled the scene as a news van skidded into the drive. Perfect. Paparazzi witnesses to my own personal apocalypse.

Finn didn't want to do this. Not really. It was risky, and we didn't know if we'd be just ash afterward or would combine into some angelic alien being. But like me, he couldn't deny we were players in a bigger game. We were meant to do this, even as we worried it wouldn't work, if it would do nothing more than kill me and feed his Arrazi appetite.

The expectant eyes of the Arrazi and Scintilla were on us. I looked around me at those faces, especially at the faces of the people I loved. I loved them enough to do this. I just wish I had more time to say good-bye. My eyes found Giovanni holding Claire, and a puff of a cry escaped my lips. His eyes shone with tears, and he nodded, *Go.*

There was no time to say good-bye to anyone else. Everyone's toes were off the cliff. How could we expect them to fulfill their destiny and fly if we weren't willing to do so first? My faith in the vision didn't mean I was happy about it. I didn't want to be a martyr, a prophet, or a savior.

I was just a girl...

I wondered how others had felt walking knowingly into death for some version of a greater good. I was no saint. A part of me resented it even, to die for people who would deny me and my sacrifice even after I was gone. I resented it even as I took one tentative step after another toward the boy who'd had my soul in his hands from the moment we met. Would the traces of fear and resentment and grief I felt nullify my sacrifice? Would I die for nothing, like my father, mother, Mari, and countless others? Did intention count?

If so, then I intended to die so that their lives weren't lost for nothing.

Could one girl and one boy join souls and save the world?

Even across the distance, Finn's amber eyes lit on me and burned me up from the inside out. If he felt fear, he was hiding it, probably for my benefit. The love in his eyes was the magnet pulling me forward. I could almost pretend it was months ago, it was California, and I was walking with the bloom of love in my chest toward a boy. Just a boy. Not my enemy.

My *wholemate*.

Finn's foot shuffled forward. Chilean dust billowed like memories. We'd had history on three continents, but it felt bigger than that. I wondered how many lifetimes we'd played this drama out. How many lifetimes had all of us played this drama out?

"I'm so afraid," I whispered when we were arm's length apart.

"I know, *críona*. My heart. I am as well." His eyes glassed over and his lips tilted up in a lopsided smile. "Maybe our fear isn't real."

"Of course it's real!" I trembled from my core outward. My lips quivered as I spoke. It felt real.

"Give to me like you've done before, luv. I'm here to receive you, to catch you. It's all I ever wanted—to give love to you and to receive your love."

We reached out and grasped hands, each taking a breath as big as the winds over the Andes.

"You love. I love," Finn said, radiating the gentleness and peace I'd always felt and seen in him, who he *really* was. "That's right here, right now. Fear is just the worry that you'll lose that love or that you'll lose something in the future. But right here, right now, all that's real is *love*. Let's *be* that."

Our pulses vibrated and rippled through our bodies. I could feel him, feel his tenderness and the depth of his commitment to do anything for me. Ironically, he could not save me, but together we could save the world. The heart was the stone thrown into the oceans of earth. Love, pure love, rippled outward.

"Okay," I said, squeezing his hands and looking into the forever depths of his eyes before taking one last glance at the perfectly messy heavens above us.

Would the world forget I ever existed, when the wind scattered me to the stars?

"Your eyes remind me of home," Finn whispered when I looked back at him, and he placed a soft kiss on my lips. "You are my home."

"Okay." I nodded. I consciously let my heart open and felt my silver pour out toward Finn. "Let there be light."

Epilogue

Bestselling Author and Television Personality, Edmund Nustber
From the award-winning documentary, The Light Key Conspiracy

Many journalists dream of reporting from the front lines of war—not to sensationalize warfare but to find meaning in the battle—if there *is* meaning, as there often is not, and to do it justice. I never dreamed of covering a war, because I don't believe peace is made with flailing fists. But shortly after meeting Cora Sandoval, I found myself in the middle of a supernatural conflict that's raged on for thousands of years and which, unbeknownst to the world, threatened our very existence.

During the climax of the final battle between the Scintilla and the Arrazi, I risked death to chronicle their story and their truth—a truth that had to be seen—felt—for the world to fully comprehend its gravitas. The final moments between these ancient peoples was recorded on video, by me, and now you can see for yourself the cosmic ramifications of their actions.

It was the most transcendent and awe-inspiring moment of my life.

These two brave souls, complete opposites of the other in the most essential way, put their fears aside in the midst of battle. Mysticism, faith, and research congealed into a theory that, by willingly joining energies, they could heal the world. Guided by faith in that principle, they walked tentatively toward each other to become the physical representation of "unification of opposites."

For many tense moments, it appeared as though nothing was happening. They stood motionless, with their hands clasped, and gazed lovingly upon the other. Soon, to my astonishment, a visible ball of light hovered between them at chest level and undulated like a ghostly specter that grew in size with every breath. Their energy expanded into two spirals of light, which fused together into a third spiral, and then exploded in one loving white mass of light above us as incandescent as the sun.

The silver-white light arced overhead in what we soon realized was an enormous spiral. Reports later confirmed that this spiral phenomenon was seen hundreds of miles away. Like a great explosion, the energy rippled outward and mushroomed over everyone present and infused our bodies with the most—sorry, I get…emotional…speaking of it. Descriptions are nearly impossible… It was simply the most profound and staggering sensation of *love*.

It *was* love.

To paraphrase the author, Dylan Thomas, these two

raged against the dying of the light.

Their spiral was the first of many as more brave ones followed suit in the dewy garden of that Chilean ranch. Even those who seemed intent on power, war, and annihilation of their enemies heeded their inner call to *be* so much greater, to *do* a much greater thing, and *have* the power they truly craved.

It was done for *us*. To effect massive change in the world. A promise made many lifetimes ago, and finally fulfilled in the hopes that mankind and the earth we inhabit would benefit.

In the weeks since my first broadcast, these celestial events have happened all over the world from Norway to Mexico and have left Earth, and the people upon her, greatly altered.

Their gift to humanity.

I leave you with a quote from Dante Alighieri: *"...and those blithe souls flashed out like comets streaming from the sky, Whirling in circles round determined poles. And even as wheels in clock escapement ply, In such fashion geared that motionless, Appears the first one, and the last to fly."*

Acknowledgments

Trilogy is one small word for such an enormous undertaking. Writing this series has been one of the most gratifying challenges of my life. Even now, I wonder if I managed to properly convey what I first envisioned. A writer rarely feels like they've truly bagged that beautiful and fluttering bird of an idea.

To Sydney and Cooper, thank you for believing in me and for your steadfast support during the ups and downs. Only you have been on the front lines with me all the way, and I'm so lucky to have two brilliant and amazing souls by my side.

Jason, you bring so much light and love into my days. My world is a brighter place because you're in it. I could not have a better partner in adventure and in life.

To my Tribe: Lucy, Mary Claire, and Monica (Jo), thank you for always loving me and accepting me for the epic weirdo that I truly am. Our weirds have found a forever home. Your support of my chosen path has meant the world to me.

My deepest thanks to my fantastic agent, Michael Bourret, and to my insightful editor, Karen Grove. Your faith in my stories and in me has kept me afloat during the harder times, and I'm more grateful than you know.

Thank you to Entangled Publishing for making my dream come true. Dedicated and passionate people there have helped me enormously and I'd like to especially thank Heather Riccio, Debbie Suzuki, and Stacy Abrams. Massive thanks to Kelley York for designing two of my covers and knocking it out of the park with this one.

While I dedicated this book to my mother, a secondary dedication is in order. During the drafting of ILLUMINATE, one of my literary and life heroes passed away. Dr. Maya Angelou was a lovely, saucy, brave, brilliant woman, and hearing her speak in person was one of the highlights of my life. *I Know Why the Caged Bird Sings* was one of the first books that made me want to be a writer. I wanted to speak to hearts the way she did. Maya Angelou—What a light you were in this world and will continue to be through the legacy of your words and your life.

Finally, thank you to the readers and fans of the series. Your love for this world and these characters has lifted me and motivated me, and I'm so grateful to you. Thank you for the gift.

About the Author

Tracy Clark is a young-adult writer because she believes teens deserve to know how much they matter and that regardless of what they're going through, they aren't alone. In other words, she writes books for her teen self.

She grew up a "Valley Girl" in Southern California but now lives in her home state of Nevada, in a small town at the base of the Sierra Foothills. Her two children teach her the art of distraction and are a continuous source of great dialogue. She's an unapologetic dog person who is currently owned by a cat.

Tracy was the recipient of the Society of Children's Book Writers and Illustrators (SCBWI) Work in Progress Grant. A two-time participant in the prestigious Nevada SCBWI Mentor Program where she was lucky enough to be mentored by bestselling author, Ellen Hopkins, who taught her so much about the art of writing and cured her of her ellipsis addiction.

While being mouthy has gotten her into trouble at times, she's happy to give characters the freedom to be as mouthy as they need to be. Tracy is a part-time college student, a private pilot, and an irredeemable dreamer. Visit her at www.tracyclark.org

Discover the Light Key series...